hardcore romeo

mark nadja

Afterhuman Press

ISBN: 978-0-6151-4281-4

"…I consented to suffer, I desired to suffer, to go farther, as far as the 'emptiness' itself, even were I to be stricken, destroyed, no matter. I knew, I wanted that knowing, for I lusted after her secret and did not for one instant doubt that it was death's kingdom."
–Georges Bataille

"Whatever is done from love always occurs beyond good and evil."
–Friedrich Nietzsche

Ray Pierce stood under a blue construction scaffolding outside a club on 4th street, smoking a damp cigarette. Beneath the soles of his shoes, through the concrete, he could feel the pounding party music, like the heart of a caged animal. He'd stopped to get out of the rain, which had suddenly started driving down like steel knives following a sickening peal of thunder only moments before. It was just after midnight, and he'd been wandering the streets for hours after his shift at Staples.

As he stood there smoking, he watched the idling limousines, glimpsed a few half-familiar faces he recognized from the tabloids, along with the usual supporting cast of drug dealers and sex-escorts. All in all, a rather shabby affair. Ray would know. As a former lead writer for *AdBiz*, he'd covered more than a few of these kinds of events at the launch of some new box of soap or celebrity perfume.

In the time it took to smoke three inches of soggy tobacco, the rain had let up enough to make it to the subway entrance on Broadway. Ray took one last inhale and threw the rest of the cigarette into the gutter. That's when he saw her.

She was walking through the thickly-painted red door of the club, laughing, talking on a Nokia cell phone. She used her free hand to help her talk, her face over-animated, smiling, flirtatious, as if whoever was on the other end could actually see her. She stood beside Ray for about fifteen seconds, yammering, and then disconnected the call and dropped the phone into her bag. Her hand instantly reappeared with a tube of lipstick, slim as a rifle cartridge, which she applied slowly, as she looked out at the rain, frowning slightly. She turned, the lipstick still at her lips, and saw Ray watching.

Ray blushed in spite of himself, looked away, and turned back again. The woman was still looking at him, smiling, saying something that Ray had to reconstruct.

"Are you with the party?"

"No," Ray said, "I just stopped to get out of the rain."

"Hmm too bad."

She held out her arm and nonchalantly slashed a fatal-looking red smear across the delicate tendons of her left wrist.

"I can't quite decide. What do you think? Is it me?"

"I think it looks better on your mouth." Ray said, surprised at his own cleverness. He nodded towards the red door. "Is the party that bad?"

"Typical fund raiser. This one for the MTV crowd, so maybe it's a little sleazier."

"What are you raising funds for?"

"Ben Haskins for Senate. We desperately need him in this country right now. Don't you think?"

"Sure." She continued looking at him, the whole time with that dazzling smile. On impulse, Ray caught her wrist. She didn't pull away. He lifted her hand and peered down at the mark she'd made. "I think it could even be an emergency. Do you need help?"

"What kind of help did you have in mind?"

Ray studied her face. She looked like someone, Debbie Harry, maybe, when she was younger. Her face glowed with a kind of manic excitement. Ecstasy, maybe? The drug, that is.

"What's your name?"

"Does it make a difference?"

"No," Ray said, playing along. "Not really." He nodded towards the club. "Are you here with someone?"

She looked off somewhere unspecific. Then she returned her gaze to Ray. Her eyes were…what? He'd never properly be able to answer that question. Maybe they were like the end of a sentence that had begun so promisingly but that would always be left unfinished.

She said, "Everyone's with someone. The real question is how far would you go."

"What do you mean?"

"For love. How far would you go?"

She pointed to the posters lining the brick wall behind him. Ray hadn't noticed them before. It was the same black-and-white poster, repeated, halfway down the block, like the still of a film comprised of a single frame frozen for eternity. The only contrast on the poster was the startlingly vivid color of lipstick on the model's sensuous mouth shot in extreme close-up. Ray could see it now, the ad's tag-line, *How far would you go for love?*

"Let's see," she said. "Give me your wrist."

Ray held out his arm and watched as the woman unhurriedly unbuttoned his shirt cuff. She pushed up his sleeve and Ray felt his heart pick up speed and the sweat break out under his arms. She used the lipstick to write her phone number up his forearm. It looked like he'd put his arm through a window and cut himself on a jagged shard of glass.

"Would you go this far?" she asked, smiling up at him like a movie-star. She slowly screwed the lipstick back into the tube, it's red tip suddenly obscene, wet and shiny, retracting like a dog's penis.

"Wait," Ray said.

"Now we match," the woman said, holding up her red wrist again.

"Wait a minute."

She was already backing towards the club, smiling, waving with just the tips of her fingers.

"Ciao," she said.

And she passed through the heavily-painted red door beyond which Ray was not permitted to go.

Back at the apartment, Ray stood at the bathroom sink and washed his arm. The lipstick number smeared into a scarlet incomprehensibility as if the skin of his forearm had been peeled away. He scrubbed his arm until all but the faintest trace of red remained, the rest running down the drain with the soapy water. He'd already memorized the phone number. He recited it back to himself so that he wouldn't forget it.

He dried his arm on a towel and then he put toothpaste on his toothbrush. He brushed his teeth, spitting bits of meat and greens from some forgotten meal into the basin. Then he sprayed the crown of his head with Minoxidil. He stared at himself in the mirror. In the harsh bathroom light, he figured that he probably looked the way he'd look ten years from now. It wasn't a pretty sight.

Beth called to him from the bedroom. "Are you coming to bed soon?"

She was already undressed, burrowed under the sheets, flipping through the pages of one of the romance manuscripts she edited for Longview Press. Tonight was "together-night"—a kind of warm-up for the plan they had to move in together come spring. That was the plan, but lately, Ray had been having doubts. Lately, he'd begun to ask himself if he could really see himself spending the rest of his life with Beth. The real problem was that the answer he kept coming up with was "yes." Ray set about turning off all the lights but hers. He sat on his side of the bed and pulled off his damp socks.

Sex, like everything else with Beth, was regular, safe, assured. There were no droughts, no floods. It came like rain in temperate climates, enough to keep things from dying out completely. There were the quick and efficient blowjobs, the maintenance handjobs, the obligatory weekend morning intercourse. They usually fucked in the missionary position because it best accommodated Beth's general lack of interest. Once in a while, he put it into her from behind or she roused up the energy to climb on top. But mostly, she just lay there beneath him, face composed as if she were forming a mental to-do list for the day ahead, and waiting for it all to pass. To keep it up, Ray often thought of Beth tied up, or raped, or even strangled. He'd had thoughts like that for as long as he could remember. They didn't bother him much anymore. People, he reasoned, thought up all kinds of crazy shit to get themselves off. They just didn't go around broadcasting it to each other. That's what Ray told himself, anyway. But how could he know for sure? How could anyone? And did we, really, even want to know?

Ray set the alarm on the nightstand. He said, "Just let me check my voicemail."

He quickly dialed the number he'd memorized on the cordless, waited a few moments, and heard the woman's recorded greeting. She sounded cool and businesslike. Her name was Charlotte, the machine said. Ray stared at Beth reading and waited until the woman on the phone finished and then he hung up without saying a word.

Beth lowered her manuscript. "Any messages?"

Ray said, "Nothing. Just the ex-wife. The usual. She didn't get a check fast enough. Bitch."

At Café Fiorello where they were having lunch, Ray sat at a small outdoor table and waited for Charlotte to return from taking a cellphone call. It was the second time during lunch she'd gotten up to take a call. She came back five minutes later, weaving her way between the crowded tables, smiling. She was wearing a long peasant skirt, a tight black top, and straw sandals.

"Sorry," Charlotte said, when she reached the table, "Business. It's 24-7 when you do what I do."

"What is it that you do, exactly?" Ray asked.

"Consulting. PR, mostly. And you?"

"Magazine writer. I do an arts and business column for *AdBiz*."

"Cool." She toyed with the lime wedge in her drink. "Did you always want to be a writer? Was that your dream?"

Ray shrugged. "I wanted to write fiction, but I found I hated pretending. I tried nonfiction, but I have no patience with facts. So I compromised and became a journalist." Charlotte smiled, as if he'd told a joke. A waiter passed their table with the remains of a ruined lobster: nothing but an empty red shell and disconnected antennae waving at nothing. "You know, when I didn't hear from you I figured you didn't want to meet after all. Three calls...I'd given up hope."

Charlotte shifted her eyes down, staring at a fading water ring on the tablecloth. She looked somehow pleased. She glanced back up at Ray. "You shouldn't ever give up hope."

Her eyes were no older than sixteen. That's how it would always be, Ray decided. She could be a hundred and those eyes would still radiate innocence and sexual possibility. He was in over his head. Ray knew it forty feet away from the restaurant when he first caught sight of her. He should turn back for the shore. But he knew he wouldn't.

"I was out of town most of the month," she said. "I've been in the middle of a divorce and there's been so much—stuff."

"You're married?"

"Only in the legal sense."

"Is there any other sense?"

"We've been separated for nearly three years. But it's almost over now. Just some formalities. Is that a problem? I'll understand if it is."

"No," Ray said, after some hesitation. "Not for me it isn't."

"Good. It's been complicated. Lot's of legal details to sort out. John--that's my ex..."

"Soon-to-be-ex."

"Yes, soon-to-be ex. He was into the custom-made suits, the fancy cars, the Patek Philippe watches. He wanted the big house. That kind of thing was never important to me. But I can't give up everything I worked so hard for. I can't let him steal my entire life. It's not about the money. He's being so incredibly petty and vicious. You wouldn't believe it."

"Yeah, I'm afraid I would. You're with someone for ten, fifteen years, and it all ends up being about who gets the forks."

Ray needed a cigarette. He took a pack of Camels out of his inside jacket pocket, but put them back again, wondering if the latest no-smoking laws permitted him to smoke even outdoors.

"You're bitter, aren't you?" Charlotte asked.

"Realistic. You don't really know the person you love until you stop loving them."

"Do you think that you hate women, Ray?"

"I don't know. I always end up loving them too much to say for sure."

"I'm serious, Ray."

"Of course not. Why do you even ask?"

"Because John hated women. When you said that, you sounded a little like him."

"I'm sorry. It was a joke."

"Many a truth in jest," she said.

The waiter cleared away their plates and brought the two espressos they ordered in spite of the day's heat. Charlotte showed Ray her new shoes, a gift from her mother in Chicago, she told him. She mentioned a brand name that Ray guessed was supposed to mean something, though he'd never heard of it, and mentioned a price of several hundred dollars. She then made an expression to let him know how silly she thought it was to spend so much for shoes.

"My stepfather was quite wealthy," she said. "He died two years ago. I guess I'll be a millionaire someday."

Ray followed the line she drew with her partially exposed leg. He let his gaze travel along her calf to her delicate ankle. He lingered a moment at her silver pedicure. When he looked up again, Charlotte was already looking across the street at Lincoln Center as if she were gazing into forever. She ran a manicured finger along the rim of her water glass.

"As a little girl, my father would take me to the opera every Sunday when it was in season. The last time I went, it was with John. We had a terrible fight and he walked out on me. I haven't been back since."

"I'll take you sometime. If you'd like."

Charlotte refocused her eyes on him. "Classy Ray."

"You're beautiful. I've wanted to tell you that ever since the night we met."

She smiled, touching the back of his hand where it lay on the table.

"And now you have. Thank you, Ray. That's sweet."

She reached into her handbag and took out her cell-phone again. Ray thought that she was going to take another call, but instead she turned it off and dropped it back into the bag.

She said, "Did you know that in outer space your heart starts to shrink?"

"What?"

"It's true."

"No fooling? How do you even know such a thing?"

She laughed and Ray felt how the grinding boredom steadily eating away at his life, the boredom you can forget is even there, that malaise of everything, was suddenly and miraculously gone. This is why, he thought, we bother to get up in the morning, why we evolved out of the goo at the dawn of time, why we trouble ourselves to breathe in and out. This is why we build rockets to fly into space where our hearts shrink…this feeling he got when she smiled.

Charlotte licked her perfect teeth and the wine she was sipping was reflected on her face. "It's just one of those things you hear somewhere, I guess, and then it becomes a part of you. Don't you know a lot of useless stuff?"

"Practically everything I know is useless."

Ray took hold of Charlotte's wrist and turned her hand over, palm-up, on the white table-cloth among the bread crumbs. He traced his finger over the delicate cerulean veins that she'd garishly slashed with the lipstick that first night at the club.

Charlotte dropped her head of loose blonde curls and looked up at him again from under her thick lashes. She wasn't, however, looking at Ray, but somewhere just off to the left of him. "I'm really very shy," she said. "I hope you don't mind."

Inside an over-airconditioned hotel room on 57th street, Ray fucked Charlotte for the first time. He was lying on top of her, kissing her face, as he thrust into her. In spite of the room's chill, their flesh where it touched on their chests and bellies was covered with sweat and made squelching swamp noises as they strove against each other to reach that little bit of paradise on earth.

Charlotte pulled her mouth away. Her lips were slightly peeled back from her teeth. She looked almost wasted by illness. "I want to bite you," she moaned.

"Yes."

"I mean it. I want to hurt you."

Ray was close to orgasm. He didn't care what she did. "Then do it," he rasped. "Do it."

She pressed her mouth to his chest.

Her teeth, sharp.

"Harder," Ray moaned, wincing, talking to her, talking to himself. "Harder."

He thrust into her faster and harder, trying to stay one stroke ahead of the rising wave of pain.

He did, by cumming.

Ray stood in front of the hotel room mirror as he finished dressing. He examined the wound on his left pectoral. The half-ring of inflamed flesh was tender to the touch. He vaguely wondered if a bite from another human being was dangerous, as dangerous as an animal bite, for instance. Could it infect him with some kind of pathogen, like tetanus, or worse, AIDS?

Behind him, still naked on the bed, Charlotte was lying propped on one arm, drawing patterns on the bedspread with a finger. Between her carelessly positioned legs, a silvery streak was leaking out of her. Ray watched her in the mirror. She looked preoccupied, as if she were the only one in the room.

He had tucked in his shirt by now and was carefully knotting his tie, all part of his disguise. He broke the awkward silence.

"When can I see you again?"

"I don't know," Charlotte said absently, not looking up. "I'm going out of town for a few days. Business, again. I'll call you."

Ray figured that meant never.

Selling ballpoint pens and printer cartridges wasn't what Ray Pierce thought he'd be doing at forty. But that's what happened when the economy went south and subscription rates went down because people were accessing their news online nowadays. After eleven years at *AdBiz*, Ray had finally fallen victim to some bean counter's calculator in Accounts Payable, a sacrifice to fatten up the bottom line.

He'd gotten a decent enough severance package, reflecting, perhaps, the growing tendency disgruntled employees had lately of returning to their old places of employ and shooting the joint up, starting with the managers. After eleven dreary years of writing articles about innovative point of sales techniques for hawking deodorants and herbal diet pills, reporting on the endless shuffle of incompetent over-compensated industry bigwigs from one company to another, Ray might have welcomed the change as the kick in the ass he needed to jump-start his hopelessly stalled life.

But the layoff had come only a year after the long and acrimonious divorce with Angie and it was the last straw. He'd only just been getting back on his feet financially when Saul Makewitz called him into the office to break the bad news. It was back to the lawyers after that, another three months of swimming with Angie's sharks to adjust the settlement, another ten grand added to Ray's already x-rated legal bill. So what? Now it would take forever and a day to pay off instead of just forever.

There was truly nothing like divorce court to rudely awaken a married man to just how little he actually owned in the eyes of the law, especially if the ex-love-of-his-life were determined enough to take it all. And Angie had proven herself as determined as cancer. Ray had heard that infidelity could do that to a woman, turn her into a terminal illness, *but her own infidelity?* Ray hadn't expected that—not Angie's cheating or her righteous indignation when she'd been caught at it. She felt entitled to her affair and defended herself so aggressively that Ray himself nearly came to believe that the only way his ex-wife could possibly have reconciled herself to Ray's mere existence was to screw a fellow counselor in the family crisis center where she worked.

By the time she'd had her day in court about all Ray had left was the right to keep working to pay her more until, at last, he finally caught a break and dropped dead at his desk. To that end, he took an almost grim satisfaction in donning the red Staples polo shirt and guiding people to the printer cartridges for not much better than minimum wage. Living well is the best revenge unless you have a parasite living off of you. Angie's twelve percent of what he was earning now was a lot less than her twelve percent of what he was earning before. She was convinced that Ray had gotten fired just to spite her. The expression she wore that last time in court was truly something astonishing: her mouth drawn to a tight red button straining to hold back hell itself. Ray savored the image like the trophy head of some exotic safari animal in his mental Hall of Revenge. Divorce, in Ray's estimation and experience of it, seldom made a human being out of anyone.

Truth was, Ray had tried to get another job in the industry. At least until all his old contacts stopped returning his embarrassingly frequent and increasingly desperate calls and all his leads ran into dead ends. For the last six months, he was drifting through the job at Staples just to keep his nose above water and for the boxes of stolen envelopes. He discussed possible new careers with Beth that seemed as realistic to him as fairy tales, while eating his way steadily through the last of his severance and then his meager savings. Something would have to be done and soon, hence the talk of moving in with Beth, a prospect that still filled him with dread, like walking into a crypt you suspected was going to be slammed shut behind you, burying you alive.

After meeting Charlotte and her expensive shoes, Ray wished he'd put a little more effort throughout his life into becoming a rich and successful bastard. It really was important. Women like Charlotte didn't come cheaply, and they didn't stay cheaply either. No, they did not, not in the long run anyway. But he wasn't considering the long run anymore and hadn't in a very long time.

Thinking of Charlotte now in the middle of aisle seven, Ray touched the place on his chest that she'd bitten. Under his red Staples polo shirt, the bruise ached in a way that awakened his memory of

the pleasure that had accompanied it. By afternoon that pleasure had
turned a spectrum of all the purple colors, like the horizon on the last
day of earth. You could still see the small marks of her teeth framing
the lurid wound, the shape of her mouth like the gate to some
perverse pleasure garden. With his hand in his pocket, he subtly
shifted his hard-on to a more comfortable position.

"Eat your heart out," Ray muttered under his breath.

He was addressing the world in general.

He was punishing Beth for what Angie had done. Beth, who
didn't deserve it. Angie, who didn't care. He was punishing himself,
too, but in a much more complicated way. At least that's what Ray
was telling himself when a midde-aged guy with a grave blanket of
scorched-looking hair laid across his otherwise bald head interrupted
Ray's meditation to ask where he could find those little copper things
that hold loose-leaf pages in a report together.

At that moment, life, real life, seemed very, very far away.

A week later, Charlotte took him back to the carriage house in
Montcrest where she said she was living until her divorce became
final. The carriage house was situated in the back of a large faux
Tudor mansion in the hills above the tidy upscale commuter suburb.
Charlotte fumbled with the keys to the door and disabled the alarm.
Ray followed her inside. The place was neat and well-decorated but
the fact that it had previously been some kind of garage or barn was
left otherwise undisguised. There were two floors—the upper one a
converted bedroom loft—but they didn't make it that far. Charlotte
pulled Ray towards the daybed in front of the French doors. They
undressed each other desperately, dragging each other down onto the
cushions.

"When you showed up at the diner this morning and said you
were sick," Ray said, between kisses, "I thought you were trying to
tell me you'd changed your mind about us..."

She'd been almost a half-hour late. Ray sat at the counter while
he waited over a third cup of coffee and figured he'd been stood up.
The one good thing about New Jersey is that you could still smoke in

the restaurants and he'd been chain-smoking the entire time. He was
finishing what he'd decided was going to be his last cigarette when
Charlotte finally showed up. She slumped onto the stool beside him
as if she were exhausted, like someone had pulled her plug. She was
sniffling and announced almost aggressively, as if she thought Ray
would challenge her, that she thought she was coming down with
something. Ray ordered her some tea and somewhere in the middle
of sipping at it, Charlotte apparently had a sudden change of spirit
and invited him back to the carriage house.

Now she put a finger to his lips. "Sssssh...Let's not talk. Lie
back and let me take care of you."

Ray reclined against the pillows as Charlotte straddled him. She
reached around behind her and fondled his cock.

"How do you want it? In my mouth, my hand, inside me?"

"Inside you."

She smiled. "I was hoping you'd say that."

She guided him between the damp folds of her outer sex and
slid slowly backwards onto his cock. He reached up and played with
her tits, her brown nipples puckering up. She rode him so hard, so
hungrily, that it was difficult for Ray to feel anything at all at first. He
had to concentrate for a while to find his rhythm and then it all came
back to him. He grabbed one of her hands and put the tips of her
fingers between his lips and sucked at them. They tasted like the
inside of her. She watched him carefully, gauging, as he got closer to
orgasm. He held her gaze as long as he could until he finally had to
shut his eyes against the blinding white light on the other side of his
orgasm.

When he opened them again, Charlotte was coming back from
the bathroom with a damp towel. She knelt beside Ray, who lay there
like a corpse on the daybed, and gently wiped his groin.

"I didn't know if I should cum or not," he said, when he could
finally speak.

"I want you to do whatever you want," Charlotte said softly.
"Always."

"What about birth control?"

Charlotte focused her attention on what she was doing with the towel. She seemed to be avoiding Ray's eyes. "I've had an operation," she said.

She sat back on her heels and pointed to the scar on her lower abdomen. She traced it almost fondly with her finger, as if it were the engraved signature of someone she loved.

Or a name on a tombstone.

"See?"

Ray had, in fact, noticed it earlier. But now he turned over on his side to take a closer look.

"They thought at first it might be cancer. Of course, I was scared to death. Between the divorce and being sick, it was almost too much to handle."

"But it wasn't? Cancer, I mean."

"No."

"Do you mind if I touch it?"

Charlotte looked up and met Ray's gaze. She nodded. "If you want," she said softly.

Ray traced the path of the scar along Charlotte's belly. He touched it delicately, the way Charlotte had just done, as if the scar marked the place of some new surgically implanted erogenous zone. And, sure enough, she closed her eyes, savoring the touch. Without opening them, she continued to talk.

"I was shocked when I first saw it. The doctor didn't tell me the scar was going to look like that. You don't think it's ugly, do you?"

Ray looked at the pink plastic zipper that disappeared into her light brown pubic hair. "No, it's sexy. Everything about you is."

And he meant it.

"Does it bother you...that I can't have babies?"

"No, of course not. Why should that possibly matter?"

Charlotte shrugged. "I don't know. It might bother some men. Maybe I'm not woman enough for them?"

"That's ridiculous," Ray said. "You're more than enough woman for any man."

She laid her hand on his. "Thank you, Ray," she whispered.

"I mean it."

A shivering tear was running over the roundness of her cheek.

Ray wondered if someone had told Charlotte she was inadequate, her husband, her father, maybe, some fucking man or other, someone had damaged her in some way, that was clear already; maybe that was why she seemed so oddly orphaned. He was angry at the man who might have hurt her, but Ray also knew that anger was ambiguous. If he were being honest, he was just as grateful to whoever had hurt Charlotte, because otherwise she wouldn't be here with him.

Sometime later rain began tapping against the French doors. They'd fallen asleep together. Ray woke first and looked across the gloom that had leaked into the room while they slept. The ivy covering the windows trembled. Beside him, Charlotte stirred.

"It's raining.

"What time is it?"

"Almost seven."

"*Seven?*" Charlotte sat bolt upright, like she'd just waken from a nightmare. "Shit, why didn't you wake me! I have to go."

"Go?" Ray sat up reluctantly as Charlotte bounced off the daybed. He watched her frantically searching the floor for her panties. She was utterly indifferent to her nudity, bending in front of him as if they'd already been married for a decade-and-a-half. "What's the big rush?"

"I have a dinner engagement with a friend," she said, now down on all fours. "You've got to leave."

"Hmm, a *friend.*" Ray meant it to sound like a joke, but somehow it didn't quite come out that way.

"Yes, really, a friend." Charlotte stood up, her discarded panties hooked on her fingers. "That's her picture on the bookshelf. Joan owns this place. Her and her husband."

Ray rolled off the daybed, stepped into his pants, and crossed the room. He picked up the framed picture that Charlotte indicated, one of several on the built-in bookcase. In the photo he saw a plain, nondescript, white woman and a cherubic, bearded, middle-aged Indian man. Her husband, no doubt. And between them, somehow dominating the camera's attention, stood a tall, tanned, smiling man who looked like someone Ray should recognize, but didn't. He had that well-bred "money-look" that was more than the sum of his expensive clothes, impeccable grooming, and obvious self-confidence. It was the look that only generations of unlimited power could give a man.

"She was with me at the party the night we met," Charlotte said.

"Everyone's with someone," Ray recalled.

"Huh?"

"Nothing, just something you said that night. I guess I should be relieved. I figured you were with a man that night. I must have missed your friend. But that wouldn't have been hard."

"What do you mean?

"I don't know. She's a little eerie looking, that's all."

"That's not a very nice thing to say."

Ray was thinking that the woman in the picture had a vacancy about her, like a burnt-out light bulb. It was a color photograph but she looked like she was in black-and-white.

"She's just a bit faded, that's all. Like your complete opposite. I guess it's not hard to guess who the guys hit on when the two of you are out together."

"Okay, Ray. Knock it off. Don't make fun of her."

Charlotte crossed the room and yanked the picture from his hand. Ray was taken off-guard by her reaction. He watched as she carefully returned the framed photograph to its place on the book shelf.

"Hey, I didn't mean anything by it. Don't be upset. Really, I was just joking. I'm sorry."

Charlotte was looking at the trio framed there with the kind of wistful tenderness usually reserved for those no longer around.

"She's my best friend. I owe her so much...this place, it's hers. Her and her husband, Rudra. He's a multi-millionaire. Computers and stuff. When I left him, John took control of the business, the house, everything. He was so angry. I was terrified of what he might do next. I was practically homeless." She turned back to Ray. "Do you have any idea what that's like? Joan took me in when no one else would. I owe her everything."

"I'm sorry. Really I am. Listen, if you invite me along, I'd like to meet her. What do you say? Dinner's on me."

"Not tonight. Maybe another time."

He expected her to turn down the offer. He wasn't entirely disappointed, feeding the wife of a multimillionaire couldn't be cheap. Ray was standing beside Charlotte now, testing her shoulder with his touch, as if her rejection might burn him. She didn't pull away, but didn't respond either. He looked passed her face at the photograph.

"Who's the other guy, anyway?"

"That's Ben Haskins."

"The senator?"

"Why yes, of course." The smile flickered on her lips, but didn't quite ignite. "He's going to be the next president."

Ray wondered if maybe he'd misread Charlotte's expression before. Perhaps the wistful tenderness wasn't directed at her colorless friend and her Buddha-like husband after all, but at this ageless guy with the perfectly greying temples of a soap opera doctor. What's more, perhaps it wasn't a look of wistful tenderness, but of unrequited sexual longing. Ray felt a knot of jealousy twist inside him. Millionaires, senators, future presidents…what the hell was he doing here?

"Listen, forget I opened my big mouth. Okay? I don't want to ruin what happened this afternoon. Really. It was…amazing, you know, like something you only see in a movie."

Charlotte looked up at him, eyes shining, but with what emotion it was impossible to say.

"Yes it was," she said, searching his face for something. "It *was* like a movie, wasn't it?"

"I'll call you?" Ray said, hopefully.

"Yes, do that."

That evening, on the drive back to the city through a steady drizzle, he hoped he hadn't already ruined everything. He hoped he'd see her at least one more time before she dumped him, because dump him she would, that was a certainty, and Ray would've had to be a fool to think any different.

Three nights later, they met again in Jersey. They sat by the window of a toney seafood restaurant that Ray couldn't afford. Across miles of black water, New York City was a fragile string of twinkling lights. Someone started playing the piano: a slow, sad tune with a lot of space between the notes, as if the song could end anywhere, at any time.

Charlotte asked him, "What were you like as a little boy?"

"What makes you ask?"

"I think you can tell a lot about a person by knowing what they were like as a child."

"Really?"

Even through the windows, over the clattering of forks and knives, over the piano music, Ray could hear the lonely clang of a buoy in the dark.

"Stop stalling," Charlotte said, "Tell me. What you were you like?"

"Pretty much the same as I am now."

"Come on, you must have been different in some way."

"I was smaller."

"Very funny." Charlotte took a sip of her Cosmopolitan. "Would you say it was happy, your childhood?"

Ray shrugged. "Would anyone say that?"

Charlotte considered the question for a moment. "My father tried to commit suicide three times after my mother left him. I found him one afternoon by following the trail of blood to the bathroom. He was sitting in the empty tub, naked, with his wrists and throat slashed. I had to keep him from bleeding to death until the ambulance got there and somehow keep my kid brother distracted in the kitchen. I was sixteen"

"Christ, I'm sorry. That must have been horrible."

Charlotte smiled, tossed her curls. "Stuff happens. That's what I do. Take care of things. What was your father like? Tell me the earliest memory you have of him."

"Let's see….when I was five or so, we'd gone to the shore one summer vacation with my grandma. We'd driven all day to get there and we were all exhausted. My parents had brought a pizza back to the little beach house we'd rented for dinner and dad gave everyone a single slice. I looked down at mine and I remember I was disappointed. Everyone else's piece looked bigger, even my brother's. I felt like I'd been gypped. I was so hungry and that slice of pizza looked so small. I said, 'Is this all I get?' My father took my head and smashed my face into the pizza that was still in the box. I had to sit through the rest of dinner in front of everyone with cheese dripping off my face. I've always had trouble asking anyone for anything after that."

Charlotte started laughing. "That's pretty funny."

Ray, taken by surprise, began laughing too. "Yeah. I guess it is. My father was quite a comedian. Too bad I didn't appreciate his sense of humor at the time."

"That's the spirit Ray. Things change. Hey, would you like to go to Paris with me? It's so romantic there. That's the place we ought to be."

"This is kind of sudden, isn't it?"

"Life's short."

"You're serious, aren't you?"

"Yes. As soon as the divorce is final, we'll fly out there. What do you say?"

"Sure."

"I mean, why not, right?"

"Exactly. Why not?"

After dinner they walked around the side of the restaurant, down to the dock where the pleasure boats rocked and pulled at their lines. They stood on the creaking walkway under the stars and Ray heard the same buoy as before clanging away in the dark. Along the horizon the rising wind seemed to momentarily blow out the Manhattan skyline before it sputtered back to life. Charlotte was dressed in a tight leather skirt and a light blouse with a lot of small buttons. Ray pulled her close and kissed her.

"I think I should tell you something," she lisped.

"What's that?"

"I have trouble with the T-word."

Ray looked down, his mouth now in her wind-tossed hair.

"The T-word?

"Trust. Everyone I've ever loved has betrayed me."

"You can trust me. I won't betray you."

He kissed her.

"You should know that I'm very boring in bed."

"Huh?"

"I'm boring in bed."

"What do you mean?"

"I'm not interested in girls. I'm not interested in anything kinky."

Ray didn't know why she was telling him any of this now. Was she setting down some kind of ground rules, or did she suspect something odd about Ray? Was she trying to smoke him out?

"Your ex-husband..." he kissed her again. "Did he make you do things like that?"

"Yes, Ray, he did. If that's the way you are," Charlotte said between kisses, "if that's what you're into, I'm probably not the girl for you."

Ray could feel her trembling against his body, but whether it was the cold, or disgust at the memory of things she'd done to make her husband happy, or remembered lust that made her shake so uncontrollably, he could only guess.

"You can trust me," he repeated.

"Can I really?"

"Of course."

Ray tried to kiss her again, but Charlotte burrowed closer against his chest, still shivering.

"I hope so," she said into his jacket. "I'd like to think I can trust you. I really want to be able to trust someone. People use each other. They treat each other like objects. When they're done with them, they throw away those they once wanted so badly, like they were used cars or empty bottles. Have you ever done that to anyone Ray?"

"No."

Ray thought of his defunct marriage, already lost somewhere in the past. He'd gotten out of it, left it behind, and started walking. What could describe it better than a stalled car on an endless highway? What good was his ex-wife Angie to him now? She might as well be a broken-down Ford with a shot transmission or an empty bottle of Bud Lite. Of course, she regarded Ray the same way, except that for Angie, he was still good for a few extra miles of hard driving, as long as those support checks kept rolling in.

"What is it you tell your girlfriend about us, anyway?"

"My girlfriend...?"

Earlier that week, Beth had gone to Las Vegas for a book convention. Ray hadn't given her a second thought, except whenever she left a message that had to be returned. He considered lying to Charlotte and would have, he'd done so already, after all. But considering what she just said about trust and the way she was looking at him now, Ray knew it would be a long-odds gamble. She worked herself free of his arms and took a step back. She seemed to be reading the calculations in his eyes as fast as he could make them.

"Be careful Ray," she said levelly.

"Okay. I was going to tell you. How did you know?"

"These days a girl can't be too careful. I've got to protect myself. I have a lot of people depending on me. I have a lot of responsibilities. "

"You had me investigated?"

"You lied to me about your job too, Ray."

Ray raised his hands in mock surrender.

"Busted. Look, I meant to tell you. I really did. But everything was moving along so fast. And I did work at *AdBiz* for a long time. The Staples thing is a little embarrassing, but it's just temporary. I really more or less just started."

"I have to be able to trust you, Ray."

"You can."

"But the girlfriend. The job. You lied about those things. What am I supposed to think about that?"

"That's different."

"Is it, really?" Charlotte asked.

"Yes. I wouldn't lie to you about anything important. Or about anything at all anymore. Please believe me. It's different, now. After tonight, I mean."

She looked at him closely for a few moments. What she said next surprised Ray, because he was so sure he'd already fucked things up beyond saving. "I believe you Ray. I really do. I honestly believe that everything's different now. I really do believe I can trust you."

Somewhere on the drive back to the carriage house it started to lightly rain. Then the night-sky cracked open along a blinding white fissure. Torrents. The streets were swept with great white curtains of water. The traffic lights on the highway shorted out and blinked red or yellow over desolate intersections. Charlotte had her head down in Ray's lap as he struggled to keep the car on the road against the rising wind and slick conditions. She looked up, her hand around his wet cock, when she felt him close. "Don't cum," she said, "don't cum yet." And then she ducked her head back down and sucked him into her mouth again, doing everything she could to finish him off.

Back at the carriage house, they stood by the lit pool, pulling at each other's clothes. The rain had let up but continued to fall in a warm steady drizzle that soaked them within seconds. Ray unzipped Charlotte's leather skirt. She moaned, stepping out of her red mules. Her blouse buttoned from behind, twenty or thirty tiny buttons, that Ray had trouble working with his wet fingers, as if he were trying to unbutton her backbone.

"Get this fucking thing off," Ray swore, pawing at it.

Charlotte helped him pull the blouse over her head, tiny pearl buttons ricocheting all over, and Ray impatiently yanked down the cups of her black lace bra. Her pale tits glowed ghostly in the pool's

underwater light. Kissing her bare shoulder, tasting rain and flesh,
Ray happened to look up at the main house. He saw something
flashing in the upper corner window of the Tudor. At first, he
thought it was just light reflecting off the glass, but then he saw it
again, a sharp metallic glint, and a telltale red light steadily blinking.

"Pay attention to me," Charlotte said, holding his head between
her hands, and kissing him hard.

Ray glanced passed her. There was a slight movement of the
curtain, a little jerk. It was gone almost as soon as he noticed it. But
looking closer, Ray now saw a dark ambiguous shape in the window.

The blinking red light.

"Wait a minute..."

"What's the matter?"

"We're being watched."

"You're imagining it."

"The hell I am. Look!"

He tried to turn Charlotte around by the shoulders, but
she fought against him,clinging to his neck and kissing him even
harder, grinding her face into his.

"So what?" she growled. "Ignore him. He's harmless. It's just
his way of getting off. Just look at me, concentrate on me."

"For crissakes, wait a minute."

"Fuck me."

"I can't do this."

"Sure you can Ray. Don't wimp out on my now. Don't look at
anyone, at anything but me. Feel me, Ray." She reached down
between his legs and pressed her wet body against his. She did a slow
dance as she held his cock against her damp flesh. "Look at me," she
whispered urgently. "Really look at me; really feel me. We're the only
ones in the world, Ray. It's just the two of us."

Ray slipped his arms around her. This was insane, but he did it.
He pulled her close and kissed her. At first he felt self-conscious and
awkward and that made him angry. He kissed her again, almost out of
sheer spite. If this is what she wanted, Ray told himself, he would
give it to her. If he thought she would shock him, he'd surprise her.
Craziest of all, Ray felt himself responding. His cock was still in her

hand and Charlotte was rubbing it along her scratchy cunt. Ray eased
back and then thrust into her. He slipped in easily. She was soaking
wet. They danced together like that, slowly, in the rain.

"Oh that's it," Charlotte moaned, faking it, "that's it, oh yes, oh
god, that's it…"

Ray watched her rain-spattered face as he fucked her. Her eyes
were closed, her hair matted, but she kept her face in view of
whoever was standing in the window behind them, licking her lips.
She did this even after Ray slipped his hands under her ass and lifted
her off her feet. She wrapped her legs around his hips, locked her
ankles at the small of his back. The rain dripped off her toes. She
kept her head turned away from his kisses and it took a while for it
to dawn on him. *She's conscious of the camera angle.* That's when he
unloaded inside of her.

They were in the kitchen scavenging for a late-night snack. Their
clothes, meanwhile, were tumbling dry in the laundry room down the
hall. Charlotte had brought Ray a robe to wear from a closet by the
guest bathroom. It was one of those white terrycloth robes that came
as a courtesy with certain hotel rooms. The name of the hotel was
stitched in gold thread inside an ostentatious crest over Ray's left
breast: The Excelsior, and, apparently, it was located in Chicago.
Charlotte had wrapped herself in a blue throw-blanket, loosely knit,
through which Ray could see generous squares of her damp flesh, as
if she'd pulled a net around herself she could easily escape.

"You're probably wondering why I let him do that," she said,
tossing a bag of instant popcorn into a state-of-the-art microwave
you could have easily fit a good-sized six-year-old. She slammed shut
the titanium door and stood staring at the complicated keypad, clearly
puzzled. "You're probably thinking it's a little strange."

Ray took a bottle of champagne from the refrigerator and
found two glasses. Except for three other champagne bottles just like
it, the refrigerator was empty as a stretch of Antarctic tundra, the
yellow "energy-saver" tag from the store still hanging from one of its
bare wire shelves. Watching Charlotte frantically throwing open the

cabinets in search of what had turned out to be a lone box of popcorn, Ray saw that the cabinets were likewise empty. The kitchen, with its shiny unused range and spotless sink and countertops, might have been a display kitchen at Home Depot. Whatever else Charlotte did, she obviously didn't spend a lot of time at home cooking pot roasts.

"Yeah," he said. "I was thinking something like that."

"Since Joan left him, he has no one to fall back on. So I try to, you know, look after him a little."

"She left him? When did that happen?"

"About two months ago."

Ray popped the plastic cork on the champagne bottle, filled the two glasses, and handed one to Charlotte. "She doesn't mind you putting on a show for him?"

"Rudra and I go so far back."

"Go back how?"

He took a sip of the cold champagne. It was so dry it seemed to evaporate on his tongue before he could swallow it.

"We're not fucking each other if that's what you mean. Christ, Ray, is that all you think about?"

"Well, what *do* you mean?"

"Rudra helped John out of a tough spot."

"What kind of tough spot?"

"If you have to know, it was a botched operation that could have sent John to prison."

"Your husband's a doctor?"

"A surgeon, yes."

Ray refilled their glasses. "So you entertain him sexually to repay the debt?"

"That's a crude way to put it, Ray."

"How would you put it?"

Charlotte put down her glass and lifted herself onto the butcher block counter, readjusting the blanket around her shoulders, but she didn't manage to cover very much.

"I'm repaying the compassion of a good friend who stood by me when I was in need. That's how I'd put it."

"I'm surprised that you were able to stay friends with his wife. Most women would be jealous."

"I told you, we're not having sex. Rudra is harmless. If it makes you feel any better, he's impotent, as a baby. Diabetes. It's such a shame. It's destroying his marriage."

"Yeah, I guess that does make me feel a little better."

"You mustn't say a word to anyone. He'd kill me if he knew I told anyone."

Ray lifted his glass. "Who would I tell?"

Charlotte shrugged. "Whoever."

"What I don't understand," he said, "is why you continue to perform for him? After all, you're splitting with your husband. He can repay his own debts."

"Sometimes it's a good idea not to burn your bridges. Besides, that's not the way it works."

"Not the way what works?"

Charlotte stretched out her legs and examined her toes. "You know how rich people are."

"No, I don't," Ray said. "I've written about them from time to time, but I don't really know how they are. Tell me."

"They buy and sell people like us."

"People like us? What are you talking about?"

"He owns me."

"He what?"

"Damn, that's the fucking popcorn," Charlotte cried.

The oppressive smell of scorched butter suddenly filled the room. Charlotte jumped off the counter and Ray followed her to the microwave, which was making lots of funny sounds, as if something were thrashing around inside. Charlotte yanked open the door and stood there, staring helplessly into the microwave. Ray reached around her and yanked the burning bag from inside, cursing as the sizzling butter burned his fingertips. He threw the bag into the glistening stainless steel sink, figuring it was probably the only thing that had ever been there. They both stood and stared at the torn bag as it belched puffs of black smoke like a ruined lung.

"Shit," Charlotte said. "That was the last bag of popcorn, too."

"That's okay. I'm really not that hungry."

"You're upset."

"Yeah, just a little."

"We can order out."

"Not about the popcorn, Charlotte."

"Oh."

Charlotte started looking through the cabinets again. She found a brand-new red plastic bowl. She tore away its wrapper and began picking through the popcorn in the sink.

"Come on," she said at last. "Let's go upstairs. We'll watch a movie and I'll try to explain everything."

Charlotte carried what was salvageable of the burnt popcorn in the plastic bowl and Ray followed her upstairs to the bedroom. She asked Ray to pick out a movie from the DVD library while she changed into something sexier. The loft bedroom was sparsely furnished in oak and dominated by a sophisticated home theater system: a large screen descended from the ceiling in front of the king-sized bed and speakers were mounted in each corner of the room. Ray looked through DVDs on the wire tower beside a mirrored chest of drawers. The DVDs were stored in identical black cases marked only by what looked like some kind of 15-digit serial number. There must have been over two hundred of the slim black cases.

When she came out of the bedroom, Charlotte was wearing a pink baby-doll nightie and fresh lipstick. She frowned when she saw Ray still puzzling over the rack of plastic cases. She padded over on bare feet.

"They're all unmarked," he said. "I don't get it."

"It really doesn't make a difference," she said, impatiently. "They're all good." She picked out a plastic case seemingly at random, glanced at the number, and handed it to Ray. "Here, pop this one in. It's one of my favorites."

Ray laid the disk into the tray of the DVD player and climbed onto the bed next to Charlotte. She was already sitting propped up against the pillows, the plastic bowl of semi-burnt popcorn between her thighs, her ankles crossed Indian-style. She inclined a handful of popcorn and blackened kernels into her mouth and started to chew.

"Press play," she said, crunching.

The film started somewhere after the opening credits and it was difficult to understand exactly what he was seeing, but it was immediately clear that it was no Hollywood production. On the screen Ray saw grainy footage of what could best be described as some kind of medical procedure. There was a patient strapped on a gurney and two figures in surgical scrubs. The faces of the latter were obscured by the usual cloth masks and obscured even further by the thick plastic safety goggles they wore. The patient, on the other hand, was female, that much was obvious. She was unconscious and breathing through a clear plastic face-mask which blurred her features but was surrounded by a halo of golden hair. She wore a typical green hospital gown that had been cut, probably in an earlier scene, to expose her breasts, in a way that reminded Ray of the famous rape scene in the movie *A Clockwork Orange*. Her legs and feet were bare. The operation seemed to be taking place in a basement: Ray could see rough cinderblock walls and, every once in a while, the corner of a billiards table made it into the camera's range.

"What the hell are we watching?" Ray asked.

Ray had been expecting porn, quite possibly of the homemade variety, but what was on the screen simply defied classification.

"Sssh…"

Ray watched as the doctor stepped forward and bent over the patient. Between his gloved fingers, gripping it like a pen, he held a silver scalpel. The camera zoomed in as a red line instantaneously followed the path of the scalpel across the exposed flesh of the woman's defenseless belly. The nurse assisting dabbed up the welling blood. The production value seemed so poor, so low-tech given the quality of even the cheapest cameras available nowadays, that Ray wondered if the film had been intentionally shot to look this inept. Even so, Ray could clearly see the exposed layers of yogurt-like fat, the blue-grey bulge of an intestinal fold extruding through the incision.

Ray winced. "Jesus…"

"Don't you like it? This was John's specialty."

"His specialty?"

"My husband liked to film his operations."

"This can't be for real."

Charlotte took another handful of scorched popcorn. "Oh it's for real."

"Is that allowed?"

"He's not in a hospital, Ray."

The doctor lay the scalpel aside. He pulled apart the incision, opening up a kind of dark pocket in the patient's body that immediately flowered with blood and glistening viscera. He yanked so hard the unconscious woman was jerked several inches off the table. Ray was uncomfortably reminded of someone opening up a raw turkey for stuffing. With one gloved hand, he held the edge of the pocket open and with the other he reached inside, his arm getting lost in the muck bulging from the wound. It struck Ray that he was being far too rough, that he was going to irreparably damage something very delicate inside the woman. He seemed to be rummaging around impatiently inside her body as if he were looking for something he'd lost.

"I don't understand. I don't--"

"Don't you, Ray?" Charlotte said beside him, licking grease off her fingertips. "Or is it that you don't really want to understand?"

Ray watched the screen with a queasy fascination. The doctor had pulled his hand out by now. His arm was slimed, shiny, covered with blood and stray bits of tissue all the way up to the elbow. Ray didn't see it at first, it was indistinguishable amongst all the gore, but the doctor had something in his oozing hand. He held up his trophy for the camera which zeroed in on the object: a shapeless lump of meat the color of dripping red earth.

"What the hell is that?"

"What's it look like?"

"Stop playing games, Charlotte. Answer me."

"I'm not playing games, Ray."

"Why are you showing me this?"

Charlotte didn't answer, didn't say anything. Instead, she rolled over onto top of him, breathless, her hand reaching behind him to firmly grab his testicles. With the other, she pulled down the frilly front of her nightie and one of her pale breasts flopped out.

"Fuck me, Ray."

"What the hell are you doing?"

"Fuck me."

"Are you crazy? Get off me."

"Fuck me."

"What the fuck are we watching? Answer me. Is it for real?"

"Fuck me."

"Was that you on the table?"

Charlotte pumped his genitals painfully. Ray struggled to get out from under her, but her hand tightened warningly around his balls.

"What's the matter, don't you want me? Don't you find me sexy?"

"Charlotte, for crissakes…"

"What's the matter with me?" She was sobbing now, growing hysterical. "Aren't I attractive enough? Am I too fat? Too old?"

Charlotte brought her other hand to his face. At first, Ray thought it was the stench of the burnt popcorn grown suddenly worse. But then he saw the remains of the crushed ampoule between her fingers.

"Breathe," Charlotte said. "All the way in."

Ray turned his face away from the gagging stench. His throat and nasal passages burned like he'd snorted gasoline and she'd just lit a match. Tears and snot ran down his face.

"What was that?" he choked. "What did you do?"

"Try to relax," Charlotte cooed, her hysteria replaced just as suddenly as it had come on with a babygirl coquettishness. She traced his lips with her finger. "Just let it happen. Do you feel anything?"

"No."

"You will, it'll happen, ride it out, baby. Just relax…"

It happened at almost that exact moment, taking him by surprise.

"Goddamit! *Fucking goddammit...*"

"Oh yeah honey, exactly. Oh yeah..."

"Char..." Ray gagged, his eyes bulging.

"That's it, baby, I want you hard. I want you to fuck me three or four times a day. I want you hard all the time. I need to be penetrated. I need your cock inside me."

Ray felt like something had gone off inside him, a leap, an errant rhythm that sent his whole body racing with nowhere to go. His surprise had turned quickly to alarm and then terror. He clutched at his chest, feeling a horrible burning, as if a tree with thousands of tiny branches had suddenly burst into flames inside his ribcage.

"God—I think I'm...having a heart attack."

Charlotte had gotten Ray lined up and was inserting him into her cunt. She rocked back and forth as if she were praying, taking him in half-inch by half-inch.

"Yeah, honey, have heart attack. Go ahead, do it."

"No dammit, I mean it," Ray was gasping. "I can't breathe. I think I'm really having a heart attack."

He'd sat up on his elbows, but froze there, willing his heart to slow down. The crazy thing was that Ray was hard, harder then he could ever remember being. His erection felt enormous, preposterous as an animal's.

Charlotte's eyes flicked open.

"So what," she spat, "so have a fucking heart attack. What difference does it make? What the fuck do I care? Don't be such a goddam pussy, Ray."

She put her hand on the center of his chest and pushed him back down. He fell back willingly. She leaned over, holding Ray's wrists to the bed. She'd managed to get the first half of Ray's cock inside her by then.

"I want you on Viagra," Charlotte growled into his ear, "I want you to have a penile implant. My husband was impotent. Did I tell you? He couldn't put it inside me. He couldn't get it up."

She was thrusting wildly, impaling herself on the remaining inches of Ray's cock, and he'd forgotten all about dying. Ray thought his erection must be tearing her apart.

"He couldn't do it with me. He had to see me with another girl. With another boy. That's what he needed. You don't want that, do you? That's not what you want to see, is it, Ray?"

Charlotte gasped, out of breath, but she didn't cum. She looked down at him from under a fringe of sweaty curls.

"I'm not into other girls. Are you into other boys? Is that it? Is that what turns you on? Are you a fag--"

Ray felt as if he wanted to orgasm, but he couldn't. Was that the price he had to pay for this unnatural erection? His cock had no feeling, as if it weren't even his anymore, as if it were no more than a bone dildo grafted onto the front of his body. She'd rendered him grotesquely priapic and hopelessly impotent at the same time. It was as if Charlotte had turned him into some kind of bizarre love-doll. She was still holding his wrists over his head and her lips were curled back in a contemptuous sneer.

"I asked you a question. Are you a faggot? Is that what you are? Am I too aggressive for you? Do I intimidate you? Are you afraid of me?"

Ray didn't answer. There was nothing he could say to her. She wasn't talking to him, anyway. But who was she talking to? Was it her husband, a past boyfriend, her father, an uncle or a teacher, a rapist, all men? Someone had stripped her, abused her, turned her into the creature who was fucking him now. Her husband, the doctor, was he the first, or only the last in the chain of men who had dehumanized her?

Charlotte was sitting back, straddling Ray's thighs now. She desperately mashed her tits against her chest and violently twisted her nipples. She ground her crotch against Ray's and panted and licked her lips and bared her teeth like a wild animal. Ray could feel her wetting him. She seemed to be straining for an orgasm she couldn't quite reach and that drove her to even more frenzied efforts. The look on her face transfixed Ray with its pure ferocity. Her eyes were squeezed shut, tears streaming down her face, and she forced out words that sounded like they were spoken in another language through her clenched jaw. Ray was certain that she was no longer even aware of him. That, if asked, Charlotte wouldn't have any idea who it was beneath her.

Ray stared into her face, which was wild with spite and hatred, and when she opened her eyes again, he knew that she wasn't seeing him, not sharing his reality. She stared straight through him, through the wall above his head, through eternity itself. Her eyes were as beautiful as they were empty, like an old church abandoned by faith. He was inside her body and yet he couldn't reach her. He couldn't cum any more than Charlotte seemed able to cum. They were fucking each other to death and yet it occurred to Ray that neither one of them could have been any more utterly alone.

He must have fallen asleep at some point, exhausted by the after-effect of whatever aphrodisiacal drug Charlotte had administered and the freakshow exertions it inspired, because Ray suddenly found himself being shaken awake.

"What the fuck--" he yelped, his heart throbbing like an open wound.

Charlotte was sitting up on her side of the bed, ramrod straight, staring into the darkness as if she'd just seen a ghost.

"Charlotte, what's the matter?"

"Sssh….." she inclined her head, listening. "You have to go," she whispered after a tense interval of utter silence. "You have to leave right now."

"What are you talking about? Why?"

Ray reached over to turn on the bedside lamp.

"Don't! No lights!"

"Okay, okay."

On the nightstand, the digital clock read 4.03am. Ray pressed his fingers to his throat to check his pulse. His skin was clammy and unshaved. His pulse stuttered like a rabbit's. "Baby, please tell me what's going on here?"

He raised his hand to stroke her back, but Charlotte jerked away as if he were going to stab her.

"What's wrong?"

"He doesn't want you here."

"Who doesn't want me here? Your husband?"

"Rudra."

"Are you kidding? What do you care what he wants?"

"It's his home."

"For crissakes, you're a grown woman." Ray pushed himself up on one elbow. The room still smelled nauseatingly of charred butter. "You can have someone over if you want. I thought you said there was nothing going on between you."

"Please," Charlotte said, clearly agitated. "I can't explain it all right now. Just go, okay? I don't want any trouble."

"Trouble? From who? From Rudra? Are you afraid of him? Do you want me to take care of that pervert? I'll do it right now, Charlotte."

"Ray, just go, alright? Just fucking go."

"Why? Because you think you owe him? You don't owe him a goddam thing, Charlotte. If anyone owes him, it's John. Let him pay the bastard back."

"You don't know what the fuck you're talking about, Ray."

"I want to help you."

"You can't. No one can. If you really want to help me, you'll just go like I asked."

"Fine." Ray stumbled out of bed, cursing. "Fine, if that's what you want."

In the dark, he stumbled his way downstairs to the laundry room. He yanked open the dryer and pulled out a jumble of clothes. By the patio light streaming through the small window above a shelf of laundry detergents, he sorted his clothes from Charlotte's and hurriedly dressed. When he left the laundry room, he saw that Charlotte had followed him downstairs. He sat on the edge of the daybed to tie his shoes.

"This is fucking ridiculous. If I'm walking out of here wearing your panties, it's not my fault."

Charlotte didn't answer. She didn't offer any further explanations.

"Do you mind if I at least take a leak before I dash off in the middle of the night?"

Ray stomped passed her, went to the toilet. When he finished, Charlotte followed him silently to the front door. Ray turned toward her in the doorway to say something, to tell her that he'd call her, that he could see her the following day, but she simply said "goodnight Ray" and closed the door before he could answer. He heard the locks engage and he stopped his hand from reaching for the doorknob.

"Fucking psycho," Ray grumbled.

He walked noisily down the path of crushed stones to the driveway where his car was parked. He passed the lit swimming pool. He passed the flower-beds. Everything was wet and humid like the world was in the middle of a dangerous fever. Judging by the corpse-like hue of the sky, he figured it was only an hour or two before dawn. As he unlocked his car, Ray looked up to the Tudor mansion where he'd seen Rudra at the window with his camera hours before.

There was no one at the window now: only a blue glow from what might have been a computer monitor.

Ray raised his middle finger towards the window. Juvenile, yes, but let the bastard know Ray knew he was watching, just in case he was. Ray climbed into the car, gunned the engine, and pulled out of the driveway, raising two rooster-tails of gravel. He'd gotten halfway to Manhattan and had reviewed the evening's bizarre events about a dozen times already. He fought the impulse to turn the car around at every U-turn and traffic light and head back to the carriage house to set things right, but he knew that would only make them worse. He knew the rational thing to do was to cut his losses and leave Charlotte alone just as she'd asked. Play it cool. Make her call him back...

Ray stuck with that idea for ten miles before he grabbed for his cell phone. He thumbed her number. A call couldn't hurt too much. He could pretend he just wanted to be sure she was okay. She seemed so upset when he left, etc.

Who was he fooling, he thought, as the phone rang. Three, four, five times. I'm doing exactly what she'll despise, acting smothering, needy, domineering. Like her husband, probably. On the other hand, he counter-argued, would any man just leave without demanding an explanation? Six, seven, eight times. No answer.

That made it worse.

Where was she? Was she not answering because she knew it was him? Did she think he was looking for reassurance? He had to set her straight about *that*.

It's a mistake, a mistake, a mistake, he thought, each time he called, and each call meant to undo the harm done by the call before it. He finally left a message and instantly regretted that, too. The worst mistake of all, he thought, as he stuttered and stumbled his way through it. Ray drove the rest of the way into Manhattan. He saw the sun slowly rising up the length of the Empire State Building like a fatal blood clot. He felt miserable, and then more miserable, and it just kept getting steadily worse from there.

Two nights later, Ray was still waiting for Charlotte to call back. He sat at the kitchen table, drinking. He'd been doing it for hours. The cordless phone sat next to his glass. Silent as a dead mouth. He stood up, walked to the window overlooking 12th street, and watched a police car racing towards Broadway, it's siren streaking like the tail of a doomsday comet. Another emergency, he thought, aimed for someone else. When the siren faded, he staggered back to the table and sat down heavily. He poured himself another drink.

He hadn't heard from Charlotte since the night she showed him that disturbing homemade medical-sex video. And Ray *had* found it disturbing, not at all erotic. For all his thoughts and fantasies, he'd never seen anything like what was on that DVD and the realness of it shocked and sickened him. Because it was real, wasn't it? That scar on Charlotte's stomach proved as much. It corresponded exactly with the place where he saw her husband draw the scalpel across her unconscious flesh. Even if she'd needed the operation, what kind of doctor would perform it on his own wife in a basement—and film it for his sexual gratification?

It was difficult enough to know what to make of what he'd seen on that DVD, not to mention what reasons Charlotte could have had to show it to him in the first place. And now that she had, what was he supposed to do about it? What was he supposed to make of her vanishing act? She'd cut off all communication between them and hadn't returned any of his calls. He'd already left a dozen messages scattered between her home, office, and cell. In each one, he tried not to sound weak, pissed off, angry, desperate—and he feared he'd sounded all four.

Ray picked up the phone, dialed her number again, and listened to her voice on the answering machine. Her crisp businesslike tone had a disorienting unreality to it after what she'd shown Ray. How could she be so cool, so normal, so sane-sounding under the bizarre circumstances of her life?

Ray hung up before the beep.

"Fuck."

He grabbed his drink and weaved a crooked path to the living room couch. He dropped down onto the cushions, threadbare and flattened under the weight of his first marriage, sloshing gin-tonic over his hand, and lit a cigarette. The fart-worn couch was about all he'd salvaged out of his marriage to Angie and he'd spent countless a lonely night on it, staring up at a ceiling as blank as his future, and wondering where his life had gone wrong. Ray slurped at his drink and picked up a copy of *Maxim* that had been delivered six months ago.

There was a photo-spread of Anna Kournikova in an orange bikini at the center of the magazine. She was splayed out on the polished teak deck of a yacht with the smug look of a Slavic Mona Lisa who could earn millions just to have men gawk at her. The toenails of her suntanned feet looked like they were painted with Wite-Out to match her strappy, high-heeled sandals. Ray half-heartedly tried to masturbate to the picture before giving up in disgust.

The phone rang at 1.14 am, half-scaring the shit out of a half-drowsing Ray. When he recovered, he fumbled the cordless he was so eager to answer it. The phone slipped out of his hands and onto the floor and he was literally on his knees when he put the receiver to his ear and questioned it hopefully, "Hello?"

The last person he expected, or wanted it to be, was Beth. Just the sound of her voice instantly doubled his depression. He would rather it had been anyone but her. She wasn't Charlotte more than anyone else wasn't Charlotte.

"Hi Ray. Sorry to call so late, but we just got done taking two of the authors out for dinner and drinks and you know how those things can drag on. Were you sleeping?"

For a few wild seconds, Ray was so flustered he considered simply hanging up. He'd pretend that he'd been half-asleep and accidentally disconnected her. It was almost the truth, after all. Then he'd pull the phone out of the wall or thumb the dial tone and shove the phone between the couch cushions. He was planning it all out in his mind when Beth interrupted by asking, "Ray, are you still there?"

"Yes, I'm here," he said automatically. It occurred to him that all his most successful Beth-conversations had occurred automatically.

"I just wanted to call and say 'hi.' Are you okay? You sound a little…off."

Ray gulped the gin-tonic and desperately flipped through the pages of *Maxim*. "I'm okay." Christ, he didn't want to have this conversation with Beth right now. "Just tired."

"I'm sorry. I won't keep you long."

There followed a long silence, pings and electronic echoes in the trunk lines like they'd picked up a broadcast from another planet.

"You're not saying anything," Beth said, sounding peevish.

"You called *me*."

"That means you have nothing to say to me?"

"For crissakes, Beth."

"Have you been drinking?"

"A little. Just to relax. What's that got to do with anything?"

"I just thought you'd be happy to hear from me."

"I am Beth."

"You don't sound it."

"How about we get off of this, what do you say?"

Beth didn't answer. Ray felt a despair building inside him that seemed to span lifetimes. He tried to change his voice, to sound like someone else, someone he imagined Beth would actually like. Oh Jesus, he felt like the first man who ever lived, as old as that, and just as exhausted. "How is it going out there anyway?" he croaked out in sheer desperation.

"It's going really well. Actually, that's part of what I called to tell you. I'm going to have to stay out here an extra three or four days. They're flying Jenna Corolla out tomorrow, the new historical author we're trying to sign. She had that #1 *New York Times* bestseller last year. Anyway, it's a huge opportunity for me. She's ready to jump ship at Random House to work with me if the terms are right. Roger wants me to stay out here a couple of extra days to show her the sights and to go over the outline of her next novel. You know, show my enthusiasm."

Ray had turned to that double-page spread of Anna K; damn, it was so detailed you could see the droplets of moisture on the molded brown globes of her perfect ass.

"Are you listening to me Ray? Did you fall asleep?"

"I'm listening. Sounds great, Beth, it really does."

"I'm sorry I won't be back by the weekend like I said. I couldn't help it."

"It's fine."

"I can't tell if you're pissed off or not. But I'll make it up to you when I get back. I promise, honey. We'll celebrate. This is going to be good for both of us. You'll see."

"Sure."

"You'll behave yourself until then?"

"Sure."

"Of course you will."

"Beth?"

"Yes?"

"Did you know the human heart shrinks in outer space?"

"What"

"The human heart shrinks."

Beth laughed. Had *she* been drinking? She sounded "off" herself, now that Ray   thought about it.

"Beth?"

"Go to sleep now, sweetie."

"Okay."

"I'll call tomorrow."

"Yes."

"Love you."

"Okay. Yes. Love you."

Ray hung up the phone and lit another cigarette. This news from Beth, what the hell did it mean? And what the hell did he care? He hadn't slept more than five hours in three days and his consciousness seemed to consist solely of a single closed loop running a three-minute movie: *That Last Night with Charlotte*. He needed an intermission. Ray thought of the leftover Xanax prescriptions he had stashed in an old shoebox under the bathroom sink. He'd been prescribed the pills during his divorce to cope with not being able to cope. At the time, it had seemed a miracle on the order of Jesus and the loaves that the world hadn't run out of tranquilizers before Angie ran out of ill-will. But, alas, it had happened. Hard as it is to imagine, even the end of the world must happen one day, and so did the divorce with Angie.

It was a Tuesday afternoon when Ray's lawyer called him at the office to tell him the believe-it-or-not news: Angie had settled. It wasn't a trick this time either. She signed the latest settlement agreement after finally, if reluctantly, accepting the fact that the judge assigned to their divorce just wasn't going to sentence Ray to the guillotine. Her acquiescence to settling for everything hadn't come a moment too soon. Ray still had four-hundred-fifty-seven pills left.

It was this cache that Ray carried out from the bathroom to begin the night's grim festivities. There was an antic detour first to the utility closet in the hall to retrieve a screwdriver to deal with the child-proof caps and then the chimpanzee-like operation of stabbing and prying and hammering to get the little brown prescription bottles open that nearly frustrated him to give up altogether. How the hell do drug addicts acquire the patience, he wondered. But Ray persevered in the end and emptied the bottles into the shoebox like so many pale blue breath mints and popped two with a fresh gin-tonic.

On the TV, which had been playing an x-rated DVD with the sound turned down the entire time, a blonde and a redhead were having sex with two hairy-chested guys in a paneled rec room. Ray popped another two pills and fast-forwarded. Now the two women were having sex with each other and two masked men in an outdoor redwood tub. He wondered how he could still be awake. Another four pills. Fast-forward. The blonde's on her knees giving expert oral sex to a biker. Another six pills. Fast forward. The redhead's licking the blonde's ass. Her hands are tied. Bikers all over the house. It looks like a party, but less happy. His consciousness seems indestructible. Another gin-tonic. Ten or eleven more pills. Ray passed out with the remote in his hand.

Ray woke to the smell of his whole world burning, like the Last Judgment had finally come. The stench filled his dreams, reminding him of the burning popcorn a few nights earlier, but this was worse, a lot worse, and it filled his lungs as he lay there gagging. He gradually became aware that he was lying in a squelching puddle. The couch under him soaking wet. He sat up, disoriented, trying to figure out just what the hell was going on. He put it together slowly, like a simpleton working a five-piece jigsaw puzzle. The ashtray on the coffee table was filled with crushed cigarettes. He must have passed out with a lit cigarette. That seemed the likeliest theory, especially when, shifting his ass to the side, he could see all the way down to the springs in the charred cushion. Christ, he could have set himself on fire, burned down the whole place. What a fucked up way to die. He didn't remember a thing, but somehow he must have managed to get up, fetch a pitcher of water from the kitchen, and put out the burning cushion. This he deduced from the presence of the plastic pitcher, which he practically tripped over as he struggled to his feet, and the sloppy trail of spilled water he'd left on the rug leading from the kitchen.

Ray stumbled to the bathroom with the still-smoking cushion under his arm and threw it into the bathtub. He ran the tap and watched the last embers among the blackened springs and filler blink out. When he went to swipe his hand over his unreal-feeling face, he discovered the burnt-out cigarette still between his fingers. He tossed the butt into the toilet, took a piss on it, flushed.

Back in the living room, the porn movie was still playing. He sat down on one of the remaining cushions to watch. The party had turned markedly uglier. More women had turned up. Some of them bikers. They seemed to have commandeered a school bus full of cheerleaders who, surprise, looked like hardened hookers. Ray reached into the box of pills. He took out another small brown bottle, uncapped it, and shook out a couple of pills. He swallowed them with what was left in the glass on the coffee table.

He shook out a few more pills, picked up the empty glass, put it back down. He dry-swallowed the pills.

He shook out a few more.

Repeat.

The scene on the TV had turned into an apocalyptic orgy. The screen was filled with countless writhing bodies: men and women, bikers and cheerleaders, victims and victimizers, it was impossible to tell them apart. The faceless people fucking each other on the screen, when they could be seen as separate people at all, seemed to be engaged in some kind of unending war of all against all. They seemed to be killing each other. Ray, watching, felt disembodied. He wanted to fast-forward but he had the feeling that there was nowhere to fast-forward to. This is the way it ended, he thought, the way everything ended. He'd lost the remote anyway. He watched, wondering if he were hallucinating. On the screen, the orgy had become a moving carpet of flesh with anonymous arms and legs that moved as if swimming, but went nowhere, a sprawling, hungry unicellular organism that was digesting everything into itself, a cancer cell eating up the world, converting everything into a malignant sexual act.

Ray would recall the following as if it were a dream, and it may even have been a dream, it was all as ambiguous and full of jump-cuts, freeze-frames, and flashbacks as a dream. He was lying on his back, in bed, and the cordless phone was in his hand. He was talking to someone, but exactly who, he didn't know. The man on the other end asked him the same question again and again because Ray was having trouble remembering it, or remembering to answer it, whatever.

"How many pills did you take?"

"I don't know."

"Listen to my voice. Don't hang up the phone. Stay awake. Don't hang up. Are you still there? Ray? Are you still there?"

Who could he have been talking to?

"Yes," Ray slurred, literally dozing between words. "I'm still here," he said, momentarily waking up.

"There's no telling why she hasn't called. Sometimes these things just happen. Ray? Ray? Stay with me, Ray."

He may have hung up that point; at least, he didn't remember any more of the conversation. He wondered if he'd called a suicide hotline. He wondered exactly what he might have said. If he'd called a suicide hotline, wouldn't they have some way to trace the call? Wouldn't they have sent someone to check on him? Wouldn't an ambulance be screaming its way to him?

Ray was in the street then, walking through the city. It was cold. Was he wearing a coat? He remembered sitting on a bench in the park (which park?) shivering, crying, his hands in his pockets. In the pockets of a coat? He remembered stepping off a curb and nearly getting clipped by a cab. A brief argument. A man shaking his head and waving the palm of his hand at Ray. "You crazy, you crazy." He remembered trying to buy cigarettes at a news kiosk, yelling at an Arab shopkeeper, pounding his fist on a countertop. "911, 911," Ray was screaming. And then he remembered running, spurred by a sense of urgency and fear. Had he stolen something? Attacked someone? Had the police been called?

He remembered stopping to catch his breath, leaning against an old-fashioned lamp post, his hand on the cold green metal when a dark sedan pulled up beside him. The passenger door swung open and the driver, a man he'd never seen before, leaned across the seats and said, "Get in, Mr Pierce. Hurry. Let's go home now before you do something you'll really come to regret later on."

Every window in the apartment was open when Ray woke up, shivering, under a quilt that hadn't been on the couch the night before. He peeked under the covers and found himself naked without any memory of how he'd gotten that way. Blackouts are like that, he thought, philosophically, even as he touched, cringingly, around his crotch and ass for any tell-tale sign of unremembered sexual activity. All clear so far, he thought, unable to suppress a shudder. He pulled the quilt back to his chin and huddled among the stench of ashes for a while longer trying to figure out just what the hell had happened the night before. He was also hoping to avoid facing any unpleasant consequences for as long as possible. The first of these was the man he could hear whistling in the kitchen over the sizzle of something frying in a pan.

"Up and at'em Mr. Pierce," the man said, now standing, as if on cue, in the doorway of the living room. "Breakfast is ready."

He was the man, quite probably, Ray thought, who'd appeared out of nowhere the night before—the bearded man in the leather jacket and slouch hat who he dimly recalled was driving the sedan that had pulled up at the curb. This morning he was wearing a pair of jeans and a black wool turtleneck, an apron that Beth sometimes wore when she stayed over was tied around his waist. He was a stocky man, about middle-aged, with thin greying hair styled long and braided down his back in a pony-tail, like an aging hippy. He was holding the frying pan and flipping the contents with a spatula.

"Hope you like omelets, Mr. Pierce. It's the house specialty."

Ray sat up and felt his stomach do an awkward back-flip. He gathered the quilt around his shoulders and stared at the floor between his bare feet for ballast. When he looked up, he saw the table in the dining area had been set for one. The man had found a vase somewhere in the apartment and stuck a small bouquet of gerbera daisies in it as a centerpiece. The flowers looked incongruously happy, all considered.

Ray's mouth tasted like an Egyptian tomb. "Who the hell are you?"

"First things first. Make yourself decent and grab yourself a cup of coffee. We'll get to all that later."

Something had happened last night, that much was clear. But the revelation of exactly what sort of situation Ray had embroiled himself in with this stranger was obviously going to have to wait until the man was good and ready to tell him. Ray was in no condition to argue. And, to be honest, he didn't think he could handle too much new information at the moment. The bearded man watched a beat longer than necessary as Ray staggered, naked under the quilt, everything raw and flapping, down the hall to the bathroom. He returned a few minutes later in sweatpants and a bathrobe to find the bearded man sliding a generous portion of omelet onto the plate he'd set at the dining table. He nodded Ray towards the kitchen.

"Grab yourself a cup of joe and come eat while everything's still hot."

Ray couldn't argue with that. He desperately needed some caffeine. He dutifully fixed himself a cup, which was waiting, freshly brewed, in the carafe of the coffee-maker on the kitchen counter. He walked back into the living room sipping the thick brew. The bearded man pulled out a chair.

"Have a seat Mr. Pierce."

Ray sat.

"Do you think we could shut some of these windows? It's like a fucking morgue in here. I'm freezing."

"I think it better if we keep them open," the man said with a tone that kept Ray from getting up and closing them himself. "The fresh air will do you good, I suspect. Help clear your mind. Now, please, eat. I'd say you need nothing at the moment so much as a hearty breakfast. It's been a long dark night of the soul."

Ray looked down at his plate: a western-style omelet with all the fixings, side of hash browns, buttered toast. He may have felt nauseous when he first sat up on the couch, but now, almost inexplicably, Ray felt ravenous. Come to think of it, he couldn't remember having had a proper meal in the last three days. He looked up at the bearded stranger who'd taken a seat across the table, sipping coffee out of a mug. His beat-up leather jacket thrown over the back of his chair.

"Where'd you get all the food?" Ray asked, chewing over a forkful.

"I did a little shopping while you were sleeping."

"Who the hell are you? Are you a cop or something?"

"Eat."

Ray forked up some fried potatoes. "You're not having anything?"

"I'm good, Mr. Pierce." He motioned impatiently at Ray's plate. "Now, less questions, more eating. Don't let your food get cold."

Ray chewed and watched the bearded man watch him. What the hell kind of weird shit was this? Who the hell was this guy? What kind of trouble had Ray gotten into, anyway? Was this guy some kind of cop? A detective, maybe? Christ, just what had Ray done the night before, anyway?

"How's the grub?"

The omelet, he had to concede, was delicious. Ray nodded, around a mouth full of it, "Great." He still expected to feel queasy, hung-over, sick. But somehow he didn't. He took a sip of coffee. "Where'd you learn to cook like this, anyway?"

The bearded man looked pleased. "Did a stint in the southwest as a short order cook. Good to know I haven't lost my touch. Always helpful to have a skill in case things get a bit dicey. And things always get a bit dicey. You never know when you'll need to go underground." He waved off the question Ray was about to ask "Please, keep eating. Don't let me interrupt you. I guarantee you'll feel better with some good eats in you."

It was true: Ray felt weak, hollowed out, as if he'd been drained of just about everything inside him. He set about cleaning his plate in silence for a few minutes. Between mouthfuls, nearly through with the omelet, he managed to ask the man his name. This time he got an answer.

"The name's Sam," he said. "Sam-I-Am. Mind if I smoke," he asked, even while lighting up a thin brown cigarillo.

Ray snorted between forkfuls. "Sam-I-Am? Is that supposed to be some kind of joke? Am I on a surreal version of Candid Camera or what?"

"It's not a joke Mr. Pierce. We're not on television."

Ray reached for a slice of whole wheat toast. "So I wake up and there's a strange guy named after a Dr. Seuss character in my apartment making me breakfast. Sounds like some kind of joke to me. I don't mean to be unappreciative, but if you're not here for the laughs, just what the fuck are you doing here?"

"How much do you remember of last night?"

"Not much. Was it that bad?"

"Very bad."

"How bad?"

"You don't want to know, Mr. Pierce. Trust me on that. You really don't. Suffice to say, that you tried to kill yourself. That's bad enough, don't you think?"

"That's bullshit. I didn't try to kill myself. It was an accident. I got fucked up with the booze. I couldn't sleep. I only meant to take a pill or two to relax and I got confused. It was an accident."

"There are no accidents, Mr. Pierce. You were acting on a subconscious urge—the same kind that has people miss a stop sign, or wander into a bad section of town, or neglect to protect themselves during risky sex. There are as many ways to kill yourself as there are stars in the sky."

"That's absurd."

"Is it really, Mr. Pierce? Think about it. And while you're thinking about it, drink your orange juice. Vitamin C is important."

He hadn't intended it, had he? Of course not. And yet, it shocked Ray to realize how close he'd come to actually killing himself, even if it were just an accident. But more than merely shocking him, it intrigued him, too. It was unreal, in a way, to think that the events of the night before actually might have constituted a suicide attempt. Because he couldn't discount the possibility entirely. What seemed even stranger and more inexplicable to Ray was that a decision like that could be made without his conscious consent, as if some invisible part of him had made it for him, had taken it upon itself to murder him all on its own.

"Well what difference does it make anyway?" He drained the orange juice in one long series of swallows. He couldn't remember the last time he'd had it freshly-squeezed. He put down the glass and wiped his mouth with the back of his wrist. "If I'd managed to succeed, I probably could have spared myself a lot of pain and anguish later on."

Sam tapped the ash from his cigarillo into his empty coffee mug. "Suicide is a sin."

"I don't believe in god."

"I don't mean that kind of sin. I mean sin in the way spilling oil into the ocean is a sin or destroying the ozone layer is a crime. Life is a precious resource, Mr. Pierce."

"Please. You're going to have to do better than that. Life is precious? That's the lamest cliché in the book."

"But it *is* precious, Mr. Pierce."

"What the hell is so precious about it? Love, sunsets, all that crap?"

"Oh no no no. You've completely mistaken me, Mr. Pierce. I mean the energy, the force, the mysterious whatever that pumps your blood, that drives the green fuse through the flower, as the poet says, that which without it, we're each of us nothing but a lump of insensate meat. *That* is precious, the most precious commodity on earth. You shouldn't just throw that away. It's not…well, it's just not economical. There are many who'd pay dearly for it."

"Just who the hell are you, really? Where did you come from? Are you from the suicide hotline? Did I call that last night by mistake?"

Sam laughed. "Suicide hotline? That's a good one. Well, you might say that, after all, I suppose. In a very loose manner of speaking, that is."

"Is this what they usually do? Send someone around to the house to undress you and tuck you into bed and then make you breakfast the next morning?"

"No, Mr. Pierce. Usually they send the police around and you go for a mandatory visit to the psych ward for a lot of unpleasant chit-chat and maybe a Thorazine vacation. You might consider yourself lucky in this regard." He passed over a plate. "Have another slice of buttered toast."

"So to what do I owe my good luck?" Ray took a slice from the plate. "What did I do to deserve this extraordinary treatment? What makes me so fucking special?"

"She isn't worth what you're contemplating, Mr. Pierce."

"How do you know what I'm contemplating?"

"Why you told me yourself. You told me a lot of things last night."

Ray felt himself flush.

"Don't be embarrassed. It's nothing I haven't heard before."

"Then maybe you wouldn't mind telling me."

"I'm afraid I'll have to decline that request a second time, Mr. Pierce."

"She showed me a DVD. It looked like a real medical operation. I mean, there didn't seem to be any way it could have been faked."

Sam shrugged. "Difficult to say, nowadays. So much can be faked, even by amateurs. But I know the kind of people you're dealing with. They don't have to fake things. They play some very strange games. They often go outside the country, use girls displaced by this or that catastrophe. Illegals, housecleaners, orphans, prostitutes. These things happen all the time. This is the real world, Mr. Pierce."

"She said her husband was a doctor. He looked like he knew what he was doing. She said he'd operated on her, but, aside from the scar, she seems to be perfectly okay."

Sam crushed out the cigarillo and seemed to be looking for something in the ashes. "He's not a doctor. He's a music industry executive."

"He's a what?"

"That doesn't mean he's not capable of safely doing a little erotic elective surgery on the side."

Ray felt something cold slithering inside him. "How do you know this? How do you even know who I'm talking about?"

"It's my business to know."

"What is your business, dammit? I asked you that already but you didn't answer me. Are you some kind of cop? A private investigator?"

"Consider me your own personal cupid."

"This is totally fucked up."

"Oh that it is, Mr. Pierce, that it most definitely is. Life is just as fucked-up crooked as a snake and every bit as poisonous. Did you know that he's still living in the so-called marital home? And do you know just where that so-called marital home is? It's about three hundred yards from the carriage house where she's fucking your brains out."

"Is she having an affair with me? Is that what this is all about?"

"I'd say you had a far more pressing worry, Mr. Pierce."

"You mean if her husband knows."

"Even more pressing than that. If she *wants* him to know."

"Christ…"

"She's playing a head-game with you, my friend. That's my opinion. If I were a betting man, and, by the way, I am, I'd tell you to take your chips off the table as soon as possible. You're in over your head and the game is fixed. You haven't got a prayer of winning this one."

"I don't think quitting is even an option at this point. I'm in love with her."

"Oh no you aren't, not really."

"I beg to differ."

"Excuse my frankness, but you're thinking about women is all wrong, Mr. Pierce. What you're looking for doesn't exist. Trust me. I know we've just met, but I wish you'd take my advice to heart. You should consider women a pilgrimage to something else, not a destination. You're confusing the map with the territory, my friend."

"You're wrong. It's as if I've been looking for her my entire life. Now that I've found her, I'm supposed to just give her up?"

"Oh, I'm not saying it's easy. Just the opposite. It's likely to be the hardest thing you've ever had to do. I'm only trying to spare you some major pain later on. I'm only trying to save your life."

"Maybe I don't want to save my life. Maybe I don't need you to do me any favors."

"Fact is, Mr. Pierce, you're in a lot of trouble. More trouble than you can imagine. I'm leaving the country for a couple of days, so unfortunately there's not much else I can do for you at the moment. Persia, as it happens. There's some…well, frankly, there's some business there I've got to attend that just can't wait. But let me leave you with two parting words of advice: *forget her*. She's nine ways to hell and no way back out." Sam smiled, shook his head. "But you won't listen, will you?"

"I think you already answered your own question."

"Didn't think so. Guys like you never do. You're all alike. *Romantics*."

He consulted his watch—a heavy-duty military-looking timepiece—and stood up from the table. "Well I've got to be running." He swung the well-worn leather jacket from the back of his chair, slipped it on, and patted the pockets. He took out another cigarillo, lit it, the match-flame actually wavering in the cold breeze coming through the open windows. "Do what you must, Mr. Pierce. Ultimately, we all do. You've been warned. If you require my help, you can always contact me here and leave a message. I'll be sure to get back to you. In a nick of time, hopefully."

He laid an embossed card on the table. Ray saw nothing but a name and a number.

Sam-I-Am.

555-6731

"Just try not to get into too much trouble too soon. I'm not a miracle worker, you know." He set the slouch hat on his head and smiled but there was nothing reassuring or friendly about the expression. It was more like the smile of a running chain-saw blade. "And if you absolutely must do something before I come back to the States, then do it very, very carefully." He touched the brim of his hat with a thick, sun-bronzed finger. "Good luck."

As it happened, the very next day Charlotte called with a lame excuse about why she hadn't been in touch. Ray didn't question her on the phone because he didn't want to get her angry. He didn't want to give her a chance to hang up and slip away once again. So he waited until she was safely sitting across from him in the dark lounge of the Paramount Hotel before pressing her on the matter. She was sipping a Manhattan and wearing a gray pinstripe pants suit, white silk blouse, and black pumps.

"I told you already, Ray. What is this, an interrogation? I had a consultation with my lawyer about the divorce. After I left his office I was pretty upset. I just felt like I needed to hole up alone for a couple of days. I left a message on your cell. Didn't you get it?"

"I didn't get a message. I checked. Several dozen times in fact."

Charlotte treated him to a "confused look" but hardly gave it time to register before growing annoyed again. "Are you saying I'm lying?"

"I'm just saying that I didn't get any call."

"Look, Ray, I told you from the start that my life is very complicated. I have other obligations. If the time we have together isn't enough, maybe I'm just not the girl for you."

"It's not that," Ray said, quickly backpedaling. "I just want to know…I want to know how I'm supposed to think of you."

"I don't know, Ray. How do you think of me? Do you want to see someone else? Is that what you're trying to say? Go ahead, if that's what you want, if I'm not good enough for you."

"No, dammit, that's not what I'm saying." He was suddenly aware of people looking and lowered his voice. "I'm saying I want to see more of you. Only you. That's the point."

"I don't like jealousy, Ray. Both my husbands were insanely jealous. I won't live like that again."

"Both? You were married twice?"

"Three times. I didn't tell you that?" Charlotte paused, as if she were thinking through a chess problem of moderate difficulty. She waved her hand. "It's not important. I was married three times. One time it only lasted four months, so I don't really count it. Three times. Big deal. Does it make a difference?"

"No. I guess not."

Did it—matter, that is? Ray wasn't sure. Maybe it did.

"John is a very violent man, Ray. He's used to getting his way in everything. We should have been divorced long before now, but he can't stand that it was me who finally walked out. That I made the decision and not him. He's a control freak. This divorce--I don't know how else to put this, but it could get dangerous."

Right, the current ex, not even an ex proper, the music exec and part-time erotic surgeon. He could be dangerous. Ha. Ray was thinking of what Sam had told him about the guy living right down the street from the carriage house. A thought suddenly occurred to Ray that he really wish hadn't. *What if it were Charlotte's crazy maniac of a husband who was watching them at the window of the Tudor mansion, not Rudra, after all?*

"Does he still love you?"

Charlotte bit the end of the thin red straw that came with her drink. "No. It's not about love. Like I said, it's about control. He wants to control me, even after three years. He left me with nothing, nothing, not even a car. Now he wants everything, even personal gifts from my father and stepfather, things with sentimental meaning that he wants only for the money. He's got all this stuff stashed away in safety deposit boxes and all tied up in litigation that's costing me a fortune. You can't imagine. I told you that before Joan took me in I was nearly homeless. I meant that literally. I'd been renting a room from an old woman who threw me out on the street for no reason and tried to steal my clothes and sell them. He put her up to it, Ray. I'm sure of it. What other explanation is there?"

Ray didn't see them at first; the lounge was too dark. But Charlotte had started crying. Fat tears were rolling over her cheeks.

"I've been through a divorce. I can't believe the system would allow that to happen to a woman."

"Are you saying I'm lying?" Charlotte snapped, her wet eyes suddenly glaring. "He's got the judge bought, that's what my lawyer thinks. Drugs, porn...I'd walk into the kitchen at three am and find him cutting lines of coke at the table with these organized crime-types. Bags of it, Ray, like baking flour. Do you know how much that's worth, what certain people will do for that kind of money? You can't imagine what it was like. I'd lock myself in the guest room and stay there all night. I'd wait until I saw them leave from the window the next morning. I was always afraid one of them might come back to the house to rape and kill me...and when things really got bad between us, I figured maybe John wouldn't care, maybe it would just be easier for him to get rid of me that way...maybe he'd even pay someone to do it."

"Why didn't you leave sooner, go someplace else, start a new life..."

"It's impossible. Where would I go? What would I do? How could I leave everything I worked for behind? Once, while I was taking a bath he broke into the room with a revolver. He put one bullet in the cylinder and put the gun to his temple and pulled the trigger and it just went click. Then he said, 'This is in case you're thinking of leaving me.' He pointed the gun at my face and pulled the trigger again. This is the kind of man we're dealing with, Ray. Don't you believe me?"

No, Ray thought. *I don't.* Fact was, he didn't know what to believe. Just because her husband was living down the street, just because she might still be with him, because she might even still love him, that didn't mean what she was saying wasn't true either. Love could get messy, as messy as getting your brains blown out, Ray was thinking. That Sam-I-Am guy was right. He was going to have to be a lot more careful than he had been with these people.

"But you did...finally. You left him. Didn't you? You're not still with him, are you?"

"No, I'm not still with him," Charlotte said. "But I didn't exactly leave him."

Charlotte bit her bottom lip. She looked up at him with great big daddy-please-don't-be-mad-at-me eyes. Ray couldn't shake the conviction that a lot of men made a sharp left turn into a dark universe of pain when they looked into those eyes. They'd believe anything, forgive anything, offer her anything—they couldn't help it, the response was hardwired into their genes. Here it comes, Ray thought, and tried to steel himself for anything. But Charlotte surprised him; he should have known that she would. He should have known that, with her, there would be no preparing for what would come next.

"I didn't leave him. He sold me."

They left the Paramount and took a cab to Central Park. Charlotte told him she didn't feel comfortable talking in the lounge anymore. In the back of the cab, Ray kept himself from asking any more questions about Charlotte's relationship with her husband. At least for the time being. They got out at 69th and began walking northwest across the park. The sun, like a balloon full of diseased orange blood, was taking a big splashy dive behind the Time Warner Center on Columbus. On the footpath between the trees, it was already halfway to twilight.

Charlotte immediately struck out on a tangent that Ray knew climbed towards the reservoir, but then she veered left to a series of switchbacks that climbed through a steep wooded hill. It was a warm night and Ray was sweaty and winded almost immediately. He was shocked at how out-of-shape he'd apparently become. Then again he couldn't remember the last time he'd actually done any regular exercise. But still. His heart, slamming against his breastbone, issued a sobering reminder that he was already at an age when suddenly dropping dead in your tracks of a heart attack wasn't completely out of the question.

"Did you know," Charlotte called over her shoulder from about fifteen feet ahead of him, "That rhinoceroses don't have sphincters?"

She stopped, turned around, and smiled. She looked like Jennifer Anniston tonight, but only in this one particular photo that Ray had seen on the latest cover of *Entertainment Weekly*. A shot in which Jennifer Anniston didn't look much like Jennifer Anniston herself. "Well did you?"

Ray tried to disguise the fact that he was panting from exertion. He'd pulled even with her at the top of the hill. Charlotte was leaning against a tree, staring up at the sky. She looked dreamy, like a heroine in a Maxfield Parrish painting.

"One of those useless facts you happen to know?" he managed to croak out without quite sounding like someone drowning.

"Yes, I guess it is a useless fact. But maybe not to the rhinoceros."

Charlotte looked down from the sky. Her eyes had taken some of the stars with them, or so it seemed. Ray gazed at them, dazzled. Christ, had they really just been having that conversation about her abusive husband back at the bar? Had they really just been talking about him selling her? Ray wanted to forget about all that, like you want to forget about an ominous physical symptom, a lump somewhere or a trace of rectal bleeding, talk it away, tell yourself it was nothing. That moment didn't seem real—or was it this moment that didn't seem real? She laughed—and her laugh was so carefree and girlish that it didn't seem anything could really be so terribly wrong with the world.

They continued walking, but at a slower pace, hand in hand. The ground had leveled off but the path required attention: it was studded with rocks and roots and creeping vines. Insects rose out of the wild grass in stinging clouds, the last of the season, most likely, still seeking sweat and blood. Ray's pulse had calmed to a manageable gallop and he paused on the trail to light up a cigarette. He was smoking a lot lately. Drinking, too. And, then, of course, there were the pills. He'd cut down on all of that tomorrow, he told himself, soon, anyway; that is, unless something really stressful happened. They walked in silence for a few minutes more before Charlotte asked him out of the blue, "If you could have the perfect house, what would it be like?"

Ray shrugged. It was the kind of question that Beth might have asked. The kind of question she probably *had* asked him a thousand times already in one form or another. It was a far more interesting question coming out of the mouth of a woman like Charlotte because Ray couldn't quite imagine her living in a house, being married, all the rest of that boring routine: even if she had done it three times already.

"Something with a view of the water I guess," he said, which was his standard answer and yet it also happened to be true. *A tent in the park, if you were in it*, he was thinking. "An ocean or a lake. You?"

"Nothing fancy. I'd like a small house with a white picket fence around it, just like in a storybook, and lots of plastic sunflowers in the front yard. Out back, I'd have a squirrel run. Yup, it would be the kind of place that friends could just drop by and hang out and have coffee and talk. The kind of place where no one would have to ask, 'Where are the ashtrays?' I want a normal life, Ray. I want all the normal things everyone says they want, but are never satisfied with."

Ray looked at the end of his cigarette; then he threw it into the weeds.

"I don't know what should be so hard about having that, if you really want it. Sounds like a pretty realistic dream to me."

"Is that how your marriage was?"

"I'd say it was more like living in someone else's dream. One day you wake up and look at the shower curtains, the bedroom set, the paintings on the wall and you say to yourself 'Who picked all that out? I hate it.' You look at the two cars, the house, the yard. You don't know how you ended up with any of it. You feel like you stumbled into the wrong story. You look at the person you married, the person you're sharing your life with, who you thought knew you better than anyone…and they don't know who you are at all. They're stuck with some version of you back from 1987. You could grow a second head and they wouldn't see it. They see some person they've fixed forever in their mind so that they don't have to bother seeing you at all anymore. You've become invisible to them. And that's really what they wanted all along, to absorb you, to swallow you up, to turn you into them. It's like being a ghost among the living, except that no one's really living. You're inhabiting a haunted house."

"That's a pretty dark view of life, Ray."

"Sorry. I'm probably just exaggerating. Maybe it doesn't really have to be like that, after all."

They rounded another bend and the path unrolled in front of them between inky blue trees that all but blocked out the sky overhead. Ray hadn't meant to say any of what he'd just said, and wished he could take it back, it sounded too depressing, too fucked up. He tried erasing the impression his words left, but it was like trying to pick up your footsteps in a snowy field.

"There are just so many things about people, especially the ones you know and love the most, that you wish you hadn't seen. But I guess I don't have to tell you that. I mean, you said your husband sold you. I'd have to think that things don't get much darker than that."

"I like to focus on the positive, Ray."

"The positive?"

"John had a sickness; correction, he *has* a sickness. It was the drugs and the women and the kink. He needed the thrill. He needed it more and more. He couldn't just be satisfied with love anymore. I tried, Ray. I really did. But I wasn't enough. The women who participate in those films—they don't come cheaply. John owed a lot of money to all the wrong people. He borrowed from Rudra to pay it back, and then he borrowed more and more and eventually Rudra wanted it paid back. Even friendship has a price."

"And you were the price?"

"Rudra has all the money he could ever want and John had none at all at that point. I was the most valuable thing he had."

"He's a doctor," Ray said, knowing perfectly well that he wasn't, not according to Sam-I-Am, anyway, but a music industry exec, which was even better. "He's got to have some money. It's what you're fighting over in the divorce, isn't it?" But was she even getting a divorce? That was in question, too. Ray realized that he could easily be trying to understand one lie with another lie.

"We're talking *money*, Ray. Real money. John was a pretender. He didn't have that kind of dough. Do you know what a life costs? How valuable that is?"

"And Rudra wanted yours?" Ray recalled again the conversation with Sam. This was the second time in as many days that someone pointed out the value of a life. "I thought you said there was nothing between you two?"

"There isn't, not the way you're thinking of it. He wants me like you'd want a painting or a baseball team. I'm an acquisition, Ray. That's what rich people do. They acquire things. Yeah, I guess he'd fuck me if he could, but he can't get it up, remember? We always want what we can't have. That's part of the allure, what drives up the price."

"And you went along with this insane idea? You let your husband sell you?"

"No, I didn't go along with it. I suggested it myself. I saw it as a way out. For both of us. I was certain that John would eventually end up killing me if I didn't find some way to leave. Rudra, in spite of it all, is an old friend of mine. I knew he'd never hurt me."

"And Joan didn't object?"

"I told you, she'd already left him at that point. If not physically, then in her mind. She was having an affair with a professor in Princeton. She was just as happy to know that Rudra was preoccupied. Harmlessly preoccupied, I might add, which made it all the more palatable to her."

"And now your husband wants you back? Even though he agreed to sell you?"

Charlotte shrugged. "He's crazy, Ray. You can't make sense of insanity; if you try, you'll go insane yourself. What he's done is eating him up inside. People like him...they don't consider the consequences of their choices. Now let's stop talking about this. I came here to show you something cool. Follow me."

Ray followed Charlotte off the main trail, down a short stony incline, to a narrow shelf of packed mud.

"Look," she said excitedly, pointing into the gloom. "That's what I wanted to show you. It's one of my favorite places in the city."

Across a brackish swamp of dead roots and felled trees, Ray saw what looked like a magic castle out of a fairy-tale. It was covered in leafy vines and all but disappearing in the dying light and Ray knew that logically it must have been some kind of old barn or way station or even a garage for park department vehicles from bygone days but there was something eerily enchanting about coming on it like this, at twilight, as if it might be some hidden Camelot.

"Jesus, I've been through this park a million times. I've never see that before. That's amazing..."

And it *was* amazing, the way the world seemed to reveal its secrets when he was with Charlotte, how it seemed to have more stars in it, more undiscovered doors, more dreams, more adventure, more *life*. Ray would miss the world she opened up to him when she was gone. And she would go, Ray never doubted it. He was just trying to hang on as long as he could, which was all anyone was doing, wasn't it? It would be hard to go back to the drab life he'd lived before, it would be almost like dying. The other night such a return seemed impossible. Thus, if he were to believe Sam-I-Am, a motive for Ray's half-assed suicide attempt when his banishment from Charlotte's world seemed imminent. But inevitable and imminent weren't the same thing and for the time being, Ray was glad that Sam-I-Am had come along and saved his life. Ray wouldn't have experienced this moment if he hadn't. For the time being, Ray agreed with both Sam and Charlotte, life *was* precious.

"Isn't there a bridge or something?" he asked, scanning the black poisonous-looking water that separated them from the enchanted-looking building. "How do we get over there?"

"I'm afraid this is as close as we get."

Charlotte was standing against him, looking into his face, as if studying it for the first flicker of arousal. Her hands were working at his belt, pulling down his zipper.

"Charlotte."

"Ssssh..."

What did he want to tell her? That he loved her? That he'd die without her? That he'd been thinking of what he'd seen on that

DVD? Whatever it was, she didn't want to hear it. She saved him from making a mistake.

She was holding his genitals like a flightless bird in her cupped hands, petting it, soothing it. They were standing on wet ground; it squelched beneath Ray's shoes, but Charlotte was going down on her knees. She was whispering, as if to his cupped genitals, as if trying not to frighten them away, the warmth of her hands and breath hypnotizing him, so that it took a moment for him to register exactly what she was asking him to do.

"Force me," she whispered hoarsely.

"I don't understand."

"Make me do this. Put your hand in my hair and fuck my face, Ray. You've got me out here alone. It's jungle-time, Ray. No laws. Force me to my knees and rape me."

She was stroking his penis, whimpering.

"Call me a bitch Ray."

"Charlotte it doesn't have to be this way."

"Don't psychoanalyze me, goddammit. Fuck me."

"Charlotte..."

"Rape me..."

"Damn you..."

"Ah, that's better," she said, as Ray tangled his fingers in her curls. "Whore—say it Ray. Call me that."

"Whore."

"Like you mean it, you pussy."

"Whore," Ray repeated, like he meant it. And he did.

"Suck my cock you whore."

"Suck my cock you whore."

"Shut up bitch."

Ray hesitated, confused.

"Say it Ray."

He did.

"Harder."

"Harder."

"Your fingers in my hair, Ray. Tighter. Hurt me...oh...a little..."

"Sorry."

"Never say you're sorry, Ray. Never. Never."

She was moaning now, kneeling in the mud in her designer pants suit, licking him, the whole length of his cock, from the base of the balls to the tip, and talking to him in between.

"Suck my cock," she said, alternately mewling and growling, "suck it....mmmm....or I'll kill you. Suck it.....mmmmm....bitch. Say it....mmmmm....say it. Or I'll.....mmmmm.....kill you."

Ray said the words and others besides, said them without thinking, as if that language of cruelty had always been there, dormant, and he'd only needed to tap into his secret fluency, like one of those Pentecostal spastics who spontaneously began speaking in tongues. He closed his eyes and tightened his fingers in her hair some more, feeling her body stiffen, and pulled her head towards him. Charlotte moaned and took him in her mouth with a muffled whimper. Ray kept on talking, an x-rated glossolalia, and felt his orgasm building like a fuse at the end of which the world, as he knew it, was about to go *boom!*

Beth was standing over a pot of boiling pasta. She wore a pair of cut-off jeans that showed off her Pilates-trim thighs and one of Ray's dress shirts knotted under her petite tits. He slipped his arm around her waist and strummed her tight bare midriff with his fingers. There was a hooked paring knife on the cutting board which she'd just used to peel a cucumber for the salad. Something about the blade's shape, like the beak of some ferocious microscopic predator magnified to the thousandth power, made Ray think of the scar on Charlotte's stomach. He found himself unconsciously tracing the same scar on Beth's tanned, toned, unblemished belly. The smell of garlic from the simmering Bolognese sauce filled the apartment.

"Looks great," Ray said, staring into the chaos of the roiling pot.

Beth leaned back against him, her tight ass molding itself to his crotch like some kind of weird mask.

"Just thinking how nice it would be if we were living together. We could do this all the time.

"Yes," Ray said tonelessly. "All the time."

"I was talking to my real estate agent friend, Kate, and she says there are pretty affordable places out in Park Slope. We can even barbecue out back there. Have a small yard. Plant tulips. You know, even raise a family if we want."

It was the same kind of thing that Charlotte had said in the park—the dream of the house with the white picket fence: the fantasy of a normal life. The problem was that Ray wanted this normal life with Charlotte, and probably for a very simple reason: that with Charlotte such a life would always be out of reach. But with Beth, such a life was something less than a dream: it was a grim inevitability.

That morning they'd slept in and read the *Sunday Times* together amid the sleep-warm bed sheets. Eventually Ray turned Beth over and she handed back the tube of lubricant and, after sufficiently slathering her up, he entered her from behind. He slipped easily into her greased cunt as she knelt on the crinkling, spread-out papers. Ray fucked her over stories about truck bombs exploding in Baghdad, rising cancer rates, a corporate stock scandal, and a jealous wife who'd run over her husband with his own Mercedes. When they were done, they had breakfast at the downtown Pane Quotidien and strolled around SoHo. The whole time Ray was thinking, "Why can't this be Charlotte?" They talked some more about living together over cappuccino at Ferraro's in Little Italy; but this time the conversation didn't have the semi-speculative tone it always had on previous occasions. There was an unmistakable urgency to the way Beth was talking about it now, like she was discussing symptoms of a disease that Ray hadn't been taking seriously.

"I don't want to live alone anymore, Ray. I'm tired of coming home at night and looking at the same four walls."

Ray stared at Beth with a blankness he fancied very much like one of the walls she was talking about. "We said we'd talk about it…"

But Beth wouldn't be put off this time. "We've been talking about it for months. I want to do more than talk about it, Ray. I want to know when it's going to happen."

"We both agreed I had to get another job first."

"No, that's what *you* keep saying. But why? I was thinking about it. You can move in with me and immediately cut your living expenses in half. You could still be looking."

Ray felt his frustration building. "What's the rush all of a sudden?"

"When I was away I realized that I had nothing to come home to, *no one* to come home to. I'm not so unusual, Ray. I'm not being unreasonable. I want what everyone wants. I want security. I want someone to grow old with. Someone to love and to love me. Someone to spend my life with."

Someone to love, Ray thought, that about sized it up, not just for Beth, but for plenty of people. Didn't that sum up, to some extent, Ray's first marriage? And was there really anything wrong with that? Could everyone expect to be struck by lightning? If magic were commonplace, it wouldn't be magic. Love, for most people, was exactly the negotiation of needs that Beth was seeking. Someone to share dinner with, take care of you when you were sick, hold you in the night. Living alone was no picnic. It ground you down after a while. You got tired of searching, of pretending you weren't searching, of waking up at three am in a cold sweat wondering if you were going to die alone. You needed someone to go on vacation with, you needed someone to touch your private parts. You needed someone to love even if you had to change the definition of what you meant by "love."

"Let's do it," Ray said, surprising even himself.

Beth looked as if someone had just offered her an outrageous line of credit she was certain would be denied, but had applied for anyway. Seeing the expression on her face, Ray found himself wondering if she'd been about to dump him.

Really? Do you mean that?"

"Really. Of course I mean it. Why are you so surprised?"

Beth had tears in her eyes. "Because it's always been so hard to get you to talk about the future."

Ray thought about that: the future. He pictured it something along the lines of an endless, pale-green hospital corridor with closed doors. At the end of it, the room reserved for him. The room he'd never leave. He could do worse than travel that lonely corridor with Beth.

He said, "Maybe that's because I didn't see myself as having a future until now."

Beth was no fool. She had to know that he'd been seeing someone else. Ray could tell by the way she looked at him when she thought he wasn't paying attention. He could tell by the way she kissed him, handed him a cup of tea, undressed in front of him. He could tell by the way she laughed and touched her hair. The way her face pinched up when he checked his cell phone or email. The only thing that hadn't been tainted by her suspicion was the way that she fucked him; if anything, that had gotten somewhat more energetic of late, taken on an unaccustomed sense of urgency and obsessive presence.

Ray had picked Beth up at the airport four days earlier. That same morning, he'd fucked Charlotte at the Savoy Empire Hotel in the upper 70s. She was staying at a suite Rudra had rented for Joan. Charlotte's friend was recuperating after several hours of extensive plastic surgery. Ray had called the day before to tell Charlotte that Beth was flying in the next morning and that he wanted to see her before she came back to Manhattan.

"It'll be our last chance to get together for a couple of days at least."

Charlotte sounded annoyed. "I can't get away. I promised Joan I would stay with her while she recovered from the surgery. She doesn't want to see Rudra and she can't stay by herself."

"I have to see you."

Ray rode out the bumpy silence. He wasn't sure how Charlotte would take what he'd said: as a demand, as a plea, as passion…

After a while, she said: "Meet me in the lobby at seven. Maybe I can slip out for a coffee."

Click.

Ray arrived a half-hour early. He sat in an overstuffed leather armchair and wore a black trench coat. It had rained all day and was raining then. There was half an unlit cigar in his hand. He stared at himself in the floor-to-ceiling mirrors across from his chair. He looked like a mourner at the side of an open grave of everything he'd ever loved. Charlotte wasn't answering her cell. It was seven-forty-five. Ray was convinced that she wasn't going to show up. He'd already asked at the front desk: Joan either wasn't registered, or she'd used an assumed name. Then, at eight-fifteen, Charlotte came through the sliding glass doors, walking hesitantly, arm-in-arm, with a heavily bandaged Joan to the check-in.

"Hi toots," Charlotte said, looking up from an Amex slip as Ray approached.

Ray glanced at Joan—she seemed completely out of it—and what was visible of her face under the gauze was bloated, red, and unrecognizable. She looked like a prize-fighter who'd gotten the pulp beaten out of her. Ray turned back to Charlotte. Like him, she was dressed in all black, her hair straightened by the rain, her cheeks flushed. She looked ten years younger and more excited than he'd ever seen her look, like a cherubic Christina Aguilera.

"I can't leave her," Charlotte explained sotte voce. "I'm sorry. The doctor said she needs someone to stay in the room. She's had a really tough time of it, poor thing. I'm glad you came, though. Just give me a few minutes to settle her in. We're in fifteen-ten."

Ray nodded. "What about her?"

Joan stared off into space, seemingly oblivious.

"The suite is huge. I'll put her to bed. She'll never even know you're there."

Ray leaned forward and whispered in her damp ear. "It's great to see you. I've missed you."

Charlotte squeezed his hand. "Give me ten minutes, okay?"

Ten minutes later, Ray knocked softly at the door to suite 1510. Charlotte answered after some minutes passed with a finger to her lips.

"I just got her to sleep," she whispered.

The suite turned out to be surprisingly drab for such an ostentatious looking luxury hotel. Ray walked to a window at the back of the main room and looked into a courtyard of dead vegetation and dingy brick. The surrounding towers of the hotel, grim and prison-like, blocked out most of the sky. Behind him, Charlotte was pouring white wine into a pair of champagne flutes with the hotel's supercilious crest stamped on them.

She said, "If it were up to me, I would have chosen a better place. Everything here is so cheap and cheesy. Why don't you sit down and get comfortable?"

Ray crossed the room and stopped at a lavish bouquet on the dining room table.

"Rudra sent them. I've been on the phone with him practically the entire day giving him a blow-by-blow account of Joan's surgery. At the same time, I'm taking calls from Allan down in Princeton. I'm exhausted."

"It's not easy being you," Ray said, only half ironically.

Charlotte handed him a glass of wine and sat down in an armchair. All the suppressed energy he'd seen down in the lobby seemed to have suddenly left her.

"You can say that again."

"What the hell did they do to her, anyway?" Ray asked, taking a seat across from her on the couch. "She looked terrible."

"Face-lift, eye-tuck, lips, cheekbones, the works. She needed it all. I told her she might as well go for it while Rudra is still paying. Boyfriend or no, she's going to be a woman on the loose in the world again. She's going to need to look her best."

"What were they trying to do, force her into visibility?"

Ray had practically mumbled the words under his breath, but he'd spoken loud enough for Charlotte to hear. This time she didn't seem upset in her friend's defense, the way she had back in the carriage house. Instead she playfully stuck out her tongue.

"Don't be bad," she said. "Hey, I'm starved. Do you want to order some food?"

She bounced up out of the armchair, suddenly energized, and crossed the room to a small desk.

"Sure."

Ray barely had time to make a suggestion before Charlotte was flipping pages in a thick hotel binder filled with ads displaying menus from local restaurants.

"What do you feel like...Indian? Thai? Greek? Chinese? French? They have everything in this neighborhood."

"Thai sounds good."

"Exactly what I was thinking."

On the phone, Charlotte was staring at herself in the mirror over the desk and talking a mile-a-minute to whoever was taking her order. She ordered a smorgasbord of food—green curry, red curry, double-cooked pork, chicken and beef satay, coconut shrimp, sweet rice, brown rice, vegetables in peanut sauce—more food than it seemed they could reasonably eat in four meals. Ray leaned back and sipped his wine and stared blankly at the carpet.

Charlotte plopped back down in the armchair, breathless, the phone still in her lap. She stared at him for a minute or two as if she didn't recognize him, not just who he was, but *what* he was.

"I'm so tired," she finally said. "Pooped. Maybe I'm coming down with something. It wouldn't surprise me. On my way to the hospital this morning to pick up Joan, I was sitting at a red light and I got rear-ended by a girl who could only speak Polish. She was so upset that I just told her to go. Then I called my insurance company, they informed me that they'd dropped my policy. For no reason. I think John had something to do with it. Maybe he cancelled it."

"Wouldn't they have told you if he had?"

"I really don't know, Ray. All I know is that my attorney called with more bad news. I have to make walk-through of the house for the final divorce settlement. I can't go back into that house again. I just can't do it."

"I'll go with you."

"That's sweet, thanks, but that won't work. It's got to be someone we both agreed on in the original suit. That means it's got to be Dmitri. My brother is being such an asshole. He has absolutely no loyalty. Last time, he ended up talking to John about business the entire time. Can you imagine? There's some good news, though. Rudra told me over the weekend that he'll pay all my legal bills. Isn't that great? They're over a hundred grand already. By the way, I've also decided to stop seeing my therapist."

"What the hell's going on, Charlotte. Can you tell me? Because I really haven't got a clue."

In spite of her manic state, Charlotte looked almost deflated. Her face, in the dim light of the room, looked ashen. Suddenly she didn't look like anyone anymore, but like a deflated, exhausted, middle-aged woman.

"Well, life's a mystery without enough clues, isn't it? Who said that?"

"I don't know."

"Me either. Hmmm...Maybe nobody said it until just now. Is that possible? Did you know that medieval Japanese women used to blacken their teeth to look chic?"

"Tell me. I know that you don't think I can help, but I'll do whatever it takes. I promise you. Do you need to get away? We could disappear for a little while. I'll tell Beth—fuck, I'll tell her something. I'll tell her to go to hell. Christ, I don't care..."

"That's sweet, Ray, very romantic, but I can't go anywhere, not now. What I really need..."

"What? What do you really need?"

"Some time to myself. I need to go into myself for a while. I need some time to think. I need to go into a hole."

"Just so long as this hasn't got anything to do with us."

There was a long silence and Ray knew he'd fallen into some kind of inextricable trap. Still, he couldn't help but ask the next

question: it was as irresistible as looking at the fortune inside a
fortune cookie.

"It doesn't have anything to do with us, does it?"

"I can't answer any big questions right now, Ray."

"And just what the hell does that mean?"

"It means exactly that. I can't answer any big questions."

"But you said..."

"Things change, Ray."

There was a sharp knock on the door and Charlotte was out of
the chair before Ray could say another word.

"That's the food," she called over her shoulder, already halfway
across the room. "I'll get it. Don't worry about it. This is what I do. I
take care of things."

Ray stood up slowly and walked to the back window with the
bottle of wine. Something had broken open inside his brain and a
thousand poisonous thoughts wriggled out. He pushed aside the
curtain on the window and looked down into the barren courtyard.
The square of dirt and weeds was illuminated by a half dozen or so
high-intensity floodlights. Behind him, in the doorway, Ray listened
as Charlotte joked and flirted with the Thai delivery boy.

The table was covered with take-out containers, paper-plates, two
flickering candles, and the remains of a third bottle of wine. They'd
eaten the food between sloppy kisses and drunken groping,
Charlotte, perched on his lap, feeding Ray pad thai noodles and bits
of highly seasoned meat on the end of her chopsticks. Ray didn't try
to resume the conversation that had been interrupted by the delivery
boy. He moved discretely around the topic during dinner like it was a
trap full of nails, disease, and explosives set to spring at the slightest
whisper.

It was simple cowardice on Ray's part, he realized that. He
didn't want to hear what Charlotte had to say, even though he knew
he was only putting off the inevitable. He unreasonably hoped the
whole thing would simply go away, like seeing blood in your urine.
And then, too, when her tongue was in his mouth and her warm flesh

was moistening in his hands, it was hard to imagine that it wouldn't somehow all work out in the end. The "truth" of the body, and all that. He wasn't fooling himself about *everything*, was he? They were clearing the table when Charlotte herself reopened the topic.

"What I was saying before, about us…"

Ray felt himself freeze in the act of reaching across the table for a carton of sweet white rice.

"Well, the fact is, Ray, I just don't know if I can have a relationship right now. I don't know if it's a good time."

Ray stared down into the box of rice, gripped by the absurd desire to count each grain.

"You're mad aren't you," she said, helpfully. "You want to leave."

Ray was surprised at just how clear and calm and cold he felt inside. He exaggeratedly put down the rice, crossed the room, and picked up his black trench coat from the back of a chair. He felt exactly as if he were in a stage-play and were following the directions in the script: *RAY puts down the rice, crosses the room, and picks up his black trench coat from the back of the chair.* In other words, he felt completely unreal, as if he were faking, as if none of this were really happening. He made it to the door without a word. He didn't trust himself to speak. He'd walk downtown to a bar and drink himself into a stupor. He'd call up Sam-I-Am, throw himself in front of the Q-train, go home and wait for Beth and the rest of his life to kill him like a bullet to the temple. It hardly made a difference. He'd already opened the door to the hall and oblivion when Charlotte shouted angrily behind him.

"Go ahead. Leave! Leave just like everyone else leaves me."

Ray turned around, uncomprehending at first. Charlotte was coming towards him, hands out, drunkenly pushing him into the hall. Everything happened so quickly after that. He dodged her blows and grabbed her wrists, kicking the door shut behind him.

"Go," Charlotte shrieked into his face. "Just go!"

He shoved her back into the room and walked her up against the wall.

"What the hell are you talking about? I'm not leaving you! You're throwing me out! I'd never leave you."

"We can't do this anymore," she sobbed.

"Do what?"

"Love each other."

"You're just drunk," Ray said, letting go of her wrists, almost relieved. He hugged her, petting the back of her head as she sobbed a soaking patch onto his shoulder. "You don't know what you're saying."

She lifted her head and stared at him for a moment and Ray had a damn

good idea what was coming, but it surprised him with its incongruity all the same.

"Fuck me."

He wanted to talk, he needed to talk. But he did what she asked because he wouldn't get anything else out of her, nothing he wanted to hear anyway, and the rest, lies. That, and the trust that he had in the act itself. Glands don't lie. They don't tell the whole truth, not even a significant part of it, but they're honest as far as they go. Ray reached under her skirt and yanked down Charlotte's panties. She was already wet to the touch. He pulled up her black sweater and worked one of her tits out of its bra cup. He put his mouth on her nipple: it tasted slightly acrid, like she'd dipped it in some kind of poison distilled from tree bark. She reached down for his zipper when he straightened up to kiss her mouth and Ray heard her make a kind of small animal moan when she reached inside his pants and touched the tip of his cock with her thumb pad.

"Put your hands around my throat," she said huskily.

Ray, numbly, did as she asked. His fingers laced behind her neck, he placed his thumbs on her windpipe.

Charlotte bucked up against him. She worked herself up on tiptoes and whispered into his ear. Ray felt his blood go cold.

He nearly let her go, *nearly*.

"Squeeze," she whimpered. "Squeeze…"

Her eyes were shut and her lips quivered, showing her teeth. She'd managed to get his cock out, and Ray slid it inside her, shoving her against the wall with each thrust. Now her hands were at the front of his shirt, pulling it open. Ray could feel her breath under his thumbs, wheezing in and out. He could feel her pulse, too, pounding under his fingertips. He put his mouth over hers and tasted the bone-taste of her teeth. It would be easy, so ludicrously easy, he thought, to push a little too hard. Her windpipe felt as fragile as a paper cup. It seemed to Ray that, if he concentrated, he could punch through it with his thumbs just as easily.

He suddenly let go of her neck, his cock buried inside her, and laid the flat of his palms against the wall.

Charlotte gasped for air. She'd ripped open the front of his shirt. She groaned. "I want to see it."

"What?"

"Blood on your flesh."

"Do it."

With his hands still against the wall, Ray stood as if he'd just been arrested for some invisible crime, arrested for everything, and continued thrusting into Charlotte. At first, it felt like a kiss, hot, hard, and passionate. It took a while for Ray to register the pain, the searing white agony of her kiss. He stuck a balled-up fist in his mouth to keep from screaming. But whether it was pain or pleasure he was trying to silence he couldn't say.

The next morning Ray woke up first. He found himself lying on the couch and holding Charlotte protectively, cradling her in his arms from behind. She was still wearing her panties and bra. They were simple cotton panties with strawberries printed on them, like something an adolescent might wear. He ran his hand lightly over her golden skin. He propped himself up on an elbow and looked down at her sleeping face and saw no sign of the wild passion of the night before: she looked completely innocent, almost angelic.

Charlotte stirred and opened her eyes as if she had sensed him looking at her. She smiled up at him, turned, and snuggled in closer. Her skin smelled of warm bread, flowers, and cinnamon. She let him go and stretched like a cat, arms over her head, toes curling.

"Mmmmm…." she purred. "I'm glad you didn't go last night. I like waking up with you."

Ray leaned over and licked her nipple.

"I like waking up with you too."

She gave him a thoughtful look. "I liked that you forced your way back inside last night. I like it a little rough sometimes, you know?"

"I don't know what the hell I'm supposed to think," Ray said. "About any of this."

"I know. It's so confusing."

"What are we supposed to do? Are we still seeing each other or what?"

"I want you to go talk to him."

"Who?"

"John. I want you to tell him to leave me alone."

"I thought you wanted me to stay out of it."

"I've changed my mind. You aren't scared are you? You aren't afraid of him?"

Damn sure he was.

"No," Ray said.

Charlotte smiled. She lifted one of his hands. "You have such pretty hands, like the hands of Christ." She fixed him with one of those stares that Ray knew well enough by now presaged a total non-sequiter, usually involving some variety of totally inappropriate sexual act. He wasn't mistaken. "I want you to fuck me before you go. Right now. I want you inside me."

Ray slid her under him with one arm, and with his other hand separated her thighs. He was already hard, had been hard for the past hour, pressing up against her warm sleeping flesh, re-running memories of the night before.

"I can barely get my arms around your shoulders," Charlotte murmured, letting her eyes close when he was inside her. "I feel so safe with you lying over me like this. Like nothing could ever hurt me. Like you'd protect me from anything."

"I'd never let anything hurt you," Ray murmured, wondering if it had finally come time to prove it.

He was soon holding her wrists down on either side of the pillow, slowly fucking her, easy, gentle, trying to let his cock speak the poetry in his heart, if one could bend one's mind around anything so preposterous, when a voice called out weakly from the door behind them. Ray stopped, his cock buried all the way inside her on the thrust, and craned his head round to see Joan standing in doorway of the bedroom. She was wrapped up in a robe, her face still swathed in bandages, and she looked like something out of the movie *The Invisible Man.*

Ray realized that Joan couldn't see them. She was looking off in the wrong direction for one thing.

"Charlotte?" she said again, her voice quavering. "Where are you? Why aren't you in bed next to me?"

Charlotte squirmed out from under Ray and peeked over his shoulder. She cleared her throat. "I'll be right there. I'll explain everything. It's okay, honey. Please go back to bed, the doctor said you have to stay quiet."

"Charlotte, who's that? Who's there with you?"

"It's no one, baby." Charlotte stifled a laugh. "Please go back to bed."

"I can hear someone."

"It's just my friend Holly," she said, snorting with mirth. "She stopped by to say hello. She's just leaving."

"I didn't want anyone here…"

"I'm sorry. She was just going. Please go back to bed. I'll be right in."

Charlotte had pushed herself out from underneath Ray by now and was retrieving her clothes from the floor. She was giggling like they were in a scene from a bedroom farce. She motioned to Ray to get dressed, that she'd be back in a moment. She gave up trying to put on her sweater and stumbled towards the bedroom in her bra and skirt. Joan stood there, still looking bewildered, facing in the direction from which Charlotte's voice had last come, while Charlotte approached from the opposite direction. Ray pulled on his pants, feeling like a jackass. The whole encounter was unexpectedly turning into a kind of embarrassing joke.

Charlotte led Joan back inside the bedroom, murmuring to her consolingly. Ray was dressed by the time Charlotte returned.

"I'm sorry," she said, blocking another laughing fit with the back of her hand as she led him to the door. "I feel like we're a couple of teenagers who just got caught by their parents."

"Sorry if I put you on the spot."

"Never mind. It's my fault. I asked you up. Let's just lay low for a few days. We have to figure this all out"

"What you were saying about your husband..."

"Forget it. I was just talking nonsense. I could never ask you to do something like that. I was still half-asleep, just sleep-talking, just wishful thinking. Forget it, okay?"

"No, I want to help. I'll have a talk with him if you really want me to."

Charlotte stared deeply into his eyes, regarding him carefully.

"Will you?" she said softly. "Really?"

"Yes. Of course."

"You promise?"

"I promise."

"Oh Ray," Charlotte exclaimed, and stood on tiptoes to kiss him, throwing her arms around his neck. She looked up at him with bright adoring little-girl eyes. "Call me after you've talked to him. Don't let me down. I'm depending on you. Oh Ray. You're my hero now."

They ate dinner by the window at Beth's place, overlooking First Avenue. The sounds of Saturday evening traffic drifted up from the street. Almost regularly, a siren passed: usually an ambulance or a fire engine accompanied by a flashing police car. It was always surprising to Ray how many fires and medical emergencies and crimes there were in the city. It seemed that fires were breaking out or people were suddenly taken ill or being shot or stabbed or beaten or robbed every ten minutes.

Sometimes Ray imagined what it would be like to know the sirens were coming for him. He imagined it as something of a relief.

But a relief from what?

What would he have done—or had done to him—for the sirens to be singing for him? What was he guilty of? He couldn't say exactly. Because it seemed to Ray that we were all guilty of something.

How far would you go for love?

Ray didn't eat much. He put the food in his mouth, chewed it, swallowed. Repeat. He tasted nothing. He hadn't had much of an appetite for days.

"Aren't you hungry?" Beth asked. "You've barely touched dinner. Didn't you like it?"

"My stomach's bothering me a little."

"Maybe you should go to the doctor and get it checked out."

"It's nothing."

"That's what you always say. It's always nothing. According to you, there's nothing ever the matter. Doesn't it matter to you that *I'm* worried? Did that even occur to you?"

Ray looked back from the window, surprised at Beth's outburst. Not that she'd have one, of course, but that she'd have one now, when things were going relatively well.

"You're always worried."

"Do I have anything to worry about?"

And he knew that in her own cryptically passive-aggressive way Beth was giving him a chance to talk, to admit that he was seeing someone else. If he said nothing now, it meant that the affair was over, that Ray had decided to end it once-and-for-all. That's how Beth decided to handle the matter. Don't ask, don't tell. But don't fuck around anymore. Ray understood that. She wanted to move in together, move forward, start a new life. What had happened before was ancient history. She was asking Ray if he was in love with someone else. She was asking him in a round about way if he was still fucking someone else and, if he was, to cut it out from this moment forward.

"No," Ray said, "you have nothing to worry about."

And he meant it, too. Yes, he did. Because the whole situation with Charlotte was getting a little too damn weird for comfort. A little too damn weird, period. A little too damn weird—and a little too damn *real.* She'd raised the stakes with this business of confronting her husband. For all Ray knew, he was walking straight into the middle of some kind of bizarre lover's quarrel and he'd be the one caught in the crossfire. Dying for love was one thing; but dying for someone else's love didn't hold much appeal for Ray. And that was only one possible twist in a situation as tangled as a bowl of linguine. The dramatis personae in Charlotte's life were steeped in the kind of major dysfunction you usually only found in Greek tragedy, and not just any one of them either, but all of the Greek tragedies put together. Ray was having second thoughts and then some about just how exciting he wanted his life to be. Maybe a quiet life of weekend shopping trips, missionary sex, and watching HBO specials wasn't so bad, after all.

"Do you promise, Ray?"

"I promise."

Ray was no private detective. He had no idea how to follow someone. It was a lot more complicated than it looked on TV. Charlotte's husband lived in the marital home on the same block as Rudra, about three hundred yards from the carriage house, just as Sam said. But three hundred yards in Montcrest separated the bona-fide mansions from the mere million-dollar homes that Rossi owned. The mountain street was long, tree-lined, and picturesque, running along a wooded ridge that fell away into a chasm. There was no shoulder to the road and no sidewalk: it wasn't the kind of neighborhood that encouraged parked cars, strollers, or amateur stakeouts.

The plan was to get a glimpse of this maniac who produced music for a living and played doctor on x-rated DVDs at night. Ray wanted at least an idea of what the hell he was dealing with before dealing with it, or, as he promised Beth, not dealing with it, and devoting the rest of his life to standing in a backyard in suburbia grilling burgers on the new redwood deck. The problem, though, was that this just wasn't the kind of situation where you casually knocked on a guy's door one afternoon and told him to bugger off because you were now screwing his wife. Fact was, Ray had been loosely keeping an eye out for the bastard ever since Sam-I-Am told him he was living down the street from the carriage house, but more to avoid running into him than anything else.

If truth be told, Ray would have preferred to avoid a direct confrontation altogether: after all, he didn't see what possible good could come from it. Ray was far from being a tough guy; he was actually quite the physical coward, as well as all the other kinds of coward one could be. But Charlotte had upped the ante and inspired a desperate recklessness in him. All that aside, however, as Ray saw the matter, scouting out the competition was only the safe and sensible thing to do.

So he sat in a parking lot at the bottom of the ridge smoking cigarettes and listening to the car radio hoping to spot John Rossi's silver Lexus descend the hill on its way into town. But it didn't happen. Not for days. Ray began to wonder if the man worked at home—or worked at all. Maybe he'd left town on business. That would explain things, except whenever Ray rolled by the house at night, he saw lights blazing in all the windows.

It was on one of those drive-bys that Ray ended up attracting the attention of the local police. They pulled him over and ran his license, took down his plate numbers, and asked what the hell he was doing cruising the area. There'd been complaints, etc. Ray denied that he was doing anything wrong, said that he was just visiting someone in the area, and when they demanded to know who, instantly realized his mistake. He switched stories, said he was just in the habit of driving along the scenic road to relax. The cop in charge offered that he didn't think it would be very relaxing to travel fifty minutes from Manhattan to drive up and down a narrow ridge road in the pitch-black. He called in back-up and before Ray knew it, he found his car surrounded by a half-dozen Montcrest policemen, hands on their holsters, as if they were expecting a shoot-out at the OK Corral. They made him get out of the car, they frisked him, they searched his trunk, they had him take a breathalyzer test. As Ray explained for the fourteenth time what he was doing in the area, he thought about what Charlotte had told him about her husband having connections inside the local police department. It didn't help either that he'd been pulled over directly in front of Rossi's house. So much for not attracting attention. If Rossi hadn't called the cops himself, he no doubt saw him being rousted at the end of his driveway; that is, if he was even in residence. Ray still hadn't caught sight of the man.

They let him drive off nearly a half-hour later with a warning not to be seen in the area again unless he was visiting someone willing to vouch for him. Ray was sitting at the counter of a local restaurant the next day trying to come up with a new plan. He considered paying a visit directly to John Rossi, pretending he was looking for an address in the neighborhood. That might get him to the front door. But then what?

He was mulling over his incomplete plan, finishing up a fifth cigarette with a third cup of coffee, the ruins of an egg-and-ham breakfast in front of him, when a man in a navy peacoat slid onto the stool beside him.

"What the fuck do you want?"

Ray turned. "Are you talking to me?"

The man looked didn't up. He sat hunched over the counter, staring at his folded hands. He was thin, dark-haired, unshaven, about Ray's height and weight. Nervous-looking.

"Why are you following me?" the stranger grumbled.

What surprised Ray was that the guy looked just as pale and scared as Ray figured he must look, but that couldn't be, could it, because at least this guy had the balls to walk direclty up to him. Ray didn't need to ask, didn't need any introduction. He recognized the haunted look in the guy's eyes immediately. He'd been seeing it a lot in his own lately.

It was Charlotte's husband.

"I just want to ask you a few questions."

"What the hell for?"

"It might clear up a few things."

Rossi looked up from his folded hands and fixed Ray with those burnt-out eyes and then nodded toward the pack of cigarettes on the counter beside Ray's coffee cup.

"Help yourself."

Rossi shook free a Camel and lit it with Ray's Bic.

"Let's go somewhere a little more private," he said through a cloud of smoke.

They moved about ten feet away to a polished wooden booth about the size and shape of a double-coffin. Rossi motioned over a waitress who looked like she was auditioning for the part of a waitress in a fifties film. He ordered a coffee. To be accurate, he didn't have to order it. The waitress simply brought it to the table. As if Ray hadn't noticed, John Rossi made a point of pointing out just what that meant.

"They know me here," he said flatly. "They'll remember that I was here with you. If something should happen to me."

He didn't seem to be joking either. Ray tried to micromanage the little muscles in his face. All the ones that would have given him away.

"Isn't that why you're here?" Rossi continued, stirring a cup into which he hadn't put any cream or sugar. "To beat me up? To kill me? What is it she wanted you to threaten me with? Financial ruin? Public humiliation? Blackmail? Murder? Her lawyers tried all of it, except the last."

"I'm just here to talk. No threats."

"Oh yeah?" A smile twitched at the corner of his mouth, more like a post-mortem spasm than anything else. "Why should I trust you?"

"Because if I really planned to kill you, would I be sitting here wasting time talking? Sipping coffee?"

He shrugged. "Maybe. What choice did you have? I found you at the counter, remember? Not the other way round. You're not very good at this, are you?"

"I don't know what the fuck you're talking about."

"Oh no? Maybe I should be the one waiting for you with a baseball bat."

"Is that a threat?"

Rossi shrugged. "Does it make a difference?"

"I didn't come here to cause any trouble."

The man laughed bitterly. "Oh that's priceless, Mr. Pierce. It really is."

That sent a little jolt of electricity through Ray's spine. He frowned. "How do you know my name?"

"I've seen you hanging around in town, cruising by the house. I called the police last night when I saw you driving up and down the street. They gave me your name, address, phone number, even how many points you have on your driver's license. So the local cops know about you, too. As incompetent as they are, even they wouldn't be able to fuck that lead up."

"What lead?"

"I've had my eye on you for weeks, Pierce."

Ray was incredulous. "You've been stalking Charlotte."

"I went past the carriage house. Yes. After all, it's only natural, don't you think? To be curious who is fucking your wife? You haven't been too subtle about it."

Ray thought that this was where it was going to turn ugly. Of course, that was inevitable. No matter what he was pretending, John Rossi was still in love with his wife. It was painfully obvious. Ray could feel it coming off him in waves, like the aftershocks of a massive explosion. Everything in the man was teetering on the brink of collapse.

"You *are* fucking her? Aren't you?"

"That's none of you goddamn business. That's not relevant here."

"Isn't it?"

"You two are separated. You're getting a divorce. You threw her out of the house, for crissakes."

The expression on Rossi's face made him look physically ill, like he had AIDS. "Is that how she tells it?"

Ray watched him compulsively tearing an empty packet of Sweet'n'Low into pink confetti. His hands were long and narrow and almost delicate, the hands of a musician or a surgeon. The hands of Christ, Ray thought, with a weird déjà vu. His thin tapered fingers were trembling. The cuffs of Rossi's coat had ridden up and Ray noticed something else weird: the man's hands and wrists were completely hairless. Not naturally hairless either. The guy waxed his arms.

"Who said I was sleeping with her, anyway?"

"You don't have to tell me you're fucking her," he said. "I know you are. I can see it in your eyes."

"I told you, that's none of your business."

Rossi sighed. "You're right. But having her fuck partners harassing me is."

"You're the one issuing the threats, buster. You're the one with the problem letting go."

He favored Ray with another one of his sick smiles. "Is that what she said?"

"Yeah. Among other things."

"Other things meaning what?"

"You sold her for crissakes. How about that for starters? Isn't that enough?"

Rossi shook his head. "She told you that? And you believe it? She's crazy."

"You're the one that's crazy. After what I heard about you, they should lock you up in a rubber room forty miles under the earth"

"You know something, you're right about that. Did she tell you that as well? That I'm crazy? I had to check into a psyche ward for nearly six months after she left me. They called it nervous exhaustion. It was what they used to call a mental breakdown. Do you know what it's like to live with a woman like her? To hear strange men on the answering machine, to find credit card charges for day-stay motel rooms, to smell another man's sweat on your wife's skin? And she didn't make any secret of it either. She wanted me to know. Yeah, I was crazy. You show me another man who loves a woman who acts like that who's *not* crazy. You come back to me in six months and tell me *you're* not crazy, too."

"I don't believe you," Ray said, without much conviction. What he was thinking is how close he'd come to a visit to the nut ward himself that suicidal night. "What happened or didn't happen in your marriage is irrelevant now. What is relevant is that she doesn't want to see you any more."

"If I never see that crazy bitch ever again it'll be too soon."

A lie. Ray could see it a football field away. "So then why are you still living right down the block?"

"You might just as well ask why she's living right down the block from me. What do you want me to do, abandon the house she abandoned? Give up everything I worked for?"

"What's the matter? You don't want to give up the amenities? I'll bet there aren't a lot of houses on the market with a home operating room in the basement? I saw the DVD, *doctor*."

Rossi looked genuinely taken aback. "She shouldn't have shown you those. She really shouldn't have. Dammit, she must be more desperate than I thought."

"You butchered her, you goddam sick fuck."

"She's lying. I never touched her with a blade."

"You're saying that wasn't you?"

"I don't know which tape you watched. There must be a thousand of them. Consider that for a minute."

Ray thought of all the DVD cases he'd seen in the rack at the carriage house. "You're telling me she's not the only one? What, that's supposed to make it better?"

"It's supposed to make you think."

"Think that you found other victims besides your wife? I don't give a damn what you do with anyone else. Just leave her alone. She doesn't want to see you. You say you don't want to see her. As I see it, the problem's solved. I pay for my coffee and wish you a happy life. I leave. That's it."

"That's really how you see it, Mr. Pierce? Everything as simple as that? Pardon me, but you don't know shit about what you're involved in here. You really think these people are just going to let it go at that?"

"What people?"

"The kinds of people who make those kinds of DVDs."

"Those people are you."

"Think again, Pierce. This isn't even just about some kinky video. It's worse than that. You have no idea. You tell Charlotte that I've got an email stored on my computer. Every thirty-six hours I have to log on to my account or that email gets automatically sent to someone who'll be very interested in the truth. It contains the contact information of someone who'll spill the whole story of what's going on if something should happen to me. So nothing better happen to me. Do you understand?"

Ray wasn't sure how the conversation had taken this abrupt U-turn. He was here to threaten Charlotte's husband and this last bit sounded suspiciously like a threat boomeranging right back at him.

"Yeah, I understand. No one wants anything to do with you, pal. I guarantee it."

"You'll tell her? About the email?"

"I'll tell her."

"Or I will."

"I'll tell her. Don't worry."

Let Rossi save a little face at the end, that was Ray's thinking, don't back him into a corner. All in all, he couldn't have imagined it going as well as it had. So far, anyway. No sense in pushing his luck. He'd been prepared to play any one of a half-dozen roles with Rossi but the man had gotten the drop on him and presented an entirely unexpected script. Ray was improvising, not his strongest suit, and Rossi was probably lying through his teeth, but the important thing was that he'd confronted Charlotte's husband and could report back to Charlotte a hero. All in all, a good day's work. Ray reached into his pocket for his wallet and put a five down on the table.

"Coffee's on me." He slid out of the booth. "No hard feelings. Everyone goes their own way. If it's any consolation, I've been through it myself. Divorce, that is. It's not easy. But you'll survive. Everyone does. Have a good life, Mr. Rossi."

And he really did feel a kind of animal sympathy for the man slumped in the booth. His very being radiated misery. Ray had been there, might soon be back there again, but he wasn't there at the moment, and that put him one rung up. He could afford a little magnanimity and fellow-feeling. It felt good to be on top for a change.

"Fuck you," Rossi said weakly.

Ray smiled, hoping he looked cooler and more in control than he felt. He headed for the exit as if walking over brittle ice, half-expecting Rossi to follow him out to the parking lot. Ray's fists were clenched, his heart was hammering, and his shoulders ached with tension waiting for something to happen. He was ready for it, as much as you could be ready for such a thing. But it didn't happen. *Nothing happened.* Rossi didn't leave the restaurant and Ray sat in his car and put his hands on the steering wheel and waited until he stopped trembling. *Well, that went better than expected,* he kept muttering to himself. But he wasn't very convincing. He realized that the meeting with Rossi unnerved him *because* it went better than he could have expected. If trouble hadn't come, that was only because it was still on the way, waiting for a better chance to fuck him up. And it meant that it would probably be coming at the very moment—and from the very place—he least expected.

They sat on the couch watching Matt Damon in *The Talented Mr. Ripley.* Beth seemed to be enjoying the movie, but Ray could barely endure it. He flipped through the personals of a free copy of the *New York Press* that he'd picked up from a bin on 57th street earlier that day. He read an ad posted by "a seductive and submissive 45-year-old cross dresser looking for understanding men or couples to play with." A little further down he saw one for "a married white professional man, 38, who wants to give afternoon blowjobs to well-hung black studs. Satisfaction guaranteed." There was a 54-year-old SJM who wanted to be humiliated, degraded, and abused by a very dominant woman, couple, or group, to serve as "a doormat, spittoon, urinal, toilet, or lackey." Who were the people behind these ads, anyway? Were they any different than the people you met everyday on the subway, at the office, or lying in your own bed?

Beth turned from the television to see Ray studying her.

"What's wrong. Don't you like the movie?"

"I've seen it before."

"You have? When? At the video store, I thought you said you'd never seen it."

"Maybe I haven't. Maybe it just seems like I have. Maybe it seems like I've seen a movie just like it ten thousand times before."

Beth looked at him funny. "Are you feeling alright, Ray?"

"Yeah, I'm fine. I can't stand Matt Damon, that's all. I can't stand that premeditated toothy grin of his. He gives me the creeps."

"I thought you liked Matt Damon?"

"No Beth. You like Matt Damon. I hate him. I've always hated him. How could you possibly think I liked Matt Damon?"

Beth seemed genuinely hurt. "I don't know. I thought it was Ben Affleck you hated."

"No. I merely can't stand Ben Affleck," Ray said, having given some genuine thought to this topic, as unlikely as it might have seemed, and, thus, the passion of his response. "There's a difference. You see, Ben Affleck is simply too one-dimensional to inspire an emotion as significant as hatred. But Matt Damon offends me on many levels and in several dimensions. I truly hate him."

"Are you sure there's nothing else wrong?"

"I'm sure," Ray said, annoyed at Beth's prescience. "Why do you keep asking me that?"

"Because," Beth said, "you won't even look at me. You haven't looked at me all night."

Ray felt pissed off, put-upon. It was the way he always felt after two or three days in a row of Beth. That was, apparently, his Beth-limit. His Beth saturation point. Wasn't it enough that lately he was pretending to love her, even though he was desperately in love with someone else? Wasn't it enough that he was compromising? What the hell else did she want from him, anyway? Dammit, she was never satisfied and that was going to be their downfall. He was never satisfied either. No one was ever satisfied. Ray was being irrational, true enough, but people weren't rational, life wasn't rational, and, most of all, love wasn't rational. Isn't that what the poets and songwriters said, for crissakes? Isn't that what was supposed to be so great about love? Shit, when you came right down to it, nothing was rational.

Here, for instance, was an ad from a married white male looking for an older gay couple to touch and service him. He was available late in the afternoons in Manhattan.

"You're imagining that," Ray said, "I've looked at you many times tonight. I'm looking at you right now, for instance. See?"

Now it was Beth's turn to stop being rational. Her voice grew sharp and witchy. Christ, they already sounded like they'd been married for ten years. Pretty soon, they'd be bickering about whose turn it was to unload the dishwasher. Just listening to her, Ray felt a smug justification that he was having an affair.

"The hell I'm imagining it," she said, "I know when I'm being looked at, and when I'm not. That's why I just turned. Because I could sense you looking at me and it was the first time all night."

"Did you know," Ray said, suddenly remembering something Charlotte had told him, lying in bed during one liaison or other, "that the human eye makes movements fifty times a second?"

"Cut the shit, Ray. I wish you'd just tell me what it is that's really bothering you."

"It's Matt Damon I'm telling you." Ray forced himself to laugh, but suddenly felt so drained he thought he might suddenly just slump over, boneless, like bag of dirty laundry. "I really can't stand that phony bastard. He's awful. He makes Brad Pitt look like a real actor. Look, Beth, I'm too tired to have this argument. Maybe you're right. Maybe I should see the doctor. Maybe I am sick or something. I'm going to bed."

"Ray, don't do this."

"Goodnight."

He heaved himself up off the couch and headed for the bedroom. It took a Herculean effort.

"Ray don't."

He paused near the door. "Don't what Beth?"

"Cut me off like this. I'm not done talking."

"Maybe not. But I'm done listening. Good night."

"Ray—" and so on and so forth up the scale to hysteria. Ray left the room as it peaked in a shriek that sounded like a skinned cat.

Ray sat at the vanity in Beth's bedroom and accessed his hotmail account on his laptop. He looked at himself in the mirror as he waited for the account to load. Whatever kind of mirror Beth had, it sure made him look terrible. His eyes, for instance, looked like the site where two black death comets had shattered into a billion pieces. Ray dipped his pinkie into an open jar of some kind of "vanishing" cream that Beth used and dabbed it around the discolored flesh. He'd have to make an awful lot of himself disappear to look any better.

He really *didn't* feel well lately: queasy and feverish. He hadn't been sleeping much. Smoking. Drinking. Always on edge. He scrolled through his inbox and didn't find a reply from Charlotte. Of course, she hadn't called him back at the office like she said she would. He'd emailed her several times over the last four days and hadn't received a single response. Had her husband gotten in touch with her after all? Had Ray's little talk precipitated a meeting between the two? And if so, was it a threat from Rossi that had resulted…or worse, a reconciliation? Were the two of them fucking right now? Was Ray just a means to bring them together again?

Ray opened up an old email Charlotte had written him: a short, almost off-hand message to say "hi" and an attachment announcing some kind of democratic party fund-raiser she was involved in. She'd never been much on writing him email and it occurred to Ray that maybe it was because she wanted to leave as little trace as possible of their affair.

Four days—for a woman like Charlotte, that was like four lifetimes.

If it wasn't her husband, Ray was certain that she'd found someone else to sleep with by now. She wasn't the kind of woman who could bear to be alone.

"What are you doing? I thought you were going to bed?"

It was Beth—she'd come into the room without Ray hearing her. Ray quickly logged off his email account and began shutting down the computer. She'd calmed down, or yelled herself out. Either way, she looked smaller, tired, resigned.

She pointed over Ray's shoulder. "What was that?"

"What was what?"

"What you were looking at?"

"Nothing," Ray said. "Just some spam I opened by mistake. I logged on to see the weather report."

"The weather? Why are you interested in the weather all of a sudden?"

Christ, Ray thought: is this what it was going to be like? Was she going to question everything that he said? Everything he looked at? Every move he made? He hated the way he always answered her in spite of himself and the cringing, childish, fearful way it made him feel inside. What was he afraid of, anyway? Of losing Beth? Of facing her anger? Of being caught?

"I wanted to see if I should bring an umbrella with me tomorrow."

"Why…what's going on tomorrow anyway?"

Ray was disgusted with himself, but he couldn't stop answering her questions, couldn't stop lying. It was almost like a challenge now to see who would give up first.

"I wanted to take a walk downtown at lunchtime. I need to start getting a little more exercise. I need to get back into shape."

He got up from the vanity to keep her from asking any more questions. He went to the bathroom to get ready for bed. He undressed, took a shower, and spent a long time brushing his teeth. When he came out, Beth had taken his place at the vanity and was putting some of the erasing cream on her face. She was staring at herself in the mirror but talking to Ray.

"So what did it say?"

"What did what say?"

"The weather report."

Ray felt a little better after the shower. He felt more spiteful, anyway. He was determined not to let Beth win at whatever game she was playing.

"The weather looks good," he said, cheerfully, as he made his way to the bed, wondering how he could get out of having sex with Beth again. "There were smiling suns wearing sunglasses in every box."

They lay beside each other, not touching, not talking, wide awake and staring at the ceiling. The window was open and the sound of the street below drifted up. Ray heard another siren speed down First Avenue: another poor bastard on his way to the hospital or the morgue or the lock-up. Ray tried not to move, to pretend that he was already asleep. It was impossible. In the quiet between them, you could hear every swallow. Beth broke the silence first.

"I don't want to fight anymore."

"Okay," Ray said dully. He was relieved, though; he was relieved that Beth hadn't wanted to continue talking like she usually did, hadn't demanded answers to any difficult questions.

"I guess what I'm saying is I'm sorry."

Ray didn't answer.

"Did you hear what I said? I said I was sorry."

"Yeah. I heard."

"Well, are you sorry?"

"Yes," Ray said. "I am."

"I just want everything to be okay between us. We have so much planned together, so much to look forward to."

And Ray knew that Beth felt that she might have ruined things tonight. She'd worked so hard to get their relationship to this point that she was willing to overlook a meaningless affair. She had rationalized to herself that Ray was just nervous about commitment; after all, he hadn't gone through that disastrous divorce all that long ago. Ray knew that's how Beth was talking herself out of being angry and resentful. He knew that she was telling herself that it wasn't that easy meeting straight men in Manhattan willing to settle down, that she wasn't getting any younger, that she wanted to get married.

"You *are* looking forward to things, aren't you, Ray?"

"Yeah, of course. But I'm really kind of tired right now. I'm kind of looking forward to just falling into unconsciousness."

There was silence again. And Ray felt Beth's hand on his thigh, moving up towards his crotch. She slipped her hand under his waistband and touched his cock gently, fondling him with her fingertips. Ray made no effort to respond and he didn't respond. He just lay there staring up into the darkness feeling her hand fluttering around his genitals. After a while, Beth said, "Do you want me to stop?"

"Stop what?" Ray asked.

"Ha-ha." Beth elbowed him in the ribs. "Don't be a jerk Ray."

"No," Ray said, stretching out again. He laced his hands behind his head. "Don't stop. Keep doing what you're doing. Keep doing exactly that. Don't stop."

She continued to rub, stroke, squeeze, and tickle his penis until Ray slowly, almost grudgingly, began to get hard. He pulled his pants off as Beth turned to the nightstand to get out the jelly and vibrator. She kept her hand wrapped around his cock, as if afraid that it, and Ray, might disappear. She slathered the jelly on his erection and on her hot, dry pussy. Is this the way it would be? Yes, playing Nostradamus and peering into the future, Ray could foresee that this is exactly how it would be. Beth straddled him and turned on the vibrator. Ray reached up and mechanically massaged her tits under her nightie. She took one last look at him and closed her eyes.

He wondered what Beth thought about when they had sex, what she saw when she closed her eyes, what finally made her have an orgasm. Was she like one of those people whose personal ads he read in the *New York Press*? Was she looking for a man to crawl on his belly and lick her dirty toes? Did she want a lesbian affair with a tattooed leather-dyke? Did she want to do it with two guys? Three? Did she want to be gang-raped, kidnapped, pierced, pissed on? Was she one of those nameless, faceless people calling out to other nameless, faceless people with desires that couldn't be named, that shouldn't be named, let alone fulfilled?

Ray knew they would never discuss what she really thought about when they fucked because they had so many other things to discuss: 401K plans, what color towels to put in the bathroom, what dreadful Hollywood blockbuster they were going to see on that Saturday night, whether they needed to buy more orange juice. They had to discuss tomorrow, and the next day, and the day after that. And that was one thing Ray never had to discuss with Charlotte: *tomorrow.* That's what made her so sexy, so irresistible. He never had to discuss life with Charlotte because there would never be a life with Charlotte.

With Charlotte, there was always no tomorrow.

Between the squeeze of Beth's cunt, the vibrator, and his own unspeakable thoughts, Ray came thinking of something else.

It was almost a week later before he saw her again. Charlotte said she'd been in Arizona on business. She was brokering an exciting deal she couldn't wait to tell him about. They met for lunch at Foley's in the Renaissance Hotel. Ray had managed a window table overlooking Broadway, which lie beneath their feet like a snake gorged to immobility on cabs, busses, and anarchic noise. Around them rose a canyon of advertising: flashing signs for cell phones, sneakers, Cadillacs, flat screen televisions. Charlotte was picking at her lunch—a pair of thirty-dollar crab cakes. She'd barely touched her wine. She had that manic look that Ray had seen before, as if the world weren't turning fast enough. Ray wondered lately if maybe she were on drugs.

She was wearing a tight, sheath-style silk skirt with a Japanese print. Her top was tight and low cut. She wore black lacquer sandals with a short high-heel.

She told him about the new business venture that had her so jazzed: two young associates of Rudra had an idea for a new TV show. It would be about a small-town, the kind of small town that hardly exists in America anymore, if it ever did, but that everyone still misses all the same.

"You know," she said, "the kind that used to be on old sitcoms in the early sixties."

There'd be a local barbershop, a post-office, a general store—the whole works. And the businesses would all be run by these loveable local characters. The police chief would come into the town diner and tell all his problems to the waitress and then in would walk the bumbling mayor and then the floozy with the heart of gold, because, in this town, even the worst people are the kinds of people you just shake your head and laugh about affectionately.

"But that's not the best part," Charlotte said excitedly, "the best part is that you can go to your computer and actually buy stuff in a virtual online version of the town. All the stores will have their own webpage and all the stuff you see in the town, it'll be available to buy. And the people from the show will have regular postings at the site, too, so that you can read up on all their doings, even when the show isn't on TV. And the site will be up 24/7 so it'll really be like everyone's really part of this imaginary town, part of one big pretend village. Isn't that great?"

"Sounds interesting," Ray said. He'd heard of ideas that he'd thought were equally moronic striking it big, so he didn't trust himself to judge. As far as he was concerned, everything was pretty much as stupid as everything else. How could you discriminate?

"You might want to write about this," Charlotte said. "You could do a freelance piece for *AdBiz*."

"Maybe," Ray nodded, trying to decide if he she looked like a slightly rounder version of Reece Witherspoon. "I'll think about it."

What he was really thinking about, though, was whether Charlotte seemed any different than the last time he'd seen her. Did she seem like she'd met someone else? Had she talked to her husband in the meantime? Why the total disconnect from where they were the last time they talked?

"I've brought you a numbered copy of the prospectus for reference," Charlotte said

With her freshly manicured fingers, she tapped a thick sheaf of papers bound in a clear plastic binder with the title "HometownUSA." She'd pulled it out of her handbag and placed it on the tablecloth between them.

"If you have any extra money, you might want to get in on this yourself, Ray. I've been around business long enough to know a golden idea when I see one. And this is the golden egg *and* the goose that laid it. If Rudra is willing to put up his own money on something…you can bet it's the closest thing there is to a sure thing."

Ray dragged the prospectus towards him over the crumbs of their bread selection. He pretended to regard it with some consideration.

"I don't have to tell you, it's confidential," Charlotte added. "For your eyes only. Don't let anyone else see it, okay?"

"Sure," Ray said, thinking of the last $2,217.68 left in his bank account. He hadn't been back to Staples since the night he attempted suicide. Somehow, even after trying to kill yourself, selling push pins and glue sticks didn't take on any new meaning.

"And you'll really think about investing?"

"Yes."

"Promise?"

"I promise."

Charlotte stared at him with pinwheel eyes. "My mother insisted I wear braces as a child," she said, apropos of nothing.

"What?"

"It's true. She said that nothing was more important to a woman than a devastating smile. My mother was a model, did I ever tell you that? A real beauty. She taught me how to smile. She'd stand smiling next to convertibles and luxury sedans dressed in bikinis at car shows. This is what she taught me…"

"I had a talk with him," Ray said, meaning Charlotte's husband, of course. "We had a kind of conversation."

"I know. You told me in one of your emails."

"I didn't know if you'd even read them. You never answered any of them."

"Sorry. I was working like a fiend."

"Aren't you curious what he said?"

Did he even need to tell her, that's what Ray really wanted to know.

Charlotte picked up her fork and poked around her plate. She bit her lip and looked up, like a schoolgirl getting news on her crush. "Well, what did he say?"

"He said you were lying."

She shrugged. "That figures."

"He said he wasn't the guy in the movie, never hurt you, isn't trying to screw you over in the divorce." Ray hesitated before saying the next part. "He claims he doesn't want to see you anymore."

"And you believe him?"

Ray shook his head. "Not even with the time of day."

"He's a lying bastard, Ray."

"Yeah." He watched Charlotte's face carefully, trying to see through all that light, trying to see to the woman behind it. "He claimed to have some information that could damage the people you work for. Damage Rudra and Joan, too, I suppose. That was the implication. He seemed to be afraid someone was going to kill him. If that happened, the info would be delivered."

"Typical John. He was playing headgames with you. Oh Christ, he's so fucking sick. Can you see why I had to get away from him? Why I'm so terrified?" Charlotte reached out and touched his face. "There's just something about you…"

"Really? What is it? Tell me. What about me? I'd really like to know."

"I'll never forget this day," Charlotte suddenly burst out, "I want to marry you! I want to spend the rest of my life with you."

Charlotte stared at him, eyes shining, almost trembling with excitement, as if suddenly possessed of some emotion too great for words. It all struck Ray as somehow very wrong. Some kind of performance. He wasn't that far gone as to believe what she was saying. There was nothing special about this day. Maybe Charlotte had missed him after a week's absence and had come to some kind of conclusion that she needed him, but Ray didn't think so. Maybe it was just the excitement about the business deal. Or maybe it was something else he didn't know about, something that had happened that she hadn't told him. Still, he couldn't help but wish that there was some grain of truth in what she'd said about wanting to be together.

"Marry me, huh?" he said, trying to maintain a sense of ironic cool. "Are you serious?"

Charlotte vigorously shook her head *yes*.

"Right now I'd settle if we could just see each other a little more. Your husband did point out something interesting, though."

Charlotte speared a cherry tomato and popped it into her mouth. "What's that, Ray?"

She chewed, swallowed. It was something that had been nagging at Ray since Sam had first mentioned the buying and selling of people that morning at his apartment.

All those DVDs on the rack...

But Charlotte didn't seem to be listening to him. She was touching his bottom lip, tracing it's outline with the tip of her fingernail. She had that spaced-out look again that Ray had begun to associate with all their sexual encounters. It suddenly seemed unreal to be sitting among businessmen and tourists eating their lunches and talking about erotic surgical procedures and slave contracts. Or was it the other way around? Maybe what was unreal were these other, seemingly normal people sitting here with their ordinary, everyday, ho-hum lives.

"Charlotte?"

"Huh?" She seemed as if he'd woken her up out of a dream. "I was just thinking," she whispered, "I want to put an object between our mouths so I can see your lips sucking on it." Her other hand had by now slipped underneath the table and began tracing the outline of Ray's penis through his pants. "I want to tie you up, baby, make you helpless..."

Ray felt a hidden door inside his mind pushed open a crack, and he caught a glimpse of the familiar shadowy images inside: the rope, the knife, the sacrificial altar. He saw an anonymous heap of suffering flesh suspended from a ceiling. He saw himself cast aside. Charlotte leaned forward, her breasts brushing against him, her cleavage separating. He stared down into the chasm, catching her scent. She whispered into his ear, her breath feverish and jungle-moist. "I want to penetrate all your orifices."

She had her thumb just below the tip of Ray's engorged cock—and he knew that with just one more flick... Somehow it gave him the courage, the desperation, really, to ask the question he'd wanted to ask all along.

"The woman," Ray said, the words sounding choked, "the woman being operated on in the film you showed me that night. That wasn't you, was it?"

Charlotte looked almost embarrassed, like a girl caught making out in her room. She smiled shyly, but beneath the table, her hand, alternately halting and coaxing, wasn't shy at all.

"You have to understand something, Ray. By that time he'd taken so much out of me. You can only take so much out before you kill a person. There's a finite amount you can give up. A spleen, a couple of inches of intestine, a gall bladder, even a kidney...you reach a limit, Ray. There's a point beyond which you can't love someone anymore."

Ray refused to be derailed, but it wasn't easy staying on track. "You were the other woman, weren't you?" he said, losing focus, not sure he even wanted to stay focused. "The one helping in the operation."

"Yes, that's right."

"He forced you to do that?"

She leaned over and whispered into his ear.

"No, Ray. You don't understand. I wanted to do that. I liked it."

Charlotte looked at Ray as if she were momentarily lost. Had she even meant to say what she just said out loud? Had he heard her correctly?

"Oooh, poor baby, what are you going to do?" Charlotte teased, holding his loaded, hair-trigger cock under the table. "You can't leave here like this!"

"You'd better...stop," Ray said, gritting his teeth. He gripped his knife and fork until his knuckles whitened. "I'm going to lose control."

Charlotte looked down at his lap. Then she looked up at him with a look impossible to describe. Her voice was urgent and insistent, but with a touch of coldness.

"I *want* you to lose control, Ray. You should wear a condom from now on. Always. Just in case...for times like this. In public."

Ray felt lightheaded. He was having difficulty breathing, as if the air had somehow thickened.

"Look how hot you are..." Charlotte said.

"Let's rent a room. We can go upstairs," Ray said. "It's been such a long time since we've been together. I can't wait."

"I have a better idea," Charlotte said. "Meet me. Tonight. There's a club downtown, on the lower east side. Two am."

"That might be a little difficult..."

Charlotte squeezed his cock and winked: "*This* is a little difficult..."

"Okay," Ray said, "I'll do it. I don't give a damn. I'll think of something. Beth can screw it."

"Oh Ray," Charlotte mock-pouted, "that's not nice." With her hand still wrapped around Ray's cock, she flirtingly asked a passing busboy for the time. When he answered, she turned back to Ray. "I've really got to run. Meeting downtown in a half-hour."

And just like that, the pact concluded, Ray knew that they were leaving that secret twilight room, that place where he always lay prostrate with his earliest and most potent gods and fantasies, that holy of holies, and entering the real world once again. The air was becoming clearer, the lights brighter. Ray could hear the sounds of the other diners: their knives and forks and conversations. He could see the neon billboards hanging over Broadway. Everything was becoming normal again. Everything that had happened five minutes ago seemed impossible. Under the table, freed from her hand, the crisis had passed. For now.

On the way out of the restaurant, they passed a small podium where a pretty Hispanic girl stood like a slave tethered to the pillar behind her. It was an image suggested by Charlotte as they approached, whispering into Ray's ear, as if to remind him how close that x-rated room still was, how the door to taboo could open practically anywhere. The girl's purpose was to greet guests and take reservations. Charlotte took a complimentary matchbook from a clear crystal bowl on the podium. She said to the girl: "Excuse me. But I just had to tell you. I absolutely love your hair.."

The girl unconsciously touched her hair and then blushed when she realized that she had. She smiled adorably. She wore too much lipstick, Ray noticed, but it made her smile look sexy in a clueless way. "Oh…thank you."

"Could you tell me where you had it done?"

"I have a friend who works at that new place on twenty-third. *Schisms?* Have you heard of it?"

"No, I'm afraid not," Charlotte said, and reached out and touched the girl's hair herself; she wound one of the girl's loose auburn curls around her finger. Charlotte bit her lower lip and studied the hair wound around her finger as if considering something. She looked back up at the girl. "I'd been thinking lately of doing something different with my hair. Maybe I'll try something like this. I just wonder if I can pull it off. It just looks so cute on you." She turned to Ray, "What do you think honey?"

Ray was at a loss. What he was watching was another act. There was no other word for it. All he could think of to say was something like, "Very nice."

"If you want," the girl said, her head slightly lowered to compensate for the tension Charlotte had on the hair wound round her finger, "I can give you the address of the place where my friend works. If you tell her I sent you, she'll give you a discount."

"Oh that sounds wonderful," Charlotte said, releasing the hair. "Is your friend as delightful as you?"

The girl blushed again under her dusky skin. Charlotte handed her the matchbook she'd just taken from the bowl. "You can write the address and number right on here. And don't forget to put down your name and your friend's name, too."

The girl wrote down the requested information on the inside of the matchbook and handed it back to Charlotte.

"Thanks so much," Charlotte said, and when she took the matchbook away a twenty-dollar bill appeared between the brown fingers of the Hispanic girl, just as if it had been a magic trick.

"You're very welcome, ma'am," the girl said, smiling, nodding her head.

"Ciao!"

As they headed for the elevators, Charlotte said, "I really liked her. She has promise. Nice hands, strong teeth." She handed the matchbook with the girl's name and number to Ray. "Keep this. We might want to make a reservation with that girl sometime."

Inside the elevator, Charlotte said: "You see, Ray, it's not so hard."

Ray was leaning against the wall. "What's not so hard?"

"To make connections between people. That's really what I do. I get people together."

They were alone in the brightly-lit metal box hurtling straight down without a single stop. They would reach the lobby in less than a minute. Charlotte stood against the opposite wall staring at Ray. She seemed to be growing increasingly agitated.

"Fuck me," she said.

"You're kidding, right?"

"You heard me."

"Now?"

"Now. Fuck me."

Ray looked up at the panel of rapidly flashing numbers. "There isn't time."

"Pretend that you're taking me to my execution and this is the only chance you'll have to rape me before they strap me in a chair and give me a lethal injection."

Ray simply stared at her.

"Look, does this make it easier?"

Charlotte pulled down her top and exposed her tits and stepped out of her sandals. She put her hands behind her back, as if they'd been cuffed. "Does this?"

It was happening again. In spite of himself. Ray felt something shift in the fabric of reality. The door nudged open. With a little effort, it wasn't so hard to imagine that they were in some kind of corporate version of hell and that Charlotte was his condemned prisoner.

"I'm so scared, sir," Charlotte said in a small voice, pretending to tremble. "I don't want to die."

Ray crossed the elevator car, yanking his fly down. He was fully erect. He pressed up against Charlotte, shoving her against the wall. He hiked her skirt over her hips. He opened her pussy by separating the smooth globes of her ass. Charlotte's head thunked against the fake wood panel. She moaned as Ray jerked her damp panties to the side. Her eyes fluttered open. She was looking over his head to the corners of the elevator as he entered her. She whispered in his ear, "Can they see us? Do they monitor these things?"

Back at his apartment, Ray sat on the undamaged half of the couch smoking cigarettes and staring into empty space. He tried to concoct a plausible excuse for not spending the evening with Beth, but the best he could come up with was that he wasn't feeling well, a fever, probably, and that he wanted to just hole up alone in his apartment. It was the kind of lame-ass excuse Charlotte had given him, even the expression was the same, but Ray decided it would have to do.

He was relieved when neither Beth nor her assistant at her office answered the phone and he could simply leave a message on her voice-mail. His relief changed to annoyance ten minutes later when his phone rang. Certain it was Beth calling back for an explanation, Ray wasn't going to pick up, but in the end he figured it would be easier to get the inevitable confrontation over with as soon as possible. He picked up the phone, but the voice on the other end wasn't Beth's. Ray felt a wave of absurd good humor at the sound of the unfamiliar voice, until, that is, what it was saying sank in: "I know all about you. I know what you're up to."

Ray tried to disguise the convulsion of sick fear that passed through him. With cool incredulity, he asked: What am I up to, then?"

The voice said: "You know what you're doing. You shouldn't have let it get to this point, if you cared about her. If you knew what was good for you."

It didn't sound like Charlotte's husband, but that was the first person he suspected. The voice, obviously disguised, was scrubbed of all specifics like gender.

"Is this some kind of joke?"

Ray expected hard talk, threats, warnings. Instead what he heard was almost a forlorn plea: "Why don't you let her go? You don't love her. Why won't you leave her alone?"

"Who the hell is this?" Ray demanded.

He asked the same question two more times before he concluded that whoever was on the other end had hung up. But Ray was wrong. The line was still open. He realized this just before hanging up himself and as disturbing as the call would have been if it had been terminated, it was even more disturbing to realize that whoever was on the other end was still there. Whoever it was on the other end was listening to Ray breathe, listening to Ray think, listening to Ray sweat, while on his end Ray heard nothing but dead air.

At two am, Ray met Charlotte at an after-hours club in Alphabet City. From outside, the club was invisible, nothing but a heavily painted and repainted red door in a wall of faded brick that anyone not knowing any better would have taken for some kind of service entrance, but some people did know better, and these stood in a short queue outside waiting for admittance. It took Ray a while to recognize it without the construction scaffolding and limousines, but this was the entrance to the same club where he'd met Charlotte by accident two months earlier; if Charlotte remembered, though, she gave no sign of it. And, sure enough, when Ray brought it up, she just looked at him uncomprehendingly a moment or two before saying, "Really?"

It was clear that Charlotte had no connections at the club, or she didn't choose to use them, but she charmed her way passed the steroid-and-Armani enhanced doormen all the same and dragged Ray in her wake. Inside, they found themselves in a massive open space towering upwards on all sides like an ex-apartment building gutted of all its floors and apartments by a vicious architectural cancer. A series of metal catwalks were bolted along the interior walls, an elaborate weblike structure of cages and steel balconies that were inhabited by outrageously costumed dancers that Ray figured were probably recruited by the club from the surrounding East Village environs to provide atmosphere. They were visible only periodically, as a series of spotlights played pell-mell up and down the walls like plague sores, lending the entire club the look of a large central hall in the mansion of an hallucinated hell.

"This place," Charlotte shouted, "is so not happening anymore."

The main floor was a seething mass of young bodies, an almost indiscriminate collection of eyes, arms, bellies, and backs without beginning or end that reminded Ray of that x-rated video he was watching the night he tried to off himself. The crowd seemed to pulsate along with a concussive soundtrack that wanted to crush every thought in Ray's skull to nonsense. They skirted their way around the crowed to a bar that looked like a plexiglas altar and was lit from within by a blue-red phosphorescent light. The flagrantly gay bartender was stripped to the waist like a professional wrestler, or like one of those models on the covers of the ridiculous romance books Beth edited. He served them toxic-colored drinks in large red plastic cups and eyeballed Ray with a bewilderingly instant distaste. It must have been the same—and only—drink he served to everyone because he handed them over without waiting for an order. A Jim Jones cocktail, Ray thought, club-style.

"I'll bet you don't dance," Charlotte said.

She was dancing in front of Ray as she said this, doing a little shimmy-down. She was wearing a short, white knit dress and gold heels with rhinestone straps across the insteps.

Ray shook his head, "No."

"I knew it. I'll teach you."

Charlotte closed her eyes and slipped a hand under her dress. She was masturbating herself, or pretending to, touching herself, in any event. If there was any doubt, she put her fingers under Ray's nose as proof, or for inspiration, it was difficult to say.

"This is what dancing is really all about," she screamed. "Dance with me Ray."

A request Ray answered by shuffling his feet and holding onto Charlotte's wildly gyrating hips; she had abandoned herself to the music as if she were fucking an invisible demon. Ray felt like he usually did when trying to dance, more like he were suddenly possessed of an extra half-dozen limbs or so, and a few odd feet thrown in, to boot. Charlotte leaned over and shouted something into his ear, pointing at a girl at the end of the bar. She was a more or less average-looking girl, late 20s, short dress, high-heels, long dark hair parted down the middle. It was a while before Ray understood what Charlotte was asking.

"Do you?"

Ray shrugged, moving his weight from foot to foot, like he was shouldering a sack of rocks. "I guess," he shouted back.

"Come on, you can say. I won't be mad. Promise."

Ray lifted the red plastic cup and took a sip of the drink. The club blurred and he squinted at the lone girl. "Yeah," he said, "she's okay. But I like that one better."

He extended his cup in the direction of a black-haired, punk-looking Asian girl in a short, blue-paid schoolgirl's skirt, platform boots, and a stud in her lower lip. She, too, looked to be in her 20s, but had a harder, cooler look than the long-haired girl. She was dancing with a tall black couple, or more likely, they were dancing with her. The girl seemed oblivious to anyone else's presence.

"So that's what you like?" Charlotte grinned, and ground against him. "Do you want to see me dance with her?"

"You don't have to—"

"I'm going to dance with her."

Charlotte slipped out of Ray's hands and angled her way across the floor. She approached the girl with a friendly smile and started dancing beside her, doing a little bump-and-grind that shook the girl out of her autistic solo-routine. Charlotte was still holding her cup and she offered it to the girl, who sipped at it. Charlotte fluttered her fingers over the girl's exposed stomach, tracing the tattoo around her navel, and playfully tugging the piercing there. Ray could see the girl suggestively licking the neat black bow of her lips in response.

The connection, Ray thought, *had been made.*

They continued to dance for a while and then Charlotte shouted something in the girl's ear or kissed her, or both, and jutted her chin in Ray's direction. The girl looked over, nodded, and just like that, they were both walking toward Ray. Charlotte had her arm around the girl's waist, casually possessive, and Ray couldn't help thinking that it was all just too goddamn easy.

"This is Miki," Charlotte said, making the introductions, when they walked up. "She likes to party. Let's go to a party place."

In the cab, Ray felt vaguely sick to his stomach. After almost no deliberation, it was decided the "party" would be held by default at his apartment, Miki living with a jealous black bouncer on parole from some violent crime or other and Charlotte's situation, well, just too complicated to go into. At his place, Charlotte took him off into the kitchen and told him to mix up drinks and just relax. She lit up a joint she produced from somewhere and gave his ass a reassuring squeeze. "Everything's going to be cool," she said. "Trust me." Then she joined the girl on the couch, or rather, on half the couch. She shared the joint with the girl, who'd already made herself comfortable, her legs draped over the couch arm and her head now in Charlotte's lap. As he stood at the kitchen counter pouring gin into glasses of diet Sprite, Ray could hear the messages from his answering machine: three or four messages from Beth asking him how he was, where he was, and finally, angrily ordering him to call her back immediately. Charlotte kept hitting the playback button letting the messages replay over and over. She and the girl were giggling and snorting like a couple of cruel teenagers at a pajama party.

By the time Ray brought the drinks into the living room, Miki was already high and half-undressed and kissing Charlotte deeply on the mouth. Charlotte had the girl's plaid skirt flipped up over her waist and her hand was playing in her shaved crotch.

"Jesus," Charlotte said, amused, "don't any of you girls have pubic hair anymore? God, you'd think a real live wild beaver was an endangered species or something."

Ray stood there feeling awkward and stupid with a drink in each hand. He'd only been involved with group sex twice in his life and one of those times hardly counted: a drunken party-turned-orgy back at the university that Ray had both entered and left a virgin. Damn good thing, too, since the entire episode was later reclassified as a rape. The second time had been in a German brothel during a bicycle trip across Europe. He hadn't been much older, and only a little more experienced. Two Polish whores—more woman than Ray knew what to do with at the time—an overwhelming tidal wave of flesh, mouths, breasts, thighs, hands, etc. He generally remembered it as a short and all said humiliating experience.

Seeing Ray enter, Charlotte jumped up from the couch, leaving the Asian girl with her skirt hiked up around her waist. "Take over for me, Ray. I want to put on some tunes."

The girl took one of the glasses from Ray and pouted. She called out passed Ray. "Does *he* have to stay? I'd really rather he didn't. I'd rather it was just the two of us."

Charlotte laughed as she looked through Ray's skeletal CD collection. She'd taken off her panties and had them balled up in her left hand. "Did you hear that, darling? Miki wants a girl's night only. It's okay, don't pout, honeykins. I still want you." Charlotte turned back toward the couch. "Don't worry about him," she said to Miki. "He's perfectly harmless."

Ray sat down heavily next to the girl and sipped at Charlotte's drink. He absently kneaded one of Miki's small tits with his free hand. In spite of what the girl said, she didn't object to Ray's mashing her flesh around. Not that there was much to mash around. She didn't have much more up top than a boy. Ray tried to get turned on by looking over her body. Besides the navel tattoo, she had a ring of barbed wire and roses inked around her left biceps. And, on her waist, just above her right hip bone, what he'd first mistaken for a large bruise or birthmark turned out to be yet another tattoo: a black scorpion in some kind of notched circle, like a brand trademark. They hadn't flipped her over yet, but he felt fairly certain there would be some more illustrations on that side, too. Ray felt idiotic, uninspired, and unaroused. He wanted to call the whole thing off. He had the strong intimation that picking up this girl had been a terrible mistake. He undid his pants and reached inside. His penis lay shrunken in it's nest of hair like a dead baby bird.

In the meantime, Charlotte had put Rammstein into the CD player and switched the TV on to CNN. The dour, German heavy metal music made a disconcerting soundtrack to the video clips of two smiling generic-looking politicians campaigning against each other for some office or other. They grinned and waved in front of cornfields or in malls, on aircraft carriers, in school rooms. Charlotte watched the TV, swaying to the fascistic techno beat and nibbled a cold slice of leftover pizza she must have found in the fridge.

"Haskins just has to win," she said, chewing. "We need that seat to take control of the Senate. The fucking right wing has had a stranglehold on this country long enough."

Charlotte turned from the TV. She asked the girl: "You're for Haskins, right?"

"Who's Haskins?" the girl slurred, licking around the inside of her glass.

"He's only one of the most liberal voices in Congress. The next Ted Kennedy. He's for civil rights, abortion rights, gay rights, animal rights, all the good stuff."

"Politics," the girl said incredulously. "Fuck--who pays attention to that bullshit anymore?"

Charlotte smiled a dazzling smile, "Rock the vote," she said.

"Generation Whatever," Ray said, trying to make a joke, but unsure what joke he was trying to make. "You're forgetting how young our friend is." He turned back to the slumped-over girl. "How young are you anyway?"

The girl glowered at Ray, didn't answer, and Ray wondered if she even heard him. He stopped mushing around her tit.

"You're for Haskins, right Ray?" Charlotte asked.

"Sure," Ray said. "I'm for him." He'd managed to work a finger into the girl in spite of her foul expression, but it didn't feel good: like he'd stuck his finger into something dangerous, like a wet electrical socket.

Ray flopped his head back on the couch and stared at Charlotte. He saw it in her left hand then, all but concealed in the balled-up panties: the scalpel. His heart, lulled into a metronomic torpor, suddenly woke up and began pounding.

"See," Charlotte said, "Ray is very obedient. He likes what I like. He does what I tell him. Don't you sweetheart? He's very eager to please. He'll do whatever I ask, won't you baby?"

Ray looked up, questioningly. "Can I see you a minute. In the kitchen?"

"Why don't we show this girl how accommodating you can be?"

The drunken girl slumped further down on the couch, spread her legs wider, and began snorting and giggling for no apparent reason. Ray vaguely wondered if he were tickling her. He pulled his finger out of her cunt, having forgotten it there. Looking at her now, Ray decided that she'd somehow lost all her allure somewhere between the club and the apartment, like a shell you take home from the beach. It looks pretty and exotic lying on the sand; not so great on your window-sill. Ray suddenly felt like punching someone in the face.

"Come over here Ray," Charlotte said sharply and she put her fist to her mouth, as if she, too, were about to start giggling uncontrollably. "But...ummm... come over on your hands and knees. Like a good doggie."

She winked at him, as if something were up. Ray had been keeping a careful eye on the balled-up panties in Charlotte's hand. He couldn't see the scalpel anymore, but he knew it was still there somewhere. It made him nervous not seeing it, and, of course, having seen it in the first place. He slid off the couch, onto his knees, as if he were going to do push-ups, and scooted across the floor to where Charlotte stood. He felt like a moron but they were all so high that human dignity really didn't seem to be a priority at the moment.

"Good boy," Charlotte said, reaching down and tangling her fingers in his hair. "You see," she said over his head. "He'll do whatever I say."

Behind them, the girl burped, "Groovy." She wasn't paying that much attention anymore.

"You can stand up now doggie," Charlotte said, "Evolve. Just like you were a human being."

Ray got to his feet and Charlotte ignored the words he was mouthing. She nibbled the tip of her finger, thinking of what to do.

She said: "Strip."

Ray hesitated.

Her voice was sharper the second time. " Do it, Ray. Take off your clothes."

Ray undid his belt and dropped his pants. He pulled off his shirt. His socks and underwear came next.

He stood there naked.

Charlotte handed him her panties.

In the same hard, cold voice she said: "Go ahead. Put them on. We don't want to see your disgusting thingie."

Behind him, the girl on the couch barked out a laugh and said something like "thingies are fucking gross." But Ray wasn't paying any attention. The scalpel was now naked in Charlotte's fist. The girl couldn't see it because Ray was standing between her and Charlotte. He put the panties on. They were tight and the seams stretched, but they didn't rip. Charlotte's eyes were round and jazzed. It was crazy. He had a hard-on all of a sudden.

"What are you doing with that blade?" Ray asked under his breath. He was trembling.

"Calm down, toots. Don't be a party pooper. I just want to have some fun with this girl." Charlotte didn't bother to keep her voice down. She ran her hand through her hair, the hand with the scalpel. "Turn around and show our guest how cute you look."

Ray turned around, feeling ludicrous. Charlotte patted his ass.

At this point, the girl had reached between her legs and she was listlessly pushing two fingers in and out of the naked hole at her center. She wasn't paying attention to what was going on. She was back inside herself, like she was on the dance-floor. The way she was fingering herself made Ray cringe. It was too rough, maybe it was the drugs that had desensitized her. She looked as if she were reaching into herself for something. She was masturbating alright, but it looked as if she were trying to pull herself inside out.

"Dance for us Ray," Charlotte said, dancing herself to get him started. "Come on, baby. Be our go-go girl."

She grinded up against Ray for a while and then she joined Miki on the couch, watching her masturbate, before making out with the girl. Ray moved around for a while, not exactly dancing, but not stopping altogether. He made it to an armchair and dropped into it, watching Charlotte and the Asian girl kissing. He'd lost track of the scalpel. Charlotte didn't seem to have it anymore. Ray wondered where it'd gone to. He kept reminding himself that it was very, very important to know that.

After a while, they ended up in the bedroom. Charlotte told Ray to stand by the bed and masturbate while she and Miki made out on the bed. Ray was still wearing the panties. He rubbed himself through the scratchy pink lace without much enthusiasm. He'd already lost his erection. Charlotte and the girl climbed onto the bed and started kissing and fondling again. The girl had lost the rest of what little clothes she was still wearing. Naked, she definitely didn't look so hot anymore. She seemed too skinny and too white, almost genderless, bony even, like she must be sick or on drugs. Ray was reminded of a raw supermarket chicken that had somehow come gruesomely back to life, but stamped with black tattoos.

They didn't pay him any attention, lost in their mutual explorations. They quickly worked their way into a "69" position, heads between each other's legs, eating each other out. To get turned on, Ray tried to pretend that he wasn't there, a tactic that had helped him in the past when having sex. He imagined, for instance, that he was watching a porn film.

Eventually, Charlotte looked up from the girl's skinny thighs, her eyes scrunched tightly closed. Her face was wet from the girl's pussy and the girl's likewise with the juices from hers. Charlotte crawled blindly forward, turned around on all-fours, and scooched back between the girl's widely forked legs to do a little solo. She worked at it that way for a while before coming up for air with a pained expression. Then she squirmed her way up, pressing her body against the girl's, and, finally, hovered over her, pushing the girl's shoulders back into the mattress.

"Oh my god," she exclaimed dramatically, staring at Miki with saucer-eyes, "I just have to have you!"

Charlotte told Ray to get onto the bed. Ray thought for sure that this time the girl would object, but she didn't. At Charlotte's direction, Ray sat behind Miki and wrapped his arms around her, playing with her nipples. They felt weird, like wads of chewing gum you've had in your mouth too long. To his surprise, Miki leaned back into Ray's body and sighed contentedly. Her eyes were closed; she dropped her head onto his shoulder. Charlotte glanced at Ray and shrugged. He figured the girl must be pretending he was someone else, another girl, probably, or maybe she had just zoned out. Meanwhile, Charlotte ducked back down between Miki's bony thighs. There was a slight smile playing on the girl's lips, but if you looked closely, it could almost have been a grimace, as if she'd been left out in the cold for a very long time.

Charlotte stuck two fingers up to the second knuckle into the girl's wet asshole. The girl moaned and shivered. Ray wondered where the scalpel was now. He hadn't seen it for a long time. He dutifully kept playing with the girl's nipples. He kissed the side of her neck. There were tattoos there, too: a line of fanciful kanji saying god-only-knew-what.

The girl was moving now, thrashing a bit, moaning. She spread her toes, painted a metallic BMW blue, and started pedaling her legs in slow-motion. Charlotte had gone under the hood again and was making loud lip-smacking sounds, like she was slurping soup, between the parted legs. The girl was making a lot of noise herself. She moaned. She farted. She cursed. She seemed about to cum. Charlotte came up briefly to say, "Hold her Ray. Hold her tight goddammit." She put her head back down but after awhile the slurping noises suddenly stopped again and the girl was making a weird strangled sound. That's when Ray looked up to see what was wrong. Charlotte looked back at him from between the girl's forked legs. She was holding the scalpel between her fingers.

The girl had opened her eyes for some reason and seen this, too. She'd been momentarily stunned but she now started hitting Ray with her sharp elbows. She very understandably tried to smash his nose with the back of her head. In anticipation of this reaction, Ray pressed his face tightly against her shoulder to protect himself. The girl's skin suddenly smelled bad, like parts of the Jersey Turnpike. Instinctively, he sank his teeth into her sinewy shoulder just to shock her into settling down. In the meantime, Charlotte had climbed up onto the girl's knees to help control her thrashings. She stroked the side of the girl's face with the fingers holding the scalpel.

"Sorry love," she said. "Don't be so upset." Charlotte looked from the girl to Ray and back again. "There's nothing to be afraid of. Is there, Ray?"

"No," Ray muttered numbly.

"You can take your hand off her mouth," Charlotte said. "You're smothering her."

Ray was surprised to find his hand clamped hard across the girl's face. He didn't remember putting it there in the first place. He reluctantly took it away certain she would scream and ready to clamp it back on. But the girl didn't scream. She didn't make a sound.

"We're just playing a little game," Charlotte explained. "It's harmless, really. I'm going to explain and all I want you to do is listen, okay? If you don't like the rules of the game, you're free to go. I promise. Does that sound okay to you?"

The girl quickly nodded her head. She sniffed some snot back into her nose. She seemed to have settled down, but Ray was thinking that it was just an act.

"Good," Charlotte said. She smiled her bright everything's-going-to-be-great smile. "What I want you to do is simple. I just want you to blow my boyfriend while I cut him. It's okay, I'm a doctor. I know what I'm doing. This is just the way we get off. You see, we're sort of vampires. Well, not really. There's no such thing as vampires, of course. We're not psychos. We just like to play. Its like a Goth thing, you know?"

To Ray's surprise, the girl really seemed to be considering what Charlotte was saying, as if it really made sense. Maybe it was the reassuring way Charlotte said it. The girl, nodded, "Yeah I think I get it."

It was a bit freaky, she admitted, but she'd been involved in freakier scenes. Ray figured she was still bluffing. Could there really be anything freakier than this? He thought that she might just be waiting for an opportunity to make a run for the door.

"Let her go, Ray."

Ray shot Charlotte a look.

"Let her go."

Charlotte rolled off the girl's legs and Miki squirmed out of Ray's arms. She slid down to the end of the bed. She didn't run. She could have tried, but she didn't. She sat on the end of the bed wiping her mouth and glaring at Ray.

"Okay lover," Charlotte said, winking at him. "Here we go."

She turned back to Miki.

"Are you ready?"

"You're gonna cut him?"

"Yup."

The girl sneered. "I'm ready."

Charlotte straddled his waist and told Ray to put his arms over his head. Ray did it, why, he didn't know. He could feel the girl pulling the panties down. She pulled out his cock and balls. He felt the girl's small, warm mouth on him.

He still thought Charlotte was lying, that she was trying to trick the girl, but he wasn't sure. Charlotte told him to relax, that it wasn't going to hurt. She winked at him again. She held the scalpel like a pen and her tongue poked out at the corner of her mouth like a schoolgirl concentrating on drawing her capital letters. Ray didn't think she was really going to cut him right up to the moment she drew the thin line across his left breast.

It didn't hurt, just like she promised it wouldn't. At least, it didn't hurt the way Ray might have expected it to hurt, the way it looked like it should hurt.

He stared down at the incision with a sense of unreality. The blood welled up along the horizontal line almost instantly. It seemed in an awful rush to leave his body. Charlotte made another careful stroke with the scalpel. This time she drew another diagonal line. It bisected the first line to form a little "x." The second cut just missed his nipple. The blood rose up from this cut just as quickly as the first.

The blood looked vibrant, oddly alive, *alien*. Ray had the strange sensation that the life it represented wasn't even his own.

Ray looked up from his chest. Charlotte was leaning over him and staring at the bloody cross she'd drawn in his flesh and her face seemed to be transfigured: she looked as beautiful as the pictures Ray had seen of medieval saints and martyrs when they were burning at the stake. Meanwhile, the girl between his legs was dutifully licking, ministering to both Ray's cock and Charlotte's now exposed cunt. Ray could feel the girl's mouth alternating between them, as if she were trying to connect them, spark some kind of highly unstable and unpredictable chemical reaction, and she would be the catalyst.

Charlotte muttered something in a guttural voice that Ray didn't understand: it sounded like a foreign language. She leaned forward and licked the blood off Ray's chest and lifted her head again. Her face was contorted, as if it were melting. She was panting and groaning in a way that Ray had never seen before. She didn't look beautiful or transported anymore. Her forehead was corrugated and her lips were peeled back in a grim sneer. Her eyes bored into his without giving any hint that she was seeing a thing. She looked brutally ugly the way only the insane can be ugly. She looked like something caught in the middle of a transformation, a transformation between a human being—and something else. Ray knew she must finally be close to an orgasm.

Close…

She was sucking at the wound on his chest again, the red x over his heart, like a jackpot marked on a treasure map. The warmth of her mouth sucking there trumped even the sensation of the girl's mouth on his cock. Charlotte's mouth and his wound seemed to form a new sexual organ uniting them in an act more intense and more intimate than anything Ray had ever experienced.

Ray, too, was now speaking a hoarse gibberish as if he were temporarily possessed. He was saying crazy things and they got crazier as he neared orgasm. Charlotte was sitting up and fucking him now. She had abandoned Miki's mouth, pushing the girl roughly away, and eased back on his erection, her pussy sopping wet from Miki's saliva and her own arousal. Ray lost track of the girl for a while, lost track of everything. Then he saw her small hands covering Charlotte's tits, like some kind of exotic tropical sea-creatures had attached themselves there. The girl's small, black-painted mouth was sucking on Charlotte's neck as she stared down at Ray with a raw hatred that, compared to the savagery he'd seen on Charlotte's face a moment earlier, seemed like little more than childish petulance. And the whole time Charlotte was tracing incoherent arabesques of silver in the air with the scalpel.

Ray was out of his mind. In other words, he was cumming. He had no idea what he was saying, or maybe, it was more that he didn't care. He wasn't even sure if he were speaking out loud, and if so, how loud. It was more like the leaking out of a black monologue from the darkest texts of his desire. What he was saying now were like those sex adverts he'd read in the back of the free newspapers and the compulsion to expose himself to public view was identical, just not as anonymous. He knew that he'd regret whatever he admitted now come morning, but at that moment, morning would never come.

Charlotte got rid of the girl. Ray could hear them talking by the door in the other room as he lie there, feeling like airplane wreckage. Charlotte told her to take whatever cash was in Ray's wallet and forget about what she'd seen. "It's no big deal," the girl kept saying. She'd regained her cool with the first crack dawn. Everyone did, when they realized they were going to survive. Like one of those super rollercoasters that are perfectly safe no matter how terrifying they seem, and, of course, deep-down, you know this all along, even though you've screamed your ass off the entire ride. It's just easier to believe when the ride is over.

After the girl left, Charlotte showered and after she showered she came back into the bedroom to pull down all the blinds, keeping the light at bay for a few hours more. She had a meeting with some computer people back in New Jersey. She was telling Ray this as she slid earrings into the tiny pinholes in her ear lobes. She was already late. She click-clacked over on her olive-green velvet pumps and kissed Ray on the forehead and then the sound of her heels faded down the hall. And then the door closed behind her.

Ray didn't move for a long time. The crisscrossed lines of blood that covered his chest had dried to a dark, weblike crust. He opened his eyes after a while and stared at the ceiling. Each pit in the paint seemed to him as detailed as a crater in the surface of the moon. He whispered in the lunar landscape, *"Why am I still alive?"*

Hours passed.

There was no answer.

Life goes on, often unfortunately so. Ray eventually got out of bed. He tried to call Beth but her line was busy. He walked to the kitchen. He poured out a glass of orange juice, but the taste of it sickened him, and he spit out the very first mouthful in the sink. He tried to call Beth again; this time the phone rang unanswered. He hung up when her message started. She's pissed off, Ray figured. He'd call later.

In the bathroom mirror he assessed the damage: the cuts on his chest weren't nearly as deep as he'd thought. The dried crusts of blood had made it all look much more dramatic than it really was. Still, Ray figured he needed to tend to the wounds somehow. He should keep them clean at the very least. He poked gingerly around the sensitive edges of enflamed flesh. He found himself oddly reluctant to do anything that might erase the mark she'd left on him.

In the shower, he carefully soaped himself. The dried blood washed away and the soapy water stung. Around the drain at his feet, the water ran pink.

Ray patted himself dry.

He had some rubbing alcohol in the medicine cabinet, less than half a bottle, leftover from something or other. He finished cleaning the cuts out with that. He wadded up pieces of toilet paper and soaked each wad with dabs of alcohol. He touched it to his skin. The wet tissue was cold for a second or two, and then it burned like a lit cigarette. Each time he touched the paper to his skin he closed his eyes until the pain eased. When he was done, the waste basket was filled with blood-tinted crumpled toilet paper, like a dozen pink carnations.

Under the fresh shirt Ray wore, the crisscross cuts on his chest felt tighter, and stung like a corset of thorns. But it wasn't all bad. Somehow, it even felt weirdly satisfying, a constant reminder of the reality of Charlotte. Before he left the apartment he called Beth one last time: her line was busy again. He decided she was punishing him.

She would probably keep it up for a day or two.

They were sitting in the café section of the Barnes and Noble bookstore at Union Square. It was two days since that crazy night with the girl from the bar. Charlotte said she could squeeze Ray in between a dentist appointment and an interview with a potential

client at the Paramount at seven pm. She was thirty-five minutes late.
Ray drank coffee while he waited and flipped through a book of
Helmut Newton photographs. When she arrived, Charlotte was
wearing a conservative navy suit and matching pumps. She was
drinking a bottled fruit shake.

They made small-talk for a few minutes. Charlotte seemed
perfectly ordinary, like any middle-aged businesswoman, content to
keep things on the level of superficialities. It was frustrating, this
charade of normalcy. Ray was burning up with questions. He stuck it
out for as long as he could, playing it cool, but finally leaned across
the table, cutting her off in the middle of some blather about her love
of African-American fiction.

"I've got to talk to you about the other night."

"What about it?"

Charlotte sucked at her straw, staring up at Ray from under her
sunglasses. It made her look like Sue Lyon from the movie version of
Lolita, but more cosmopolitan.

"You scared the shit out of me."

"What do you mean?"

"Don't play games--you know exactly what I mean."

"Not really."

Ray drew a cross over his chest with his forefinger. "You cut
me."

"Oh that...did it freak you out? Be honest."

She was so open and frank, acting as if it were the most
perfectly natural thing in the world, that Ray felt almost silly for being
so goddamn dramatic about it.

"I wasn't expecting it."

"I guess I got a little carried away. I didn't hurt you, did I?"

"No."

"I guess I should have said something. I have a bit of a blood
fetish. I find blood sexy. It's so much more intimate a body fluid than
any other. Don't you think? I mean, if you think about it? Bleeding
can be such an act of giving. It can be so beautiful when done in the
spirit of love. Does that make me weird?"

Weird? Ray wondered how to even qualify it anymore. It seemed to him that they had passed beyond the merely weird some time ago. Weird was in the rearview mirror by now, but small, you had to look for it very closely. It had all but vanished.

"I'd be lying if I said that seeing that scalpel pop up in your hand all of a sudden wasn't a little unsettling. After all you told me about your husband, after seeing that video…"

Charlotte cocked her head. "Wait…what did you think I was going to do to that girl, anyway?"

"I don't know."

"Tell me the truth. Did you think I was going to kill her?"

"No," Ray said, glancing around at nearby tables because Charlotte's voice was not lowered the way you should lower it when you talk about killing people in a public place. "Of course not."

"You did. Admit it." Charlotte was laughing. "You thought I was going to kill her."

Well, what was he going to say? He'd answered "no" because that was the kind of thing you said to the woman you loved when she asked you a question like that. Because anything else would be unthinkable.

"I wasn't sure what you were going to do."

"Oh toots, that evening was for you. You mean to say, you didn't know that? Oh boy. No wonder you're so upset. Poor thing. I thought I'd put on a little show for you. I thought you'd enjoy it. I hope you didn't misunderstand. You weren't scared, were you?"

"That's not the point. I'd just appreciate knowing what the game is."

"You *were*," Charlotte said, "Oh Ray, you were scared. It's okay to admit it. I didn't let you know what I was going to do because sometimes it's better not to know. It's better to be surprised. Sex is all about letting go. It's all about sacrifice. Like the French say, *la petite morte*. I believe in that, Ray. I really do. Giving oneself up totally to whoever—or whatever—one loves. Don't you?"

"Yes," Ray said, and the truth was he did. "But you have to be careful. Things could get out of hand."

"I won't do anything you're not ready for. I promise. You have to trust me, Ray."

"Trust you?"

"You do trust me, don't you?"

"I want to trust you."

"I'm so glad we're talking about this, Ray. I'm glad it's out in the open. Really. I think its so important." Charlotte let her eyes wander briefly around the café section before settling back on Ray. She leaned across the table. "Don't you think, for instance, that some women were born to be raped? I know it's not fashionable to say that, not PC or what have you, but let's talk honestly. I mean, don't you sometimes see women working in Radio Shack or shopping in supermarkets or even hanging out in a place like this...really beautiful, sexy women and you think to yourself, what is *she* doing here? She should be someone's slave. Don't you think to yourself, 'I'd just like to take her.'

"I'll bet you even had a woman like that in your office. She's so pretty but she just looks so dull and lifeless sitting behind a desk all day, working on spreadsheets or whatever, so bored with her drab life. Don't you get the sense that the real purpose of such women isn't being fulfilled? These women are a gift. These women belong to the gods, Ray. In the old days, you know what they'd do with such women? They'd decorate them with flowers and sacrifice them. That's what they were born for, Ray. To be offered up. They'd come alive on the altar. Don't you think it's possible that you'd be doing a woman like that a favor by taking her away from reading a computer screen all day or waiting tables?"

"Times are different," Ray said tightly.

"Are they? Are they really any different? Hmmm...I wonder."

Charlotte looked at the book open on the table between them: a naked woman wearing only a gas mask and stiletto heels crawled across a polished floor on all-fours.

"I love Helmut Newton," Charlotte said. She touched the black-and-white photo with her fingertips, glanced back up, the reflection of photographed naked flesh in her eyes. "Life is so boring,

Ray. Even fucking is so boring, after a while. It lacks intensity. It lacks the spirit of sacrifice."

Either she's crazy, Ray thought, or she thinks I am. Some kind of trap, that's what she could be laying for him. She seemed to be going out of her way not to say something. He had to be careful.

"Do you think I'm crazy Ray" she asked, as if reading his mind. "I see life as a ceremony, as a sacrament. Is that insane? We could be priest and priestess of our own religion."

"What religion would that be?"

"Love," she said softly, laying her hand on his, "is something so much deeper, so much more communal, than most people can experience: it's beyond all boundaries, all reason, all comprehension..."

"I don't understand what you're trying to tell me. Why don't you just come out and say it."

"We passed a barrier the other night, Ray. Don't try to tell me you didn't feel it too."

"What kind of barrier?"

"Am I wrong about you, Ray? Tell me if I am and I won't bother you anymore. But I don't think so. I have an instinct for this kind of thing. How far would you go, Ray? Would you do anything for love?

"I don't want to rape and kill anyone, if that's what you mean. I draw the line there."

"You don't have to rape and kill someone. There are other kinds of sacrifices.
Other kinds of gifts. Do you love me, Ray?"

"Yes." Ray ordinarily would have considered it a mistake to tell a woman like Charlotte this, but this was not an ordinary moment. "Yes, I do."

Charlotte smiled. "I know you do."

"What about you?"

"I could love you Ray. I do believe I could."

"If?"

"Make me an offering."

"What is it that you want?"

She softly touched her fingers to the back of his wrist.
"Oh, you know what I want, Ray. You know."

To Ray's relief, Beth finally returned his call. He'd realized in the
intervening days how much he still needed her. It was shocking,
really, how much he needed her, like you need gravity, for instance.
Beth provided a sense of normalcy, even if three-quarters of the time
he was bored to death by it. Her absence over the last few days left
him feeling at loose ends, like nothing was quite real anymore. Beth,
love her or leave her, was reality itself, and Ray understood that he
needed to get back on an even keel with both. He needed some
insurance against the insanity of the last few days.

She was distant and cold when they met. Ray was expecting
that. That he figured he could handle. Beth had been busy, she
claimed, working with the new author she'd mentioned meeting
during the book convention in Vegas. She told him her name again
when it became obvious that Ray didn't remember who the hell she
was talking about. That night, after all, he'd been in the process of
committing suicide.

"Jenna Corolla."

She said it with a note of annoyance that Ray found annoying.
"Right, yes, of course. Jenna Corolla."

They saw a foreign movie in the East Village about a man in
love with a comatose woman and then they had dinner in a quaint
little Italian restaurant on First Avenue. Ray had black linguine. Beth
had something with a pink sauce. They split a bottle of wine that
seemed to help melt the wall of ice between them.

"I love you Ray," she said, "but you're making it so fucking
hard."

She looked at him with an exasperated, but not entirely
disgusted expression.

Ray, inwardly, breathed a sigh of relief. She wasn't going to
dump him, not yet, anyway. Her un-Bethlike silence all evening had
given him some cause to doubt. He hadn't already fucked up
anything beyond repair, after all. Her attitude gave him hope that he

might still be able to patch things up, like a life-raft in the middle of a shark-infested patch of open ocean. He was clinging to her.

"I know," Ray heard himself saying, "I'm sorry. I haven't been myself lately."

"A friend of mine said that maybe you were getting cold feet."

"Maybe."

"Another flat-out told me you didn't love me."

She peered at him from over her wine-glass as if she'd been told exactly what tell-tale give-away to look for in his face.

"That's just bullshit."

"Is it?"

"Of course."

"I need to know that I can depend on you. On us. I need to know that you want the same things I do."

"Yes, I do."

And he did want the same thing: he didn't want to be alone. He was afraid of facing a life of microwaving dinners for one. At fifty-five, at sixty, the life he was leading now wouldn't be freedom any more. It would only be the sad lonely shuffling of someone who'd missed the carousel. If that's not the way it really was, that's the way it looked. Besides, a man needed someone around to call the ambulance when he finally had his heart attack. That's the way Ray saw it, anyway.

"I wasn't myself the other night," he said. "I didn't want you to see me the way I was."

And that, too, was true enough.

"Are you better now?"

"Yes."

"Because if you're sick, Ray. I should know. You at least owe it to me to be honest. That's all I'm asking."

But that wasn't really true. She was asking for more.

A lot more.

Later, at Beth's apartment, Ray undressed in the bathroom and came to bed in the dark. He slid under the fresh sheets and pressed up against Beth as closely as possible. But it didn't work. She managed to slide her hands between their bodies and over his torso.

"What's this?" she asked, feeling the taped gauze-patch.

"Nothing."

She pushed him away and rolled over on her back.

 "Let me see."

"Don't..."

Beth turned on the bedside lamp and propped herself up on one elbow. At its deepest point, Ray had finally had to tape a pad of medical gauze over the wound. The webwork of cuts surrounding it had healed up enough to look like little more than scabbed-over scratches. Beth touched the coppery-stained bandage with her finger.

"What happened here?"

Ray said, "It's really stupid. I stopped by to see Eric; he took in a stray cat, if you can believe that, as if the guy can commit to anything. Anyway, I was holding the damn thing and the tea kettle started whistling. The cat went nuts. I didn't let go in time."

"What happened to your shirt?"

"What shirt?"

"The shirt you were wearing when this happened."

"What difference does that make?"

"I'm curious. What happened to the shirt?"

Ray sensed a trap, thought it through, then saw it.

"I wasn't wearing one."

Beth looked up from his chest. "You weren't wearing a shirt? Why not?"

"I'd spilled some beer on myself earlier in the evening. I guess I was a little tipsy. You know how those bulls sessions go with Eric. So I took it off to let it dry. What is this, anyway, the Inquisition?"

Beth didn't say anything else, not about the cuts, anyway. She reached over and switched off the light and they made small-talk for a while. He wondered if she believed him, or if she were just biding her time to bring the subject up again in a day or two, like a detective returning to a suspect with new questions, wearing him down. Ray got her turned around after a while. He kissed her on the neck and behind the ear and then he played with her tits. He lightly ran a test-finger along her slit and found a surprise: she was actually wet for a change.

He entered her, after a few more preliminaries, easily from behind. She sighed and pushed her ass against him. Her flesh felt smooth and cool.

Ray worked it in and out, in and out. He let his imagination drift, nudging open the secret door, letting the blue light in. It was Charlotte who walked into the room, she was standing by the bed, the scalpel in her hand. He was seeing things from her perspective. There were two bodies on the bed, joined in the midst of sex, white and vulnerable looking, crisscrossed with thin red lines. "It's okay," Charlotte was telling them in a soothing voice. "Just relax. Let it happen. Everything's going to be okay. You two are bleeding out nicely." Stunned, Ray came, unexpectedly, in a hot rush and held Beth close, whimpering, breathing in her Beth-scent, and when it was over, he began apologizing profusely.

"It's okay," she murmured, "it felt good anyway."

But Ray slipped down under the sheets, ignoring Beth's half-hearted protests, and prompted her onto her back. He kissed her belly, the insides of thighs, and Ray heard her sigh. He had never done this before, never wanted to, but he couldn't face Beth, not yet. Beth was a gooey, salty mess between her legs, the heat radiating out of her in waves. Ray had to overcome his initial squeamishness. Her clitoris was swollen, hard as a peanut still in its shell, in the middle of all that muck. He licked her, tasting the bitter salt taste of his unmanifested generations. He pushed his tongue inside her, feeling veins, the tunnel of ridged muscle. She took a long time, longer even than usual. Ray's jaw began to hurt and he had to keep gulping his foul-tasting saliva and whatever else was squirting from Beth's cunt, but he refused to give up. Beth seemed almost trying to defy him, trying to resist having an orgasm. She seemed to be fighting against it, fighting Ray, determined to defeat him. But between his tongue and two of his fingers, she finally gave up. She sighed, shuddered, and had what Ray figured must have been at least a minor orgasm, unless she was an even better actress than he thought.

They lay together side-by-side afterwards, holding hands, for a long time in the dark. Traffic passed.

Then Beth said, "I've got to fly to Maine on Friday. That's where the new author lives. Now that the contract is signed, I've got to sit down with her and talk about the book."

"This is sudden."

"I meant to tell you earlier tonight. Fact is, I just found out about it this afternoon."

"How long will you be gone?"

"A week. Maybe ten days. We'll talk when I get back. Assess things."

"Okay," Ray said, chastened, but grateful.

A week, he was calculating, *that would have to be enough.*

Over the following days, Ray found himself looking in a completely different way at women on the subway, at the grocery, at the dry cleaners. At lunchtime, he strolled towards Central Park. Using a small digital camera, he surreptitiously took pictures of passing women from a strategically inconspicuous spot on a rocky hill, overlooking a bend in the asphalt trail below.

Charlotte wanted an offering. These things weren't accomplished so easily. It wasn't like they showed it in the movies. Ray hadn't been truly aware of it before, but women were extraordinarily cautious; they left behind trails, like breadcrumbs, so that others could come after them if they unexpectedly disappeared. It wasn't any wonder that when women went missing the first suspects were always those who knew them best.

Who else could get close enough to capture them?

Ray thought for a moment of Beth. She would make an easy victim. She'd go off with him without too much of a fuss. But, of course, they'd come looking for him right away.

At a Starbucks on Astor Place, where he stopped for coffee after a day of hunting, Ray saw a woman sitting at the counter who caught his eye. She was alternately organizing the directory on her cell phone and staring moodily out the window at the passersby emerging from the subway station. Ray felt as if he recognized her from somewhere, but from where he couldn't quite place, the memory lying tantalizingly just beyond of reach. But it was as if she were somehow sending him a message, odd inasmuch as she never so much as noticed him, but broadcasting it unconsciously all the same: *choose me, choose me, choose me.* She wasn't even the prettiest woman he'd seen that day, and yet he felt a powerful attraction.

Puzzled, Ray watched her surreptitiously, trying to solve the mystery. He was sure that he didn't know her from anywhere, that he hadn't ever seen her before, in spite of the nagging sense of familiarity. It took him a while and when it came to him, and then only much later, trudging up Lexington at one am, it surprised him so much he pulled up short and simply stood there in the street for several minutes, not even realizing it had begun to rain, and wondered what it could possibly mean.

If I'd been born a woman, he realized, *I would have looked just like her.*

In a café-bar on Sullivan street, Ray met Eric for an early dinner. Eric Mondee was a screenwriter Ray knew from the days when Ray still had pretensions of being a novelist or a poet instead of chasing down fatuous stories as a hack magazine writer. Unlike Ray, Eric had never married, never needed to worry about making mortgage payments, or weather-proofing the deck, or shopping for china patterns. He never had a woman in his life for longer than six months before he started the process of breaking up with her and starting over and he never seemed to worry about dying alone on a kitchen floor at three am with an aneurysm, at least not so as he ever mentioned it. For all his extra time, Eric had managed to produce only one screenplay that actually made it into production with a major studio; but, through judicious penny-pinching, mooching and stiffing friends, lovers, and relatives, he'd been successfully living off the sale of that one miserable screenplay for the better part of the last two decades.

"So what do you make of it," Ray asked, sipping a gin-tonic. "Have you ever heard of anything so fucked up?"

Eric munched a steak fry. "I'd have to say that on just about any top ten fucked-up list I've come across, she's got to make the top three. Listen, your girlfriend sounds like she's got a lot of problems. That's pretty clear."

"But what are they?"

Eric shrugged. "Most likely you'll never know for sure. And be glad. I know it's tough to see it this way, but you should consider yourself lucky to experience something like Charlotte. But you should consider yourself even luckier to be rid of her."

"I'm not feeling particularly lucky right now. Can't sleep. Can't eat. Can't work…"

"Yeah, exactly. Now try to imagine living an entire life of that. Because that's what it would take. You'd be a basket case if it didn't outright kill you."

Ray thought briefly of John Rossi. He was a basket case, or so he would have Ray believe. Maybe he wasn't lying, after all. The café was packed: tourists, business people, couples, friends, the after-work happy-hour crowd. Ray scanned the room and spotted a fragile-looking blonde sitting alone in a booth. She was delicately eating a burger, shoes off, one leg crossed under her, and writing in a purple journal.

Something about her…

"Thing is, when I'm with her," Ray said, his eyes only reluctantly unsticking themselves from the blonde, "I never feel more alive; it's like life starts the moment I see her, and ends the moment she leaves. It's like a movie."

Eric laughed. "Movies aren't real, Ray. I should know. First thing you learn writing screenplays is that no one goes to the theater to see real life. They've already got one of those. They're going to the theater to get the hell away from it. They go to see something better than life."

"That's how it is with her. Like things are better than life. Dammit, Eric, if I could just keep her in one place long enough, I might be able to figure her out. But she keeps blinking on and off, like a fucking star or something."

Eric sipped his martini. "Isn't that always the way? The ones you can have bore you to death. The other ones—the ones you dream about—you follow them forever without ever catching up. Light and shadows."

"Someone gets her in the end, though. Someone already did. Three times."

"No one keeps a woman like that," Eric said emphatically. "You only get her like you get cancer. Temporarily."

Ray's eyes had drifted back to the woman writing in the purple journal. It was the damnedest thing. He was imagining that she was really a man: his long legs shaved smooth, his toenails painted. He'd have been given hormone shots to enhance the breasts inside his skimpy pink t-shirt. She looked almost familiar. Who was she? Eric? Ray shook his head as if to shake the thought out, like it was water in his ear. Nutty is what it was, like thinking that girl at the Starbucks counter reminded him of himself.

"What's the matter?" Eric asked.

Ray turned and stared at him blankly. "Nothing," he said slowly. "Just that, well, did it ever occur to you that they told it to us all wrong?"

"Everything 'they' tell us is wrong. What in particular?"

"That it's the man who really sacrifices everything for love? Not the woman. Think about it: just about every great poem or film about romantic love is written by a man. All those novels where a woman desperately loves a man until it ruins her…just about all of them were written by men. Have you ever known a real woman to love a man that way?"

"Sure," Eric said, "I guess so. Then they turn seventeen and grow up." He motioned to the waiter for another martini. "Sexually attracted, I can understand, Ray, even obsessed. But tell me, what exactly is it you think you love about this woman anyway? I'd really be interested to know. Because from what I can gather, if she doesn't end up killing you, she's going to end up putting you in jail."

"I don't know," Ray admitted, poking the garnish on his plate with a toothpick. "That's the most frustrating part. Why do we love someone? If you could explain it rationally, is it really even love? If it's a list of qualities you could tick off like features of a car or digital camera…you know: it's reliable, looks good, affordable…it would be easy. But would that be love? If it were just a matter of someone being good for us…"

"So you've gone for a psycho?"

"I'm trying to say that maybe love is precisely what's *not* good for us, what's against our best interests. How far we're willing to run counter to our own natural selfishness and instinct for survival…maybe that is what measures how much we love someone. If we're willing to sacrifice ourselves for them."

"I'll revise that. It's *you* who've gone psycho."

"She's damaged goods or she's a goddess, or maybe she's both. She's like a woman with the sun trapped inside her burning from the inside out."

"And to think you gave up writing poetry."

"Did I tell you she wants me to find someone for a threesome?"

"A threesome? That sounds promising, Ray. Very promising. Are you making me an offer? If you promise to keep to your end of her, I might consider it."

Ray looked back at the woman with the purple journal. She'd gotten up from the table and was packing her carry-all to leave. Ray followed her with his eyes as she headed for the door.

"Sorry," Ray said, distractedly. "Female. She wants another girl."

He turned back to Eric and seemed to be having trouble fixing his features. It was like looking at a plate of soft dough with some dark shadowy spots floating around in it.

Eric whistled softly. "Wow. Looks like you've finally hit the jackpot. What about, Beth?"

"What about her?"

"Aren't you moving in with her?"

Ray shrugged. "I'm sure this will be over by then. And, you know, I go on with my life, right?"

Eric tapped him on the arm and wagged a pretend paternal finger at him. "Just so long as you remember that, Ray."

"That reminds me. I told Beth I got scratched by a stray cat that you took in. It was the only way I could explain these cuts on my chest."

"Cuts? What cuts?"

"Sex got a little rough. Charlotte left some marks."

Eric lifted an eyebrow. "Hmm. I see."

"So just in case you run into Beth and she asks. You know, about the cat, make something up. Say you found the owner or it ran away again. Whatever. It probably doesn't make a difference. I don't think she believed me anyway. She's been acting weird lately. I think she suspects something."

"Smart girl."

"I'll have some time to operate, though. She's going to Maine for a week or so to work with some new author she signed up named Jenna something. Corolla, I think."

Eric paused, the fresh martini halfway to his lips. "Jenna Corrolla? The romance author?"

"Yeah, that's it. You've heard of her?"

Eric laughed. "Sure. It's one of the best-kept secrets in the industry."

"What is?"

"Leon Szorkin," Eric said. "The 800-pound Pulitzer-prizewinning gorilla of political fiction and father of new journalism himself. *He's* Jenna Corrolla."

"You're kidding."

"No kidding. He apparently gets his jollies penning these steamy eighteenth century historical potboilers. Go figure."

"Are you sure?"

"Yup. His wife is a member at the Writer's Union. She's got a desk there, sits right next to me, writes these tiring, long-winded and, most importantly, unpublishable female coming-of-age memoirs. You know the type." Eric made a distasteful face, like he'd just tasted a bad chive in his steak fry dip. "I see her all the time. She's been spitting nails lately. Seems the old man is having another affair. That in itself isn't news. But this one seems serious."

Ray could feel the blood sluicing down the big veins in his neck, leaving his face the color of a corpse.

"Dude, you're not looking so good."

"Fuck."

"Hey, what are you thinking…"

"I don't know…"

"You don't think…"

"Dammit, Eric. I don't know."

The next day, Ray sat on a bench in Washington Square Park at lunchtime making a list on a yellow legal pad:

No friends

No friends of friends

No one in the building

No former business associates

No co-workers

No one on the regular subway route

No one on the Palm Pilot

No ex-girlfriends

No ex-wife

No Beth

No one Beth knows

The list ran on like this for almost two full pages. Who else was left? He couldn't use a call girl: they'd get his credit card and address before they even showed up. Picking up girls at clubs seemed inefficient and fraught with its own complications—friends and other witnesses, including other clubgoers, bartenders, cab drivers, etc. Prostitutes—street whores weren't usually lookers, and they were full of disease and drugs.

No one Eric knows.

Ray underlined this sentence four times and tapped his pen against the pad. Could it be true? Could Beth really be cheating on him? For some reason, Ray hadn't even considered the possibility, but it made perfect sense. She was unhappy and suspicious. She'd warned him. She probably wanted some kind of revenge.

But how long had she been cheating? That suddenly seemed of crucial importance. Because just as he tried to console himself that, after all, he'd deserved her betrayal, it struck him that maybe he really hadn't, which made him doubly angry. He remembered Beth telling him that she was staying an extra few days with Jenna Corolla at that convention in Vegas. That was weeks ago. Had the affair started then—or even earlier? Had it started even before he'd met Charlotte on the street outside the club that night?

If Beth were really having an affair, Ray wondered what had prompted her to tell him about Jenna Corolla in the first place? Had she somehow wanted to get caught? Or were her motives darker? Did she want to hurt him, to humiliate him? Had she planted the clues like a time-bomb to go off when Ray least expected it? Did it make her cum more violently in Leon Szorkin's arms to know that Ray suspected? Did she get wet talking openly to an unsuspecting Ray about her lover when they were eating dinner or watching TV or riding the subway together? Was this what love was really all about? Was Eric right? Was Ray going insane?

Ray needed to clear his head. He took the car out of the city and drove the length of New Jersey, as far as the Garden State Parkway would take him, all the way to Cape May. He walked along the beach and stared out at the horizon; there was nothing to see by the time he got there but the night. And a thick humid fog kept him from seeing even much of that. The air was so sodden and heavy it felt like he could scoop a chunk of it out with his hand. Ray made his way back up the beach and into town for a drink. On the way he passed stately old Victorian houses, renovated and converted into bed-and-breakfasts for romantic getaways. The kind of place Beth would love, but it was Charlotte that Ray imagined fucking on one of those fairy-tale canopied beds.

The main street was lined with boutique restaurants and overpriced bars that catered mainly to tourists. Most of the tourist shops were closed by now—windows filled with polished seashells and ceramic lighthouses, and crap like that. Ray turned off the main drag and walked until the houses started looking shabby. He stepped into a yellow brick bunker isolated beside a dimly-lit municipal parking lot. He sat at the bar and ordered a gin-tonic. The TV mounted over his head was tuned to a newschannel: it seemed that Haskins was up four points.

It was a gay bar, as it turned out: the lisping voices, the catcalling, the rainbow flag. A muscular man, middle-aged, dressed in improbably tiny cut-off jeans sat down a stool away from Ray. The man took a long pull on his beer and wiped the foam from his greying handle-bar mustache. "Hey smiley," he said, in a jocular voice tinged with flirty faux Hells Angel malice, "it's not the end of the world."

Ray happened to be looking at his face in the mirror behind the bar and above a silent audience of bottles; he'd been going eyeball-to-eyeball with his own misery for maybe an hour now, maybe more, it was impossible to say. *It's not the end of the world.* People said stuff like that all the time, but Ray wondered how did they know it wasn't? Maybe, from where you were sitting, it really was the end of the world. Maybe you'd just returned from burying a child or you'd just found out your wife was having an affair or the doctor had called back moments ago with a diagnosis of Stage IV cancer. How did people know? They didn't, of course. They didn't even think about it. They just assumed the world was spinning on the way it always did, if it was spinning that way for them, since they considered themselves to be at the center of it. But the end of the world came every day for someone. The apocalypse was occurring all the time. Ray reluctantly broke his stare-down with himself. He slowly turned to the fag sitting next to him and said, "Why don't you make me? Smile, that is."

Ray didn't mean it as a threat, but there must have been something unsettling about the expression on his face. Mr. Handlebars put up his big hands and mimed backing up, as much as one could do that on a bar stool.

"Hey, just trying to be friendly pal."

Ray tried to correct the misunderstanding, but that didn't come out sounding right either. "I just meant," he said, "why don't you amuse me in some way? Tell me something funny. Work for it, a little?"

He was only making things worse. His voice sounded hard, angry, and aggressive.

"No offense, okay," the man said. "I said I was sorry. I didn't mean to upset you."

Eyes were on him. Ray heard a lisping voice sotte voce off to the right advising the man to leave Ray alone. A boyish-looking man in a silk shirt.

"He's just drunk."

"Some people…"

"Closet case…"

He wasn't, though, was he? Drunk, that is. Ray had returned to his contemplation of the face looking back at him from behind the bar. There was something not quite right about it, like he'd forced a few extra pieces into it. He felt frozen to the stool. The bartender came over, wiping a glass. He didn't look directly at Ray, but off to one side, as if Ray were sitting beside himself one stool over.

"Maybe you should leave now."

Ray nodded, staring into his glass, at the colorful squiggles between the ice. He didn't seem able to move. It was as if gravity were sucking his ass into the stool towards some irresistible black hole in the floor of the bar. Two pair of hands grabbed him then, one on each arm, and yanked him upright. He got his feet under him as the bouncers marched him double-time to the door. They didn't throw him into the street, not exactly, but he ran into a mailbox all the same. He felt the bruise in his side when he turned onto the parkway ramp, and, after that, whenever he pressed his foot on the accelerator, all the way back to Manhattan.

Ray caught up with her as she was leaving the Writer's Union on East 4th. He'd been waiting for her across the street, sitting at the counter in the window of a small natural foods store, where he'd been picking apart a carrot-and-coconut health muffin for the last forty-five minutes. He left the ruined muffin behind and hurried out of the store. "Excuse me," he said, as the woman climbed up the curb. "Can I have a word with you?" She turned toward him with a look that might have been reserved for a walking-talking pile of dog shit. Ray knew that look instinctively: it was the face of a woman who'd come to hate a man at first sight.

Diane Glickstein was a bottle-blonde at the very bottom of the bottle: her hair, like so much else about her, was stripped to the color of nothing and nowhere. Her face had been nipped and tucked, cheated and peeled, and god knew what else beyond any identifiable human age or expression. But she wasn't so much ageless or expressionless, as she was completely unrecognizable. Whatever she might have looked like before, she looked like the frozen scream of that woman now. The most vibrant part of her face were her lips, which had been injected so many times her mouth looked like a decaying fruit.

Ray said: "Can I talk to you a minute?"

"Who the hell are you? I don't talk to strangers."

"I'm not exactly a stranger. I think we may have something in common."

She pulled down a pair of large sunglasses that had been perched on her head. "Oh yeah?" she snorted. "And just what could that possibly be?"

"Your husband."

That knocked her back a beat, but when she recovered, she came back even harder. "Fuck him," she said, with the compressed force of a fist. "I don't want anything to do with that prick."

"Let me buy you a drink and maybe we can talk about it."

"I don't drink with strangers either." She lifted the sunglasses, puckered one eye, and glared at him, as if trying to recognize him from some society page or other. "Who are you, anyway? You never answered me. One of his fucked-up friends?"

"No. Just the opposite. He stole something of mine."

"So?" she laughed, not that it sounded like one. She let the sunglasses fall back onto the reconstructed bridge of her nose. "What's that got to do with me?"

"I think he stole something from you, too."

Ms. Glickstein opened her mouth to say something, but nothing came out. So she closed it again. Then the fat diseased fruit that it was disappeared entirely, as if she'd eaten it herself. Ray couldn't see her eyes anymore behind the large dark glasses, but he could sense she was sizing him up. The fat red fruit popped out of her face again, as if she'd only been sucking its poison and it had agreed with her. She looked almost, well, hopeful.

"Is he in trouble?"

Ray thought abut it for a minute. "I'd say yes." He nodded toward the natural foods market. They were standing right outside the red-awninged door. "How about if I buy you a carrot juice instead of a drink and we can talk about it?"

"No," Diane Glickstein said: "Let's go for that drink."

She'd already put away three apple martinis and she was working on a fourth. They were sitting in a sushi place on 9th, at a table by the window: it suddenly started to rain. People passing on the sidewalk were rushing passed holding newspapers and briefcases over their heads, or struggling to dig umbrellas out of their bags. Diane Glickstein decided she was hungry and ordered a twenty-eight dollar sushi platter. Ray was starting to get the feeling that she'd tricked him into some kind of bizarre date.

"I'm sorry," she said, blowing her nose noisily. She'd informed him only moments before that she had a sinus infection. "I'm sorry but I'm very angry. Obviously."

"It's okay," Ray said. "I understand."

"Do you...do you really? Fifteen years I've lived in the shadow of that sonofabitch. I've put up with his selfishness, his ranting and raving, his ex-wives, his children from other marriages, his hair transplants, his stinginess, his intellectual abuse, his drinking, his polyps, and his fucking affairs. Yeah, his many, many fucking affairs, but this time he tells me out of the clear blue he's in love with the bitch. *He's in love with her...*"

Her voice had risen to a screech that drew the startled attention of those at the tables nearby.

Diane didn't seem to notice. She gulped down a sob along with her sickening martini. "Do you know what it's like for a woman my age? Do you have any fucking idea? I just turned fifty-nine..."

Ray would have liked to have been able to say something helpful, something complimentary, but there wasn't anything he could say that wouldn't have been a pointless and obvious lie. This woman wasn't fishing for compliments. She didn't give a damn what Ray thought about her. She was beyond all that. Just the opposite. Ray had the distinct impression that Diane Glickstein was one insincere and badly executed platitude from leaping across the table and planting a chopstick through the center of his left eye.

"Do you know where your husband is?"

"You bet your ass I do," she spat. "He's in Maine—at our vacation lodge. He's with his fucking girlfriend I'm sure." Not yet, Ray thought, she's not with him yet, but she's packing, goddammit, probably right this very moment, and I'm driving her to the airport. "The shithead is fucking his editor. Can you believe that? He writes books pretending to be a woman for fun and he's fucking his goddamn editor. But you knew that, didn't you?"

Ray didn't feel sad, or even angry. He felt a kind of numb resignation, as if he'd been trying not to see something for a very long time, something he knew had always been there, like a mole or birthmark on his back, maybe, that had suddenly and inexplicably gone bad.

Ray said: "How long? How long has it been going on?"

"On and off. A year. I begged him to stop. He would for a while and then he started up all over again. He can't stop, you understand." A sick grin carved itself into Ms. Glickstein's patched-up rotting face. She looked like an evil pumpkin left out too long on some forgotten stoop. "Because this time it's not just the sex. *He's in love with her.*"

She could be the one, Ray thought. She'd be easy. She was bitter, finished. She had nothing much to lose. But Ray looked at her tired body, at the spotted, spoiled flesh of her cleavage, and realized she was passed using even for that. What would that be like, Ray wondered, to no longer even be good as a sacrificial offering? He felt something like sympathy for the woman, tinged by fear of his own mortality, because it wouldn't be too long anymore before he was too old for that as well, but it didn't last too long, the sympathy, that is.

She said: "So what are you going to do about it, anyway? Are you going to do *anything* the fuck about it? Men, *real men*, seem to be in short supply in the world nowadays."

Ray didn't answer.

"Are you going to let him get away with it? You're not going to let him get away with it, are you?"

She leaned forward over the table, her spotted, red-taloned hand grabbed at his wrist like the claw of some horrible endangered bird.

"Tell me," she hissed. "Are you going to hurt him? I wouldn't mind, you know. I wouldn't care if you killed the both of them. I swear I wouldn't tell a soul."

Then she started sobbing uncontrollably, the waddle of flesh under her augmented chin violently trembling. People at the other tables were pretending not to be looking like they only do when they're watching every move.

Ray called for the check.

She invited him back to her place as Ray walked her east in search of a cab to pour her into. It was still raining, lately it seemed to be always raining, and Diane was close to hysterical, crying and cringing against Ray with every crack and roll of thunder. Her drunken body felt surprisingly soft and light leaning against his own, as if she were hollowed out, a fragile bubble that could burst at any moment into nothingness and feathers.

The streets were bleary with rain and headlights. Ray finally spotted a cab on 23rd and flagged it down. He propped Diane up as the cab pulled to the curb. He yanked open the door and helped her inside. She protested when he stepped back onto the sidewalk. She begged him to come back with her.

She reached out of the cab door, that red-tipped claw trying to snag him.

"I don't want to be alone. I don't. I don't!" she wailed and the thunder boomed and she wept even more pitifully. Ray told himself he was just making certain she got home alright, but he knew that wasn't true at all.

This is a mistake, he thought. *A mistake, a mistake.*

He let himself be pulled in. He slid onto the damp seat beside her.

She lived in a doorman building near the U.N. on one of those hushed leafy streets lined with dark sedans sporting diplomatic plates. The minute Ray stepped out of the cab he felt as if he'd popped up on a dozen hidden surveillance cameras that were no doubt monitoring the neighborhood. The apartment was on the 17th floor—a large maze of dimly lit rooms insulated from the reality of the city outside. The dark gleam of the furniture alone told Ray all he needed to know about the financial status of the Szorkin-Glicksteins. He stood there dripping on a five-thousand-dollar doormat as Diane turned on the lights from a master control panel, illuminating a world Ray would never know.

"I'm getting this apartment," Diane slurred, waving around a talon. "You can take that to the fucking bank." She walked into a door jamb. "No," she cackled mirthlessly, "Correction. *I'll* be taking that to the fucking bank. Wait in there."

She pointed at a room off to her left.

Ray stepped into an octagonal-shaped study filled with floor-to-ceiling bookcases. Seven walls of books, broken up here and there with a rain-spotted leaded window, and the whole chamber solemn as one of those niches in a church where you find a plaster saint. A two-hundred-gallon aquarium, surreally-lit, filled with blindingly white sand and exotic coral, emitted a comforting hum from its place in the wall. Inside the tank, large flat fish drifted passed the glass like colorful dinner plates in an underwater china cabinet. Ray turned and saw an old-fashioned roll-top desk under the only bookless wall. On the desk sat a running computer, its plasma screen as garishly colorful as the fish tank, only smaller, and full of fauna of an even stranger, human type. A pornographic website, obviously, but even close up it took Ray a while to fully comprehend what exactly he was looking at.

"Find it interesting?"

Ray jerked around. Diane was standing in the doorway dressed in a red silk kimono that had fallen, somewhat unfortunately, open in front, exposing her from stringy jugular to withered crotch, and whether her grim exposure was due to drunkenness or desperate lewdness, Ray couldn't say, and wasn't sure he wanted to know. Her pussy was trimmed to a landing stripe of crippled-looking grey fur. Ray thought it looked like a mouse someone might have pulled, broken-necked and dead, from a trap.

"They're underage," he said, distractedly.

"That's not all. Look a little closer."

The look on her face was twisted, like she was now sucking all the bitterness in the universe through a straw and had decided to smile through it all the same.

Ray bent over the computer screen. They were only kids, most of them barely developed, in some cases not developed at all, flat as boys. You missed it at first, eyes drawn to the close-ups of sodomy, outrageous as war-crime photos, all those swarthy muscled cocks plunged into smooth and childish flesh, those hairy fists where they shouldn't be, not in a thousand years. Terrified eyes, bloodied assholes, the bodies positioned on warehouse floors, or in bathtubs, or hanging from doorways, or posed in coffins…it was hard to get passed all that. But when he did, Ray understood what Diane Glickstein wanted him to see.

"I think I should get going."

He started away from the desk.

"Going?" she barked. "Who said you could go anywhere?"

"Listen, Ms. Glickstein…"

"Shut up, shut up, shut up," she shrieked, holding her wrists to her ears.

"Calm down," Ray said, "for crissakes, stop screaming."

"Fuck you, you piece of shit! Who the hell are you to tell me to stop screaming? I'll fucking scream if I want!" And then she did to prove it. "Who the hell are you?"

"Okay, scream all you like. It's been a long night. I don't blame you. I want to scream, too. I apologize. I shouldn't have come. I don't know what I was thinking. I probably shouldn't even have gotten in touch with you. I'm leaving now."

"What is it, do you think you're too fucking good for me?"

Ray looked at her, uncomprehendingly.

"Is that what it is? You're too high and mighty? You think I need you to suck my tits? To fuck my pussy?"

"No, ma'am. I'm sure you don't..."

"Let me tell you, you fucking faggot, I can get anyone I want."

She started towards Ray, veering too far to the left, and sent an antique lamp with a lot of crystal dangling from it crashing to the floor. There goes a thousand bucks, Ray thought. She let out a squeal and stooped to pick up the lamp, but gave up the attempt. Ray thought she'd topple over and pass out; it was wishful thinking. She managed to stand upright in stages, like you'd unfold a beach chair. It was a slim address book bound in red leatherette that she'd been going for. This time she snatched it off the table and shook the book at Ray, like the slab with the Ten Commandments.

"A phone call away..." she spat at him, "I can get anything I want. I can get any *one* I want. Men, boys, girls, twosomes, threesomes. I can get a man who'll let me piss in his mouth, a girl who'll rape me with a dildo and a Doberman. I don't need to have the body of a twenty-two-year-old to get to fulfill my desires. I can buy the body of a twenty-two-year-old, a different one every night. I can buy it and my husband will pay for it all..."

Ray stood frozen to the spot, transfixed by the woman's rage—and the gun she had suddenly produced from the deep pocket of the kimono.

"Ms. Glickstein," he said quietly, like trying to move a wasp's hive without disturbing its angry contents, "You don't want to do this." He said this not having any idea exactly what Diane Glickstein wanted to do, knowing only that *he* didn't want her to do it, whatever it was. "I'm not your husband. You're not angry with me. It's him you want to kill..."

"Don't you fucking dare tell me what I want to do. You're evil. You've got it inside you. I can sense it."

She was holding the gun level with Ray's gut. He could feel his intestines squirming as he anticipated the bullet, his hands going automatically to his lower belly, the sucking hole in his squishy insides. He wanted to double-over.

"I'm going to make him pay—you'll see," she said bitterly. "My phony-baloney enlightened macho husband…he not only likes to write as a woman, but he likes to see little boys dressed like girls and raped. This is how he gets off. He talks to these freaks on the internet." Diane Glickstein pointed over his shoulder with the gun. "I have his emails, his chats, his message posts…or, maybe should I say, my lawyer does.

Ray glanced again at the computer. That's what he'd seen alright: beneath the makeup, the wigs, the panties, the lingerie and fetish gear, the waifish underfed-looking bodies were undeveloped for a reason beyond the fact that they were underaged—they were the bodies of prepubescent boys.

"I even have photos of him in action. Would you like to have a peek?" she barked out a laugh. "They're really something to see. Now *that's* obscenity."

"Spare me," Ray said, and meant it.

Diane had let the gun drift away from his stomach. She seemed to be lost inside her own incomprehension. Ray took the opportunity to start edging sideways, thinking he could make it passed her and out the door of this insanity. But his movement summoned Diane back to the here and now. She jerked the gun towards Ray.

"Where the fuck do you think you're going, anyway? You haven't fucked me yet. Don't you want to? Aren't you man enough to fuck me?"

"Maybe another time," Ray said. "I'm really not feeling very well right now." And he wasn't. His gut was thrashing around like a basket of crabs. "I think I'm going to be sick."

The woman sneered at him. "How about now?" She held the gun to her head. "Can you fuck me now? Do you want to fuck a dead woman, you sick bastard? Does that turn you on?"

Ray did a quick mental calculation of what might happen if she blew her brains out, if he'd get dragged into an investigation of her death. But she apparently changed her mind about blowing her own brains out because she fixed the gun on him again.

"Get on your knees," she said. "Now!"

Ray, still thinking of an out, sank down to his knees. It would be ironic if she shot him instead of her husband; after all, Ray was guilty of looking at similar websites himself on occasion, not the kid stuff, but the violence fetish. Of course, he wasn't *just looking* at it, was he? He wasn't the only one either. How common was it, anyway? This connection between violence and taboo and eroticism? TV shows like CSI, all those lingering camera shots of pretty victims in their negligees, horror films, serial killer books, salacious news reports of missing co-eds…wasn't it all a form of erotic death, even if most people weren't honest enough to admit it? Sex and violence, violence and sex, maybe it's just how we were made. Diane Glickstein walked towards him on her chunky-heeled silver slippers. Her old toes were scrunched together like fat sausages with lacquered helmets.

"They'd suspect you killed me," she said, "at least for a while. Murder-suicide. My husband fucking your woman…maybe it was your idea of revenge." Diane Glickstein laughed. She pressed the gun to Ray's forehead: he felt its cold steel kiss like a hole already in his skull. "Or," she said, "I could kill you in self-defense…or out of my terrible grief. Women get off for things like that all the time, you know. No one wants to believe a woman could kill someone in simple cold-blood."

Diane was standing so close to Ray now that her grey pussy was scratching his face. It smelled almost as dead as it looked.

"Lick," she commanded.

Ray felt his stomach shake, the crabs all tumbling.

"Lick," she barked again, and ground the gun into his temple.

Ray screwed his eyes shut and touched the tip of his tongue to her pussy: it tasted scorched and metallic. He forced himself to lick it, the wiry strip of hairs scraping his tongue like steel wool. He thought of making a grab for her wrist, or wrapping his arms around her thighs, planting his head into her mid-section, and tackling her. But he didn't do either of those things. A different plan was taking shape in his head. He continued to lick her pussy until she'd had enough.

"Stop it," she said, sobbing, "for crissakes, just fucking stop it."

Ray sat back on his heels.

Diane Glickstein stood over him, trembling all over, and the gun was hanging down by her side, pointing at the floor.

"Get out," she said dully, like a robot whose plug someone had suddenly yanked.

Ray climbed slowly to his feet. His mouth tasted like the floor of a slaughter house. He could feel the sharp hairs between his teeth.

"We could do it together," he suggested quietly, trying not to gag. "Blackmail him."

"Get out," she repeated softly. "Before I kill one of us."

Well, it was an idea. The way Ray figured it, though, he could blackmail Leon Szorkin with or without Diane Glickstein's cooperation. Judging from the apartment, there was enough to go around. It would be a kind of poetic justice, fucking over the man who was fucking his girlfriend. He only wished he could tell Beth what a sick manipulative fuck she'd chosen to cheat on him with. He would, eventually, when he was finished proving what a sick manipulative fuck *he* could be, if sufficiently motivated.

On the way down to the lobby, Ray thought he really might throw up. By the time the elevator doors opened, he'd broken out in a cold sweat.

He dashed out into the deserted street; it was still raining. He held his contentious gut all the way to 37th street. He stood hunched, facing the marble wall in a recess of an office building off Park and tried to vomit, but nothing came so he gave up and bought a package of wintermint Rolaids and a Snapple Raspberry Iced Tea at a Duane Reade. He rinsed his mouth out with the Snapple and chewed four of the Rolaids. He walked on. The fresh air eventually made him feel better. He caught a cab somewhere along Broadway. From the back of the cab, he tried Charlotte on her cell phone. He called her at the carriage house. He called her at the office. There was no answer anywhere.

Tapping his fingers on the steering wheel, Ray accelerated passed a flatbed truck loaded with fertilizer bags. On the radio, a conservative talk-radio host was trying to explain away the eight-point lead that Haskins had inexplicably opened up in the latest public opinion polls. Ray jerked the car back in front of the truck and ignored the long blast of the air horn as they rocked on the shocks. Beth splayed her hand on the dashboard and jammed her flip-flopped foot on an invisible brake.

"Jesus Christ Ray," she yelled, "what the hell are you doing?"

"Driving."

About ten miles back they'd gotten stuck in traffic bottlenecked around an accident: a car crushed flat as a profile and burned black. Fire engines all over the fucking place, two jack-knifed trucks, state troopers, glass, a twisted guard-rail, and three ambulances.

Someone, Ray thought, *must have lost control.*

Beth glared at him. "What the fuck's the big hurry anyway?"

"I don't want you to miss your flight."

Beth yanked down the sun visor. Checked her face for something, a stray eyelash, smudged lipstick, a sign of guilt, maybe? She flicked away whatever she found with a pinkie. She snapped the visor back up.

"Well, I'd like to make it to the airport alive."

Ray ignored her. He zipped passed a Lexus with New Hampshire plates like it was standing still. The storm the night before had scrubbed the sky a flawless blue, like a bed on which were laid a few skeletal clouds; it matched the weather of his mind.

Ray took a turn onto a long curving off-ramp. Up above, large green signs directed them to gates, parking lots, shuttle buses. The airport lay off to the right like a great bowl of concrete, glass, and steel. They whooshed passed a speeding black limousine like a coffin with darkened windows.

"You know," Beth said, "you're not going to be able to reach me at the house. There's no telephone up there. Jenna doesn't keep one at the lodge. Writer's quirk, I guess. You don't know how eccentric they can be."

"Oh really," Ray said, checking the rearview. Nothing seemed to be gaining on them.

"Um…yeah. And Maine's outside the roaming range of my cell."

All this said, Ray noted, in a rush. Trying, she was, to get it all out of the way, like swallowing something nasty.

"So I guess that means you'll be incommunicado?" That last word made Ray smirk, impossible to use it seriously, but he couldn't help showing a little irony.

"Well, there's always email…and I should be able to get away and call you from a payphone in town once a day or so."

"I see," Ray said, passing a van with Japanese writing on the side and a painting of a dancing shrimp. "But not from the house. I understand."

Ray put a cigarette in his mouth. Tensing up, waiting for Beth to object. But he didn't light it and she kept quiet. He eased the car into the right hand lane and passed under the sign for domestic flights. His cheekbones ached. He suddenly realized that he'd had the same expression on his face for, what, twenty minutes? Time to change it. But it was like assembling a puzzle with no clues and a bunch of missing pieces. What the hell was he supposed to look like right now, anyway?

"You're acting very strangely, Ray."

"Am I Beth?"

"Yes, you know goddam well, you are. I don't like it. If I knew you were going to be like this, I'd have hired a car service."

"Is that so? Sorry about that."

Ray failed to yield, failed to reduce speed, failed to watch for pedestrians.

She turned in her seat, furious-looking. "Is there something you want to tell me? Something you'd like to talk about?"

That was a dangerous question. That was like bringing the match really close to the fuse. He thought of what he'd learned about Leon Szorkin the night before. What he knew was like a sunrise inside him; holding it all in was almost impossible. There was no way to act perfectly naturally. If he didn't see Beth off soon, it would all come exploding out of him.

"You know Beth, all considered, I'd have to say no."

He pulled up to the front of the terminal, brakes screeching, nearly rear-ending an airport van. He popped the trunk and jumped out of the car before Beth could complain some more and began yanking her bags from the back. She came round the other side. She was dressed in a light-weight white sweater and off-white drawstring yoga pants. She'd had her hair cut; there was bright fresh polish on the nails of her fingers and toes. *For him*, Ray thought, and never wanted Beth more than at that moment. He retrieved a luggage cart and Beth started in again.

"I really don't appreciate your attitude. This isn't the way I wanted to leave things between us."

"No?" He began piling the bags on the cart, throwing them onto the cart would be a more accurate description.

"I thought it would be good for us to get a little perspective. I thought it was what you wanted anyway. A little space, a little time alone. You can't expect me to go on like we've been."

Ray wrestled up the last bag. He signaled an airport red cap with a ten-dollar bill.

"You're all set."

"Where are you going?"

Ray had walked back to the driver's side, leaving Beth standing with the red cap beside her luggage cart. "To park the car."

"You'll meet me at the gate, won't you?"

"Bon voyage," Ray said, waving her toward the entrance.

"Ray? What the fuck is that supposed to mean?"

"I think, it means have a good trip."

"You asshole, you fucking miserable bastard..."

Ray peeled the car away from the curb. He finally found the right expression for his face: it looked like murder.

Ray sat at the airport bar and watched the big planes taxi on the runway. They lifted off and landed, lifted off and landed. The sun had begun to set and it looked like the edge of the world consisted of a line of burning flamingoes. He tipped a glass of beer towards his mouth and thought about absolutely nothing. A 727 climbed into the sky as if it were moving in slow-motion and would fall back to earth at any moment. Ray pictured himself hardly flinching if it did, his face warmed by the resulting orange fireball.

After dropping Beth off, he'd parked the car in an underground lot and took his time walking back to the terminal, purposely taking the longest, most circuitous route possible, insuring he'd be late. He'd calmed down considerably since leaving her at the curb and, almost regretful, had gone to where her plane had boarded, after all, on the off-chance that she'd missed her flight on purpose to wait for him. That wouldn't have been like Beth. She was too practical to miss something like a booked airline flight. And, to tell the truth, Ray hadn't wanted her to do that anyway, but if she had, he'd have had to acknowledge…well, what exactly? That, maybe, just maybe, she might really love him? He didn't know if he'd go that far, to say she loved him, but it would have definitely colored things somewhat, it would have tinted them, at least, it would have given him something else to consider. Because if she loved him, even if there were a possibility…well, the fact was that Ray didn't want her to love him, not really, not when it came right down to it, did he? That would have made things too ambiguous, too complicated. As it turned out, he needn't have fretted. True to form, Beth hadn't waited, she'd gone ahead as scheduled, as expected, as she always did. Even though Ray was relieved to see all those empty seats, Beth not waiting for him in any of them, he also felt all hashed up inside, his first unscripted reaction to what he was surprised to discover was a visceral disappointment. If she had waited…well, there was no point in thinking about that, she'd spared him the trouble of conflict. She'd made things simple. There was no reason to turn back now.

He hadn't even noticed the woman who'd come up to the bar and taken the stool next to him. She was there when he turned away from the window overlooking the runways: blonde, mid-20s, dressed in a peasant skirt made of some kind of frothy material, like a ballet tutu. A tight black t-shirt under a denim jacket. Big tits. Ratty sneakers. Her face small, pretty, like a doll's porcelain face, but with a smattering of freckles, as if to prove she were real.

"Excuse me, I didn't mean to bother you."

She was hunched under an enormous camping backpack, complete with rolled sleeping bag, like she'd just trekked across Antarctica, and she was in the process of slipping the thing off her shoulders. It had nudged him, apparently, or she thought it did, hence her apology. Ray hadn't noticed, but figured that was why he'd turned round in the first place.

"I got bumped in Miami," the girl said. "Can you believe it? Some kind of security thing. Now I've missed my connecting flight. It's been a nightmare trying to get home."

"Tough break."

Ray reached out to help relieve her of the awkward pack, which she was having trouble squirming out from under.

"Thanks."

"Where's home, anyway?"

"Stillwater."

Ray didn't, but his face must have asked the question.

"That's Oklahoma. You know, where the wind comes sweeping down the plain." The girl held out a small, pale hand tipped with delicate pink nails. A slender gold band with a little engraved heart captured her right middle finger. "My name's Juliet."

"Nice to meet you. Paul White."

"Nice to meet you, too, Paul. Shit, what am I going to do? The next flight isn't until tomorrow. I guess I'm going to need a hotel for the night unless I decide to camp out here at the airport. Do you think they'll comp me a room? Aren't they supposed to do that? For that matter, who do I even ask?" She laughed. "Sorry, I guess I'm freaking out a little."

"Understandable." Ray lifted his beer. "But these kinds of things always work out. Care for a drink while you freak out? It helps. Guaranteed"

"Maybe a 7-Up."

"That won't help much. You're twenty-one, aren't you?"

"Twenty-six." She lit up the freckles with a smile and winked a large green cat's eye. "Relieved?"

Ray, tongue-tied and annoyed by the fact, motioned the bartender over in what he hoped passed for suave, and, thankfully, the bartender wasn't a prick and cooperated. Juliet ordered a Corona. She delicately squeezed the lime and licked each of her little pink fingertips. On the TV mounted above the bar, a couple of talking heads were debating the upcoming election. There was a graphic showing Haskins ahead in two polls, but his lead had shrunk to four points. In a third poll, he was dead-even.

"So what were you doing in Miami?"

"Visiting."

"Family? Friends?"

"Boyfriend."

"Oh. That's nice."

"Well, not exactly a *boyfriend* boyfriend"

Ray arched a calculatedly quizzical eyebrow. "Not exactly?"

He tried to keep his tone light, distracted, and maturely amused. The key to successfully flirting with girls who could almost be your daughter, Ray had recently discovered, wasn't to try and act *their* age. They were young—they could get a real twenty-year-old if they wanted one of those. It took awhile to bend your mind around the idea, but if there were anything at all attractive about Ray to a kid like Juliet, it was precisely what he had that they didn't—it was the decay of him that was alluring, the ten-car pile-up he'd become.

"Oh you know…" Juliet made a gesture with her hand, like a leaf caught in the updraft of a bonfire. "He's a grad student at FSU. He's doing PhD work in philosophy. So, like, how serious *can* it be?"

Ray started calculating, weighing the options. He took another pull from his beer. "What do you do?"

"You're going to laugh," she said, leaning forward. The tabula rosa of her perfect forehead brushed his coat sleeve. "You see, I really shouldn't talk. I'm no better. That's the thing. I'm a grad student, too."

Ray laughed.

Juliet mock-pouted. "See I told you you'd laugh."

"I'm sorry. What's your field of study?"

"English lit."

"Oh well, you can afford to support the both of you then. You don't know how many millionaire Chaucerian scholars I run into."

"Right. Can you think of anything more useless? I mean, outside of philosophy? I'm carefully preparing myself to be completely irrelevant in today's world. Think about it? Could I be any more expendable?"

Not really, Ray thought, staring at her over his glass. Do we ever really see anyone? What color were this girl's eyes, for instance? Not green, not really…something changeable, hazel, maybe, with some kind of splintered caramel-colored pattern in the irises that kept growing and shrinking like…what?

"Excuse me," Ray said.

He reached into his pocket and took out his cell phone, unfolding it in front of him on the bar. He peered at the screen, but he was just pretending.

He moved the phone this way and that, trying to line her up in the viewfinder without making it obvious. It helped that she was looking up at the television now, and then out the window, politely waiting for him to be done presumably checking his messages. She turned back when he snapped the phone closed, her smile right back where it was, as if habitual. One of those perennially sunny personalities that you came upon sometimes that seemed to Ray totally incomprehensible, as if he'd come upon another species altogether. Had she never heard of war, train wrecks, cancer, earthquakes in India that swallow up fifty-thousand in an afternoon?

"Anything important?" she asked.

"No. Just the office, but it can wait." He flipped open the phone again, shaking it, pointing it right at her. "Dammit, I think my battery is running down." He took three shots of her smiling vacantly and slipped the phone back into this pocket. "Anyway, where were we?"

"You were going to tell me what you do. Not a grad student, I'll bet."

"I'm a magazine writer. *AdBiz*. Financial analysis and trends, stuff like that."

"Really? Cool. I don't think I've heard of it though. Sorry. Of course, I've been reading nothing but Emerson for the last three months. I can tell you, *he* doesn't get much circulation nowadays. So what do I know?"

Ray smiled, trying to keep it cool. "Its okay. Most English majors wouldn't have. It's not in the syllabus."

"Anyway, like what do I need to read a financial magazine for? Right? I won't be making any money. What did you study in school anyway?"

"Me?" Ray laughed, and this he really did find funny. "English lit."

He wouldn't have thought of it exactly this way, but Ray was giving the girl a chance to escape the trap he'd set for her. He'd excused himself to the restroom and left Juliet at the bar sipping her beer. If she were smart, if she had the least sense of self-preservation, she'd take the opportunity to get away. He emptied his bladder into the urinal and felt, as he did every time he took a piss lately, like he had a sore rubber ball at the bottom of his belly. Prostate problems, already? His ill-fated father had died of that, three-quarters of his pelvis eaten away by the time he did anything about it, and then it was too late, at fifty-eight. Ray peered into the bottom of the urinal at the little yellow circle hoping not to read his fate in a tell-tale string of floating blood. So far, so good. Ray shook off the last drops, tucked himself away, and thumbed Charlotte's number into his cell phone with the other hand. She didn't answer, of course.

Phone still pressed to his ear, Ray drifted over to the mirrors above the sink, always a bad idea in a public toilet. How the hell did they do it, these mirrors? Show a man the portrait of his innermost soul? What apocalyptic misanthrope, what modern-day desert prophet, was responsible for reflecting back these stark, unpleasant truths? No one needed to see himself as he really was. No one.

Especially not in an airport men's room with a few drinks in him. A human being just wasn't made to endure it.

Ray looked, in short, like open-heart surgery when it was going particularly badly. He wondered if this was the way he actually looked all the time if only he were provided enough light and no distractions.

"Her name's Juliet," Ray said into the phone, staring fascinated at his own head-on collision of a face. Dammit, it was impressive. He should be lying in a morgue. "Juliet...Christ I forgot her last name. Maybe she didn't tell me. I guess it makes no difference," Ray heard himself laughing, but it was more like a nervous stutter. "She's twenty-six. Dirty blonde. Greenish eyes, about five-five. Maybe one-twenty, hard to say, too many clothes, but she looks like she has a good figure under them." Someone in one of the stalls flushed a toilet. Ray lowered his voice. "She's on her way to Oklahoma. She'll be on a plane tomorrow. So we have to...decide. I've sent you some digital pics. Let me know what you think."

Ray wet his hands under the tap and smoothed his hair back, trying to resurrect the gel he'd applied that morning. Hair came off on his hands. Shit, he was going bald, too, just like dad, and right on schedule. No stopping any of it, either. He washed and dried his hands under the hot air blower, or, more accurately, got them dry enough to wipe on the thighs of his pants. When he went back out to the bar he felt a little dip of disappointment deep in his gut; the girl was still waiting for him, just like he knew she'd be, making the mistake we all made, believing that nothing really bad could ever happen to us because, after all, we were the star of the movie.

She called back within the hour, first time ever. Ray was on the turnpike approaching the exit to the tunnel and Juliet was sitting beside him, seat reclined, feet propped up, thumbing through an airport magazine, something with Jennifer Garner on the cover. A few miles earlier, just to make conversation and keep things normal, he asked what he always asked when the subject of Jennifer Garner came up: "Is that James Garner's daughter?" No one Ray had ever asked that question seemed to know the answer and Juliet didn't either. Maybe, in her case, she had the good fortune of being just too young to remember James Garner.

Charlotte's voice on the other end of the phone doubled-up his heart-rate instantly, just like it always did.

"Yes or no answers only, Ray. Understand?"

"Yes."

"Is she with you?"

"Yes."

"Does she know your real name?"

"No."

"Very good, Ray. Oh baby, she's wonderful. A real find. She's gonna be a pop star. Nervous?"

"A little."

"Yes or no answers, Ray."

"Yes."

"That's okay. That's natural. It's your first time. I guess you offered her a lift. Dinner in the city, maybe?"

"Yes."

She'd accepted the offer easily. By then, Juliet was working on a second beer, a light drinker obviously, getting touchy-feely with Ray, bumping up against him when she told a joke or Ray said something completely unfunny. She was talking about her father, deceased, who'd spent his last years in an alcohol-induced dementia. It was a sad story and Ray said so, but she giggled inanely all the same. He suggested she accompany him to dinner, see a little of Manhattan since she was so close, and, after all, the alternative was a crummy airport meal. It didn't take any convincing at all. She seemed as enthusiastic about the idea as he was apprehensive.

Charlotte approved. "Nice, Ray. Very smooth. Sure you haven't done this before?"

"No."

"That was a joke, Ray." Charlotte chuckled. "She seems comfortable, not suspicious?"

"No. I mean, yes…yes and no."

"I understand. Good. You've got a natural gift, Ray. You've got a real gentleness about you that women trust. I noticed that immediately. They take advantage of it, I'll bet, in the long run. That's okay. You just have to learn how to turn it around. Make it work for you. You're a good guy. That can be a powerful tool, Ray. Believe me, I know."

"Yes."

"Okay, now listen, Ray. This is what you're going to do. I'm your sister. You understand? I just called, this call right now. I'm telling you I've had a meeting cancelled and you're going to repeat what I'm telling you out loud. 'Damn sorry about the meeting, sis. I know how important that was.' Go ahead, Ray. Say it."

"Damn sorry about the meeting sis. I know how important that was."

From the passenger seat, Juliet looked up, eyebrows raised in courteous pseudo-concern, from a centerfold of this year's Top Ten Spring Hairstyles. Ray held his finger over the speaker and mouthed the words "my sister."

"How about I cheer you up with dinner out? Your choice. My treat."

Ray repeated, "How about I cheer you up with dinner out? Your choice. My treat."

Juliet smiled, nodded, and returned to her magazine.

"The Paramount?"

"The Paramount?"

"See you then."

"See you then."

"Good work, Ray. Now it's just me and you again. We're back to yes and no. Understand?"

"Yes."

"It's six pm. You're going to take her back to your place. You've got to pick up something there before dinner. Some file of papers for me. Make something up. Divorce papers, maybe. I'm going through a divorce, which is true, of course. Keep it real, as close to the truth as possible. That's always the best way. Less to remember. Understand?"

"Yes."

"Encourage her to use the shower. Get her cleaned up. Give her a drink or give her a joint if she's amenable, just to mellow out. Let her rest up. She's got a long night ahead of her. Got all that?"

"Yes."

"Oh that's good Ray. That's excellent. I knew I wasn't wrong about you, baby. I knew you could do it. It's not so hard, Ray. Really, it's not. You'll see. Now you're going to be a good boy until I get there, aren't you? No playing without me, right?"

"Right…yes, no."

Charlotte laughed. "I know you won't. I believe you. I trust you, Ray. I really do. Trust is everything. You can see that now, can't you? We have to trust each other. Now, just relax. We're in the home-stretch, baby. Just do as I say and it'll all be cool."

"Okay, yes."

"Ciao, toots. See you soon. Smooches."

Ray thumbed off the phone and slipped it back into his pocket. He turned to Juliet and apologized. He explained, as off-handedly as possible, that there'd been just the slightest change in plans.

"I think I can see the resemblance. Yeah, I definitely can." That was Juliet talking, looking from Ray to Charlotte, from Charlotte to Ray. They were sitting around a faux oriental coffee table in the plush Victorian chairs of the Grammercy Hotel lounge sipping cocktails. Elaborate chandeliers of flickering candles hung from the ceiling, seemingly hundreds more candles flickered in wall sconces, in colored votive glasses, on polished tables, in every nook and cranny. The place looked like a movie-set for a Kenneth Anger film where Satan would show up as a rock-star. Moving in and out of the bruised shadows, pretty cocktail waitresses in slinky party gowns flashed like dangerous exotic fish, the kind that could poison or electrocute you on contact.

Ray wondered if it were true, did he and Charlotte look alike, or was it just the suggestive power of claiming they were siblings that worked on Juliet's mind? Ray couldn't help but think of that theory that people usually fall in love with those who resembled themselves,

seeking union with their cross-gendered double, and, in the process,
proving that we essentially never escape self-love.

They'd started with drinks at the Paramount, as planned. Ray
sat there nursing a gin-tonic, trying to pace himself for what
promised to be a long night, and watched Charlotte work her magic.
Juliet liked her instantly, who didn't? Charlotte's smile encouraged,
her touch excited, her enthusiasm was infectious. Ray imagined that
Charlotte must be good at whatever exactly it was she did, selling ice
to Eskimos, fire to the devil, water to a drowning man, etc.
Convincing people to give up things, particularly money, that seemed
to be the most accurate description Ray could come up with so far to
describe what Charlotte did. If it were possible to personally talk to
each and every voter, he didn't doubt that Charlotte could get
Haskins elected president by a landslide.

Dinner was at the Hudson, a quick change of plans, but
Charlotte said she felt inspired.

"Follow your bliss Ray," she said when he shot her a
questioning glance.

"Yeah, follow your bliss," Juliet echoed, wearing Charlotte's
arm on her shoulders like an exotic snake she was naively
underestimating.

And Ray saw how it was, how Charlotte had enlisted Juliet to
her side, that's how comfortable the girl was getting, that she thought
it was girls against boys. Women, after all, trusted other women. The
sister thing, too, had worked like a charm. Whatever reserve of
caution Juliet may have still felt about Ray had fallen utterly away.
Who wouldn't trust a sensitive guy having dinner with his sister in a
time of need? It was a stroke of genius.

Eating at one of the restaurant's Japanese-style communal
tables, Ray listened to Charlotte spin the story of her divorce-in-
progress. In this take, there was no violent husband, no drugs, no
frozen assets, and it wasn't that Ray necessarily found it suspect that
Charlotte might want to change or omit details of something so
personal with a virtual stranger, but what he did find disconcerting
was that the story Charlotte told now was every bit as believable as
the one she'd originally told him. If not more so, especially inasmuch

as it corroborated John Rossi's story, more or less. Her husband's "psychological breakdown," as Charlotte called it, had required him to be hospitalized, but when he refused treatment, well, what was there to do? His erratic behavior, the days he went missing, the calls to pick him up from "god-knew-where-this-time, in god-only-knew-what-state," the multiple suicide attempts...

It was only on the advice of her deeply concerned family, friends and therapist that Charlotte, broken-hearted, exhausted nearly to the state of breakdown herself, but still determined to do whatever it took, was persuaded at last to leave him. And even then, she did it only for his own good, finally convinced that her long-suffering Anna Karenina-like self-sacrifice was merely enabling his self-destructive behavior. She couldn't watch him destroy himself any longer. She didn't want to see him commit suicide. It was all just too painful.

"That's so sad," Juliet slurred.

She could be an actress, Ray thought, not for the first time, watching what he knew was a performance, and at some point he realized that Juliet, still sympathizing, was cooing and tsk-tsking personalized endearments and that meant Charlotte was using her real name tonight. The way he figured it, that could go both ways, it could mean everything was going to be okay, or that it didn't matter, because things weren't. There wasn't going to be any in-between, though, that's what Ray figured; it was going to be all or nothing, and which one he wanted, the all or the nothing, seemed irrelevant, out of his control, like he was watching a car accident develop.

In the middle of dessert, Charlotte interrupted whatever they'd been talking about with that electric look that Ray knew signaled an upcoming break in the linear narrative, some quantum leap Charlotte was about to make that would change everything.

"Let's go to the Grammercy Hotel. The lounge there is so cool."

They'd cabbed it downtown, wandering around the dark leafy square of streets around the Grammercy Park itself, looking for the hotel. Charlotte claimed to have once owned a condo in the area, or she still did, it was impossible to decipher. She was pointing vaguely up to a tall brown building with ornate molding, like a filthy wedding

cake, which reminded Ray of that horrible song no one could ever
forget, the one about leaving a cake out in the rain. Charlotte
mentioned the name of an architect that seemed completely made-
up. But aside from that, and the fact that she inexplicably didn't seem
to be able to locate the place she'd so meticulously described as her
home of eight years, Ray doubted any of it could be true, that she'd
really lived here when she said, if ever: the chronology, like so much
else, just didn't match up. She walked up to a guy unlocking a silver
Acura and flirtatiously asked him for directions to the hotel bar. The
guy pointed around the corner. Juliet noticed nothing. She said
admiringly, "You're sister is really something."

That's how they ended up here, ensconced among the votive
candles, like a Sadean tableau, Juliet looking like a lot of space had
opened up between her eyes, Charlotte whispering into her ear,
massaging her shoulders with both hands, and Ray watching them
with a smile that felt like it would slide off the side of his face if he
wasn't careful.

"Your sister is so cool Ray," Juliet kept repeating, like a mantra,
which seemed to be her answer to whatever Charlotte was
whispering, and Ray could only try to keep that smile hanging on his
face and answer with variations of "Yes, I know."

"What do you say we take this party home?" Charlotte
suggested.

"Home," Ray repeated the word as a question.

"To the carriage house."

He felt an unspecified relief not to be going back to his
place.

"Okay."

"I have to be at the airport tomorrow," Juliet piped up, as if
she'd been forgotten, as if she'd forgotten herself, and just
remembered her own presence.

"Oh of course," Charlotte said. "It's a much quicker drive to
the airport from my place; isn't that true, Ray?"

It wasn't true, none of it was. Ray signed the credit receipt that
had meanwhile come to the table and they left, all three of them, with

Ray already feeling as if he'd made a series of very fatal mistakes it was already way too late to correct.

Back at the carriage house, Ray searched the kitchen for something to party with while Charlotte and Juliet danced to a disco compilation on the stereo. The pantry was still empty, except for a can of condensed milk and half a box of ginger snaps hiding in the back of the last cabinet he checked. In the fridge, he did a little better: three more bottles of that mid-priced Brut champagne in the vegetable crisper. Each bottle was festooned with red-white-and-blue ribbons and tagged with the name and date of a recent Haskins fund-raiser.

Ray carried the bottles into the living room area. The girls were dancing the way girls often made love with each other in lesbian porn movies made for guys, as if they were doing masturbating alone in front of a mirror with a guy watching.

Ray watched. He'd surreptitiously popped a Viagra on the ride back from Manhattan to forestall any anxiety-induced malfunction of the equipment and his cock presently felt like a wet sweatsock full of silver dollars hanging inside his pants. He popped the cork on the first bottle of champagne, sucked up the eruption, and passed the bottle, still foaming, to Charlotte. She sucked at the bottle, fed some to Juliet, and the two girls kissed noisily and sloppily.

Ray opened a second bottle, same as before, but hung onto this one, watching the girls dance, drink, and kiss, as he drank. After a while, they collapsed onto the daybed and Charlotte pulled Juliet's suddenly bare feet into her lap, massaging them. She held up one of Juliet's feet as the girl nursed, oblivious, on the champagne bottle.

"Did you consider this girl's toenails when you picked her up?"

"What?"

"The shape of them, Ray." She playfully bit Juliet's big toe and the girl giggled, snorting champagne. "Ohhh, so precious." She looked up at Ray. "Don't tell me you didn't notice. It's details like this that are so important. So much can go wrong. You did good."

Ray had no idea what she was talking about. Charlotte began sucking the girl's toes.

"Come keep us company Ray," she said between toes.

Ray sat on the other side of Juliet, putting his arm loosely around her shoulders. The way her head flopped against his chest, he thought she might have already passed out, but when he put his mouth on hers, she kissed him back hungrily, her mouth like one of those single-cell organisms that you see on television science shows that assimilate other single-cell organisms in their vicinity.

"Feel her up a little Ray," Charlotte encouraged, "for god's sake, don't be shy."

Sliding his hand under Juliet's shirt, Ray felt the girl's smooth warm belly. It wasn't toned or rippled with muscle or anything like that, just a soft, rounded girl's belly, slightly protruding, like a girl's belly should be. He stroked it a while and moved up to the cups of her bra, pulled the material aside, and rubbed a plump nipple with his thumb.

"Ummm…mmmm…" the thing that was Juliet's mouth said into his mouth.

Charlotte jumped up. "I know what we need!"

She went over to the book case, rummaging around among a stack of photo albums, causing the pile of albums to topple and vomit a cascade of photos across the floor. Ray stopped paying attention to Charlotte for a while, one of his hands, somehow, having made its way under Juliet's ass, one finger nudging its stubborn way inside her. Then Charlotte was front and center again, cutting three lines of coke on a copy of *Time* magazine with a picture of a saluting Haskins stepping out of a jet over the caption: *Can He Save Us?* Ray felt the crease in his forehead deepen and his heart do a back-flip. Charlotte was cutting the lines of coke with the scalpel.

Charlotte dipped her head to the magazine and breathed the line up in one hungry inhale. She tried to say something but her eyes pinwheeled, she gave up, and she sank back on the couch smiling and licking her gums. The scalpel, still in her hand, lie on the couch by her thigh.

"Oh, mmmm, candy-time," Juliet cooed, and sat up.

"Say trick or treat little girl," Charlotte murmured.

"Twick or teet…" Juliet leaned over the coffee table and breathed up a line.

Charlotte recovered. "Your turn Ray,"

Ray managed it and found Charlotte's tongue in his mouth. Her tongue slid out, slid back in, slid out again. Her face—who did she look like now?—pulled back into focus, but she wasn't looking at him, but beyond him, to Juliet, who was somewhere.

Charlotte: "I hope we're not shocking you, Juliet. But Ray and I don't believe in boundaries. We may be brother and sister, but we're also lovers. Ray and I don't believe that anything's forbidden between us. Do we, Ray?"

"Uhnnnn….hmmmnn…" Ray said.

Meanwhile, Charlotte used her finger to paint the girl's lips with the last of the coke. She rimmed Juliet's nostrils with her finger. Juliet didn't protest the tip of Charlotte's finger in her nose. Charlotte puckered her lips in a sympathetic pout. She cooed, "Is that a problem for you, baby? We don't scare you? Do we?"

"It's cool," Juliet said, smearing the words. It was uncertain whether she understood anything at this point. "Ish all good…"

Whatever the girl said next was swallowed up by Charlotte's voracious kiss. It took a while for Ray to realize that Juliet had by now truly passed out because for a time he must have passed out, too. When he came to, his fingers were still inside the unconscious girl.

"Help me get her pants off, Ray."

Charlotte had slid to the floor, ineffectually yanking at the expensive designer jeans Juliet had changed into after showering at Ray's place, and Ray was trying to work the zipper, trying not to snag it on her panties. It seemed absurdly difficult to get the pants off her, but they did, needing a break to share a joint and making judicious use of Charlotte's scalpel to separate some of the seams in the denim. When they were done, Juliet lay back against the cushions in her pink panties, legs splayed, mouth open, her jeans in ruins, snoring lightly.

Charlotte climbed up onto the daybed opposite Ray, Juliet between them, and collapsed into herself, staring sightlessly into the middle distance for a while. Then she shook herself awake and she and Ray stripped off Juliet's bra.

"You never know about the nipples," Charlotte said absently, poking at one with her ring finger. "Sometimes they're just, I don't know, too diffuse."

Ray kissed Juliet behind the ear.

Charlotte was doing something, pushing at the girl's shoulder, trying to turn her over from the looks of it.

"Give me a hand, will you?"

Ray pulled Juliet towards him and Charlotte scooched up behind her. The girl's breasts mashed flat against Ray's chest and her mouth, sagging open, drooled a little. Ray licked her lips, tasting something bitter, the drool probably, and heard her moan a little. It was easy to miss, but Juliet was moving in cooperation with whatever Charlotte was doing behind her, finger-fucking her, probably. Ray shimmed her panties, already half off, down to her knees, and without even meaning to, his penis slipped inside her. Surprised, he pulled it back out. Then he put it back in for a while.

"Taste this," Charlotte said, her face popping up over Juliet's shoulder.

Ray was sitting beside the action now, his head in his hands. He lifted his face, which felt all punched up, like an old boxing glove. He unthinkingly licked the proffered finger. Then he sucked it into his mouth like a peppermint stick.

"Her ass?" he asked speculatively after he'd sucked the flavor away.

Charlotte nodded. "Bingo!"

Ray felt dizzy again, probably nodding off for an unspecified time. When he focused again, it seemed some frames of the film were missing.

"Look at this girl," Charlotte was saying, super-excited. She was holding the sides of Juliet's mouth open with her thumbs, giving the girl a gaping idiot's grin. "She's such a treasure. I mean it, really *look* at her."

Ray squinted, really trying to see what Charlotte was talking about. Juliet was sprawled on the couch, naked, except for the panties around her ankles, her trimmed pussy yawning open, folds of pink like an octopus mouth. Ray leaned forward and peered deep into the dark hole of Juliet's mouth. She was drooling copiously over her chin with her mouth held open like that. Charlotte leaned forward, too, and kissed Juliet complicatedly on her open mouth, sucking in her tongue.

"No life is wasted Ray," she said, lifting her head and looking at Ray seriously, "if it's fully appreciated. Do you understand me?"

"Yes," Ray said, not sure if he did, but thinking he might. He had a fistful of Juliet's hair in his hand and he was breathing in its scent: coconut and strawberry, sweat, cigarette smoke, and something else mixed in, something unnamable—Juliet, maybe? Charlotte looked up from another oral exploration of the girl's still pried open mouth. "You can't say you understand, Ray, not really. Not until you've tasted her molars."

Ray pressed his face against Juliet's and Charlotte put her hand on the back of his head and held it down firmly. He could do nothing else, so he probed around inside her mouth with his tongue. He felt the little ridges of her back teeth. He did that for awhile.

They turned her over after that, stuffed some pillows under her hips, and took turns giving her head. Juliet came around at several points, once muttering something like "Hey guys hey" and another time taking Ray's penis in hand and attempting to feed it into her mouth, but otherwise she confined herself to being passed out.

"Do you see what I mean Ray?" Charlotte said after some more awkward gymnastics, as if they'd been having a continuous coherent conversation. She stroked the inside of Juliet's thigh, dipping her head down to take a deep breath of her cunt. "This girl's an adventure. That's what other people can be."

She smoothed her hand over Juliet's body, tracing her tits, her belly, her thighs, "Like distant worlds, strange planets. They're waiting to be discovered. Do you have any idea yet what I'm talking about?"

"Yes."

Ray's erection hadn't abated through any of this. Charlotte was now holding it in her free hand; it fit there, it seemed, so perfectly you might almost think the hard-on belonged to her.

"Do you? Do you really know what I'm talking about?"

She abandoned her exploration of the girl and leaned over Ray's lap.

"Yes," he answered, breathing heavily, feeling Charlotte licking all around the head of his cock, and then closing her lips over it. And it was true: he really did, he believed he understood. He didn't, not really. He would, though, soon enough, and then he'd wish he didn't. But at that moment, he didn't understand a goddamn thing.

They were face to face, Charlotte kneeling on his lap, his cock buried deep inside her. It could almost have been mistaken for a form of meditation. Beside them, Juliet was drunkenly playing with herself, but not for long. Her hand fell to the couch and her head lolled forward, like a wilted dandelion. Ray grabbed Charlotte's tits as she leaned forward and sank her teeth into the flesh between his neck and shoulder. Ray had to fuck her harder and faster to outrace the pain radiating through the right side of his body and threatening to overtake the pleasure. Charlotte rocked in his lap as if she were having a visionary seizure, as if she were drifting off on a vision-quest. Her hands were around Ray's throat and she bit him on the cheeks and lips and screamed "No, no, no," and, of course, she didn't come.

Had he come yet—or had he come again? Ray couldn't say for certain. It must have been the drugs. He was still hard, his cock felt like it was made of concrete, like it was one of those ancient obelisks in the desert, carved with alien heiroglyphics. Each heart beat, every breath, seemed to take on the pattern of orgasm: build-up and release.

"How are you doing?" Charlotte asked him.

"It's like fucking in a dream. Better than reality."

She rolled off him. "It can always be like this Ray."

"What are you doing?" he said dreamily.

The scalpel was in her hand. Her eyes were incandescent. "Let's use her body as our altar."

"You can't do this."

"You can do anything. You're just afraid, Ray, that's all. Don't be."

Ray should have stopped her, he knew he should, but he just lay there, passive, as if he were in a theatre and watching a performance that you'd be a fool to think was happening for real. The cut wasn't life-threatening, Ray consoled himself with that, but that wasn't much to console oneself with. Blood welled up in a thin line beneath the bottom of Juliet's left breast, roughly where you'd make an incision for a breast implant because it's not supposed to be as noticeable there. Ray consoled himself with that, too, but that wasn't much either. Charlotte put her mouth over the cut and sucked on it. Then she looked up.

"Have a taste. Share this girl with me."

"You shouldn't be doing this Charlotte."

The blood line under the girl's tit was jiggling like a fat red worm.

"It's what she wants, Ray. She might not even know it herself, but this is why she's here. This girl is offering herself to us. It's a gift, Ray. It's life. Don't turn your back on it. Don't waste it."

She kissed the wound under the girl's breast again and looked up, her mouth freshly bloodied, looking redrawn somehow, the mouth of a hybrid beast from out of some grim xxx-rated porn mythology.

"Kiss me."

That kiss was a mistake, Ray remembered thinking at the time. It's the forbidden fruit all over again. The original sin.

"It's a zen parable Ray," Charlotte said, breathlessly. "You're hanging over a ravine with a man-eating tiger beneath you and two rats gnawing the vine you cling to. This is life." Charlotte pointed to her bloodied mouth. "This is life," she repeated through her twisted mouth, that malignant talking strawberry, "Are you going to taste it, or are you going to waste it?"

Ray stepped out of the bathroom, toweling his hair dry. Charlotte was standing in front of the mirrored wardrobe, posing, and checking her voice-mail on her cell phone. She was wearing a silk robe with a japanese pattern, something with flowers and herons, or maybe they were ibises. She winked and blew Ray a kiss.

"What's up toots?" she said cheerily.

Ray glanced over at the bed to survey the damages. They'd managed to stagger their way up the stairs to the loft at one point in the evening, god only knew how, they were all so trashed. Juliet was still lying among the tangled sheets, snoring raggedly, sound asleep. There was a crusty line of dried blood under one tit and some incidental bruising here and there, but nothing too bad, everything considered. Ray checked his watch and started to say something but Charlotte held up a finger. She was apparently listening closely to one of the messages. Ray sat on the bed and put his hand on Juliet's bare thigh, trying to shake her awake.

That got Charlotte's attention. She immediately folded up her cell phone. "What are you doing?"

"Waking sleeping beauty here. She's got a flight to catch."

"Let her sleep. She needs the rest."

"But her flight. It leaves in less than two hours."

"She can miss it."

Ray felt a little flip in his gut hearing that. "I don't get it."

"I need her Ray."

"What the hell's that supposed to mean?"

"I want to hang on to her for a few days."

"Hang on to her?" Ray looked down at the sleeping girl. "Did you discuss this with her? Get her input on this?"

"Not yet."

"Don't you think you ought to?"

"That's not really necessary," Charlotte replied coolly. She was staring into the mirror again and examining the flesh around her jawline.

"You can't keep her against her will, Charlotte. What the hell are you thinking?"

"Calm down Ray."

"Calm down? That's kidnapping you're talking about."

"Who said anything about kidnapping? For crissakes, stop being so dramatic." Charlotte turned from the mirror. "I'm just going to borrow her for a few days. I'm sure she won't mind when I explain it to her. I can be, you know, very persuasive if I want to be."

She'd reached into a drawer in the wardrobe and pulled out a couple of those plastic ties the police used instead of handcuffs during riots. Charlotte crossed the room and climbed one-kneed onto the bed. The girl stirred and Charlotte stroked her hair.

"Hey baby, good morning," she said brightly. "How are we feeling?"

Juliet mumbled something and Charlotte snuggled up behind, cuddling, gently rocking her. She nipped Juliet's shoulder, nuzzled her neck. "Mmmm, you taste good." She kissed the girl's shoulders, fondled her bottom. Juliet backed closer against Charlotte's warm body.

"This is crazy," Ray said quietly, " I can't let you do this."

"Do what, Ray? I haven't done anything yet. I'm just going to convince her to stay. There's no law against that, is there? Now why don't you go home if you don't want to be here. If you're not into this, why don't you just leave? I don't need you anymore. You've served your purpose. Go away."

Charlotte's words stung, no doubt about it, the way she could turn on him, cold like that, reminding him, as if he needed reminding, that she could drop him on a dime. Crazy as this scene was, Ray didn't relish being shut out of her world, because once that door shut he knew instinctively it would never open to him again. And now that he was involved, he needed to stay close; it was the only way he would be able to exert some control over the situation. But he needed to think this new development through and he had to get away for a few hours to do it. Charlotte was right, nothing had happened yet, so what was he getting so bent out of shape about? This was a fucked-up situation, Ray was sure of it, but so far nothing that couldn't be fixed. Maybe it just seemed fucked up from Ray's small perspective. Maybe, and he kept telling himself there was a real reason to believe this, his apprehensions were nothing more than a bourgeoisie overreaction and this was standard operating procedure in Charlotte's world.

"Fine," he said, trying to muster some resolve. "I'm outta here."

He half-expected her to call him back as he headed toward the door, but she didn't. On his way down the stairs he took a last glance back at the bed. Charlotte was still lying spooned against a naked Juliet, rocking her, softly singing what sounded like a lullabye into the unconscious girl's ear.

Yeah, maybe this was all normal in Charlotte's world.

Yeah. Right.

The moment he left Ray felt better, but that didn't last long. He drove back to Manhattan and had lunch in a café on Houston. He spent a leisurely afternoon strolling around Soho. By late afternoon, he missed Charlotte. He was worried, too, about what was going on at the carriage house. He called eight times, left three different messages, but Charlotte didn't return his calls. She must be mad at him, he thought. He tried not to think the worse. He tried not to. The problem was that he couldn't decide which of the many different awful possibilities he was considering would qualify as the *worse*.

Charlotte returned Ray's calls two days later. They met at the Sony Public Space on 55th. They sat at a small metal table surrounded by potted trees and the usual lunch-hour crowd of businessmen and tourists. She was, as usual, between appointments. Haskins was up by six with a month to go, good news, she said. "We're picking up momentum." She denied that she was angry at him, just busy, and yes, she admitted, Juliet was still with her.

"Does she have a choice?" Ray hated the jittery smile that seemed to have taken up permanent residence on his face lately, like a cockroach problem, impossible to completely eradicate.

"Everyone has a choice. Yup, I'm pro-choice."

"This isn't a joke."

"No, its not."

Ray looked around at the sunlight and ficus and men in business suits. He wondered if anyone else were having a conversation even remotely as insane as this one.

"So how did you persuade her to stay?"

Big smile. "You're not jealous, are you Ray?"

"No, I'm not jealous. It's just—never mind."

"What is it?" She leaned across the table and took hold of his wrists. "I want you to tell me everything. What?"

"We've known each other how long now, a couple of months? I haven't even spent two straight days with you."

Ray regretted the words the moment they were out of his mouth.

"You *are* jealous." Charlotte laughed and sat back. "But you're trying to be brave about it. How adorable."

"No," he said, denying the obvious, but hoping to obscure it with an equally genuine concern. "I'm worried, that's all."

"Worried about what?"

"That girl. What we did to her."

Charlotte pulled the straw out of her latte and licked it.

"What did we do to her?"

"You know."

She thrust the straw back into her drink and sipped. "No, I really don't. Why don't you tell me what we did to her?"

"Stop playing games."

"I'm not playing games. We showed Juliet a good time while she was in town, Ray. That's all."

"What's she still doing here?"

"She's giving of herself. What's wrong with that?"

Ray didn't want to ask because just asking meant something, didn't it? But he went ahead and asked anyway

"Is she okay?"

"Of course she's okay. Would you like to see for yourself?"

Ray was certain that Charlotte expected him to decline the offer.

"Yes," he said, trying to find something reassuring in Charlotte's open, innocent face, but finding, instead, something completely impenetrable, like the amoral curiosity of a child. "Yes, I really would."

The dildo connecting them was lifeless, but festooned with hyper-realistic muscles and veins of unfailingly hard rubber, and glistening with slathered lubricants, of both the organic and the manufactured variety; it was the biggest cock Ray had ever seen in his life. He had helped Charlotte into the harness himself, all the belts and buckles involved, transforming her into a man from the waist down, a kind of PVC cross-gendered satyr. Juliet, meanwhile, was propped up like a raw turkey awaiting stuffing, her face buried in a damp pillow. She let the big rubber cock enter her without a whimper of protest, let it go into and out of her, and it was startling to see how accommodating her holes had already become.

"Hold still silly," Charlotte said, as if parodying the girl's absence of complicity.

She gripped Juliet's hips tighter, steadying the bulls-eye when the girl started to topple over. It wasn't really that Juliet was actually moving of her own volition, mind you; it was the violence of Charlotte's fucking that was throwing the girl's submissive body off-center. Juliet was totally, even alarmingly, inert.

It had been three days since Charlotte had taken Ray back to the carriage house to prove to him that Juliet was "okay." That afternoon he'd found her propped on the day bed in a stained nightie, staring blankly at Oprah, and only minimally coherent. With Charlotte patiently prompting her like she was an infant, Juliet managed to cobble together a barely comprehensible sentence fragment meant to assure Ray that everything was "cool." Ray was pretty sure that nothing going on in the carriage house was even remotely "cool," that, in fact, it was all very very uncool. There were bruises on Juliet's wrists and ankles where the plastic ties had abraded her skin, but otherwise, aside from some bite marks, paling bruises the color of a battered sunset, and a scattering of partially healed cuts, Juliet seemed largely unharmed.

"Satisfied Ray?"

Charlotte had her hand around Juliet's shoulders, practically holding the girl up, making Ray think of a ventriloquist and her dummy.

"This has gone far enough. I think we should get her the hell out of here."

"But Ray, she doesn't want to go."

"I don't know what kind of game you're playing. But this is serious."

"Ask her yourself if you don't believe me. She's sitting right here. Go ahead. Ask her if she wants to go."

"Charlotte..."

"Go on."

Ray shifted his gaze to the girl sitting between them. Her lips were badly chapped and her zeroed-out eyes had kernels of white crust in their corners. A faint odor of sweat and sex rose off her, reminding Ray of a dead garden.

"Juliet?" he said, wondering if she were even in there. "Juliet do you want to go home? Juliet?"

Charlotte shook the girl and leaned close to her ear. "Sweetie, honey, Ray is asking you a question."

"Juliet," Ray said, "can you understand me?"

"Uhhhn..."

"Do you want to leave? Go home?"

Charlotte shook her again. "Answer Ray, baby."

"Do you want to leave?"

"Uhhnn..." the girl turned her head slowly and look up at Charlotte. They kissed, or rather, Juliet let her mouth go slack and Charlotte covered it with hers. Ray could see Charlotte's tongue probing the side of Juliet's cheek. When this was over, Charlotte turned Juliet's head back toward Ray so she could say, "Uhhhnn no..."

Was she afraid to tell Ray the truth, thinking she couldn't trust him? Had Charlotte threatened her? Brainwashed her? Or, most likely, was she simply too damn wasted to know what the hell was happening?

"There Ray. Are you satisfied? She's told you herself."

"Of course I'm not satisfied. She's barely conscious."

"She's of legal age, Ray. She's a consenting adult. I've got her statement on tape saying so."

And sure enough, Juliet seemed to be fully participating in their debauches if, by participating, you meant she didn't outright protest or resist in the least as they manipulated her limbs into various obscenely accommodating postures. If the evidence between her legs was to be believed, the roseate flush across her cheeks, the stiffening of her nipples and the spasm of her vagina during many of these escapades, she was more than just enduring the acts perpetrated on her, she was responding to them with genuine, if only occasional, sexual gratification.

The tripod was set up to record most of everything they did—the digital minicam becoming so omnipresent that, most of the time, Ray virtually forgot it was there.

One day, Ray arrived at the carriage house to find that Juliet's nipples and clitoris had been pierced. Charlotte explained that a "friend" of hers who owned an East Orange tattoo parlor had come by to make these little enhancements to their pet. She lifted the gauze to show him the extensive tattooing on the backs of Julet's thighs and across her shoulderblades. "A preliminary outline for a depiction from a scene from Sade's *120 Days of Sodom*," Charlotte deciphered, because the swelling and blood and smeary inks made it impossible to make out. "It's going to be fantastic when its completed." In the days that followed, Juliet was further "modified." At the corners of her mouth, and punched at regular intervals through her lips, were a series of what looked like tiny brackets of blue wire, giving her lips a sewn together look when engaged, effectively latching her mouth shut. Another day her tongue was swollen to half-plus its ordinary size around a stud, making it difficult for her to speak, not that she did much of that anyway, but for the next two days oral sex was out of the question, which, of course, she did do a lot of. So much so, in fact, that Juliet had to be repeatedly reminded that she needed to hold off on the crotch licking until her tongue healed up.

The piercings and the tattooing especially alarmed Ray because they were permanent records of what they'd done to her flesh and because Juliet was clearly not in any state to have given her consent to these modifications.

Each day, he grew more nervous upon arriving at the carriage house, wondering what he would find next.

Now, as he sat and watched from an armchair, naked, smoking a mid-sex cigarette, Charlotte pulled the dildo she was wearing almost all the way out and roughly sank it all the way back to the hilt in Juliet's trembling rump. On each pale buttock a large winged demon had been tattooed—one male, the other female—each wielding a whip of human skulls that curled suggestively around the roseate tattoo crowning the girl's asshole. Charlotte slapped the illustrated meat of Juliet's ass with her open hand. Only the hardest slaps seemed to rouse Juliet from her stupor lately. Charlotte turned towards Ray and asked, breathlessly, "Aren't you going to join the party?" Ray waved noncommittally with his cigarette. Without the drugs, he was sure that an erection would have been out of the question. Even with them, Ray doubted he could overcome his apprehension enough to feel anything for the scene playing out in front of him. "Be sociable," she said, panting, "at least jerk-off, for crissakes."

He'd never masturbated himself in front of anyone before doing so in front of Charlotte. And the act, long associated in his mind with privacy and shame, at first seemed impossible to enjoy under her scrutiny. But he knew that after a short while, she would stop paying any attention to him and his self-consciousness had therefore waned. He developed a strategy. He tried to look at Charlotte and what she was doing to Juliet the way he looked at pornography, objectifying it in his mind, distancing himself from any responsibility, like it was all pretend, and, after all, who's to say it definitely wasn't? With a little practice, it wasn't difficult. That was, after all, Ray's first introduction to the female objects of his sexual desire: glossy, taboo, untouchable. And, being eternally unattainable, they were still the most potent. Charlotte was as distant and unreachable as any of the two-dimensional women of Ray's long-cherished porn fantasies—forever alluring and forever out of reach even though he could feel the heat of Charlotte's body only a few feet away and hear the slap-slurp of her thighs making contact with Juliet's ass.

It worked again. Ray was genuinely hard now and his penis moved in and out of his fist as he sank into the old rhythm he knew so well, the meditation practiced behind thousands of locked doors, that made him, momentarily, nearly as self-sufficient as a Buddha. Three feet away, Juliet was in one of her increasingly rare awake cycles, moaning and grunting and pushing back on the dildo, meeting Charlotte's rough, punishing thrusts. Unless Ray was kidding himself, Juliet was orgasming again, her little toes curled back, that's what it looked like anyway, the flesh on her thighs trembling like milk vibrating after a thunderclap. Mounted behind her, fucking her like one of the devils tattooed on Juliet's rump, Charlotte, oblivious, kept going straight through Juliet's orgasm, her amazing eyes closed tight as if she were concentrating very hard on something impossible to see, something very far away, deep inside her, and, as always, she didn't come.

"You don't think I'm weird, do you?" she asked him two days later, as they drove back from Princeton after a ten-thousand-dollar-a-plate fund-raising dinner for Haskins backers that included the governor of New Jersey and George Clooney. Rudra was staying back at the carriage house with Juliet. "Babysitting," as Charlotte called it. Ray hadn't seen a trace of the man's existence other than an occasional stirring at the curtain of a third-floor window where the telescope and camera stood. But each day Charlotte walked the digital record of their exploits of the day before up to the main house.

"Don't worry. All he can do is watch her," she assured Ray over their roast beef dinners. "Poor guy. His testicles are fried. I keep telling him to get that implant. That's what I'd do, if I were a guy. Instead, he lets Joan take lovers and he lets his heart break. Stop worrying, Ray. Your precious little kidnap victim will be safe with Rudra."

Ray winced. He looked around to make sure that the Assemblywoman or whoever it was seated next to them hadn't overheard.

"Jesus, Charlotte, keep your voice down."

"Oops." Charlotte put her hand over her mouth in mock concern and rolled her eyes. "A slip of the lip."

"Why do you call her that, anyway?"

"Isn't that what you think she is?"

"Is she?"

"Ray, I thought we settled that."

Ray wasn't sure if they'd settled the matter or how. Was Juliet a prisoner—or a willing participant? Charlotte had invited him to ask her that again, this last time on camera, and Juliet told him she wasn't being coerced; well, she told him that after a fashion. She was eerily cogent this time, at least for five minutes or so, as if she'd been rehearsed and were reciting her lines mechanically under threat. Anyone watching the clip could see that. She reminded Ray uncomfortably of those terrorist hostages on television denouncing American imperialism while sitting between two heavily-armed guys in masks and head rags. At Charlotte's invitation, Ray asked her specifically if there wasn't someone who should be informed of her whereabouts, someone who would be worried about her. Her family? Her boyfriend? She told him that everything was "totally cool." But what did that really mean? What did any of it mean? He hadn't been rehearsed or threatened, and yet his questions seemed just as staged and phony as Juliet's responses. He was certain this videotaped "testimony" wouldn't hold up in court, if it came to that. It was, Ray decided, of absolutely crucial importance that it didn't come to that.

Just the night before Charlotte had two Chinese "escorts" come to the carriage house. God knows where she hired them from. What they'd done over the next twenty-eight hours was still a surreal smear of drugs, hormones, and deviance on Ray's staticky mental screen: only a series of vivid tableaux remained burned in his memory like signposts that indicated a descent to some of the deeper circles of erotic hell. Juliet tied to a ladder and "interrogated"; lying face-down on the kitchen table with her buttocks bloodied; curled in the bathtub with both naked whores straddling her; standing on a chair, hands tied behind her back, and a noose around her neck...

"She's kinky Ray. Twisted. Everyone is under the surface," Charlotte tried to reassure him. "Normality is only skin deep. People like us, we're just more in touch with what's underneath."

Ray wanted to believe her, for Juliet's sake, for Charlotte's sake, for his own. He'd been so sure, for instance, that Beth was normal, and there she was having an affair. Maybe Charlotte was right. Everyone had a secret. Everyone was twisted. Juliet, included. Maybe there was no such thing as straight. Human nature being all it was, and wasn't.

Ray spent the night back in the hotel room watching porn because, as Charlotte said, the special after dinner party would just bore him to tears, and, besides, she needed to network among the power-players. It was a thinly-veiled lie, Ray was sure of it. She didn't want him at the party; no doubt his presence would hamper her ability to "mingle" among whatever lovers or potential lovers were in attendance, and perhaps, more importantly, Ray would be an embarrassment, for he truly didn't belong among that class of people, never did, never would. So exactly where *did* he fit into Charlotte's life, anyway?

"I'll make it up to you later," she promised.

Later, stretched above her on the hotel bed, Ray took his "revenge," cumming with his cock buried in her beautiful face as she stuck a finger up his ass and pushed it quickly in and out. But it was like a gladiator fucking Messalina, even spewing his slime down her throat and using her like a whore, she was still an Empress, still the Moon-Queen, she was only amusing herself, only using him to play the whore. Lying beside her afterwards, she kissed him and Ray tasted his own cum on her tongue. Moments later, she burst out sobbing uncontrollably telling him a disjointed story of some man or other, not her husband, who left her for a younger woman, and Ray, holding her tightly, said, "I can't imagine what man could ever leave you."

Her body stiffened and her voice went flat and cold. "Well he did Ray. It happened."

Ray tried to tell her that he was sorry.

"That doesn't help, does it? You being sorry."

She squirmed out of his arms and Ray let her go. She rolled over, facing the wall. After a while, Ray reached over and touched her shoulder. In the over-airconditioned room, her flesh was cold as a cut of meat.

"I'm sorry," he whispered again, stupidly, because there was nothing else to say.

"No sweat," she muttered. "It's over. I'm sleepy now. I'm going to sleep."

And she did, or pretended to, almost immediately.

In the morning they fucked again, twice, but Ray had to force it, especially the second time. The night before had raised yet more questions and Ray was preoccupied and anxious to get back to the carriage house and reassure himself of Juliet's safety. They ate omelets in the hotel coffee shop and were back on the road by ten.

"You don't think I'm too kinky, do you?" Charlotte asked from the passenger seat. She was wearing dark glasses and holding a toothpick between her perfect teeth at a jaunty angle. She was on the upswing again, climbing towards her manic apex. The wind was blowing through her hair and her bare feet were propped up on the dashboard. She looked like Reece Witherspoon on those occasions when Reece looked like Scarlett Johannsen, only somewhat less "ethereal." Her bad mood from last night seemed to have completely evaporated.

"When my life is over," Ray said spontaneously, pushing up her skirt and resting his palm on Charlotte's naked thigh, (and the whole time he was perversely fantasizing about jerking the steering wheel sharply to the right and sending the car and the two of them careening and screaming into a bridge abutment), "and I ask God what it was all for, all the heartbreak and loss and sickness and death and futility, he's going to point to the way you look right now and say, '*That*—that's what it was all for...'"

"Oh Ray," Charlotte said, "That's poetry. You're a real troubadour. Thank you. I can't take off my sunglasses right now because you've made me cry. I don't know what to say."

And, as if to prove it, she said nothing as she yanked down Ray's zipper and leaned over the gear shaft. For the next four miles she performed a little oral poetry of her own.

"Where are you? Why aren't you ever there when I need you? Why isn't anyone ever there when I need them? Dammit Ray, pick up the phone. I don't know where the fuck you can possibly be. Call me when you get this. Oh, fuck you. Just forget it." That's the message Ray found on his answering machine when he came in the door at two am. Unable to sleep, he'd been walking around St. Mark's without his cell phone. He hadn't heard from her for the better part of three days. Nothing unusual about that, of course, but he could never manage to get used to it. He'd been purposely leaving the cell phone behind lately on occasion to keep himself from waiting obsessively for her to call. For the most part, that didn't really work inasmuch as he still found himself surreptitiously hurrying back to the apartment "just in case."

Wimp, Ray called himself, even as he strode quickly through the streets to his building. He couldn't help himself.

Now he nervously gulped a bottle of Powerade and flipped through four hundred channels of nothing on TV waiting for Charlotte to pick up his return call. According to the log on the answering machine, she'd called almost two hours ago. Cursing himself for leaving his phone behind, Ray could only hope that he hadn't missed his opportunity to be there when she needed him. Her phone rang seventeen times and he was waiting for the voicemail on her cell since she wasn't answering that either when she suddenly picked up. She sounded half-asleep, drugged, almost incoherent.

"Yuh, who's it?

"It's Ray. I just got your message. I'm sorry. Were you sleeping? Are you okay?"

"Uh-hunnh…" she said. There was a pause and then the sound of something hitting the floor and breaking into a thousand pieces. "Mmmmmm…?"

"What was that?"

"Something…I don't know…huh?"

"I said, I just got your message. Are you okay? Did you still want me to come over?"

Charlotte muttered something, as if she were talking to someone else in the room with her. She whispered a curse under her breath and then asked Ray in a faraway voice, "Are you home?"

"Yes."

"Good."

There was a long pause during which Ray considered that Charlotte had fallen asleep or hung up.

"Charlotte?"

"Mmmm?"

"Did you still want me to come over?"

"Come over?"

Someone was there, Ray felt certain of it. Her husband? She was talking like someone with a knife to her throat. No, no, he was just letting his imagination get the better of him.

"Charlotte, are you okay? Do you still want me to come over?"

"Yes, okay."

"I'll be there in an hour, okay?"

"I think I cut my foot…"

"Charlotte?"

She'd already hung up.

Forty-five frantic, worried filled minutes later, Ray was at the door of the carriage house. There didn't seem to be anyone else around: no cars in the driveway, no lights on in the main house, the faux Tudor looked closed-up and deserted. Somewhat to his surprise, Charlotte opened the door before he could even ring the bell. She must have seen his headlights splash across the windows. She kissed him on the threshold, her arms locked around his neck, yanking him towards her. Ray peered over her shoulder into the murky room, looking for John Rossi. She ground her crotch against Ray's, almost mechanically, as if merely out of habit, or—and the thought chilled him—as if she were trying to hide something from him. Ray suddenly felt exposed standing there in the doorway, wondering if Rudra was watching from his window.

"Can we go inside?"

She led him by the hand through the dining area, the room with the day-bed, all of it looking just as undisturbed and unlived in as ever, and through the French doors to the patio out back. There was no sign of any visitors. On the way to the patio, Charlotte grabbed an open bottle of wine on the kitchen counter. When they were sitting, Ray poured the wine into mismatched orange juice tumblers. Charlotte stared bug-eyed at her glass, her leg bouncing nervously on her toes. Ray noticed that she didn't seem to have cut her feet, after all.

"I might have to fly to Chicago," she announced, suddenly. She pulled a ginger snap from an open box on the table, stared at it a moment, and then put it back in the box. "It's my father. He may have had a heart attack."

"Damn—I'm sorry. When did this happen?"

"Sometime early this morning."

"Is he okay?"

"It's touch and go."

"Have you talked to him? How does he sound?"

"No, I didn't talk to him."

Ray waited for her to continue but she didn't.

"How did you find out?"

"His friend called me. He's with my father in the hospital. Dad didn't want to worry me. They're running some tests to find out what happened."

"Wait…so you're not sure if it was definitely a heart attack?"

"No. But he's very old and he's had a couple of heart attacks already. It could have been a heart-attack. It's hard to know how serious it is…until they do the tests."

On the table was a supposedly valuable first edition of Baudelaire's *Flowers of Evil* that Charlotte had claimed her brother, a dealer in antiquities, gave her as a gift. From the looks of it, she'd left the book out on the patio, exposed to the weather, because when Charlotte first showed it to him weeks ago it was in mint condition. Now it's cover was stained and buckled, the paper swollen—it's once perfect binding bursting like a bloated corpse. Charlotte was still talking, "Dad always seems to rally when I visit. But I have responsibilities here. I can't be away unless it's really necessary."

Over the hills that tumbled down to the river, Ray could see the skyline of Manhattan flickering tentatively through the haze. Since he hadn't eaten anything since an almond roll for breakfast that morning, the wine hit him pretty quickly. He drank some more and Charlotte leaned forward and kissed him. Her tongue pushed into Ray's mouth like someone punched him and everything was swelling.

It was cold on the patio. But Charlotte wasn't wearing anything but a t-shirt and thin red shorts, a pair of black platform thong sandals on her bare feet. She looked, surprisingly, a lot like Nora Jones, but with blonde hair, of course. He touched the exposed flesh of her upper arm: it was chilled and covered with gooseflesh.

"You're freezing." he said.

"Yes."

"Let's go back in."

"Okay," she said, but she didn't move, still jiggling her leg, as if she were stalled in neutral, her enging gunning.

Ray put his hand over hers.

"It'll probably be okay," he said.

She stared with big, glistening round eyes at nothing on the table.

"It's not really that," she said.

"What is it then?"

She didn't look up. "I have something to show you."

"This might look a little odd," Charlotte said, after she led him upstairs, "but it's really not." Juliet was lying on the bed. "This might look serious, but it's actually pretty common." She was sprawled on her back, apparently unconscious, a series of fresh tattoos inked into the bruised ridge of flesh across her belly, and all but undressed, her bra pulled down, her skirt hiked up, wearing one high-heel sandal, and no panties. The first thing that struck Ray as seriously wrong was that she was wearing clothes at all. It was the first time Ray had seen Juliet dressed in over a week. Even worse, it didn't look like she'd made the effort herself. It looked like someone had hurriedly tried to dress her unconscious body and given up somewhere in the middle.

"What happened to her?" Ray asked, "what's going on?"

"Nothing," Charlotte says, "I just gave her a little something to...relax...and she just got, you know, very relaxed."

Ray stood over the girl on the bed, looking down at her, close enough to smell what happened.

"She's peed the bed," he said, alarmed to hear himself say this, because he didn't really want to believe it and because it seemed pretty serious. He touched around Juliet's sprawled body. "For crissakes, everything is soaking wet."

Charlotte shrugged. "That happens sometimes," she said absently. "They...lose...umm...control." She was standing by the bed now, too, but she was trying ineffectually to work her arms under Juliet's shoulders. "Help me get her up will you...we have to get her out of here."

"She's not breathing," Ray said, looking up from the girl's slack face, her unmoving chest. "Jesus fucking Christ almighty, Charlotte. Did you hear me? She's not *breathing*."

"Calm the fuck down, Ray, will you? I know this doesn't look so good," Charlotte said, momentarily snapping out of her fog. "But it's okay, I swear it."

Ray repeated what he'd said just a moment ago, because, really, it seemed to be the most crucial point at the moment. *"She's not breathing."*

"She *is* breathing," Charlotte said and she said this in an almost aggravated, dismissive, I-already-told-you-this sort of way, as if Ray didn't have a lot of experience with passed-out girls and she did, which, of course, was true enough.

"I don't see anything—shit—*moving*," Ray said, his hand hovering above the girl's pale, motionless, and he hated to admit it, slightly bluish tits, afraid to touch her, afraid to feel cold, clay-like flesh and what that would mean. "This is fucked up, this is just so totally fucking fucked up."

"Put your finger under her nostrils," Charlotte said, and she sounded exhausted, at the end of her patience, like she was tutoring a retarded child, and had been doing it for ten, fifteen years. Ray hated to admit even to himself what he was thinking at such a crucial moment, but right then he found himself looking at Charlotte and noting that she looked like a freaked-out Hilary Duff. "Wet it first, for crissakes," she said and put the first two fingers of her own right hand into her mouth, sucking on them. She did this for so long a time that Ray started to think she'd just forgotten what was happening and that she was just standing there, absently sucking on her fingers. Just when Ray was about to say something to shake her out of her self-absorption and get the scene rolling again, Charlotte popped her fingers out of her mouth and held them under Juliet's small dark nostrils. Charlotte held her fingers there a moment, re-wet them, and held them there again. It seemed to take forever. Her shiny eyes were looking unseeing at a far corner of the dark room as if she were on a game show trying to recall the capital city of Chile.

She stayed that way for a while longer, frowning a little, and then she looked directly at Ray as if trying to find him in a crowd of strangers and failing, until at the very moment she'd finally decided to give up, all of a sudden, there he was.

"Oh," she said.

It would have been easy to stand around speculating whether the girl were really dead or not, easy, even to keep thinking that maybe she was just in some kind of deep drug snooze, to keep up, at least for a few more minutes, the pretence of wishful thinking. But the instant Ray tried to move Juliet all hope that her eyes would flutter open and the whole thing would just be one big scare, one amazingly tasteless practical joke, vanished. There was only one way anything could be *so* heavy and unresponsive as the body on the bed and that was as if it didn't resist gravity at all. If, in other words, it were lifeless.

Ray paced around the room in tight, frantic circles.

"We should call an ambulance," he said, as if the suggestion were a sudden stroke of unparalleled genius. "Pretend it was an o.d."

Charlotte, meanwhile, had grown increasingly calm. "We can't do that Ray."

"Why the hell not?"

"I can't bring that kind of scrutiny here. I have a responsibility to Rudra and Joan."

"Fuck that."

"The cops would never buy an o.d. anyway."

"Then screw the o.d. She died, that's all. How the hell are we supposed to know why. We didn't even know her. People die. Maybe she had an enlarged heart or an asthma attack or something. How do I know? It happens all the time."

"That won't work either, Ray."

"Why Charlotte? Why won't it work? Why don't you tell me why?"

"Because she really shouldn't have been here in the first place."

"Right, because its kidnapping, isn't it? Because she wasn't here of her own free will, was she?"

"You brought her here, Ray."

He crossed the room in a flash, like frames were missing from the film. One moment he was pacing in front of the DVD tower filled with hundreds of those psycho films and the next he was clear across the room. His hands were clamped down on Charlotte's shoulders, violently shaking her, and he was screaming obscenities into her impassive face.

"Don't pull that double-speak with me, you bitch. I told you it was wrong. I told you!"

Words failed him, all the language centers of his brain flooded with red. He'd never hit a woman before, but Ray wanted to hit Charlotte now. He wanted to punch a big empty cartoonish hole right through the center of her beautiful face, shove her head through the wall, break her nose and teeth with his forehead. She didn't even put up a fight. She let him scream and curse and shake her around like a Doberman with a rag doll, waiting for him to finish, to exhaust himself. Ray suddenly had the realization that she was used to getting hit, used to being physically helpless and had learned not to resist, and that in itself made him stop. They stared at each other, speechless, for a few seconds.

"Fuck me," Charlotte said.

Ray pushed her away from him and stepped back. "You're crazy."

The blow came out of nowhere, like a comet from deep space.

"Don't ever call me that," she shrieked.

Ever.

Ever.

Ever."

Each time she said the word "ever" it was punctuated with a clout to the side of his head. He figured he must have hit a sore spot with that "crazy" crack. He figured she must have been called that before, many times before, by many people who knew her well. These were no movie slaps either that she delivered. She wasn't big but she hit him with the heel of her hand, swinging stiff-armed from the waist, three, four, five times. Ray lost count. It all seemed to be happening in slow-motion. Ray let her do it. He grabbed his own wrists and held his hands behind his back to keep from instinctively defending himself. He felt he deserved the blows she delivered, deserved them for the goddamn weakness and stupidity that had gotten him into this fucked-up mess in the first place, and in some unexpected way it felt almost good to be hit. His glasses bent, slipped from his face, and he felt a cut stinging over the bridge of his nose. His left ear was ringing.

Charlotte stood there, panting, flushed, her eyes still blazing.

"You pussy. I thought you were a man."

"Stop it," Ray said softly.

"You pussy," she sneered.

"This isn't going to help."

"Pussy."

"For crissakes, just shut the fuck up."

"Or what," Charlotte taunted. "Or what? What are you going to do about it, you fucking pussy."

Ray shook his head and turned away. This was how they got you, he thought, women, that is. They pushed you into a corner, stood at every exit, and forced you to punch your way out and then cried abuse, rape, victimhood. He looked out the window, staring at his car in the driveway. "What the hell am I going to do now," he muttered, staring at the shiny ghost of himself in the glass, "What am I going to do?"

The question was meant to be spoken in his head, but somehow he'd said it out loud. Charlotte was right behind him, answering it.

"You're going to get rid of the body, that's what you're going to do."

"Get real. This isn't the movies."

"It's the only thing to do," Charlotte said, stealing a glance at the girl sprawled on the wet bed. "Get rid of her."

"How?"

"Use your imagination, Ray."

Ray thought it over, if you could call the rat-in-a-burning-maze panic going on in his mind right now *thinking*. Charlotte was right. Ray could see that there was no way to explain what this dead girl was doing in the carriage house covered with tattoos and bruises and piercings and god-only-knew-what-else that wouldn't cause all kinds of trouble. Getting rid of the body was a gamble. If he were caught, it would make everything immeasurably worse. Obviously. But it offered a chance, slim as it might be, that he wouldn't get caught and then nothing at all would happen, they would be home free. Ray pondered the angles a few moments more: it looked grim from any viewpoint, like a bad chess game where you could only put off losing long enough to hope the other guy made a mistake.

"Get me a pair of gloves."

"What do you need gloves for?"

"I'm not leaving fingerprints."

"Ray," Charlotte said soberly, "you've probably left fingerprints on that girl's pancreas."

Ray winced. "Just get me a fucking pair of gloves."

All Charlotte had were a pair of brick-red women's leather gloves she retrieved from a box of winter clothes on the top shelf of the bedroom closet. Ray forced them onto his hands as far as they'd go. How could he not remember that famous line from the O.J. trial, *"If the glove don't fit..."* Well, it didn't matter if they fit or not. Leaving fingerprints wasn't the only thing he was worried about. He couldn't bear the thought of touching Juliet's dead flesh with his naked hands. Not that he was going to tell Charlotte that. Somehow he didn't think she'd find his squeamishness a manly and attractive quality. Ray approached the body on the bed hands squashed halfway into the gloves, as if the girl's corpse were booby-trapped, as if it might suddenly pop up like a jack-in-the-box and say "Gotcha!" That was ironic, because as much as Ray wanted this all to be a nightmare, he'd probably drop dead of a heart attack on the spot if Juliet suddenly came back to life. At this point, her coming back to life would be scarier than her staying dead; it would be utterly unnatural, like she were a zombie back from the dead come to rip out and devour his intestines. *Guilt*, Ray thought, that's what it was. Better get used to it, pal, it's the only dish on the menu from now on. Fact was, Ray couldn't even believe it anymore, Juliet being alive, that is, that's how far he'd come to accepting that what he was experiencing now wasn't just a bad dream.

As he stood over her, Ray saw he had nothing to fear on that score. It was obvious that Juliet was dead and was going to stay dead. She was out of the game for good. How could he have ever thought otherwise? There was something special and unmistakable about even the recently dead, Ray suddenly realized. Hard to say what it was exactly. But no one, not even knocked unconscious, would lay the way she was laying. The lax expression on her face, for one thing, as if the face itself were sliding off the skull, the result of the muscles under the flesh giving up, maybe, no longer trying to convince anyone that it was happy, interested, sincere, pretty, whatever, not even trying to convince itself anymore. Ray stretched out a finger and poked a shoulder: it was like touching a mattress full of hard rubber. The girl's limbs, when he tried to lift them, bend them into an easier shape for transport, were sickeningly resistant. Ray felt a burning fist rising through him, stopping at the back of his throat. He put his own fist to his mouth, to meet it, pressed his teeth hard. When

Charlotte asked him what was wrong, he managed to croak out that
he felt like he was going to puke.

"Oh Christ, Ray, grow up."

Ray ignored her. He worked his jaws for some spit and forced
the sour impulse to vomit back down his throat. He managed to get
it about halfway down before the burning fist lodged under his
diaphragm, clutching at him. Then, with his eyes mostly closed and
holding his breath, he set about pulling and pushing at Juliet's body,
trying to position it as close to the middle of the bed as possible so
he could wrap her up in the reeking, piss-soaked bedclothes. It was as
he tugged at her that Ray saw it: the real reason they couldn't claim
that Juliet had died of an overdose or natural causes. The incision on
her lower abdomen was about eight inches long and stitched tightly
closed with a double railroad-track of thick black thread. Even now, a
gelatinous pink fluid was leaking out between the seams and a large
crusty flower of dried black blood decorated the inside of her left
thigh.

"Fuck fuck fuck," Ray sputtered, losing his ability to articulate
again, backing away from the bed. His eyes found Charlotte standing
against the wall, chewing a fingertip, like a naughty little girl. "What
the fuck, Char?"

"What?"

Ray gestured helplessly toward the bed, the girl, the scar.

Charlotte shrugged. "I guess...um...she had a little
taken...umm...out."

The burning fist in the pit of Ray's stomach was on the rise
again and this time it wasn't going to stop. Ray raced, doubled-over,
for the bathroom. The fist pushed its way straight past his gag reflex
and over his tongue and left a tracer flame of acid burning his throat
just as he flung open the toilet cover and fell to his knees on the tile.
He embraced the cold bowl and bent his head as everything inside
him hit the water.

When he was finished, Ray stood at the sink on shaky legs and
delicately brushed his teeth and washed his face. Somehow he didn't
feel any better, as if whatever was making him ill were still inside him,
sloshing around, having a party. His hands were trembling like a

spastic doing sign language when he took off and put back on the undersized gloves. He didn't even dare look at himself in the mirror. He didn't want to see whatever would be looking back. He returned to the room and it was just him and Juliet. Charlotte had gone downstairs. Ray was grateful for that. He didn't want her to see him like this. He approached the bed, gasping and light-headed, and, by dint of a lot of inefficient prodding and poking, managed to finish arranging Juliet in the middle of the sheet. He averted his eyes from the roughly stitched-together wound poised on her belly like a malevolent black centipede frozen in the light midway towards her pubes. Eventually Ray got the sheet tucked around her, and by rolling her from one side to the other, managed to wrap her up. He tucked the sheet up at both ends, head and foot, like he was making a giant human-stuffed taco, and after taking a short cigarette break, the worst finally over, worked her off the bed, and hefted her over his shoulder.

Ray was right about one thing: it wasn't like they showed it in the movies. Juliet's body was heavy, heavier than anything that weighed one-hundred-twenty pounds had any reason to be, and it was awkward, as if it had a dozen more knees, legs, and elbows than it really had. Getting her down the stairs was an ordeal. He dropped her twice and nearly lost his balance and fell down the stairs himself. He pictured himself lying broken-necked at the bottom of the stairs, their dead bodies tangled together, in a Poe-like coup de grace of justice, and it was an almost comforting thought. Each time he dropped her, Ray cringed and found himself muttering, "Dammit, I'm sorry," forgetting, perversely, that she was well beyond caring about a few cracks to the noggin.

By the time Ray reached the ground floor, his shirt was soaked through with sweat and his limbs ached. Almost out of gas, he dragged Juliet across the room and stopped to catch his breath. He asked Charlotte to hold open the front door as he tried to maneuver the body outside. It would have been almost comical if it weren't so gruesome the way Ray had to keep setting Juliet down and picking her up again, tilting her this way and that, like a couch, to fit her through the doorframe. At one point, puffing and red-faced with exertion, Ray set Juliet down and wiped his brow with his sleeve, indulging in the macabre spirit of it all.

"How the hell did we ever get her in here in the first place?" he asked.

"I don't know," Charlotte answered, as if taking the question seriously. "They're always easier getting in than out."

Once out the door at last, Ray continued to drag Juliet's body along the cobbled walkway to the car. He had to remove the spare tire and a few bags of clothes stashed there since his divorce, but he managed to fold her doubled up inside the trunk. Pushing down on something that felt like a hip and a face, Ray got the trunk's latch to engage, if only barely. He pressed down a few times to make sure: he didn't want the trunk springing open on the highway and Juliet popping up to say "hi" to whoever might be driving behind him. He was lucky. Another half-hour, he reckoned, and her body would have been too stiff to stuff inside the trunk at all. He glanced up at the Tudor, at the window at the top of the house. He couldn't see anyone there. But the moon was bright and almost full and reflecting off the glass. "Hope your enjoying the show asshole," Ray muttered. He went back inside and Charlotte offered him a drink. She seemed calmer now, more like herself. For that matter, so was Ray. Whatever had possessed them earlier to fight between themselves had evidently passed. Murder did that to you, Ray thought, brought out your worst—or brought you together. He started laughing.

"What are you laughing at?" Charlotte asked, laughing tentatively, like it was contagious.

"Nothing. Oh shit, nothing."

"Me too."

Ray drank the drink she offered—more of that damn champagne—and he let it kill the nervous humor and burn through his chest. The drink helped ground him. Ray's mind cleared. He thought through the long night ahead and already felt a tremendous exhaustion.

"I'm sorry Ray" Charlotte pouted. "About before. I hope you're not too mad at me."

"It's okay," Ray muttered. "Things got...a little unhinged."

She fumbled around at his belt, started down to her knees, but Ray stopped her and pulled her back to her feet. She looked up at him, questioningly.

"What's the matter?"

"Not right now," he said.

"Why not?"

Ray looked at Charlotte's face, all the anger was gone now, she was pretty once again, like Tara Reid, not as obviously superficial, but equally clueless. He could tell she really, truly, didn't understand.

He did his best to explain. "Because there's…um…stuff to do?"

Sometimes things happen that don't make sense at the time; only later, after other things happen, do they start to fit in and reveal their place in the overall pattern, but then, only up to a point. That's what Ray was thinking, driving east along I-80 on the way back through Pennsylvania after dumping Juliet's body at the bottom of a wooded ravine that he picked quite at random. He'd driven without any clear path for nearly three hours, panicking, lost, half his attention fixated on his rearview mirror which he expected to explode in a carnival of red state trooper lights at any moment.

Now, in retrospect, he began to consider his lack of plan an accidental stroke of genius. There'd be even less logical connection to be drawn between him and Juliet's body whenever it was found. And Ray had no doubt it would be found, probably even sooner than later, since the ravine where he dumped her was only about half-a-mile from a third-rate, but relatively well-traveled highway. Someone pulling off the road to take a leak, or catch a quickie, or illegally dump trash was bound to stumble across it. If nothing else, the bulldozers encroaching to clear the available nearby acres to erect strip malls and senior housing complexes would inevitably plow her up from the makeshift grave of dead leaves, sticks, soda cans, and broken concrete he'd scavenged together to cover her.

Bodies, it seemed to Ray, always got found. They just did. No matter how carefully they were hidden away. There just didn't seem to be any privacy anymore, no tolerance for uncertainty or secrets, in the end everything and everyone got accounted for somehow. A girl like Juliet didn't just go missing without getting found. Sam was right. A life, especially one like hers, was just too valuable.

A few other things were becoming clear to Ray, as well. For instance, the powerful sex drugs that Charlotte had given Ray were no doubt prescribed for Rudra's impotence. Ray wondered if they helped the millionaire financer get it up and, if so, had he raped Juliet during her stay at the carriage house? Or did frustration over his sexual inadequacy lead him to kill her? Imagine having millions, all the money you could ever want, the ability to buy whatever woman you wanted—a woman like Charlotte, for instance—and not be able to do something any pimple-faced teenager could do without thinking ten times a day. Ray could well imagine how something like that might inspire homicidal rage in a man.

Ray's hands were still shaking on the steering wheel. The tremors traveled up his arms, to his shoulders, hell, his whole body was shaking, as if he'd cranked the car's air conditioner to the max. He was trying not to think about what he'd just done, but that was like trying not to think about a lump you'd found under your armpit during your morning shower. He'd wrestled Juliet out of the trunk, an operation even more unsettling than putting her inside. He wouldn't have thought that even possible, but the world was full of unexpected surprises lately. Her body had time to grow even deader during the drive, and when he sprang open the trunk, the corpse seemed to awkwardly start unfolding itself, like an inflatable doll only partially inflated. He was at the riskiest point in the entire fucked-up adventure and all he wanted to do was sit on the car's fender and weep. If he got caught at that moment, there'd be nothing left but to call a lawyer and get ready for prison. His heart was trip-hammering like a cheap alarm clock. No longer making even the pretense of handling her carefully, Ray had jerked Juliet out of the trunk where she'd compressed into a dense, impossibly heavy, hard-to-grasp shape, like one of those IKEA boxes containing a pressboard entertainment center. He managed to wrestle her into a semi-standing position, her legs still bent at the knees, and danced her to the edge of the small ravine. At the worst point, the sheet partially unwrapped from her head and exposed her face to the moonlight. Rigor mortis had given her a grotesque face-lift, pulling her previously slackened features into even greater distortion. She looked like something out of the *Planet of the Apes*, only hairless and bleached and a thousand years old.

Ray pitched her forward into the chasm, sobbing, muffling a scream with his forearm, biting through his coat to gag himself. She made it only half-way down, lying on her face, some of the bed sheet snagged on a fallen tree limb. Ray had to slide down the side of the ravine, bumping along on his ass, cursing, whimpering uncontrollably, and yank her the rest of the way down. He collected a whole new gallery of scratches and scrapes he'd have trouble explaining to the cops if he were caught, the kind of abrasions that look exactly like someone struggling through some wooded underbrush with a dead body. Crawling around on hands and knees, Ray pushed around in the leaves and branches and assorted garbage for enough refuse to cover the corpse. Then he scrambled back out of the pit, earning some more scratches and scrapes, chased by a superstitious certainty, as his laboring heart thundered in his chest like destiny, that he'd suffer a massive heart attack or stroke, fall back, and rejoin Juliet at the bottom. Murder was just not a good occupation for a neurotic hypochondriac, he decided. As it happened, though, Ray didn't have a heart attack or stroke, not yet anyway, and there was no police cruiser at the top waiting to bring him to justice and now he was driving down I-80 like everything was perfectly normal except he was shaking like he had pneumonia.

He needed another Xanax, needed it an hour ago, but he forced himself to keep driving, not daring to stop at a rest area in case he'd be remembered later on by some old geezer gassing up an RV. But now, exiting the interstate, he figured he was far enough away. He spotted an industrial park with all its sprinklers going at four am and got what he thought was a good idea. He pulled into the parking lot behind one of the non-descript concrete and glass buildings, stripped off his mud-caked clothes, and stood on an impossibly green lawn in the midst of the drifting spray. With a bottle of windshield wiper

fluid, he soaped away whatever filth still clung to his body. He stood
there chattering and rubbing himself in the cold grass. Then he
bundled up his soiled clothes and threw them in a dumpster at the
back of the parking lot. He picked out a shirt and a pair of pants
from one of the bags of clothes he'd had stashed in the trunk,
swallowed that long-needed Xanax, lit a cigarette, and he was back on
the road in less than fifteen minutes.

Looking almost normal in a window reflection, Ray called
Charlotte from a gas station payphone a few miles inside the New
Jersey border while his car refueled. He might have guessed: no
answer.

He paid for the gas, bought a cup of sour coffee, and drove for
another half-hour before he realized he'd taken a wrong turn
somewhere along the way and was traveling west instead of east. At
the rest area where he made a U-turn, he spotted a Denny's and
suddenly felt hungry. He sat in a booth, smoking, and watched the
sky brighten a corpselike blue over the trees. When the plates came,
however, the wobbling eggs and flesh-pink ham simultaneously
struck him as so disgusting he wondered how he could ever have
thought of ordering anything to eat in the first place. He contented
himself instead with drinking the iced Coke he'd ordered and
smoking and watching the almost non-existent traffic and eventually
found his gaze drifting to the television behind the counter.

He saw the devastation left in the wake of a series of tornadoes
rolling through some place like Mississippi, if that made sense, if it
were even possible to have tornadoes in Mississippi. These days
anything seemed possible, earthquakes in Manhattan, civil war in
Kansas, a Martian invasion in L.A., especially if they showed it on
television. The tornado story ended and the news went on to the
upcoming elections. Haskins' lead had spiked to nine points and his
campaign was "cautiously optimistic." Ray paid the check and left.

In the front seat of the car, he sipped the icy dregs of his Coke
and watched the moon dissolving like a mint Rolaids over the
eastbound lane of 94. To relieve his stress, he quickly jerked off
under the dashboard. He found himself thinking of a girl he and
Charlotte had seen one night standing on the platform of an uptown

6 train. Blonde, big hair, she was dressed for clubbing, in tight black capris showing off slim bare ankles and a French pedicure. In the fantasy, Charlotte starred as pimp and had turned the girl into some kind of love-slave, prostituting her on subway platforms to whoever for five bucks a pop. What followed was a complicated slide-show of images that ran the spectrum of perversity—Charlotte-the girl-and a stranger, Charlotte-as-the-girl, Ray-as-the-stranger, etc etc.—all the conceivable permutations, until Ray blended into the girl forced to kneel on the filthy tiles in a recess under the stairs leading up to the street as Charlotte watched him unzipping the pants of a stranger and licking the underside of an enormous, bulging-veined cock. Bam! *Where the hell did that come from?* Ray wondered. He took another Xanax, threw the soiled Denny's napkin and the remainder of the Coke into the orange-headed garbage pail outside his window, and hit the road.

Ray figured he'd taken too much Xanax because twenty miles down the road he suddenly could barely keep his eyes open. He pulled over at a truck stop and slept until about seven-thirty. He got out of the car, stretched his stiff legs, and walked a short distance into a woods that looked exactly like the one where he'd dumped Juliet hours ago. Wouldn't it be really fucked up if it *was* the same wooded area and no matter how far Ray drove he kept revisiting the scene of the crime, like in a *Twilight Zone* episode? Ray was thinking this as he pissed against a rotten log where some wasps had built a nest. He actually found himself looking around to assure himself that it really wasn't the same wooded area where he'd dumped Juliet's body. Of course, it wasn't, but, then again, it all looked the same, all these trees, these fallen branches, dead leaves, crushed Whopper cartons, etc. Ray forced himself to stop thinking such Kafkaesque fictional thoughts. He figured there was enough to creep him out without his imagination getting into the act. Imagination, he considered, adding it to the ever-growing list, was another liability in a killer. He zipped up and walked back to the car.

He drove until he saw signs for a large mall and decided to make an unscheduled pit stop. He parked in the barren wasteland of a lot and went inside a complex that looked like a sprawling greenhouse. None of the stores had opened yet, so Ray strolled along the various levels looking at the mannequins standing on plaster tiptoes in the display windows. The escalators were all broken, or maybe they were just not turned on yet, giving the entire mall a kind of frozen, peopleless, Day-After-the-End-of-the-World look. He bought a coffee at a Dunkin Donuts that had just opened in the food court and sat on a bench at the center of the mall in a high-ceilinged atrium with skylights and a species of tall, anorectic tree that looked as if it must have been gengineered especially to live in malls. There was a fountain at his feet filled with hundreds of pennies, nickels, and dimes looking all scuzzy beneath the dead water. Ray thought he remembered hearing somewhere that the money thrown into these mall fountains was donated to children's cancer or the homeless or battered women's shelters, something like that. But he could just as easily imagine that the janitors who swept up this spare change each night put it into the janitorial weekend beer fund.

Ray called Charlotte again, this time from his cell phone, and this time, to his surprise, she answered. He wasted no words getting right to the point, just in case she changed her mind.

"I have to see you. Tonight."

She sounded vague, breathless, falsely cheerful. "It's not a good time."

"What do you mean it's not a good time?"

"No, I don't think so."

"Is someone there with you?"

"Maybe Thursday."

"Don't do this to me, Charlotte. I have to see you."

"I told you, it's not a good time."

Someone was there. Ray could hear whoever it was in the background. Maybe whoever was there was there last night, too, whoever, Ray thought might have been there when he'd called Charlotte back and she'd asked him to come over in the first place; maybe they'd been hiding somewhere in the carriage house the entire insane night, waiting for Ray to get rid of the body. The voice in the background was soft, barely a murmur, as if whoever was getting impatient for Charlotte to end the call.

"Who's there?" Ray demanded.

There was a fumbling on the other end of the phone.

"Huh?"

"Who's there with you?"

"What do you mean?"

"Dammit Charlotte."

"Not a good time…I told you…"

"Fuck you, it's not a good time. After last night…"

Charlotte hung up on him, just like that, without a word. Ray stared at the phone in his hand in complete disbelief.

"Shit," Ray said, louder than he'd intended. The word seemed to hang in the empty mall, ringing.

He called her back five times: no answer.

No surprise.

Ray slumped on the bench. He reached into his pocket and found some spare change. He threw the coins into the water one by one, maybe forty-seven cents worth, trying to figure out what to do next. Who the hell was at the carriage house with her? Rudra? The police? John Rossi? No, he didn't think it was the police. Ray threw another dime into the water, a quarter, three pennies. The fountain, like the escalators, was either broken or not turned on yet. Nothing moved. No wishes were ever answered. Where the hell did he get all this fucking spare change, anyway?

By the time Ray made it back to the carriage house it was nine that evening. He'd spent most of the day back at his apartment, lying in bed, staring at the ceiling, and calculating what to do next. The rest of time he spent uselessly fantasizing that the last thirty-six hours had all been some kind of bad dream. The only problem with that fantasy was that he couldn't wake up from the nightmare because he was already relentlessly awake. He didn't call Charlotte again because he knew she'd either tell him not to come or, worse, she wouldn't answer the phone at all and take off, disappear for days. Maybe, he figured, it was better if he just laid low and they had no contact for a while. Maybe that's what she'd been trying to tell him when he'd called earlier.

Be cool. Bide his time. Someone could be watching.

That made sense, after all. Didn't it?

From the very beginning, there'd been an illicit flavor to their relationship. Ray had tasted it. Behind every meeting, every liaison, every fuckfest, there was the nagging background sense that Charlotte didn't want them to be seen together. That they were in some kind of undefined danger. Ray still didn't know for sure whether Charlotte really lived in the carriage house, if she were really getting a divorce, or if she was even married. Fact was, he knew shockingly little about this woman after nearly three months and a murder.

Although it directly contradicted what he'd just been thinking, the best chance Ray had of seeing her and get to the truth was to just show up at the carriage house without warning, something he hadn't done yet out of respect for whatever delicacy her situation required. But now the rules had changed. After what he'd just done for her, Ray figured Charlotte owed him a few explanations. It was time, in any event, he'd decided, to pay her that long delayed unexpected visit.

Traffic out of the city was light that evening. Ray made it to the carriage house in just under half-an-hour. He pulled into the steep driveway winding around the back of the faux Tudor and saw that Charlotte's SUV was gone. In its place was a dark blue Chevy Suburban van that he'd never seen before. Ray parked beside it and lit a cigarette. Across the dark courtyard, the main house looked as deserted from behind as it did from the front. He checked the upper windows for any signs of watchers and saw no one. The porch-light outside the carriage house was burning, but that might have been set by timer to come on at dusk, same with the dim glow coming from the upstairs windows. Ray got out of the car and walked around to the front of the Suburban. The van's hood was still warm to the touch, the engine beneath ticking.

Ray looked up again at the soft glow coming out of the upstairs window of the carriage house. The lamp on the night table beside the bed. Was someone up there with her? He walked to the door and listened.

No noise from inside.

Ray pressed the bell.

Charlotte opened the door after the fourth ring. She was wearing a pair of shortie kid's pajamas that were faded and pink and way too small for her. She was barefoot and the pajama-top barely covered her tits and left her rounded belly exposed. Ray could see her scar glowing white in the harsh porch-light. Her hair, which had been getting longer lately, was clipped back with plastic barrettes. She looked so young and helpless, like Marcia Brady in *The Brady Bunch*, that he wanted to snatch her out of the carriage house then and there, take her away from whoever stood behind the dark windows of the empty fake Tudor, away from whatever the hell had such control over her, away from the whole fucking freakshow. But something stopped him. Ray wasn't exactly sure what it was. But maybe it was that somehow he felt Charlotte didn't really want to go anywhere.

She stood there, one hand still on the doorknob, and she didn't look upset or even surprised, but rather like she was half-expecting him, even though it was fairly obvious she wasn't exactly happy about seeing him standing there.

"What's up?" she asked.

Ray tried to determine if she were drunk or high or something else because she looked both sleepy and jazzed at the same time. She acted like "what's up" was a perfectly normal question under the circumstances. All Ray could do was look at her like he couldn't believe what he was hearing, which he couldn't, and repeat the words back to her, but with a completely different emphasis, *"What's up?"*

"Yeah," she said, "what's going on. Why are you here?"

"We've really got to talk."

Charlotte rolled her dark eyes. She looked down and to the left and smiled. It was the expression he'd always found so cute and flirtatious before, but it didn't fit in with anything that was happening right now. Ray wanted to take out the script and show her. "Look where we are," he wanted to say, stabbing the page with his forefinger. "Where does it say you make that flirtatious expression!" But there was no script. Or whatever script Charlotte was reading from, she hadn't made it available to him.

"It's cold," she said at last, tired of waiting for Ray to say something. "I don't have much on…"

"Can I come in?"

"I told you this isn't a good time…I'm kinda busy."

"Kinda Busy? What do you mean you're kinda busy? Kinda busy with what?"

"You know…stuff…"

Ray put his hand on the door to keep her from shutting it in his face, even though she hadn't made any move to do that. She hadn't really made any move at all. It was as if she were sleepwalking and had come to rest in the doorway and Ray was part of some incoherent and ultimately insubstantial dream she were having.

"Talk to me. Please. Tell me what this is all about."

Charlotte made a show of being annoyed, but it seemed as if she could hardly be bothered putting on an act anymore. What she said next seemed rehearsed, and, like everything else about her tonight, completely out of context.

"Look I have a life—friends, obligations, a career—if you can't *deal* with that…"

"Screw your friends and obligations. I want to know what last night meant—what am I supposed to think about *that?*"

"I really can't have this conversation right now, Ray. I've got to go—I told you, I've got to fly to Chicago. My father has had a heart attack. You're so goddamn self-centered ."

"You're lying dammit. There's no father. No heart attack."

"I don't have to listen to this."

How could he *not* have seen this coming? She was leaving town, leaving him behind with the consequences of Juliet's…what? Accidental death? Murder?

Ray was about to tell her she couldn't do it, that he wouldn't let her get away with it, but he'd forgotten about the blue Suburban. Out of the darkness, the morbid thing stepped right behind Charlotte, or rather, it's was if she'd risen straight out of the floor, materialized out of the gloom, like a Nosferatu. Or, not to get too mystical or special-effects about it, it was as if she were there the whole time and some subtle shift of the ambient light revealed her pale, almost ghostly presence behind Charlotte. She was wearing a long, plain, colorless dress that fell straight from the shoulders, a wide white collar trimmed in lace, like something they always showed pilgrims wearing, and her bookish, dour face stared at Ray over Charlotte's nearly bare shoulder. Her eyeglasses were blanked-out by the reflection of the porch light, like Little Orphan Annie's. It was the second time Ray had seen her since her plastic surgery and even with everything going on he couldn't help thinking that whatever they did to her, however they altered her features—she looked exactly the same, which was to say, completely non-descript.

She seemed to be saying something to Charlotte, talking as if trying not to move her long, thin mouth. Ray couldn't hear what she was saying, if anything at all. She was standing behind Charlotte like a grey spider and Ray was re-doing in his head the equation that never added up all over again.

Charlotte said, "I've got to go."

She said it with her lips brought together as if in a kiss, almost childishly lisping the words. Then, without further explanation, she closed the door in Ray's face, after all.

"I see you didn't take my advice."

Sam-I-Am was dressed all in black, looking gaunt and sober, like someone had just died. He was seated at the back of the club, where the hostess had led Ray, at what was no doubt his usual table, a man like Sam-I-Am looking the part of a man with a "usual table," and one situated, no less, in dramatic fashion in front of a black-draped Doric pillar. An untouched drink the color of wood varnish stood by his long, pale, almost elegant hand. The private club was in the upper 70s, twilight dark, traversed by leggy women in glittering thong bikinis carrying drink trays. From the outside, the building looked like any ordinary residential brownstone and that's exactly

what it might have been, at least the part of it that was above ground.
Sam was wearing the beat-up leather jacket and slouch hat he'd worn
that first morning at the apartment. He was smoking a thin brown
cigarillo. Ray sat down and ordered a gin-tonic from a waitress with
the flawless face of a plastic sex-doll.

"I must say, I'm not surprised to see you Mr. Pierce."

Without having to be told, Ray could tell that one of the many
unspoken rules of this sort of club was that guests from one party
didn't pay too much attention to guests in another party. Peripheral
vision was valued here: it ensured the privacy of the members. Still,
Ray thought he recognized a fatter, balder Judd Nelson in a corner
booth with all the fingers of his left hand casually inserted into the
remodeled ass of a tall young Asian "courtesy" girl.

"I'm sorry," Ray said, chastened, re-directing his attention. "I
should have listened. You were right. She's fucked up, involved in
something...I don't even know what. Man, I'm in way over my head.
I was stupid. What can I say?"

A hostess dressed in nothing but silver glitter passed by on
skyscraper heels. She was a big, well-built porn-model type with
round waxed tits that shone like pink bowling balls. At Sam's barely
perceptible signal, she stopped, turned, and approached, all smiles,
bending slightly at the knees to hear his whispered instructions. Her
hard pink tits hung in front of Sam for fingering, but Sam ignored
them. The girl looked momentarily worried, then nodded quickly,
smiled perfectly, and hastily left.

"Love," Sam said, "makes us do stupid things. Crazy things. We
lose our minds. Do things against our own self interest."

"Yes," Ray said staring at the hostess's glitter-dusted ass as she
made an x-rated performance of walking away. You could look at the
women in the club all you liked. They didn't require peripheral vision:
you could examine them as closely as a virus under a microscope if
you chose. That's what they were there for. Ray turned back to the
table. "That's it exactly."

"Let me guess. You secretly cry at sentimental movies. When
the dog comes home, the hero lays down his life, when boy gets girl
and true love prevails even in the face of disease, war, and death. You

sit there in the dark and pretend to be adjusting your glasses to dab away the stinging tears that you don't want anyone to see."

It was true. That's exactly what Ray did.

Sam nodded.

"Oh you don't have to tell me that you do it. I can see that you do. It's a kind of insanity, Love. That's how you see it, isn't it Mr. Pierce?"

"Yes."

"You're wrong, of course. That's not what love is at all. You don't know the first thing about love. But now isn't the time for that lesson. You said in your message that you were in trouble. You sounded quite...desperate."

Ray had called Sam after returning from the carriage house. After seeing Charlotte and Joan together, it all became clear. She was leaving him behind, flying off to Chicago with Joan, leaving him behind to take any possible heat if the girl were found and somehow traced back to them.

"I feel shitty about this," Ray said, "but I can't let her set me up. I can't take the fall for murder."

"Of course not."

Across the table, Sam regarded Ray with a face as stiff and dead as a totem pole: it was the kind of face that had seen a lot of foul weather. Ray imagined that generations of prehistoric worms had once lived in the pockmarks of his ancient face. That would have been centuries ago. Millennia, maybe. Now, there was no life there whatsoever. There was no fear in the man's face either, no emotions at all, which somehow calmed you if he were on your side. But that meant there was no pity in it either, which, Ray considered, would be terrifying if he wasn't on your side.

"I don't want to get her into trouble," Ray said, suddenly feeling that maybe this meeting was a mistake. Another mistake in a long series of mistakes that would lead...where? "The thing is, I don't think she's responsible. There someone else..."

"Mr. Pierce, please."

Sam held up his hand to silence him. Ray noticed for the first time that the middle finger of the man's hand left hand was missing and that it was a recent subtraction. What was left, a rudimentary stump, was half-healed and crudely stitched. Sam noticed him looking and said, "We all have our masters, Mr. Pierce," and he took the hand away. "Now tell me what happened."

Sam listened without interruption or questions as Ray told him everything that had happened from the night they brought Juliet back to the carriage house to the moment she shut the door in his face. When he finished, Sam said "Where is the body?"

Ray lit a cigarette, or tried to. He was having the hardest time hitting the flame. Sam held Ray's wrist steady, his touch firm, surprisingly gentle. Ray inhaled, exhaled, looked up at Sam through the cloud of smoke.

"Why do you need to know that?"

Sam let his wrist go slowly, lifting one finger at a time. Ray got the momentarily creepy feeling that the man was taking his pulse with the last two fingers to let go, one of them the stump. They lingered there just long enough.

"Mr. Pierce, you're going to have to trust me if you want me to help you."

"Trust you? Christ, I don't even know who you are or who you're working for."

"I believe you're innocent. Isn't that enough?"

Ray thought about that a moment. He supposed the man was right. That was enough. For now, that was everything. Who the hell else was going to believe him? Who else was going to help him?

"I need to know where the body is before it's found and the local police get involved. We don't want that to happen, I can assure you. That will make everything that much more complicated. It will be harder to protect you then, Mr. Pierce. We need to make that body disappear. Permanently. Now surely you can appreciate that."

"Yes sir. I'm just not sure I can be very exact. I was pretty fucked up that night."

"Do your best."

Holding a silver Mont Blanc that looked like an anal vibrator with the stump of his finger held out oh-so-delicately, Sam quickly jotted down the directions to the gravesite on a damp cocktail napkin as Ray narrated.

"Do you know where she is now?" Ray asked when he'd told Sam everything he could remember.

He'd been watching a blonde in stacked sandals and daisy pasties bending forward to serve an old man a yellow daiquiri. Ray found himself imagining the blonde had advanced surgical procedures performed, including breast augmentation, brow shaving, and jaw reconstruction. He imagined the tall willowy brunette allowing herself to be groped at a table of African businessmen had just started hormone replacement therapy.

"She's in Chicago now," Sam said, "and seeing a guy she hooked up with at a wedding out on Montauk that weekend you tried to off yourself. He's a real estate developer, married, three kids. The Donald Trump of Illinois."

"Her father?"

"Died fifteen years ago."

"I see."

"But none of that really makes any difference, does it?"

"No," Ray said. "Whatever she is or isn't, all the questions I can't answer, don't matter. The real mystery, the one I can't solve…" Ray looked down at Sam's hand on the table, at the part of his finger that was no longer there, "…is why she doesn't love me."

They were both awaiting SRS, Ray thought, looking again at the two waitresses, but they were already functionally impotent. They've been effectively chemically castrated, their penises limp inside their bikini-style panties. They hardly even needed the gaffe that smoothes the front of their short hobble skirts and is meant to conceal their gender when stripped to their sexy fuck-me underwear.

Sam nodded, as if Ray had finally gotten the answer to some ancient zen riddle. "That's the mystery no amount of information can answer. The hole no pain can ever fill. Did you ever consider that she was trying to save your life?"

Ray imagined the two boy-girls sharing an apartment, fussing with each other's hair and makeup, painting each other's toenails, unaware of their sublimated homosexuality as even their brain chemistry started to change. Maybe they even engage in a little affectionate hand-holding and cuddling, or some playful kissing while watching TV on the couch, playing a game of who's a hunk and who's not.

"That's bullshit," Ray said, "pure bullshit. She used me like a bag you take stuff out of until its empty and fill with trash to put at the curb."

"There are many ways to save a life, Mr. Pierce."

"What she did…it would have been better if she'd killed me. What the hell am I supposed to do now?"

"Only one thing. Do you remember Chernobyl?"

"What?"

Ray, distracted, thought he must have missed something. He seemed to be missing a lot of things lately.

"The reactor meltdown in Russia. The biggest nuclear accident in history. Do you know how they finally dealt with that?"

"No."

"Well they tried everything to get it under control. Nothing worked. All the theories, all the precautions, all the fail-safes…worthless. Finally they just flew over the area in helicopters and dumped tons and tons of concrete over the whole mess: they buried it, Mr. Pierce, in effect, that's how they dealt with the biggest man-made disaster in history. They left it there in the middle of nowhere, a billion-ton concrete tombstone, like a sphinx, a riddle no one can solve. A thousand years from now, that's what it'll still be. A mystery. Do you understand what I'm trying to tell you?"

"You want me to just *forget* her."

"Things are getting very dangerous, Mr. Pierce. He's dead, you know."

"Who's dead?"

"Her husband. John Rossi. He was found yesterday morning in a welfare motel in Eatontown, New Jersey with nothing left inside him. Three inches of esophagus…and the rest cut away."

Ray felt sick…well, *sicker*. "That's got nothing to do with me."

"Doesn't it? Think about it. You went to visit him recently, did you not? You were fucking his wife. You threatened him. Apparently there are witnesses who saw the two of you together. How long do you think it will be before the police link you to him?"

"I didn't threaten him...I..."

Sam waved him off. "This is no longer just a kinky game, Mr. Pierce. I suggest you take a trip. Take a tip from Charlotte. Get out of town yourself for a few days. Let me handle the situation here."

Ray nodded, numbly. It was all too much to take in. There was still something he wanted to know, something Sam-I-Am had alluded to during their first meeting.

"That night I called you, the night I tried to kill myself. What was it I told you? You never said."

"Some things are better left unknown Mr. Pierce. What you said that night was one of them."

"Please...please, I *need* to know."

Sam shook his head, but this time it didn't look like "yes or no." He stared at the tip of his finger, or where the tip of his finger used to be, because now there was nothing but a wound and an absence, a sense of feeling in a part of him that no longer existed. He looked up at Ray with hooded reptilian eyes that suddenly seemed to be without pupils, or all but invisible slits of pupils, a trick of the suggestive light, perhaps, inhuman eyes, transformed forever by whatever he'd seen, whatever we're not supposed to see, the mystery behind the sphinx. He knew the answer to the riddle, Ray was sure of it. *Whatever it is that we aren't supposed to know.*

Sam motioned to one of the shadowed alcoves along the wall and a nearly-naked black girl emerged, no more than a teenager, maybe less, mincing toward the table with a smile and gold-tears painted on her face. The black girl knelt by his chair, head bowed, and in cupped hands offered Sam what looked like a miniature black coffin. Only if you looked very closely, and Ray was looking very, very closely, could you see that the girl was trembling all over. Sam opened the coffin-shaped box. Ray was expecting a fine cigar. Instead, Sam held up a skeleton key.

He smiled thinly, looked back down at the girl and nodded. She seemed to stagger a little, falling backwards into herself, and only shakily recovered a semblance of her former poise.

Sam glanced up at Ray, almost as an afterthought.
"You wanted to die by her hand," he said.

Ray decided to take Sam-I-Am's advice and get out of town for a few
days. He booked a room in a bed-and-breakfast in Cape May, the
very bed-and-breakfast where he'd once planned to take Charlotte on
a surprise six-month anniversary trip. At $225 a night, it would clear
out his bank account before the week was over, but money, he
figured, was no longer an object.

As advertised, the inn was decorated with that over-the-top
romantic Victorian hoo-ha one expected in such a place. His room,
the *Belvedere*, for crissakes, was cluttered with uncomfortable chairs,
overwrought tables, a rickety writing desk, and mirrors so ornately
framed a pile of horseshit reflected therein would have looked like a
million bucks. No wonder women loved these kinds of places, Ray
thought. Ha ha ha. Somehow the mirror didn't do a thing for him,
though. Inside it's gilded borders, he still looked awful, like some guy
who lived in a boiler room.

After checking in at two, he spent the rest of that first day in an
antique wing-back chair drinking himself stupid. From the window, if
he bothered to turn towards it, he could see a cold, knife-sized slice
of the Atlantic. The next morning, when the sun came up, Ray was
still sitting there.

On the drive south, he'd called Charlotte from a public phone
at a rest stop on the Garden State Parkway, near exit 150. He had the
dim suspicion that maybe it would be better not to use his cell phone
just in case the police ever decided to seize a record of his calls.
There was no answer at any of Charlotte's numbers. He called again
at the Cheesequake rest area, exit 123, and there was still no answer.
He called a third time at a sprawling toll plaza, same result, and then
drove in a simmering funk through miles and miles and miles of
desultory swamp and stunted pine forest until the asphalt colon he'd
been passing through for hours finally disgorged him into the gaudy
cistern of Atlantic City. There among slot machines, jackpot bells,

and stoned senior citizens shuffling zombie-like with their plastic buckets of quarters, he tried again.

No answer.

No answer.

No answer.

Some time later, a little further south, Ray beat a payphone receiver to death outside a Wawa where he'd stopped for a cheesedog and a Coke slushee. The earpiece on the payphone cracked open and partially fell off, hanging by a bunch of festive-looking wires. He looked up and was startled to see a guy staring back at him in the window—all wild-eyed and dangerous looking, like one of those guys on *America's Most Wanted* who hold up convenience stores or what have you—and after the initial shock, he was even more scared when he realized that what had alarmed him was that he was looking at his own reflection in the glass .

After that first night, Ray took breakfast with the other guests of Haven-by-the-Sea, all of them coupled and shuffling around together, like handcuffed prisoners. They sat around a single table on the enclosed back porch which overlooked a riotous English-style garden that reminded Ray of something terminally malignant. By the third day, Ray was on friendly terms with a middle-aged couple from Maryland. Upon hearing they were avid birdwatchers, Ray said, "Did you know that a duck can't walk without bobbing its head?"

"No," the Sorensons exclaimed in unison, delighted.

It was true, apparently. He'd read it the day before under the bottle cap of a Peach Mango Snapple he'd bought from a vending machine in the basement. It seemed that every Snapple bottle cap had a "fun fact" underneath. He didn't know if this was where Charlotte got her little bits of quirky, conversation-starting trivia , but he figured they would serve just as well.

In the evening, Ray joined the other guests on the front porch where they all gathered regular as clockwork to watch the horizon darken like a livid sexual bruise that extended for miles. Ray, glancing at the headline of a *New York Times* someone left on a rattan end table, saw that Haskins' lead had been shaved to five. He good-naturedly polled the assembled who they were backing. They were hopelessly divided: seven were for Haskins; seven for Rexson, with Ray, the deciding vote, abstaining. Later, avoiding Scrabble and gin rummy in the parlor, Ray headed out to the bars. Just like last time, he steered clear of the tourist traps on the main drag and staggered through a series of gay bars. To a man who sat beside him in a sweaty leather joint, Ray offered the following that he'd learned from a bottle of Strawberry Kiwi Snapple he'd purchased that very afternoon: "Did you know that an ant has a more developed sense of smell than a dog?"

In between morning and evening, Ray wasted entire days slouched in a wicker rocking chair. There, in the shadows of the porch, he remained blitzed on Xanax and gin-laced Snapples while waiting for the police to come. After two days passed and nothing happened, he began to believe that maybe Sam-I-Am had come through, after all. Alone in his room at night, hunched over his laptop, Ray obsessively logged into the chatroom that was on the other end of the link that John Rossi had sent him. Just as he'd promised, actually threatened, Rossi had sent that email he said he would in the event something bad happened to him. At first, Ray thought it must be some sick kind of joke, a final "fuck you" from beyond the grave. Because he didn't expect that promised email would come to him. And because the email Rossi sent him didn't contain a detailed expose of Charlotte & co. as he claimed it would. Not exactly. What it contained was a url that when clicked turned out to be the address of a transgender sex-fetish web site. It was there, Rossi wrote in the brief accompanying note, that Ray was supposed to meet someone named "Sindy."

As usual, the opening page requested that Ray enter a "sissy nickname" before he was allowed inside. It hadn't taken him long to come up with one. He lit a cigarette, held it outside the open window since he'd been informed upon check-in that the whole inn was a "smoke-free environment," and with one hand typed in the name *"charlotte."*

Ray sat drinking and smoking and watching the fake girls come and go, eavesdropping on conversations between married men sitting in offices, bedrooms, and apartments—ordinary men who wanted to be gang-raped, cuckolded, castrated, ass-fucked, injected with female hormones, forced into high-heels, demeaning secretarial jobs with chauvinistic, sexually-harassing bosses, French maid's uniforms, bondage harnesses, latex fucksuits, etc. etc. Ray played along, giving out fake blowjobs, fake ass-fuckings, fake whippings. In between fantasies of panty-worship and nipple-torture, he kept an eye out for "Sindy."

One afternoon, on a whim, Ray pulled up a photo of Charlotte and, using some image-editing software, layered it over a photo of himself. He blurred the physical borders between them, widened his smile to encompass her smile, equalized the skin tones, dissolved his eyes into hers. He thought he'd confirm his suspicion that they resembled each other in some basic elemental way. But the resulting composite looked disturbingly unreal, like those police sketches of some heinous spree killer based on eyewitness reports that never turn out to look anything like the real suspect after all. That same afternoon, he took a long walk up the beach. He called Charlotte on his recharged cell. He got her answering machine, but this time he didn't hang up.

"Please just see me," he pleaded, shouting over the ocean waves. "I just want to talk to you one more time. I think we understand each other. I think we're the same kind of people...please listen to what I have to say. I think I know now what you were trying to tell me...I think I know what you want...When I look into your eyes I see myself...we are like the divine twins of an ancient Egyptian god, male and female...nothing is out of bounds for us, everything is permitted...I don't think I can make it without seeing you one more time, without looking into those eyes that are my eyes. I want to travel the world with you...I want to take you to all those exotic places you talked about...I want to fuck you in a pyramid..."

Ray didn't know when his time ran out, or what else he'd said, before the machine stopped recording this insane hysteria. He was drunk, lunatic, ranting into a dead phone. He left a second message, suddenly sobered up, and this one a lot more succinct: "You better call me back, you bitch, or I'm going to the cops. I'll tell them everything. I don't care. If you think I'm kidding, just try me out. You've got three days."

He hung up, then touched the re-dial button, and threw the phone as far as he could into the ocean. It made a little splash. Three seagulls appeared instantly out of nowhere and zeroed in on the spot where it disappeared almost immediately. They circled around and around until it was clear that the phone wasn't coming back up again. Ray imagined the phone sitting on the ocean floor, recording all the inarticulate gurglings, the booming hallway voices, the telegraphic click and chitter of crabs and sick dolphins and the moaning tonnage of distant lonely whales and all that depth and sad salt emptiness spooling onto Charlotte's answering machine. Ray laughed, thinking of that, and walked back to the inn.

He packed up and left that evening just before sunset. It was time, he decided, to return to Manhattan and whatever the fuck was waiting for him there.

He'd given Charlotte an ultimatum. He didn't think she'd respond too well to that, not from what he'd seen. But then again, maybe she would. He'd never given her an ultimatum before, not one that he actually stood behind. What the hell. Maybe she'd only been waiting for him to "take charge." What did he have to lose? He had no idea what he would do if she didn't call him back. He couldn't really go to the police, after all. He didn't want to think about any of that just yet. He still had three days before the deadline he'd given Charlotte and some unfinished business of his own to attend.

Meanwhile, Beth's messages had been building up everywhere: at Ray's apartment, on his cell, on his email account—even with his landlord, who delivered them along with a threat of eviction if he didn't come through with the long overdue rent by week's end. Ray called her back at home when he knew she'd be at work and at work when he knew she'd be at home. He played phone-tag with her, biding his time until he could figure out how to handle her. Finally, he had to bite the bullet. She returned his last message almost immediately. Ray picked up the phone feeling nauseous.

"Can't we get together tonight," she asked, after "Where the hell have you been" and "that means you couldn't call?" and "I don't appreciate these disappearing acts of yours, Ray" when he tried to explain how he'd needed time to think. "If you like," she softened, "I can come downtown to your place with takeout. Does that sound good?"

"I'd rather not," Ray said, inspecting the slice he'd just made in the vein looped over his left wrist. He placed the knife down on the coffee table. "I'm really beat. Maybe Monday."

"*Monday…*"

Beth repeated the word as if he'd just said Oz or Atlantis or some other mystical never-to-be found place. There's always a moment, Ray noticed, before the blood wells up when you can almost imagine that this time you won't bleed, that you're not even human, and then the heart beats and you bleed, after all. "I promise," he said vaguely.

"Ray, I'd really like to talk to you. While I was away, I did a lot of thinking, just like you. I don't know that what I have to say can wait."

"Really, Beth. I kind of just want to be by myself tonight."

Ray wondered what she wanted to tell him that couldn't wait: that they were through, that she was in love with Leon Szorkin, that she'd stopped loving him or realized that she never loved him at all?

Ray felt an overwhelming sense of exhaustion.

"Can't you just tell me on the phone?"

"No, it's too important."

It seemed to Ray that a long silence followed—in any event, he didn't recall if Beth said anything else or if he just wasn't paying attention. He was holding his wrist to his mouth, tasting his blood. What did it really taste like? Not what the novels said, not all the clichés. What did his blood *really* taste like? In a tense, brittle, almost sarcastic voice, he heard Beth say, "Are you trying to send me some kind of message, Ray? Is that what this is about?" And that's when he knew that Beth, whatever else she wanted to discuss, wasn't breaking up with him, that she'd never break up with him. An idea came to

Ray then, not a good one, certainly, but it gave him a curious kind of strength.

"No honey," he said, and his tone was suddenly light and carefree. It was the voice he used lately when he told people that camel's milk doesn't curdle or that the speed limit in New York City used to be eight-miles-per-hour or that seals only sleep one-and-a-half minutes at a time. Each and every fact to be found under the bottle-cap of a quality Snapple beverage. "Not at all. I'm not trying to send you any ulterior message. In fact, I've just changed my mind. Let's have dinner tonight."

"Do you really mean that, Ray?"

"Oh yes. Let's get together tonight."

"Are you okay?"

"Yes. Why?"

"I don't know. You sound a little…oh never mind. I'm really looking forward to seeing you, Ray."

"Me too."

They met at Lucky Chang's on First Avenue. The Asian waitresses, each one tall, slender, exquisitely beautiful, didn't escape Beth's notice. She watched them carefully: the artfully made-up faces, the exaggerated grace, the soft and submissive demeanor. "Interesting choice of restaurants," she said when the delicate sloe-eyed creature waiting their table minced back to the kitchen with their order on red spangled stilletos. "They're all guys, aren't they?"

"Oh," Ray said, looking up from his indecipherable menu. "I suppose they are."

Beth sipped her water. Ray munched a fried noodle. A statuesque Chinese beauty in a gold gown like a mermaid's skin sauntered past carrying a steaming plate of chow mein something.

"So where were you all this week? What happened?"

"What do you mean? I told you already."

"You never called."

"You said you'd be out of your coverage area. You didn't lave a landline number. Didn't seem much point in calling."

"I've been home for nearly a week now, Ray."

Ray shrugged. He was running his finger down the columns of offerings, Wo Fun this and Wo Fun that, seeing nothing.

"I guess I lost track of time."

"You could have left a message."

Ray cleared his throat.

"Or an email."

"I was feeling a bit under the weather."

"Pretty cavalier, Ray. I might have thought you'd want to talk, especially after the bizarre way you acted at the airport. I even came home a little early, did you know that, of course not, earlier than I had to, just to see you."

"Oh yeah?" Ray said, wondering if maybe things hadn't worked out with Leon Szorkin, after all. Maybe that explained the plaintive whine undercutting Beth's pissed-off tone.

"Couldn't you have at least returned my messages? I left them everywhere. I even came by your apartment. You haven't been home in days."

"Like I said, I left the city for a little R and R. I needed to get away. I needed some time alone."

Well this was Beth inside and out, just in case he'd forgotten, arguing about the same thing over and over, like a grammar school teacher repeating a question to an idiot student until she finally gets the correct answer. These kinds of interrogations used to infuriate him, but tonight it seemed almost comforting, like a mindless ritual. This senseless, predictable bickering was a luxury he was now equipped to appreciate after the lunacy with Charlotte.

"You *were* alone," Beth cross-examined. "By virtue of the very fact that I'd left town, remember?"

"Alone, alone..." Ray waved with his chopsticks, "away from the teeming masses."

"I see. You know, I tried to call you at Staples. They told me you lost your job. Or rather, just stopped coming."

"Shelving copier paper and day-planners is just not for me, I guess."

"What is for you? If you don't mind my asking. What exactly are your plans?"

"I haven't quite got around to planning that yet."

Beth seemed to be making a visible effort to keep from losing her temper. "I was worried sick about you. It wasn't fair of you to just vanish on me like that, Ray. I don't appreciate it. I don't know why you have to be so selfish. Didn't you think how upset I'd be? Where have you been all this time?"

That, too, was just like Beth: if Ray's head fell off one fine day, just rotted and came off his shoulders, bouncing around in the gutter like a cabbage out of a grocery sack, he was certain it would somehow end up being more of an inconvenience for Beth than it was for Ray. He'd never hear the end of all the sacrifices she had to make living with a headless boyfriend. She had no idea what he'd been through the last two weeks, she wouldn't understand, and, of course, he couldn't explain it to her, but it hardly mattered what he might have told her, he could have had terminal cancer or one of those flesh-eating viruses. If he fell down dead off his chair at that very moment, struck by lightning, it would somehow all be unfair to her. It wasn't so much that Beth was self-centered; she just couldn't see that anything existed outside her Beth-centric world-view. But that didn't particularly bother Ray anymore either.

"I was at the shore."

"At the shore?"

Ray knew that Beth was adding it all up again on her mental calculator. She was remembering all the trouble she'd gone through to even get him to this point. She wasn't willing to throw all of that effort away so easily: she wasn't getting any younger, after all, etc. etc. Christ, that Leon Szorkin thing must really not have panned out like she'd hoped and not in any small way either. It must have been a real Super Bowl-size disaster. She was back to thinking of Ray as a strong possibility for the future. He could almost feel sorry for her. Imagine him, Ray Pierce, a strong possibility for *anyone's* future. It was like the punchline to some kind of sick joke, the kind that featured burning babies and Princess Diana. Fact is, Ray had begun to consider that the concepts "Ray Pierce" and "the future" were mutually exclusive terms, that Ray Pierce was the opposite of something extended in time and space, that Ray Pierce was, to put it in the vernacular, a dead-end. That's how bad things had gotten for Beth: that she'd come to the fork in the road of her life and chosen the dead end. Another waitress walked passed their table. She wore an electric blue silk sheath and silver sandals. It's the feet, Ray thought, it's the feet that give them away. They can't do anything about it either. If they could only make the feet right, all our problems would be solved. We wouldn't need women at all, no more heartbreak, no more insanity. In the meantime, they'd ordered and the food had come. Ray started filling a mu shu pancake. They munched away in silence, Beth more or less only picking at her food, poking at it with her chopsticks, as if she were testing to make sure that it wasn't still alive.

After a while, annoyance finally getting the better of her in spite of herself, Beth snapped, "Don't you have anything at all to say?"

Ray looked up, his mind somewhere else. "Did you know," he said reflexively, "that the beaver can hold its breath underwater for forty-five minutes?"

Beth made an incredulous face like he'd spontaneously said something in Mandarin. "What is that supposed to mean?"

"It's a Snapple real fact," Ray said. He desperately searched Beth's face for any resemblance to Charlotte, like searching for someone familiar in a sea of strangers, but Charlotte wasn't there. "Do you know," he said, suddenly realizing what a mistake this dinner was, "what the longest one-syllable word in the English language is?"

"What the hell are you talking about Ray?"

Beth's face was so utterly vacant of any resemblance to Charlotte, he had to look away. He turned his eyes to the rain-smeared window, the crumbs by his napkin, the middle-aged bald guy sitting by himself at the next table, eyeballing a little Korean in a sequined hobble-skirt and lifting a knot of lo mein noodles like a ball of worms to his slippery pink hole of a mouth. *That's the man I should be*, Ray thought, the man I will be before too long. He turned back to Beth, her puzzled, suddenly alien face probing his for any sign of the human being she thought she'd known, identified, labeled, inventoried once upon a long time ago.

"Screech," he said.

"Ray please," Beth said, "I know you don't like to talk about these things," she forced a smile, looking like she was straining on the toilet, "as you say, I do tend to talk them to death, but I did do a lot of thinking in Maine. I know it's not perfect, but we've got something going between us that can be good, if only we'd let it, if only we'd give it a fighting chance. Do you know what I'm talking about? Be honest, don't you feel it, too?"

Looking at Charlotte, Ray thought, as he watched Beth babbling, was like looking at the sun: when you looked away, there was nothing but a hole.

Ray felt like saying something interesting like "Did you know that the mosquito has forty-seven teeth?" But he hadn't become completely lost touch with the expectations of his audience. So instead he just recited the line he'd memorized from a thousand performances of this exact type, "Yes," he said, devoid of any feeling whatsoever, "I feel it too."

Later, outside a bar, on the corner of Fifth and 25th, they kissed under a streetlamp. Beth slid her hands inside his coat, under his sweater, and her moist palms were pressed against his chilled bare skin. "Why don't you come up to my apartment for some major make-up sex," she cooed with lewd promise, her breath scorching the side of his face with desperation. "It's been such a long time."

A cab pulled to the curb as if on cue, just like in the movies, and twenty minutes later, they were on Beth's couch, feeling each other up. Ray pulled off her boots, unbuttoned her blouse, and worked her tight jeans from her skinny white legs. He smelled her familiar acrid brand of sweat. His had his hand inside her leopard-print mini-g, fingering her stubbornly dry little bush from behind. With his pinkie, he tickled the tight bud of her pursed asshole.

He was thinking of Charlotte the entire time. Licking behind a knee, he imagined emails he might write her. Nibbling fingertips and salty toes, he wondered how he could get away long enough to place a quick call to her cell. He kissed Beth the way he kissed Charlotte, except he couldn't find Charlotte's mouth in hers no matter how hard he probed and poked his tongue around. Even worse, in the way Beth kissed him back he couldn't feel Charlotte. He couldn't feel anyone or anything at all.

Lying back on Beth's bed, closing his eyes, there were stray moments when the oral sex felt very much the same, if not identical, if he forgot himself, that is, and eventually she took his full load straight in the mouth, gulping it down quickly, just like Charlotte did, like she was eating an oyster or caviar—or else, something even more repulsive, a live cockroach, for instance. Beth was trying. Ray had to hand her that, pulling out all the stops. It was the guilt, he figured, when later she turned over on her belly and pulled her knees up beneath her. Or had Leon Szorkin already taken her there, too? Given her a taste for it? The thought flipped a switch in Ray's brain. He leaned forward and spit into her crack. He did it loudly, crudely, like he was hacking into the gutter. He sucked his thumb and stuck it into the tight brown bud and wormed it inside to open Beth up. Then he got down to business.

Still willing, she nonetheless resisted it all the way to the very end, until, finally he passed the point of no return, passed the point where her body instinctively tried to save itself, to force him back out with everything inside her. She was plugged, done up, finished. She felt like a tube of hot wax glue back there, like he might be stuck inside her forever. He started giving it to her rough, as rough as he could while moving only two or three inches, and she was trying not to complain, her eyes closed, biting her lips, brow creased in little furrows that deepened each time he thrust home, as if she were accepting a beating she knew she richly deserved. Ray figured the sex probably would get better and better after tonight, but only up to a point, and then it would gradually go backward and start getting worse and worse and finally taper off to a stop altogether once Beth felt she'd punished herself enough and the long nuclear winter of her resentment set in.

When it was done, when he came a second time into the surrendered earth of her bowels, Ray pulled out and rolled onto his back against the pillows. She shimmied up against him, whimpering softly, and laid her head against his chest. Ray put his arm around her cool shoulders and absently played with her nipples, which were smaller and harder than Charlotte's.

"I can hear your heart beating," Beth murmured and Ray thought, *My heart? Jesus Christ, what an imagination.*

"Did you know," he said, thinking of the only thing he could think of to say, "that the hummingbird's heart beats fourteen-hundred times a second?"

She bit him on the shoulder, playfully, not nearly hard enough. "I'm serious Ray."

"Me too."

"I think we can be happy. I really do," she whispered, wistfully. "We can be one of the lucky ones. We've both made mistakes, but it's not too late, not too late for a happy ending."

Ray stared with wide open eyes into the darkness and thought of all the ways people managed to kill each other without even trying. He was re-running in his mind what he'd been thinking while he fucked Beth moments ago: the dim image of what he'd look like if he had breasts and were trying to reach orgasm as Charlotte, wearing the corset and dildo, fucked him from behind for one of Rudra's hidden cameras. When he climaxed, he closed his eyes and pictured himself in a double coffin, lying next to John Rossi.

Ray slid out from under Beth. He went into the bathroom and ran the water in the sink. Then he got down on his knees, put his head over the toilet, and started dry-heaving. He flushed the toilet several times and then climbed to his feet and stared at himself in the mirror. He expected to see the same old heap, the moldering ruins. Instead, for the first time in a long time, he looked—what? Ray was surprised at the answer that first popped into his head: *almost alive.*

"Are you okay?" Beth said from under the covers when he came back to the bedroom. She was sitting up, reaching over to the nightstand.

"Don't--," he warned.

But it was too late. Beth had already turned on the bedside lamp. Her gasp sounded like a rat trap snapping shut on a rat too big.

"My god Ray," she said, when she was able to say anything. "What the hell did you do to yourself..."

The wounds ran up and down his arms, scrawled across his chest, his thighs, everywhere—many of them so fresh they hadn't yet scabbed over. Each cut was like a line of poetry. There wasn't a place on his body that he hadn't cut, not a place he hadn't bled. When he closed his eyes, Ray could still feel everything throbbing. He'd carved, like poetry, what he imagined was her signature all over his flesh. There wasn't a place on his body he hadn't opened to let her in—and it still wasn't enough.

"You're sick," Beth said, but it wasn't a reproach and it wasn't pity or shock or horror. It might have been wonder, maybe even awe, but not quite those either. It was something stranger. It took Ray a while to figure out the emotion coded into Beth's tone and when he did he wasn't really all too surprised: it was jealousy. "You've lost your mind."

Ray didn't answer. He reached down to the bed, grabbed one end of the sheet, and wiped his groin.

"Do you really have to do that?" she said, disgusted. She watched as he looked around the floor for his socks. "What are you doing?"

"Leaving."

"Leaving?"

"I know about Leon Szorkin."

"Who? What are you talking about?"

"Please Beth. Don't even try."

"You don't know a fucking thing, Ray."

"I know you're having an affair."

Beth said nothing as Ray finished dressing—no denials, no excuses, no explanations. Ray laced up his shoes and stood up.

"So what," she snapped defiantly. She sat up, gathering the knotted sheets under her tits in a fist. Her eyes were lasers, resentful and triumphant. "So what if I had an affair. *You've* been having one. Do you think these last three months have been easy for me?"

"You've been sleeping with him for almost a year."

"Can you blame me? You haven't exactly been all there for me, Ray. You haven't exactly been committed. I've been starving, *starving*. I have to figure out my life. I have the right. I can't wait around forever. I need security. I have to start thinking about my future. I don't want to be alone like you do. I want someone. I need a husband." She stopped, as if she'd gone off in the wrong direction. "I don't love him. You should know that. I don't..."

Ray checked his cell phone—no messages—and filled his pockets: change, keys, wallet, all that crap we carry around. He started for the door.

"Did you hear me? *I don't love him.* Where the fuck are you going?"

"Out."

"Why are you doing this to me?"

"I don't love you, Beth"

"You don't love me? What the fuck does that mean?"

"It's not hard to translate. Ask anyone."

"You just came here to fuck me, is that it? Fuck me up the ass out of revenge and then leave? You sad, sick bastard."

Ray walked into the bathroom again, ran the water, slicked back his hair. When he came back out, Beth was lying on her stomach, naked, sobbing into a pillow. Her words were muffled.

"So you're leaving?"

"It's over."

"Just like that?"

"Just like that."

"You really don't love me anymore?"

"No."

She lifted her head out of the dented pillow and twisted her neck. Her face was a swollen ruin. "How can that be? How? You loved me once. Tell me how the fuck that happens?"

Ray wondered that himself. It really was the mystery of mysteries, wasn't it? You love someone and then you don't. Someone loves you, and then they don't.

What happens? Why does it end? Where does it go? The best explanation Ray ever heard was the one Charlotte herself provided in that hotel room where Joan was recuperating from her massive cosmetic surgery, where Charlotte had planned to break-up with him. It was, as Ray reflected later, the same thing Buddha used to say a couple of thousand years ago. The height of wisdom, according to about ten gazillion Chinese.

"Things," he said, "change."

"That's it?" Beth shrieked, "*that's* the fucking best you can do?"

Ray walked passed the bed on the way to the door. Beth was still in the same position, sobbing, but she wasn't weeping for him, it was a deep gasping feeling-sorry-for-herself sobbing. The kind of 100% genuine tears we tap only for ourselves.

That was the best he could do, it truly was. Ray put on his sportscoat. "Your ass is really bleeding."

"I don't care," Beth said, between big gulping sobs.

Ray shrugged. If she didn't care, he sure didn't. He checked his teeth one last time in the mirror by the door, and then he left.

He walked towards the subway entrance on 59th. It was still early, chilly, the leaves on the trees were starting to turn. He decided to walk through the park instead of taking the train. He pushed the ear-buds of his Ipod into his ears and listened to airplanes crashing, buildings exploding, pigs being slaughtered. He was sweating in the frosty morning cold and, as usual lately, shaking like he had a fever. All the people in the street looked like ghosts, like wisps of pale smoke and the skyscrapers themselves looked no more substantial than dark grey clouds. It was as if it were all a memory, the memory of a city once inhabited by millions, the memory of a world, of a life, and Ray thought, *I love you Charlotte. I love you like Hiroshima. After it, there's nothing.*

On Lexington Avenue, down in the 20s, Ray saw Charlotte waving goodbye to a group of friends outside of an Indian restaurant called Neelam. The night before, he'd caught a glimpse of her in the back of a white limousine waiting for a light to change on Houston. In the last three days alone, he'd spotted her in a crowded N-train at rush hour, walking hand-in-hand with a tall distinguished-looking older businessman in the upper 80s, and looking out at passersby on Sixth Avenue from a poster for a new movie called *Firefly Girls*.

Tonight, Ray was walking downtown through the October gloom somewhere on Second Avenue when she passed him walking in the opposite direction and talking on a cellphone. She was walking so quickly he only caught a glimpse of her smile, a thin fatal shimmer of it, like a stiletto under his ribs. Stunned, Ray could only stagger to a stop, trying to talk himself out of it, as if he'd seen a ghost. By the time he turned, she was already about thirty yards ahead of him.

Ray picked up his pace, bumping into passersby and crossing against the lights, as if he were in a trance. He heard someone cursing at him. Halfway up the opposite street, she turned into a small food market. Ray stood outside on the sidewalk, by the cut flowers, debating himself. Then he decided, what the hell, to go inside.

He found her standing by the vegetables, picking out an avocado. Ray was standing next to a rack of brightly colored foil bags filled with snack foods. She half-turned in his direction, as if sensing she were being watched. Ray picked up a bag lighter than air, as if it were filled with helium, and stared at it without seeing anything. She turned back to the vegetables.

Ray continued to follow her through the store, from aisle to aisle, staying discretely out of sight.

Standing behind her, finally, in the check-out line, close enough to stroke the hair brushing her jaw-line, Ray was practically crushing the foil bag he'd taken to the register with a bottle of Strawberry Kiwi Snapple. He wanted to reach out and touch her shoulder, say something to her, but he didn't. Up close, the resemblance broke down as it always did: she was clearly older, her eyes were sort of faded and enveloped in tiny wrinkled pockets, the mouth, now closed, was all wrong somehow. Her boxy cloth coat accentuated a compact, square-shouldered body and the designer jeans she wore had that kind of "off" quality that was somehow more than just the consequence of being outdated. She might have been a foreigner, Ray decided, or a dyke, or both. With the cashier, she had a brusque, no-

nonsense manner that Ray could tell was probably habitual. When she took her change, he saw her short-fingered hands and her blunt, practical manicure—the hands of a woman who wore callouses instead of rings. Looking even closer, Ray realized the woman might have been well into her mid-sixties, old enough to be his mother.

It wasn't Charlotte, of course, no more than any of the others, but it might be her twenty or thirty years from now, a widowed grandmother just back from a vacation in Italy or Greece, and Ray found that he still wanted her, just like he always knew he would, and felt a wound bleeding in some unnamed organ at his very core. He quickly paid and picked up the woman's trail, following her around the corner at 4th Street, heading east. She walked up the stairs to a brownstone and Ray stood across the street under a thin dead tree out of reach of the streetlamps. He stood there long enough to see a dark window that must have been hers suddenly light up on the ninth floor. Ray wrote down the address of the building on a slip of paper and slid it into his billfold.

Hours later, riding the 6-train back from god only knew where, he found he was still clutching the foil bag. He stared at it uncomprehendingly for a minute or two and then tore it open. Without appetite, he rode the rest of the way to his station mechanically munching blue corn chips.

Day one, day two, day three. Charlotte waited until ten pm on the last day of Ray's deadline, only two hours left. But when she finally called him back, she seemed to understand the urgency of the situation, at least the urgency Ray placed on it, and agreed to a meeting for the very next day. His threat, risky a strategy as it might have been, had worked. Ray had to admit it felt good to be calling some of the shots for a change. Not that Charlotte sounded in any way stressed-out or anxious. Just the opposite. After a brief exchange of brisk pleasantries, her invitation to meet her in southern Jersey the next day was all very straightforward and businesslike, and yet still affectionately cordial.

They met at a kitschy seafood restaurant in Point Pleasant, a seaside town about two hours from Manhattan. The kind of place with plastic lobsters hanging from fake nets draped from the ceiling. Charlotte arrived right on time, a first for her, wearing a denim skirt and platform boots. She looked like J.Lo, only younger, and, of course, less Hispanic. They sat at the counter and ate seafood gumbo off a shared plate. Charlotte's idea. She fed him mussels and shrimp speared on a seafood fork. She chatted him up about her recent doings, probably half of it lies, telling Ray that she'd just returned east, her father was okay, a false alarm, after all, and she'd only be on the East cost for a few days. She was insanely busy, crisscrossing the tri-state area, trying to rock the vote. Haskins was up by only two points in the last poll, well within the margin of error—in other words, it was a dead heat.

"But we're expecting a late bump that'll put us over the top," Charlotte said, as if she were reciting talking points on *Meet the Press*. "We're upbeat."

There was no mention about her abandoning him, of Juliet's murder, of Ray's threatening phone calls, not that they could talk about this sitting at the counter of a popular local seafood joint, but that was just the point. When Charlotte suggested they take a stroll on the boardwalk, he figured she finally intended to bring up the matter then. With the background of wind and ocean, there was far less chance of being overheard by passersby. That was smart. You never knew who was listening. Ray reached inside his sportscoat as if looking for cigarettes and pressed the 'play' button on the microcassette recorder he'd stashed there. The sound would be garbled, no doubt, but he'd take what he could.

They strolled to the end of the boardwalk, where Charlotte turned abruptly towards him, looking as if she were just about to say something of such enormity she was trembling with excitement. There, where the boardwalk terminated in a railing over a sliding pile of slimy boulders and the ocean's genital-stench of poisoned fish and diesel oil was the most overwhelming, they kissed and felt each other up with an R-rated abandon. Ray squinted opened his eyes, peering over Charlotte's shoulder and saw disgusted-looking parents steering their gawking kids in a wide semi-circle around them. As usual, Charlotte was oblivious to the spectacle she was creating.

"Ohhhh," she said, "Ohhhhhh…."

Ray knew she was faking it, but he didn't care. He slid his hand quickly inside the waistband of the denim skirt, between pale moist thighs soft as Cool Whip. He rubbed the damp patch with his knuckle and palmed her pussy. She leaned against him and Ray felt her knees give a little.

"I feel like I'm lying down even when I'm standing up with you," she said during a break for air, looking as if she were gazing dearly into his eyes, searching for something she couldn't find. Earnestly , she said: "We should go…somewhere…"

Charlotte continued staring at him , as if she were trying to decide whether to tell him a secret, and if that were the case, right now, Ray really wished she wouldn't. He figured he knew too much already. He couldn't bear to know anymore. At least not until he fucked her one more time.

"A motel," Ray suggested. "There's one up the road."

"No," Charlotte said, "I know someplace better."

Thirty minutes later they were standing in a bedroom the size of a tennis court in a sprawling estate with a state forest for a back yard. Looking out any window you couldn't see another house in any direction. The driveway alone seemed to be about a mile long and ended far out of sight of the main road. Charlotte disabled the complicated alarm system once they were inside and led Ray through a series of vast rooms like airplane hangars sparsely furnished with polished antiques and gleaming bowls of picture-perfect museum-quality fruit.

"Who owns this place anyway?" Ray said. "Celebrities?"

"Friends."

"Friends of yours?

They'd arrived at the bedroom. Ray looked around: a large sculpture depicting some kind of painful-looking erotic abstraction, a Jacuzzi for a dozen, a bed raised on a platform like an altar.

"Any friend of the cause is a friend of mine."

It suddenly occurred to Ray, "Is this Haskins' place?"

Charlotte didn't answer. Instead she said, "You know, that reminds me, I meant to ask you, are you really voting for Haskins or did you just say that?"

"I just said that," he said, "I'm really voting for Rexson."

He would have thought she'd try to talk him out of it, or be angry, but she didn't. She didn't really have any reaction at all. She nodded, as if it confirmed something.

"Hmm. Figures."

She was crouched down by the bed. She pulled open a drawer in one of the brushed steel underbed storage units and came up with a pair of handcuffs. She peeked up at Ray coyly.

"Look what I found," she said, dangling the cuffs from the crook of her finger. "I guess my friends are a little bit kinky, huh? Nowadays, everyone's got a secret."

"That was extremely childish," she said, as she closed the cuff around Ray's wrist, punctuating the reprimand with a meaningful metallic click, the other already cuffed to the headboard. At first Ray thought she was talking about the microcassette recorder that she'd apparently found going through the pockets of Ray's jacket while he was in the bathroom and which she now held, ejecting the tape inside onto his bare chest. She replaced it with a second tape, which Ray recognized the instant Charlotte pressed the "play" button as the one from the answering machine at the carriage house.

He winced, recognizing the rant. That was Ray, sounding fully cranked, no doubt about it, even if he couldn't remember saying a single word now coming out of the tape recorder. He'd left quite a few choice messages during his stay at the bed-and-breakfast, several more than even he recalled, a couple of them while so drunk and depressed they'd disintegrated into little more than slurred screeds consisting mostly of pleading and inarticulate sobbing. This one particular message, unfortunately, was all too clear, at least the part that Charlotte had cued to replay.

"...is that why you won't talk to me," Ray snarled, "because you're too busy with that kinky freak you called a parasite, a sexless leech? You'd rather be with someone who's using you, hanging onto you so she can look more attractive, less like a corpse, is that it? You'd put up with that, what did you call her, a complete void, that vacuum, just for the money..."

Ray went on like that, accusing Charlotte of betraying Joan with Rudra, of plotting to extort money from both of them, playing one off the other, of gathering evidence of Joan's affairs to use in Rudra's secret divorce filing. Then Ray ran out of gas and he started pleading and begging Charlotte to see him just one more time, etc etc etc.

"The rest is just more of the usual sad crap," Charlotte said, clicking off the machine.

Ray was naked now, on his back, except for a pair of boxers, and Charlotte pulled his dick all the way through the opening in front, and slipped a nylon cord, knotted like a miniature hangman's noose, around his balls and the base of his cock.

"What were you thinking, Ray?"

She tightened the slipknot and tugged on the cord and Ray winced a little: it was way too tight. There was an aggressive set to Charlotte's jaw, as if she were barely holding herself back from really hurting him. She looked like a little like Paris Hilton when Paris is about to say something really bitchy. Ray couldn't tell if Charlotte were serious or not, if this were yet another kind of sex-game.

"Really, Ray. What *were* you thinking?"

What Ray had been thinking from the black pit of his three am despair was that Joan might overhear what he'd said on the answering machine, causing a rift between the two women. On one level it was a spiteful and immature thing to do; and yet, on another, it was extremely effective, as are most strategies that rely on the lowest and basest of human instincts.

As if he needed proof of his plan's effectiveness, here Charlotte was, stripped to a pair of black lace panties and a matching bra. Could he have gotten her to call back any other way? He doubted it. She knelt on the bed as if to mount him, but instead backed away, feeding the loose end of the nylon rope under and around the spreader bar now between his locked ankles, which kept his thighs separated, and everything cringingly exposed. Ray looked down at the tops of Charlotte's pale breasts and the part in her hair as she pulled the rope snug and tied it off around the black bar. Ray felt his first flicker of real fear. Game or not, he really was quite helpless. He wished Charlotte hadn't brought up the subject of that phone message only after she'd tied him helplessly to the bed like this.

"I wasn't thinking, not straight, anyway," he made an effort to explain. "I was upset. You left me behind here to deal with that mess. I needed to talk to you. That girl died, Charlotte."

Charlotte tsked-tsked, reached behind herself, and undid her bra.

"Remember what I said about trust? You didn't trust me, did you?"

"I didn't know what to think."

"You could have caused me a lot of trouble with that phone call, Ray."

She rubbed a finger across her tits, like saying "come hither," the nipples obediently standing up. Ray thought of all the things he suspected Charlotte might be capable of. She was stroking his cock which was growing, like it so often did, like it did his whole fucking life, in spite of himself, at the most inopportune of times. "A lot of trouble," Charlotte repeated, "especially if Joan and I didn't have the kind of relationship we have."

Ray closed his eyes and when he opened them again, Charlotte had that zany electric look in her eyes.

"Just what kind of relationship *do* you have?"

Charlotte was staring down at Ray's mouth as if thinking about what his face would look like without it. She was making little "boo-boo" movements with her lips. She wiggled back a bit and leaned forward over his crotch. She gave the rope a little tug and licked the head of Ray's cock, which now swelled to full-size, straining against the complicated and suddenly painful cat's-cradle of nylon which imprisoned it.

"Poor baby," she said when she slid off the foot of the bed and saw the situation between his legs. "It's causing you pain and yet you can't help responding."

She walked to the side of the bed, bent over, and stared down at Ray's mouth again, staying teasingly out of reach as Ray tried to lift himself up far enough to kiss her. Charlotte pulled back, mock-pouting, and Ray fell back against the pillows.

"Is she in love with you, is that it?"

"Why don't you ask her yourself?

The door to the bedroom opened and Ray yanked against the cuffs so hard that he almost castrated himself.

"Easy toots," Charlotte soothed. "You'll hurt yourself."

Someone entered. It was Joan, of course, and she was drifting into the room like toxic smog.

"What the fuck is she doing here," Ray shouted, jerking his head from woman to woman. Rattling the cuffs and rope, he found himself bound fast. "Is this some kind of game?"

"Calm yourself," Charlotte said.

Joan had come up to the side of the bed and her eyes were staring in Ray's general direction, but it was as if she weren't seeing him at all. She was wearing, Ray noticed dejectedly, hospital scrubs. She leaned forward to say something to Charlotte, or at least that's what he assumed she was doing. Ray could see her tight, straight mouth moving, but he couldn't hear any of the words she might be saying. His gaze dropped, caught by some stray glint, a quasar of light. He felt his skin tighten. In Joan's left hand, he saw a long calibrated syringe half-filled with fluid.

"Okay, enough," he croaked. "You've made your point. Let me up. I'm not fucking around anymore. I mean it."

Charlotte's smiling eyes flicked towards him, as if just remembering his existence. She put a finger to her lips, still listening to whatever Joan was whispering in her ear. Ignoring the pain, Ray thrashed around helplessly on the bed making the spring squeak in a parody of a vigorous fuck.

"Sssh," Charlotte frowned. "Don't make such a fuss."

She delicately held the tip of his penis in the fingers of one hand, and now she used the other to lift up his tied testicles, and the very way she was doing it, Ray couldn't help but get the creepy feeling that Charlotte was making some kind of offering of them, an offering to Joan. The ghostly woman had stopped whispering into Charlotte's ear and stepped back to hold the syringe to the light coming in from the big ornate bay windows, flicking away a few air bubbles with a grey finger. Then Joan came forward, her face expressionless as the back of a mirror, and brought the needle close to the prickled, suddenly constricted flesh of Ray's shrunken testicles. Ray heard himself practically whimpering.

"This is a game, is that it...is this a fucking game because if it is I want out of it...do you hear me? Let me out of it."

"One injection," Charlotte said, almost dreamily, and she looked up at Joan and smiled her dazzling smile.

Joan had produced an alcohol swab from somewhere and she touched the square pad to Ray's flesh, obviously being extra careful to avoid any human contact. She looked up at Charlotte's smiling face, the two of them sharing an enigmatic moment above his genitals—the exchange enigmatic to Ray, that is. Joan suddenly seemed bashful, but bashful in the way that people are when they've decided that outside of only the very few things they've chosen to care about in the world, everyone and everything else is irrelevant and might as well not exist at all; and yet, there Ray lie, naked, a necessary if embarrassing fact.

Joan whispered into Charlotte's ear again and Ray strained to hear. They were so close he should have been able to catch a few words at least, but all he could hear was a low murmur. It occurred to him that Joan wasn't saying anything at all, just sensuously licking Charlotte's ear and humming, like a hive of bees, *Mmmmmm.*

Ray felt sick. He wished he hadn't eaten that seafood gumbo, it felt like it was still alive inside him, a big pot of squirming tentacles, bony sideways scrabbling legs, and clicking claws. Would they let him up, he wondered, to use the toilet? No way, they'd never fall for that. But he could try, couldn't he?

"What's going on?" he asked, groggily; it was the same question he asked a thousand times throughout his affair with Charlotte—the question he'd ask forever. "What is this all about?"

He remembered what Sam had told him during their last meeting, at the end, when Ray had begged to know what he'd told the man the night he attempted suicide. Was it possible? Could it be true? Of course, it was—it most definitely could. He felt a weird sense of calm come over him and submitted with a low groan when Joan injected him a second time with whatever was in the syringe. Around the injection site, his groin felt like it was on fire, but that only lasted a few moments, now it didn't feel like his balls were there at all. Everything in the room had taken on a hyper-clarity, as if he'd become the human equivalent of a high-powered digital camera in macroscopic mode. Charlotte leaned over him again, doing something, and for an instant she was everywhere. Ray saw for the first time the little bumps inside her excited aureoles, the one-day's growth darkening her armpits, the wispy stray hair that she'd forgotten to pluck that morning growing just above her upper lip. He picked up the sharp tang of her excitement in the air.

"Are you going to kill me," Ray asked, matter-of-factly through his mental fog. It seemed a perfectly ordinary question to ask under the circumstances. "That's it, isn't it?

The hyper-clarity of moments ago was already fading away, as if layers of distorting transparencies were being piled one over another between him and everything else.

"Sssh," Charlotte said, "Don't talk."

"I have a right to know," Ray said, fighting to articulate his thoughts. His mouth felt like it belonged to someone else, and then he realized why: Charlotte was kissing him. When she stopped, he managed to ask, "Tell me, please. What are you going to do to me?"

"Oh you know," Charlotte said coquettishly. She wasn't looking at him anymore, but staring again at Joan, as if she were looking at the moon, as if in devotion. And Ray wondered if he'd gotten it all wrong, after all. That it was Charlotte who was in love—in love with Joan. She lisped the word like a child, "...stuff..."

And the drug, or whatever it was they'd injected him with, laid another half-dozen or so layers over his senses until the whole world seemed to turn grey and staticky, like a TV out of whack during a hurricane. The last thing Ray was aware of was that the greyed-out world was really Joan leaning over him to do whatever it was they'd brought him here to do and that the sharp tang of excitement burning in his nostrils was *her*.

He heard one last word, a request.

"*Scalpel.*"

When you're unconscious, you're never really sure what happens to you and what doesn't, and let's face it, even under the best of circumstances, most of us are unconscious most of the time. Seconds slip by, hours, whole days. One day you wake up and you're thirty, forty, fifty and you're someone you never thought you'd be, your life has somehow gotten away from you. Ray woke up, naked, shivering, on top of a made bed in a small, cold motel room by the side of a highway running east and west, from somewhere to somewhere else. Outside the window, there was a view of a concrete overpass, a gigantic mute cement M.

His clothes were folded neatly at the foot of the bed. There was a brown plastic bottle of prescription painkillers on the nightstand. He needed them. He hurt all over. Ray shuffled into the bathroom, cupped some water in his palm, and immediately took two of the small blue pills. He had no memory of how he'd gotten from the mansion to the motel. He had no memory of what happened after he saw Charlotte hand Joan the scalpel. He didn't think he wanted to have any memory after that. He didn't think any memory after that was going to be a good one.

After taking a shower, he dressed gingerly, as if one false move might cause the whole tottering pile of himself to come unstitched and fall to pieces. He wasn't looking forward to it, but he knew he had to leave the motel. He felt like he could have stayed in the quiet, impersonal room, the humming air-conditioner insulating him from the outside world, for months. It reminded him of a well-kept womb but without the room service and much chillier. Ray walked to the door, took a last look around, and locked it quietly behind him. As it turned out, his room was on the first-floor. The sun greeted him like a hundred flash-bulbs and he cringed in the glare like a shamed celebrity. In the parking lot just outside the door, he found his car, unlocked, the keys waiting in the ignition.

Ray hobbled along the cement breezeway, passed a dismal line of turquoise doors, to the motel office. At the desk, the clerk took his room card, told him the bill was settled, slid over a receipt. The clerk's eyes looked elsewhere, practiced at seeing nothing. Ray asked directions to the turnpike, the parkway, whichever was closer. The desk clerk answered in limited English. There were two TVs mounted on the ceiling behind the desk: one was broadcasting a closed-circuit surveillance shot of the very scene unfolding at the desk in which Ray was co-starring, and the other a CNN report on the upcoming election showing the bump that Charlotte had predicted—Haskins was suddenly up by seven points.

Ray was on the road by three. It turned out it was a Wednesday, that's what the newspaper he bought from the vending machine outside the motel office said, along with a pack of gum he'd bought from another vending machine to get the gamey taste out of his mouth; it was three days after he met Charlotte, three days after whatever had happened at the mansion. He was in a town called Barnegat, not far from the sea. He had an erection so hard and so unfeeling it couldn't be real. As it turned out, it would be the last one he'd have for months. His groin and testicles were the color of a bloody eggplant, as if he'd been kicked by a horse, and just as tender. That was bad, but it wasn't the worst of it.

He saw it for the first time in the shower, soaping himself. He hadn't noticed it until then because you often don't see what's missing. You don't usually wake up feeling the need to take stock. But maybe you should. You just go along from day to day expecting to have what you had the day before, but there are no guarantees. Ray looked down when he felt the rough ridge of bumps under his soapy fingers. It stung, then it hurt, but the pain was nothing, completely swallowed up in the uncomprehending fear of a moment that would never really end. It's not true you scream, Ray thought later, a scream is a response, and there's no response to real terror, it steals away the breath, it elicits nothing but silence. *Something was missing.* The five-inch line of black stitches running across his lower belly marked the spot.

Ray stared out the windshield, looking for the turnpike sign that the desk clerk had told him to expect. He tried not to think too much. Right now, it seemed to be better to think as little as possible. There would be time to think later, too much time. He turned on the car radio—and turned it off again. He wished it would rain, but the sky looked cloudless and blue for the next one thousand years. They'd cleaned him up. That was pretty clear from his blanched and shaved skin. From the antiseptic stench that he tried—and failed—to shower away. But looking at his hand on the steering wheel, he saw they'd missed a spot. They'd forgotten to scrub away the ridge of dried black blood under each of his fingernails.

After the examination, Ray dressed and waited for the doctor to return. He stared at a poster on the wall in the meantime: a man cut in half to expose all that's inside a man—blood and bones and bags and tubes and valves and little pouches of diverticulosis. The doctor opened the door, sat on a small rolling stool, and pushed himself in front of Ray. He looked at a folder of notes open in his lap for what seemed a long time, but that was in reality probably only five seconds or so. Ray, waiting, stared down at the doctor's bald head. There were flakes of dead skin there, peeling off his mottled scalp as if it were the arid crust of a waterless planet.

The doctor looked up from between Ray's knees. "Well, naturally, until all the tests come back I can't say anything definitive, but on the basis of my physical examination and the preliminary x-rays, I don't think there's any immediate cause for concern. I'd don't see anything that's actually missing…"

"But was I operated on?"

The doctor cleared his throat. "You were cut open, yes. There's a surgical-type incision. But I wouldn't call it an 'operation.'"

"Why not?"

"Well, for one thing," the doctor said, looking uncomfortable, "there doesn't seem to have been a purpose—"

"But you can't completely rule out that something's missing?"

"Well, I'd say it's highly unlikely anything was taken. Anything important, anyway. If it's any relief to know, I can assure you that there's actually quite a lot inside us that we can easily live without."

Ray considered that; it was true, wasn't it? But he had other concerns at the moment. "Would you say it looked like whoever did it knew what they were doing?"

"I'd say that's hardly the point, Mr. Pierce. As I said, this wasn't an operation."

"But could it have been done by a doctor?"

"No doctor would do something like this."

"Then someone trained as a doctor?"

The doctor suddenly looked annoyed. "If you think a crime has been committed, I think you should go to the police, Mr. Pierce. I can't do anything for you in that regard."

"I can't go to the police. I'm just asking for your professional opinion, if this could have been done on a do-it-yourself basis, by someone, you know, just sort of following along in a book, for example."

"Yes," the doctor said, grudgingly. "Of course, it's possible for someone to learn how to do what was done to you without formal medical training, if that's what you're getting at."

Ray pointed to his groin: it was still swollen and bruised, looking now like a bulging inner tube. "The injection," he said. "What was it?"

"Until the toxicology and blood analyses come back, it's just impossible to say with any certainty."

"Do you have any guess what it could be?"

The doctor looked at Ray blankly for a moment. Then he looked down at his folder again, but not as if he were really reading anything written there anymore. He touched the side of his mouth with his blunt hairy fingers and then looked up. His milky-blue eyes looked much bigger behind the glasses than they did without them, like the blue yolks of some endangered species of bird.

"Like I said, it's just impossible to really say without the tests results." He got to his feet, and pushed the stool away behind him. "Almost anything could have been in that syringe from a harmless sugar solution to something, well, something much more unpleasant."

He was trying to be diplomatic, but Ray felt the doctor suspected something. Ray himself had considered AIDS, or anthrax, or some kind of ugly genetically-engineered STD—would Charlotte even have access to such things? Why not? With her connections to the rich and shady, anything was possible. He remembered Rudra, and how Charlotte told him he'd had diabetes. The injection might have been nothing more than something relatively harmless, like insulin, something to scare him. He suggested this possibility to the doctor.

"Could be, could be," the doctor said without conviction.

Ray was surprised at how relatively calm he felt—not calm, really, but sort of detached: as if he were discussing some third person with a life beyond his control. And he was, in many ways, doing exactly that, weren't we all?

"Your educated guess doc," he said, "that's all I'm asking for."

In spite of his detachment, Ray was still taken by surprise when the doctor said, "Well if I absolutely had to hazard a guess? Judging from your presenting complaints, I'd say you were injected with a massive dose of female hormones."

"Female hormones?"

"Estragon, premarin…would whoever did this have access to these kinds of drugs by any chance…was it someone undergoing hormone replacement therapy for any reason that you know of? Someone with cancer? A pre-op transsexual, maybe?"

Well, the idea that Charlotte might really be a man, that might explain things, wouldn't it? If he hadn't been to the promised land, he might even have considered it. Ray thought of Joan—she seemed at an age where she might need hormonal therapy. And then there was the scar on Charlotte's belly: a hysterectomy, maybe, the removal of her ovaries? He didn't know for sure, of course; he'd likely never know.

"Whatever it was," the doctor said, "it's my advice that you notify the police if you are concerned about this person's motives or sanity."

Ray nearly laughed—her motives, her sanity? Actually, he did laugh if anyone could call the sound that came out of his face lately a laugh anymore. "What can I expect—if it's hormones?"

"Most likely nothing," the doctor said. "One dose—even a large one—will have a temporary effect: the slight swelling and sensitivity of your breasts and nipples, as you noted, decreased libido, mood swings, maybe impotence…but not to worry," he added quickly, "unless the doses are repeated regularly and maintained over time, these effects should subside. The possibility of organ damage, especially to your liver and kidneys, is minimal, relatively speaking, with only one injection, even a fairly large one, but the tests should rule out anything of that sort."

The doctor seemed vaguely embarrassed.

"Don't worry," he said, attempting a joke, "it's not all as easy as that to become a woman."

Ray was staring over the doctor's crusty bald dome again, at the chart on the wall, at the man with the front half of him gone—the half with the face, the flesh, the hair, the sexual organs: everything that makes us…well, *us*. Without all that stuff that covers up what we are inside, Ray thought, all the tits and grins and hair-dos, no one could possibly stand to look at each other for five stinking minutes.

The doctor stood, ready to wrap things up. He had other patients to see, other deaths to hold off just a little longer. "Do you have any other questions, Mr. Pierce? I mean, questions I might be able to answer."

"No doc. Thanks."

And it was true. Ray didn't have any other questions; well, maybe none that could actually be answered. The more people talked, it seemed to him, the further away the truth got.

It was sometime after seven by the time Ray left the doctor's office. He strolled along Columbus Avenue into the upper 70s. He sat on a bench beside Theodore Roosevelt Park. It was a nice night. There was a fake Charlotte walking a pug across 81st street. It felt like rain.

So it was that Ray wasn't feeling quite at the top of his game, not quite the man he usually was, when he met Leon Szorkin for lunch, but the appointment had been made in advance and Ray was in serious need of cash. Szorkin had agreed to meet once he'd gotten the gist of what Ray wanted to discuss, but his attitude hadn't been nearly as abject as Ray expected from a man whose arguably criminal sexual secrets were just a phone call to *The New York Post* away from destroying his life. Ray was banking that Szorkin's gruff and dismissive demeanor on the phone was just a front for the genuine panic he should reasonably be feeling. He figured to see some cracks in the man's macho façade when they met and he discovered the particulars of what Ray had learned about his secret life. Ray was looking forward to the moment the famous author—and the bastard who cuckolded him—lost his balls and started squirming.

The meeting with Szorkin took place at Elaine's—the famous celebrity literary haunt where Ray once dreamed of being wined and dined by some high-powered editor at Knopf or Viking—and was set up by Szorkin himself. Ray would've expected Szorkin to choose somewhere less conspicuous, certainly somewhere he wouldn't have been recognized breaking bread with the man who was blackmailing him. As he sat there rehearsing what he would say, Ray tried not to be intimidated by the snazzy surroundings, the glimpse of famous faces, the prices on the plush menu, and the fact that someone like Szorkin moved in-and-out of such high-tone hangouts the way Ray frequented Starbucks. He hadn't considered it before, but were these the kinds of environs that Beth was used to in her line of work? No wonder Szorkin had been able to take her, keep her, and dismiss her at will. What had Ray to offer that even compared? All of a sudden Ray felt rather shabby and embarrassed to think what Beth could be thinking of him; that she could actually be slumming it by dating him, that he was, in all probability, a real step-down from what she'd once hoped for in a mate.

Ray tried to buck himself up. "So this guy writes the kind of crap that bankrolls his ability to eat $35 herb-crusted salmon balls while nodding hellos with John Grisham and stealing other men's women," he told himself over a second gin-tonic, "so what? Soon he's going to have a lot less of that money and I'll have a lot more of it."

But thinking such edifying thoughts didn't make Ray feel much better, not really, and he realized why the moment he was seated at a table right in the middle of the crowded restaurant. Szorkin kept Ray waiting twenty minutes for it to dawn on him just in case he was extra thick in the head. And then God's gift to American Letters arrived, shaking hands on his way to the table and possessing that aura of gruff invincibility that people have when you see them exclusively on TV shows, newspaper pages, and on the back covers of well-received hardcover novels.

Ray had never read any of Szorkin's books, the man was already a dinosaur back when Ray was in graduate school, but to be a well-read human being in the 21st century, he should have. Like Hemingway, Leon Szorkin was the kind of writer you'd heard of even if you didn't read. His name had become synonymous with the term "writer." He was the kind of author who transcended the world of letters and whose opinion was solicited on matters of politics and culture, whose marriages and divorces made the pages of gossip columns, whose feuds and run-ins with the law were near-legendary. It was true that Szorkin was past his prime, an old lion on his way out, but that only meant he'd be looking to his legacy, and the news that he liked looking at pictures of naked boy-girls pretending, or maybe not pretending, to be raped murder victims couldn't possibly serve to enrich that legacy, and might even still be worthy of at least a line or two on Page Six.

The man who settled in across the table from Ray was shorter, fatter, balder, and more grizzled than he remembered from the book jackets. He wore a navy-blue pinstriped suit and an open collared white shirt from which sprouted a scraggly bush of wiry grey hair.

His square head was creased with a lifetime of narrowing his eyes with contempt at everything that was wrong with the world. Right now what he saw wrong with the world was Ray. The waiter placed a scotch on the table, neat, without asking, even before Szorkin's pampered literary ass touched-down on his chair. Ray felt his hand, like the rest of his body, suddenly flush with panic as he clutched for his own glass, as if his fingers were hot enough to melt the ice in his third gin-tonic.

"Okay you little cocksucker, Szorkin opened negotiations in a measured, menacing tone, "let's get right down to business. You're going to finish your drink and walk out of here and never contact me or my wife again or you're going to end up looking like a used tampon. Do you understand me?"

Ray was so stunned by this unexpectedly savage and unrepentant opening gambit that he nearly lost his nerve altogether. The urge to run was lurking around the edges of his consciousness, not indulged, most likely, out of sheer paralysis of will. Somehow he managed to recover enough to fake a minimal façade of the most superficial cockiness. He twisted his mouth into a crooked grin and lifted his glass to cover his total confusion. He took a long swallow and put the glass down ever so carefully with what he hoped passed for ominous significance.

"You don't understand the situation Mr. Szorkin," he said, grabbing at what shreds of his nerves remained. Christ, he could feel the shirt under his arms go cold in two big sweaty patches. "You're not setting the rules here."

A thick, stubby finger stopped less than six inches from the center of Ray's alarmed face.

"No. *You* don't understand, faggot. You're pitching a fit because your woman is fucking around on you. Tough luck, asshole. That's life. Happens all the time. Get over it. You want to blame someone? Be a fucking man. Blame yourself."

Szorkin was talking none too softly either. At the surrounding tables people would be able to hear them if they really chose, maybe even if they didn't. Ray felt himself losing it: no, this definitely wasn't the way he'd scripted this meeting in his mind, not even close.

"I know about the pederastic necrophiliac shit," he blurted, "I saw those sites you frequent."

Ray paused to let the gut-kick of this revelation soften the old bastard up a little. Then he added, "I think some other people might find your interests…umm…well, a little interesting, too, especially given your super-liberal, do-gooder, crusader for the underdog image."

If Szorkin was worried, that worry didn't register in the crags and valleys, the erosions and landslides of his obdurate old pugilist's mug. He regarded Ray with undisguised disdain, like some turd dropped in his path. Ray didn't understand. Was Szorkin senile? Was he so old that he was beyond shame? Did he not understand what Ray was threatening to do? Did he think Ray wouldn't expose him? Was that possible? Had Ray gotten something wrong?

"I should kick your pathetic ass right here, you fucking pussy. Who do you think you're dealing with? Some right-wing congressman from one of the red states? Some fundamentalist religious wacko you can put to shame and destroy? Let me tell you something about how my world works, cocksucker. I'm a writer. Do you have any idea what that means? It means I can do whatever the hell I want and do you know what it's called? *Research,* asswipe, that's what. You think you can waltz in here and blackmail *me* with *this bullshit?* Do you have any idea where I've been, what I've done? Do you? Read the books, sonny boy. Do your homework. Whatever I do in my life is in service of the work, that's how I get away with murder. If you wanted to impress me with your little blackmail act you should have claimed to have found evidence of plagiarism. That's the only real crime a writer can commit. You won't scandalize anyone with my little research junket into the sexual demimonde. In fact, you and every other peckerhead can read about it in next month's *Vanity Fair.*"

He was bluffing, Ray desperately told himself, he had to be. But the man across the table looked as solid and immoveable as the side of a mountain. Ray couldn't make a dent in him.

"Your wife," he said at last, playing his trump card. He remembered Diane Glickstein's post-menopausal homicidal mania. She clearly didn't think it was just research. "She knows, too. She's ready to divorce you, blackmail you herself, and take you to the cleaners."

Bringing up Szorkin's wife might not have been the strategically smartest thing to do, Ray thought; it might easily make buying his own silence seem unimportant to Szorkin by comparison with satisfying his wife. But the situation was desperate now. He had to shake Szorkin up a little, bring him down out of his high tower and fight in the gutter like everyone else; he had to convince the self-important fuck that this was serious, that he could be hurt, that he wasn't immune, that nobody was, and that Ray, worm that he might have seemed, wasn't to be fucked around with, that he was just the man, just the worm, who could put that hurt on him. Because, after all, it was the worm that had even the greatest of men in the end.

"Diane and I have reconciled," Szorkin said bluntly. "She's decided she can get more out of life—and me—by providing a unified front. After seven divorces, I've learned a thing or two. She fully supports my work and my research. End quote."

He unfolded the starched white napkin by his plate, shook it out with a snap like the crack of a gunshot, and tucked the linen under chin as if to say "and that's that." And if what he'd said about his wife were true, maybe it really was over. A waiter had arrived with his favorite appetizer already—crabmeat-stuffed mushrooms sprinkled with crumpled feta, at least that's what it looked like—and a fresh scotch. "If you don't believe me, dickwad, why don't you call her yourself?" Szorkin held out his cell phone. "Speed dial three."

If Szorkin could condense all the hatred, hubris, cruelty, and self-love he'd felt in his entire life into one expression, it would be the hammer-like expression he was directing at Ray at that moment—and mixed in there was the man's sadistic triumph over all of it, including his triumph over Ray. He snorted and slipped the cell phone back into his jacket. Ray had come to reduce Szorkin to a trembling supplicant begging for his mercy and instead found the roles inexplicably reversed. Ray was clearly out of his league. Dammit, he thought, even the waiters in this place were out of his league. One of them, a guy who looked like Jared Leto, only taller, was talking to him, or at him. Actually he was talking to Leon Szorkin *about* Ray, asking, "And will the gentleman be having anything for lunch?"

"No," Szorkin said, clearly enjoying the moment. "This cocksucker is already full of shit. He was just leaving."

It was true, about leaving that is, and maybe the full-of-shit part, too. Ray had by now gotten to his feet, looking for the exit. He realized that no good could come of sitting there a moment longer. Ray needed to get out of the lion's den and regroup.

"Oh and by the way," Szorkin said, waiting for a sip of scotch to clear his rock-slide larynx. "FYI. I'm not the one plugging your woman."

"Bullshit. Your wife told me. She said you admitted it herself."

"I told her I was having an affair. She decided it was with your girlfriend. But she was wrong."

"I don't believe you."

"Why would I lie?" Szorkin said, grinning, looking like some evil concrete gargoyle. "Do you think I'd really fall in love with a fucking pipsqueak romance editor at some half-baked minor imprint? I tried, naturally, to fuck her. But she's the kind of principled gal who believes three's a crowd. She can only have two men in her life fucking her at any one time."

Ray ground his teeth. "Who then?"

"Normally, I wouldn't say. I come from a time when a man kept his fucking mouth shut about things like that—a matter of honor and respect. But we're living in an age of fake celebrities and reality shows, illegal wars and criminal presidents. The jackals and cocksuckers have taken over. Besides, it's an old man's prerogative to take his pleasure where he can. And, in this case, speaking strictly as a writer, I can hardly resist the irony. Take a lesson from your elders, boy. Art, like love, is cruel. Who's fucking Beth—why, that's an easy one, dickhead. That would be your screenwriter pal, Eric."

Ray suddenly felt unsteady on his feet, as if the entire restaurant were pitched to one side, as if the entire world were spinning off its axis. Little black spots floated across his vision. He passed through a blur of faces, tables, dishes, conversations, the clank of sophisticated knife and fork. At that moment he felt as if life itself were a banquet at which he were the main course. Somehow slicing through it all, however, was Leon Szorkin's obscenely amused gargle, like a toilet sucking down rocks, calling after him. "Have a nice life, asshole."

Ray walked the streets of Manhattan after dark, aimlessly crisscrossing an island of infinite possibilities and not a single kept promise, hiking from one end of the night to the other, until the empty dank hours of the thin grey dawn, stalking a city where anything could happen, and nothing ever really did. He rode subway cars without a destination, stepping off at random, and roaming the concrete underground before jumping onto another train, just like it, and just as randomly, usually shooting off in the opposite direction from which he'd just arrived. In the backs of cabs, he slipped a twenty over the plastic glass and instructed the driver to let him out wherever twenty bucks would take him.

He wandered up and down the freak streets around St. Marks, a freak himself, but incognito, a freak in sheep's clothing. He sat on park benches in Washington Square, Minetti Square, Union Square, any square. He lit cigarettes he forgot to smoke, bought papers he never read. He was waiting for something, but he didn't know exactly what. He was waiting for *her*, but even after all the time that had already passed, he didn't know who she even was. He thought about her constantly, so much so that he half-expected her to appear at any moment, passing by on the sidewalk, or sitting at an outdoor café, and when she didn't, there was always a sense that something was wrong.

The first night he saw one, he was standing on the corner of 45th and Broadway across from a "Don't Walk" sign in a vacant Times Square. The xeroxed paper was taped to the pole: her hair looked darker in the picture and she was some pounds heavier, the baby-fat making her seem touchingly young, but Ray recognized her even before he read the description and saw the name. Juliet was standing in front of a Christmas tree, holding a toy dog, and beaming a blinding smile into the camera. A surreal view into another world, disturbingly unreal, it seemed to Ray. It wasn't Christmas and there was nothing to smile about any more. There was a little fringe cut along the bottom of the paper with the same phone number repeated twelve times. Ray was the first to spoil the perfect fringe by tearing off one of the numbers. The first, apparently, to know where it was she'd gone.

Ray stopped at an all-night diner on 26th street. He sat at a table by the window, ate a stale sweet roll, and drank cup after cup of coffee. It was Election Night and he'd been a nervous wreck all day. He'd been carrying around one of Leon Szorkin's Jenna Corrolla novels. He'd bought it at a magazine kiosk in the airport the day he'd dropped Beth off, the day he'd abducted Juliet, and had forgotten all about until he came across it that morning. He'd been reading bits and pieces of it all day long, hoping to get some kind of clue. A clue, he wondered, to what? Ray didn't exactly know. He pulled the fat paperback out of his coat pocket and opened it to a page marked with an expired Metrocard. But as he read, Ray grew sicker and sicker. The main characters in the book were so full of fine and earnest emotions, so noble, so full of integrity, fidelity, and selfless self-sacrifice that he found himself at a loss as to which to marvel at more: Szorkin's powers of invention or his brazen hypocrisy. Where were these people in real life? That's what Ray wanted to know. He'd never heard anyone say the things they said or suffer or sacrifice for love the way they did in books and movies. Why was everyone pretending to believe these lies? Ray thought of all the people he personally knew: not a single one of them could measure up to these characters. He read a few more sentences in the book with growing irritation. Why did people make crap like this up? Movies, television shows, these crappy bestsellers...who stood to gain from trying to convince us that people were better than they really are? And who could possibly believe it? Yet people did, they lapped it up by the millions, and their gullibility made folks like Leon Szorkin a rich man. You couldn't really blame him. He was simply giving them what they wanted, the lies they needed to face stinking day, to face each other without puking. Ray stared uncomprehendingly at the book in his hand. Was this merely the way we'd like to be, he wondered—or, worse, was it the way we actually see ourselves? Is everyone truly that deluded?

Ray was seized with a sudden urge to rip the novel to shreds, burn it, and piss on the ashes. Instead, he slammed the book down in disgust, rattling the dinnerware.

"Everything okay pal," the big slab of a short-order cook standing at the register asked, fingertips on the counter, making his triceps twitch.

"Yeah sorry," Ray muttered, "just misjudged something, I guess."

The counterman eyeballed Ray warily, measuring him up as a potential nutcase, and pointed with his blue-black chin. He grinned, semi-malevolently. "Whatcha reading anyway?"

"Science fiction."

The counterman grunted, satisfied with Ray's answer.

They say only human beings can love. It's a lie, Ray thought. He looked at the beefy man behind the counter, the sullen waitress, the faceless customers at the other tables, hunched once again over their meals and their misery. He turned and looked at his own reflection in the window, hollowed out, ghostlike. He looked through that pale floating image into the empty street on the other side of the glass. The planet seemed unpopulated tonight. He didn't see a human being anywhere.

That's because none of us is human, Ray concluded. It's as if we were all pretending to be this creature that doesn't exist. Beneath our human masks, the acts, the fictions, the propaganda, and the lies, we're all aliens inside, feeding on each other. That was as best as Ray could figure it out. He didn't know anything for certain except this one thing. In no way in which the term was commonly understood had he ever met a single human being, not once, not in his entire life.

There was a TV behind the counter and the latest returns were coming in. Up to now, the election had been too close to call, a dead heat, the candidates within a single percentage point of each other all night long, see-sawing back and forth. But some key precincts had just reported, it was suddenly all over, they were switching live to a reporter standing by at the Crown Pointe Hotel on Madison where the victory party was already getting underway—Haskin had won by four points.

"The way to the White House would now seem to be clear for the charismatic and newly re-elected senator from the state of New York. Back to you, Reza."

"Thank you, Suprema. And now we have a projection in Ohio…"

Ray settled the check, left the diner, and stopped at the first payphone. He took out his wallet. He'd been carrying around the number without knowing why. Since then, her picture had appeared on corners all over town. He'd seen her face plastered in bus shelters, on the walls of abandoned buildings, in the tiled corridors of the subway system. Now he knew why he'd ripped it off the telephone pole in the first place. He dialed the number and a gruff, sleepy, uncertain voice answered.

"Who is this?"

Ray wondered that himself.

"Who's calling?"

The voice grew more alert, like a dangerous animal waking up from a long sleep.

"What's this about?"

"It's about Juliet," Ray said, at last.

A long silence. "Oh Christ. Oh Jesus. Who is this?"

"It's about Juliet," Ray said again, and he was crying.

"What about her? Is she okay? Where is she?"

Ray thought a moment about how to answer that. "She's not missing," he said.

"She's been found? Where?"

"She's been abducted."

"Oh Jesus, oh Christ…"

"She's been abducted by aliens."

"Who is this, is this some kind of fucking joke…"

"It's no joked. I'm one of them. I'm an alien. "

"What the hell? Oh Jesus. Please, please just tell me where she is."

"We found her," Ray said. "We took her with us. We thought she was one of us. I hope she wasn't a human being. If so, I'm sorry. I really am…"

"Wait. Don't hang up. Please…"

Ray hung up the phone, feeling numb and empty, and hailed a cab. Tonight, he wasn't wandering around the streets without a destination. Tonight, he had a place to be. He had a party to attend.

"Where to?" the driver asked.

There was only one place on the face of the planet to be tonight.

"Crown Pointe Hotel. On Madison."

The scene at the Crowne Pointe Hotel was pandemonium. The victory party had spilled out onto the street by the time Ray arrived. He wandered into the crowd like a man walking into a lake to drown himself, his old press ID affixed to his coat pocket, smiling, slapping backs all around. There's something cannibalistic about large crowds united by shared mania, and this one gobbled Ray up whole. He was happy to let himself be swallowed, he willingly allowed himself to be pushed down the long throat of bodies towards a door that led to the cavernous belly of the main ballroom. The guards let him passed, didn't recognize him as something indigestible, a poisoned morsel, and soon Ray found himself sloshing around with the roiling crowd inside.

They were all wearing the standard-issue party hats and buttons, but otherwise outfitted in the uniforms of their separate factions, a polyglot army, dressed in tuxedos and workman's overalls, evening gowns and saris, denim and turbans and tie-dye—this was America, and this was America's party, and they'd come to celebrate the victory of America's candidate. Ray circulated among the crowd as best he could, but not much circulation was possible. Over the sound-system, *Happy Days Are Here Again* was blasting and balloons and confetti were suddenly falling from the heavens and someone was shouting to be heard above it all on stage and then the audience erupted into an orgiastic frenzy of adulation.

Ray was just in time. It was the man of the hour, the man of the new century, Haskins himself, looking humble and pre-destined and boyishly earnest and iconic all at the same time. He had his arms raised in victory, in blessing, in thanks for the opportunity to lead them all to salvation. He was smiling and pointing into the boiling crowd beyond the klieg lights that must have been blinding him, pointing as if he could recognize individual faces among that dark anonymous roaring. He was pretending to try to quiet the beast he'd wakened, but only provoking it to roar louder and louder.

This went on for just as long as it was supposed to go on and then the crowd quieted right on cue, that is when the major networks signaled they'd cut live to the ballroom so Haskins could deliver his victory address. Even Ray had to admit it was an inspiring speech, punctuated at regularly scheduled intervals with wild, uncontrollable applause. Ray listened and clapped and cheered along with the others. Apparently, after thousands and thousands of years of human misery, Haskins was announcing that all the problems of the world were about to be solved. There would soon be no more poverty, no more war, no more injustice. Crime was going to disappear, racism was about to become a thing of the past. No one would ever be sick or lonely or hungry or left out on the street ever again. He'd see to it personally. Everyone was going to love everyone. Everyone was going to have everything and no one would be left wanting for anything anymore. No wonder everyone was so deliriously happy, Ray thought. This guy Haskins had all the answers. They were standing at the door to Paradise and Haskins had the key. All that was necessary was to follow him. You just wondered where the hell he'd been all this time, all these thousands of years of pointless human suffering—you just wish he'd gotten here a little sooner.

Ray stood on tiptoe, trying to peer over the bobbing heads of the crowd, peering to the right and left of Haskins, looking among the others, the chosen few, who'd been granted the honor of sharing the stage with the great man, providing background. Sure enough he saw them. There was Rudra, short and round and bearded and brown, grinning like he'd just won a prize, and, not far away, almost invisible, there was Joan, clapping tastefully, a small, self-satisfied

smile pinned to her blank face, and off to the right, only three V.I.P.s
from the Great Man Himself, Ray saw Charlotte, clapping
enthusiastically and beaming adoringly every time the senator paused
to be adored. Her face was glowing, gazing at Haskins as if toward
the sun itself; tonight she looked like the Virgin Mary, only less
otherworldly and with bigger tits, and Ray found himself wondering
if she were fucking the senator, too.

He'd begun to start shouting as he was clapping, shouting from
the back of the dark animal's throat, screaming through its roaring,
and then over it, interrupting the speech of the man who had trained
the beast. Ray was shouting things that were causing the people
beside him to become something separate from him again, something
that was causing a jostling in the crowd, forming a pocket of empty
space around him, a void, singling him out, isolating him. He was
shouting something to Haskins himself, who looked at him briefly,
smiling his charismatic smile, unchanged forever.

The men in the dark suits were coming. Ray saw them. They
were wearing their archetypal dark glasses, each wired with an
earpiece, three huge men, coordinated as one, moving quickly
through the crowd towards Ray like antibodies who'd located a killer
virus.

He didn't try to get away. There would have been no point.
That wasn't the purpose of coming here, anyway. What he wanted
was his fifteen minutes of fame, but he'd have to settle for fifteen
seconds. He was hoping for a chance to tell the truth, even if no one
believed it, even if no one would listen. He just wanted to hear the
words said, said out loud for once, just for the record, since, after all,
everything else but the truth had already been said.

But Ray knew they wouldn't give him a chance. The cameras
weren't on him. They stayed on Haskins, focused, like the crowd, on
his every iconic gesture, his every false, but noble-sounding platitude.
Every camera, like every eye, stayed trained on the future, on the
power, on the lie, *on the hope*...

Ray stood there, alone, hopeless, waiting to be arrested. He was
holding his shirt up, showing the awful livid scar on his abdomen,
and he was screaming.

"What the hell did you do? Tell me the truth you bastards! What the hell did you take from me!"

The men in the black suits were on him in moments. They grabbed him and expertly hustled him out of the ballroom as if he'd never been there at all. Meanwhile, more balloons had started falling and more confetti and the crowd was roaring and, sure enough, *Happy Days Were Here Again.*

Hustling him out a service entrance at the side of the hotel, the security contingent turned Ray over to a couple of waiting uniform cops who in turn raced him, handcuffed, by squad car to the 11th precinct. They took his belt, his jacket, the contents of his pockets, and even his shoes. They didn't photograph him; they didn't fingerprint him; they didn't question him. He didn't seem to be under arrest, not yet, anyway. At least, Ray hadn't heard them charge him with anything. But, then again, Ray had only seen people getting arrested on television, so what did he know about how it really worked?

He expected, for instance, to be put in a holding cell filled with a bunch of punks and drunks and whatever else they'd dredged in off the streets that night. Instead, he sat in his shirttails and socks at a wooden table in an over-air conditioned room that smelled of soured laundry and panic. The small room was made of cinderblocks covered in a thousand coats of thick grey paint. The parrot-faced detective who'd led him down a bewildering array of featureless corridors to this room said nothing except, "Turn around," and when Ray did so, he unlocked the handcuffs. When Ray asked if he was under arrest, if he'd been charged with anything, the detective said, "Sit down. Someone will be with you."

That seemed a long time ago, though Ray couldn't say for certain how long it had been, since they'd taken his watch along with all the rest of his personal belongings. The room was as over-lit as it was over-cold, the chair was uncomfortable, and Ray was alone except for whatever company he had on the other side of the mirror on the wall across from him. He'd seen enough of those same cheesy cop shows on TV to know they were there watching him, waiting for him to show his guilt. Ray tried to avoid what was waiting for him in that mirror: not the people he couldn't see on the other side, but the reflection of the man on his side of it—a man who, from the looks of him and if Ray didn't know any better, he might have mistaken for a lunatic.

When the door behind him finally opened, Ray turned halfway round in the chair, expecting to see the parrot-faced detective again. Instead he saw a bearded man in a dark suit, dark glasses, and earpiece. He sat down opposite Ray, looking through a folder. It took a moment for Ray to recognize him in the unaccustomed costume. The first thing he noticed was that the middle finger on the left hand was missing. When the man put down the folder, he regarded Ray from across the table.

"You're with the secret service?" Ray asked, incredulously, after thirty seconds or so of utter silence.

"Something like that."

Sam-I-Am took off the dark glasses, folded them carefully, as if still getting used to that missing finger, and slipped them into the pocket of his jacket. Then he clasped his hands together and continued to study Ray from across the table without a word.

Ray finally broke the silence once again.

"Do you think I'm an assassin? Is that it?"

Sam raised his eyebrows. "Are you?"

"You should know, shouldn't you?"

"This isn't the time for recklessness, Mr. Pierce. I should think you capable of recognizing that."

Ray laughed. "You know I really must be nuts. I've lost just about everything I can lose. What the hell do I care? What else can you do to me? Kill me? I'm not really all that attached to the future. You of all people should know that. You remember, I guess, the circumstances that brought us together?"

Sam shook his head, sadly. "The common mistake you're making, Mr. Pierce, is to assume that not being afraid to die is any kind of victory. That it frees you in some essential way from the consequences of your actions. I assure you that is not the case. Not having a reason to live only gives you that much less reason to endure the unpleasantness we can bring on you by keeping you alive."

Ray felt whatever courage he might have rallied in the last five minutes drain away, like a stopper pulled from a basin of mucky water. He was sitting in a police station, after all, across the table from a man to whom he'd admitted a host of crimes, including kidnapping and the disposal of a corpse.

"I'd like a lawyer," he said quietly.

"I'm afraid this isn't a lawyer-type situation, Mr. Pierce."

"I don't understand. Have I been arrested? Have I been charged with anything? I have rights."

Sam reached into his jacket and pulled out a slim silver case. He extracted a brown cigarillo, lit it, and blew a cloud of smoke shaped like a man-o-war in Ray's general direction. He placed a second cigarillo on the table in front of him before returning the case to his pocket.

"This isn't the movies, Mr. Pierce. This isn't a story in a novel. You don't need to be charged with anything. You don't need to be read your rights. Out here, in the real world, you don't have any *rights*. Things don't have to be fair. They don't have to make sense. Shit, as I think you've seen, just happens."

Ray felt a cold slice of fear cut right through him, as if he were a peach.

"You've got the wrong man. You know that. I came to you with the truth from the start. I didn't kill that girl and I didn't know she was going to be kidnapped."

Sam shrugged. "The physical evidence points to you, Mr. Pierce. Samples of the girl's hair and skin are in your car and apartment. Your DNA is at the site where her body was found. Your DNA is on her body. Your DNA is *inside* her body."

"And it's at the carriage house, too. Are you forgetting that? That's where she was killed. All anyone would have to do is look."

Sam inspected the lit end of the cigarillo. "But who will?" He looked from the bright burning hole back at Ray, burning a hole through the latter's patched-together calm. "And if they did, I can assure you they'd find nothing. That the place would be clean. We're professionals, after all, Mr. Pierce. Are you?"

Ray stared hard at the grain of wood in the table between his splayed hands: the swirls and whorls looked like the tortured faces of ghosts, like hell captured in the form of a desk where hundreds of the innocent damned had been sent before him. He felt the tears standing in his eyes. He was beginning to understand.

"It's all been some kind of set-up hasn't it? Right from the start?"

"Someone has to pay for that girl's death, don't you agree?"

"And I'm the fall-guy, is that it? But I didn't do it. I didn't kill anyone. It was Haskins and his whole crowd. I'm sure of it. They used Charlotte to draw me in and they're pinning the murder on me. And now you're protecting them. Why?"

"It's my job to protect him. Benjamin Haskins is going to be the next president of the United States."

"Not if he's charged with murder."

"But he won't be."

"How do you know that?"

"Because it's his time. History has chosen him and history cannot be denied. You don't think these things happen accidentally do you?" Sam gave him a curious look. "You don't really think we let—um—votes decide something like that, do you?"

Ray searched Sam's face. His expression was as emotionless as an old leather saddle.

"This is a joke, right?"

"I'm not a comedian, Mr. Pierce."

"A girl dies, I get blamed, and Haskins stands up at that podium and spouts all that humanistic hoo-ha about how much he cares, how he'll help the poor and disadvantaged, how he'll make the world a better place and he's nothing but a sociopath? Is that what you're saying? How can you defend that?"

"I don't defend it. I do my job. Ben Haskins will do a lot of people in this world a lot of good. But everything good demands sacrifice. There's always a price to be paid."

"He's not a presidential candidate. He's a serial killer."

Sam shrugged. "What is a president, anyway? Think about it. A leader has to make difficult decisions, send men off to risk death in order to kill other men, to kill women and children, to level entire cities. The difference, of course, is that a leader follows a higher calling. He doesn't do this for himself alone. If a few people must be offered up to benefit the many, you have to accept that. You have to do what needs to be done, make the necessary sacrifices. It's the way of the world, the way it's always been, and it's the way it will always be. It's the economy of life, Mr. Pierce. You mustn't be childish about it. It's love that impels a man like Benjamin Haskins, not selfishness, and he must be strong to do what he does. He needs great energy to fulfill his responsibilities. We all have a job to do. It's my duty to protect Benjamin Haskins and I do my duty with faith as well as love. Mine is not, ultimately, to reason why."

Ray remembered Charlotte talking about the human sacrifice that fueled ancient societies, how nowadays people forgot how they once lived with such intensity, or only seemed to have forgotten. Deep down, she argued, they still remembered. That's why they were so dissatisfied with the paleness of their jobs, their love-affairs, their lives. He remembered Charlotte talking about all those pretty girls going to waste, in offices, waiting tables, behind sales counters.

"Snuff films, is that it? Ritual sacrifice? You used me to help provide victims for these people's kink? Then you're going to pin the crime on me so no one can follow the trail back to them?"

Sam pinched the burning end of the cigarillo out between his fingers.

"No one's innocent, Mr. Pierce. Love always demands the greatest sacrifice of all. To find love, we must be absolutely ruthless. We must not hesitate to sacrifice others. We do it all the time. Charlotte sacrificed you, you sacrificed Beth, Beth sacrificed you, on it goes, from our first love to our last."

"Beth? How do you know about Beth?"

"Is that really so surprising? We know everything about you."

"So everyone leap-frogs over everyone else. Is this the secret of love you told me about?"

"Part of it, Mr. Pierce. But not the whole part, not the most important part. We'll get to that someday, but this isn't that day."

"But why—why get me involved? Was it all some kind of accident? Was I just at the wrong place at the wrong time?"

"You were warned, Mr. Pierce, weren't you? Right at the beginning. Did I not warn you myself? We are all endowed with free-will, but only up to a point, and then things take their inevitable course. You were given a choice. You chose not to listen. Fact is, we always have some kind of choice; it's just that sometimes the choice is between bad, worse, and worst of all. Even now I am going to offer you a choice. A fighting chance, as they say."

Ray felt a little stab of hope in spite of himself.

"Interested?"

"Yes." Ray had been eyeballing the cigarillo still resting on the desk in front of Sam. Dammit, he'd give practically anything to light up right now. "Yes, I'm very interested."

"Excellent, Mr. Pierce. You see? You've found a reason to live, after all. Congratulations."

Sam handed Ray the cigarillo, pulled out a turquoise-studded silver lighter, and Ray greedily sucked in a chestful of smoke.

"Fact is," Sam continued, "it isn't absolutely necessary for you to go down for this misfortune. To be perfectly honest, it would even pose something of a problem after your stunt tonight. Touché, Mr. Pierce. Don't, however, underestimate our resources or our resolve. You pose an inconvenience, not an impossibility."

Ray glanced over at the mirror, wondering if anyone were watching this exchange, if it were some kind of trick.

"No one's there Mr. Pierce," Sam said. "We're all alone."

Ray's eyes flickered back to the bearded man. "Can I trust you?"

"A truly useless question, don't you think?"

Ray nodded, his fingers fumbling with the cigarillo.

"Truth is, I've grown rather fond of you." Sam-I-Am said, "That's not supposed to happen in my line of work, but" he shrugged, "what can I say? I'm only human. Now I can pull some strings and get you released from here without being charged with anything. Consider it payment for serviced to be rendered. But I can't do much more. The police are focusing their investigation on John Rossi's slaying, they're zeroing in on a suspect. That suspect is you, Mr. Pierce. Consider this a warning. If you've got anything, anything at all that can save you, some ace in the hole you've been holding for the final hand, I'd use it now if I were you. This *is* the final hand. Do you understand?"

"Yes."

"It's time to show your cards, Mr. Pierce. The time for bluffing and bullshitting is over." Sam-I-Am slid his chair back and stood up. "Well, you think about it. And remember, *things change.*"

Ray reconsidered that piece of timeless advice in his current context. He stopped Sam-I-Am on the way to the door. "Just one more question."

"Yes, Mr. Pierce?"

"The wound in my stomach. What did they take out of me? You must know."

Something that resembled a smile flickered on Sam-I-Am's face, but it disappeared so quickly it might have only been a fluctuation in the cold unreality dispensed by the fluorescent lights overhead. "Think about it, Mr. Pierce. Did they take something out of you? Or were they looking for something they didn't find? The question you really should be asking yourself is, did you even have it in the first place?" He opened the door. "Good luck, Mr. Pierce."

They released Ray from custody soon after Sam left the interrogation room. A jovial three-hundred-pound desk sergeant pushed over Ray's personal belongings while joking with a black transvestite hooker, all without so much as a sideways glance. Ray filled his pockets, put on his belt and shoes, and passed through the front door of the 11th precinct an unexpectedly free man.

It was an hour or two past dawn and the streets were already starting to crowd up with people on their way to work. Ray walked up Ninth Avenue and wondered if he were being followed.

He stopped at the Starbucks on the corner of 54th and ordered a cup of coffee and a slice of almond toast. He sat by the window, ate, sipped coffee, and watched the passersby. If they were following

him, they were very good at it. On the stereo system they were
playing what sounded like a Muzak version of *Gimme Shelter*. That
couldn't be true, could it?

Ray thought about Charlotte and wondered if she'd ever really
loved him or if it had been a con all along. He wondered if maybe she
was being forced to go along with this madness just like he was.
Maybe she thought he could save her and lost faith in him
somewhere along the way. It was hard to believe that the look in her
eyes when they fucked was faked, but it was just as hard to believe
her excitement on that stage with Haskins last night was a sham.
They couldn't both be true, could they? No, he'd seen something in
her eyes, something authentic, Ray was sure of it. He was convinced
of Charlotte's deep-down goodness, but she needed help, and
dammit, if he were wrong, he'd pay, but he had to take that chance.
Because if he were right, if she were the One, and he didn't help her,
didn't have faith…

That suggestion of Sam-I-Am's—*if you have an ace in the hole, I'd
use it now if I were you*. Was he sending Ray a message? It was Sam's
duty to protect Ben Haskins, but what if he were no longer duty-
bound to do so? Was that what the man was trying to tell Ray? It was
a devil's bargain, no doubt about it, but it was the only one on the
table, and the devil was the only one still in the game.

Fact was, Ray did have an ace in the hole.

And he was going to play it now.

In the room tonight it was Mara and Samantha and Katie Lynn. Cee
Cee dropped in and then out and then in again. Dammit, Ray
muttered, in the middle of typing out a message, he'd lost track if Cee
Cee was there or not. Ellen was lurking, as usual, not saying a word.
Tammy and Sally were whispering to each other, you could tell by
how they didn't answer anyone in the room, the bitches, you'd think
this was high-school all over again, but then, that was part of their
fantasy, wasn't it? Ray leaned back in his chair and smoked a slow
joint, squinting at the monitor through curtains of smoke.

Kimmi was giving him a blowjob and Burke and Tina were watching. Tina was jealous because she and Ray spent the whole night together last night and she thought they had something "special." That's what she was whispering to Ray the whole time he was trying to concentrate on what he was typing to Kimmi, which was basically a description of how sexy she looked on her knees, handcuffed, in a white lace-up corset and thong.

They were doctors and bricklayers, lawyers and truck drivers. They were pizza delivery guys and customer service reps, computer programmers and sound system engineers and the unemployed of every kind and description.

Deni arrived.

Marcy arrived.

Ray watched Master Adam pounce on Prissy with that same old tired line, "Hey kitten how bout giving daddy a little sissy sugar tnite?" Ray knew it by heart, after all, he'd read it a thousand times by now. But it worked—Prissy was mincing over on big plastic sissy heels and acting all curtsies and coquetteries and yes sirs and no sirs just like flipping a switch.

Lara arrived.

Jenna arrived.

Briana left.

Ray didn't even know Briana had been there. Ellen sent him a private message: *Do you want me to transform you?*

Chrissy left.

Sally left.

That meant Tammy was alone so she finally got around to saying "Hi" to the room.

"Fuck you," Ray muttered, ignoring her.

Ellen sent him another private message: *Do you want me to transform you?*

They were technical writers and warehouse workers, school teachers and corporate VPs. They were husbands with wives sleeping in the next room. They were from America and Canada, England and Australia, they were men you saw on trains and in offices and on the streets everyday and you'd never know.

Ray could tell by how many times she typed "oh…oh…oh.." that he had Kimmi close to orgasm. He scrolled up to see where they were. She was humped over a desk now at work, panties soaking, a black vibrator buzzing away up her nylon-clad ass, and everyone at the office was watching, including her wife and secretary. From now on, she'd be demoted, from branch supervisor to file girl. She'd push a little wire trolley between the desks of her former employees in tight hobble skirts and high heels. His secretary would become his new boss and his old boss would start fucking his wife. It's all been a plot, you see, his wife, who's Ray in the fantasy, explains it all, as if he needs to, since it's the same fantasy every fucking night. "Look at the jiggle in his walk," the office girls, who are also Ray, collectively snigger like a Greek chorus. They give him make-up tips and advice on what color to paint his toenails. These are the fantasies that your investment banker is having or the landscaper or the guy who fills your SUV with gas on your way to work in the morning. These are men who've given up ever finding the woman of their dreams and have decided to become her instead.

Meanwhile, Deni wanted to know if anyone wanted to give her "the full salon treatment," and Marcy abjectly admitted she'd been "a bad bad girl and needed to be punished."

"What r u wearing," Cleo asked Ray, and for the fifteenth time that night, it seemed, Ray typed: red lace panties, garter, matching bra, fishnets and platform sandals.

<cleo> sexxxy ☺

Tina was fuming. She'd apologized, made Ray all kinds of promises, and then she tried to be flirtatious, and he still ignored her. Now she was threatening never to talk to Ray again. He blocked her messages, forcing her to vent her betrayal to the whole room. From the floor between his knees, or over the desk, or wherever the hell she was supposed to be at this point in the proceedings, Kimmi told him how humiliated she felt in front of her former secretary, wife, boss, et al. She wanted Ray to tell her what a slut she was, how the company would rent her out for sex parties to kinky Japanese businessmen. Christ, it really was the same thing every time, right down to the letter, all of it as predictable in its weird way as the liturgy of a Catholic mass. Ray, growing bored, asked the room just for the hell of it, "Did anyone know that despite its hump, a camel has a straight spine?"

Jenna said, Lol

Briana said, Roflmao

Carla said, Huh?

Ellen said she'd give Deni the full salon treatment if she could shave her bald and smear her with excrement. She thought this was being whispered but the whole room could hear. These are the fantasies people have but never talk about. This is what was going on in the head of your waiter, your mailman, your cable guy. This is what it's like to be a human being even though no one will admit it.

Tammy said, Yuck

Lara said, Yucky

Ray looked under the bottle cap of the diet pink lemonade he was drinking and with one hand typed, "The elephant is the only mammal that can't jump."

Jenna said, Lol

Briana said, Yeah, but what is the elephant wearing?

Tina said, TALK TO ME!

Kimmi said, arent u into me anymore? im so cloooose to cumming.

It was almost three am when she arrived and if she came on at all it was usually no later than two. They are auto mechanics and accountants, retirees and race car drivers, cops and professional boxers. Ray had been about to give up since she'd told him she'd meet him no later than midnight. When he saw her name pop up he felt his heart hit another speed. He felt his nerve endings tingle. He felt—

He sat up straight in his chair. He finished Kimmi off quickly by having his wife decide he'd make a good housemaid to her and her new hubby after castration and breast implants. He typed " and you cum helplessly like the little sissy slut u r." Then Ray scrolled up to where he saw her enter the room.

<sindy arrrives> Sorry I'm late

<charlotte> its ok
<sindy> reddy 2 play luv?
<charlotte> alwys mistrss
<sindy> gd ☺
<sindy> hm, wht will it b tnite?
<sindy> fistfuck?
<sindy> biting?
<sindy> garrote?
<charlotte? How bout 2-nite we just discss jhn rssi?

Ray was in a bar called The Boot Heel, west of the West Village, south of Canal, way south of everything, where the neighborhood took on that generic bombed-out look it did anywhere the money had long fled. He was drinking a gin-tonic and watching a game of nine-ball winding down on one of the billiard tables across the room. Downstairs, in the basement, were the sandpits and the harnesses, the crosses and cages, the pincers and the blindfolds and the whips of glistening leather. It was that kind of place. From the back rooms the sharp sounds of smacked meat and the grunt and moans of impossible desires drifted through a black-curtained doorway whenever there was a natural trough in the high tide of music pouring from the DJ cage, which wasn't often. Up front, where Ray sat drinking, the men passed the time between assignations, negotiated, rested up, posed, re-loaded.

Of the two guys playing pool, the one who looked a little less like Christian Bale, called his shot, leaned over the table, and sank the seven-ball. He chalked his cue and eyed the resulting geometry, planning his next shot. A tall man in a boxy grey suit leaned in next to Ray and asked him if he had a light.

Ray made a show of patting his pockets, shrugged, made an exaggerated frowny-face. "No," he said, "sorry."

"It's okay love." The man even shouted with a cultured British accent. "I've found my torch, after all."

He had a thick grey brush-cut and handsome rugged features. He reminded Ray of those guys you see in a glossy Sunday *Times* flyer modeling designer underwear for Father's Day sales. Beneath the expensive suit, Ray detected braided muscle and a tense kind of power that was all idle potential, like a bear trap. He looked to be about sixty or so, even with that flawlessly sculpted body, and Ray wondered how it was that there was no cheating that fact. He thought he'd read somewhere once that it's something in the eyes that give one's age away, some diminishment of light, perhaps, which made perfect sense. Maybe there was a Snapple bottle cap somewhere that explained it.

"Did you know," Ray said, at a loss, "that the ant can lift fifty times its own weight?"

"I've seen you here before," the man said, as if he hadn't heard Ray, and maybe he hadn't. "I always wanted to say hello." He held out a sinewy, but well-manicured hand. "The name's Jeremy, pleased to meet you."

Ray took it, doing a quick scan of the bar. She wasn't here yet. Was she going to stand him up?

"You're not gay, are you?"

"No, not really," Ray said. "How can you tell?"

He shrugged. "Hard to say exactly. You learn to distinguish. Let me tell you, it can all too often be a matter of survival, love. You collect a lot of broken noses otherwise."

"I suppose so."

Jeremy's gaze was amused, curious, interested. "So what are you doing here, if I may be so bold to ask, not to mention risk a broken nose."

Ray shrugged. "Looking for someone."

"Hmm, aren't we all. Anyone special?"

"I'll know when I see him."

It was subtle, the look of disappointment on his face. You could almost have missed it if you weren't paying attention, and Ray wasn't.

"Oh well," he lisped, "you never know. Sometimes if you don't find what you're looking for everywhere else, you find it right under your nose."

What Ray was really doing in The Boot Heel was playing his ace in the hole. John Rossi's transvestite lover, aka Sindy, should be somewhere in this bar, meeting him tonight. After a week of increasingly kinky computer sex, Ray revealed his identity and Rossi's referral and that's how he'd learned of Rossi's kink and his relationship with Sindy. When Ray revealed that he'd been the one entrusted with the email after Rossi's murder he established his credentials and Sindy agreed to the face-to-face meet. Sindy had the secret that had gotten Charlotte's husband murdered and she would be eager to avenge his lover's death by providing the proof that would bring the senator and his crowd down. Ray didn't give a damn whether Haskins became president or not. He had no interest in altering the course of world history; he just wanted the leverage to buy Charlotte out of their clutches—that and some millions to enjoy the rest of his life with her in whatever tropical corner of the world they decided to pitch their twisted paradise. Ray scanned the simmering crowd of cruising men. So where the hell was s/he?

Jeremy bought Ray a drink in the meantime. The music had let up a little, enough to allow the semblance of a conversation. He was a mathematics professor at Columbia and coached the wrestling team, or used to. He was an ex-wrestler himself, he told Ray, and still tried to keep in shape. He told Ray this as if fishing for a compliment, which Ray dutifully, if distractedly, fed him. Jeremy smiled, gratified. He told Ray it was one of his student wrestlers at one of the finer boarding schools back in England who broke his heart. There had been a bit of a scandal, a hush-hush dismissal, no formal charges, you understand, but nonetheless it had still been necessary to pursue his profession across the Atlantic, and at an educational level where all the lads were above the age of consent. His story of unrequited love, taking out the overtones of pedophilia, of course, was a tragic romance like any other, almost archetypal, but unless it was your story, Ray reflected, somehow it just didn't quite translate. You just couldn't feel the pain of it.

"Are you sure your friend is coming, love?"

"I'm not sure of anything," Ray said.

He looked at the man closely, wondering, could it be him? Jeremy was thumbing his lighter on-off, on-off, and Ray realized that the man didn't want it to light a cigarette. He was using it to signal something to Ray, but Ray didn't understand whatever code it was supposed to be. At last Jeremy pulled up the sleeve of his jacket to show Ray a forearm full of shiny pink scars resembling doll's flesh.

"What do you say, love?" He slid the lighter six inches across the bar in front of Ray. "Do you fancy hurting an old queen? Making him pay for the sins of his past? It's the only way it feels better."

Yes, Ray thought, isn't that the truth.

The music was suddenly louder, or so it seemed, and Ray realized that Jeremy had squared off against him, like he'd executed some kind of slick wrestling move Ray hadn't seen coming, so that Ray's back was pressed against the bar. Everything seemed to be moving in slow-motion, as if the music had been a tidal wave that had finally arrived and flooded the bar and smashed everything to bits of haphazard wreckage floating on endless miles of meaningless noise. Jeremy had edged the cuff of Ray's coat sleeve over his wrist and was lightly stroking the naked skin of his arm. He looked like he was going to lean forward and kiss him.

Ray said, "Did you know that only male turkeys gobble?"

Jeremy looked perplexed, as if he'd misheard, smiled and shouted, "Oh love, how charming" and that's when, over his shoulder Ray saw her approaching.

"That's her," he shouted back, feeling a moment of confused panic. "The one I'm looking for. She's here."

"Who?" Jeremy said and turned to take a look. "Oh," he said, with a little gasp. "Oh...I'll leave you to it then," and he obediently dissolved into the background, just like everything else.

She was huge—tall and bull-necked—her hulking shoulders and body-builders torso, pumped and vein-laced, barely contained in a red mesh tank-top and a pair of faded denim cut-offs that stretched just shorter and tighter than anything masculine. Ray was surprised at just how big she was, unnaturally big, even though she'd told him. Flesh, he thought, is always something of a shock, especially when you've been playing around in your imagination. Shocking, too, was the fact that Ray recognized him, just as Sindy assured him that he would. And now Ray realized why. Sindy was at the Crowne Pointe hotel the night of Haskins victory party. Only he'd been dressed differently. At the time he'd been wearing a black suit, black shades, and an earpiece. He was one of the secret service bodyguards who'd dragged Ray out of the ballroom.

Ray saw how the other men in the bar naturally moved aside as she approached, mincing across the floor on her wedge-heeled slides. He looked up into her broad, brutal, made-up face. She towered over him, and would have, even without the corked heels; the sheer massive width of her blocked the view of the exit and anything else behind her.

For his part, Ray had kept himself as anonymous as possible during their internet sessions. No pictures, no real names, no incriminating personal details. Just in case he changed his mind, in case he got a bad vibe about meeting her, which he was beginning to get now.

"You remember me?"

"How could I forget?" Her voice was much higher and more feminine than you'd expect coming from such a huge, steroid-inflated body. Sindy could see his surprise. "On the phone," she acknowledged, "everyone thinks I'm a girl."

Ray took a long protective swallow of his gin-tonic. Sindy was drinking a diet Pepsi because she didn't drink or smoke. She was a fitness nut, a former kick-boxer, and All-American football star before becoming a bodyguard for a presidential serial killer.

"You look just like him, you know. I'd have recognized you anywhere."

"Like who?"

"Jacqui, of course."

By Jacqui, he meant John Rossi, the name Charlotte's husband used when he was dressed in mini-skirts and platform sandals, in fishnet body stockings, in babydoll nighties and pretending to be a girl with a death-fetish.

"Relax," Sindy said. "You'll be fine. I have a sixth sense about these kinds of things."

She squeezed his upper arm, putting her entire huge hand around it with room to spare, and Ray felt goose-bumps break out over every inch of his flesh like the black plague.

Ray noted the big yoke of muscle that ran from the shoulder up the side of Sindy's neck and down the other side again. It clenched and tightened every time she laughed. Ray tried not to look too closely at the ropy veins corded through her thickly muscled arms or at her thick hands and strong blunt man fingers. He tried to imagine her as the leather-clad bitch goddess of John Rossi and other men's fantasies—the erotic destroyer these men could never find in real life. Sindy impersonated Her to finance her dream of one day becoming a real girl, a dream equally improbable, but which Ray promised to help her attain in exchange for the information Sindy would provide that Ray in turn would use to blackmail Haskins. Ray was going to help Sindy get the money to become what she wanted, as if she could ever become what she wanted. As if anyone could.

What seemed possible in the realm of fantasy suddenly seemed just as grotesque as it really was now that it was standing before him in the sweating flesh. Looking at Sindy now, Ray realized what a prison meat was, how it bore no resemblance to who we really were as it expressed itself in the shape of our desires. He felt a moment of vast sadness and tenderness for Sindy and for everyone else, but it was fleeting; it was time for sex and blackmail.

"So," Ray said, glancing down and to the side when Sindy stepped closer, overwhelming his personal space and holding both his arms now. He really had to tilt his head back far to see her eye to eye. He was reminded, with a little shock, of Charlotte's trademark flirty gesture. "Where would you like to do this?"

"There's, like, a place I go close by," Sindy said in his bizarre, gum-cracking, high-pitched valley girl voice. "It's got, like, everything us girls need."

Ray nodded. But first he ordered another drink and for all he
knew, a couple of others after that, because his memory of this part
of the evening was noticeably missing a few relevant details that
never quite came all the way back. Maybe it was better not to
remember it all anyway, like being given a powerful anesthetic to
spare one the intolerable pain of a major operation until the worst of
it was over and you could manage to suffer through what remained.
As it was, what Ray did end up remembering was almost too painful
to bear.

Almost.

That being the essential thing.

Because it's what keeps any of us suffering at all.

They ended up in a small filthy room with a bare mattress on the
floor. That's all Ray remembered of it, the room, that is. There was
no light, debris underfoot, crushed paper cups, empty bottles, fast
food wrappers and such. Ray heard lots of sidewalk noise floating up,
and Chinese voices from the lower floors as if burbling up from
unimaginable creatures far underwater. Later, he learned that the
room was in a flophouse on the Chinatown side of Mulberry street.
He was quite drunk by the time they made it to the room, staggering
really, and needed Sindy's big hand clamped around his bicep to
guide him. He was surprised that Sindy could do this cold-sober,
despite what she said about not drinking, but then he kept forgetting
that this wasn't her first time.

"Awww," she cooed from the floor as she removed Ray's
shoes, "you have such pwetty widdle feet."

Ray looked down, nearly passing out in the process. His arms
were already pulled sharply behind him and his wrists and elbows
lashed together with knotted scarves. His chest and stomach were
covered with fresh bite marks. He was wearing a pair of red lace
panties, nothing else. Sindy rose abruptly from the floor and hit Ray
across the mouth with her thick forearm. Ray felt the lower part of
his face go all crunchy and the blood sluiced liberally down his throat
like some kind of horror-movie smoothie that caused him to start

desperately gulping. He found himself suddenly lying on the floor, his one good eye at dust-level.

Sindy was wearing what looked like a PVC jumpsuit and women's platform fetish boots. She had a long blonde wig on her head. She had changed into this outfit a few minutes before while Ray sat on the mattress and smoked a joint. The jumpsuit had cut-outs for her steroid-pumped tits. She was supposed to look like Jennifer Lopez and Ray, of course, was supposed to be Charlotte. He remembered all that now, the absurdity of it, as Sindy grabbed the back of his neck and slammed his forehead against the floor repeatedly, at least four or five times, before Ray passed out. Helpless with Sindy's powerful hand clamped to the back of his neck, Ray had found himself counting the times his forehead slammed into the wood, wondering, almost objectively, how many times a human head could be smashed like that before it would be rendered a senseless and irreparable pulp.

When he came back to the world, Ray was on his back and trying to spit out hard things that he realized were his teeth. He found that he couldn't breathe properly. But he wasn't overly alarmed. It was like he was only half-watching a movie about someone he didn't care about all that much.

Ray had made a huge miscalculation, that much he understood from Sindy's monologue in the early going of this encounter, largely incomprehensible, fueled as it was by sex, grief, and rage. But the general drift of it he got. He was being beaten to a smear because Sindy believed that Ray had murdered John Rossi. He understood at least that much. Ray didn't know where Sindy had gotten that crazy idea, and it didn't really matter, but he supposed it had something to do with that fucking email Rossi had sent him. Ray wasn't going to get the chance to ask any questions or to convince Sindy of his innocence before being beaten to death, that much was clear. What a ridiculous way to die, Ray thought, as Sindy stood over him, kicking him over and over again with her heavy platform fetish boots. But then, what death didn't carry its own unique and inescapable humiliations? What death wasn't a rape?

There were catastrophic explosions of pain all throughout Ray's body, as if hidden grenades of hurt were exploding inside him, shattering bones and rupturing vital organs. Ray passed out repeatedly and whenever he came around he was too stunned to do much of anything. At some point, Sindy had pressed a knee into the small of his back and slipped an imitation Louis Vuitton scarf around his throat. Ray knew it was an imitation Louis Vuitton scarf because that's what was found embedded around the throat of his semi-conscious body much later on and, even more to the point, that's how he and Sindy always scripted it out during their online fantasies.

The whole sordid affair was nearing its climax, and that meant Sindy was inside him now, riding Ray like a calf, twisting the noose around his throat and thrusting and tearing the tissues of Ray's rectum, as Ray sputtered helplessly and strangled and drooled a bloody goatee. And Sindy hadn't forgotten her lines either, struggling to maintain her high-pitched falsetto, but just as often lapsing into the hate-filled growl of a psychotic Marine raping a third-world villager, "You know you want it, you know you want it, you know you want it" over and over like the soundtrack of a pop single in Hell. Grunting and groaning, Sindy was saying this, as she twisted the scarf tighter and tighter around Ray's throat, squeezing off his air, as his weakening fingers tried to pry the material that had become almost meshed with the fibers of his flesh. Or maybe Sindy said this earlier, right before she broke Ray's left arm in four places and shattered his left hip to powder as he half-consciously tried to scramble out of the room. Or maybe it was when he hopelessly tried to fight his way from under her bulk, his head crammed between her damp muscular thighs, face pressed to her foul-smelling crotch, as she humped his bleeding fractured mouth, nearly choking him to death on the first of his oily rank ejaculations. When he tried to pull away, Sindy had wrenched his head back so violently that at first the doctors feared Ray would never regain the ability to walk unassisted, even with the aid of crutches and special space-age aluminum braces.

Later, Ray, would-be suicide that he was, recalled with despair how he struggled for his life the entire time during this ordeal, but not because he wasn't ready to die. Not really. Betrayed by his body and its instincts, he struggled, it seemed to him, out of sheer habit, because living was all he'd done up to that point and all he knew how to do. It disappointed him. His body had its own violent addiction for survival apart from Ray's will and it jerked and arched and kicked and spat and shat itself with a ferocity that made him ashamed and his body continued to do this even long after Ray himself made the conscious decision to give up. At that point, he'd watched the unseemly struggle from a remote place inside his dying mind, rooting for the nightmare death-girl that Sindy embodied to break his untoward addiction to life once and for all.

There were gold flecks swimming behind Ray's eyes and his tongue seemed to have inflated like a pink raft, blocking his airway. There was a great roar inside each of his ears like two black trains racing toward each other and when they collided somewhere in the eternal midnight at the center of his brain, Ray understood that would be that. He would die. Ray found himself trying to calculate the moment when death would finally arrive, like one of those mathematical word problems, but it was too complicated to solve in his current brain-starved state, if train x left the station at two pm going seventy-six- miles-per-hour and train y, etc.

This wasn't the way he thought it would end. But if this is what Ray wanted now, it was because Charlotte herself wouldn't love him and wouldn't kill him. He wanted this death precisely because it was so squalid and grotesque. He didn't want to *just* die, that's what must be understood, if this can be understood at all. Death wasn't enough. Suicide wasn't enough. Ray wanted to be annihilated in an act of murderous rage and humiliating perversion that would obliterate every last trace of what he'd been and what he'd hoped from the world. He didn't just hate himself, but life itself, the emptiness and pointlessness and betrayal of it all. He hated the disappointing deficiency of it. He hated the world because he could imagine something much better and the world that existed, that he'd been compelled to live in, would never live up to it. If he hated God, or the very idea of God, it was because Ray truly believed that he could have done so much better. He hated people for much the same reason. In the end, he believed in those characters in the books and movies—the one's who love truly and died nobly—more than he believed in real people. They were certainly better than real people. Ray killed himself because he couldn't kill the world and everyone in it. Because the world was a malignancy that couldn't be cured, or stopped, because it would just go on betraying and beating and killing us all. Dying the way he was in this rotten room was a rejection of it all. It was an obscene joke. It was like taking a shit on life itself.

His last memory was of his body finally giving up the fight. He was conscious of meekly going through the last pale motions of protest. Just a formality, it seemed, at the very end. Death always wins. Death always fucks you up the ass. He could hear Sindy still whining and grunting and slobbering above him like a sick animal. A revelation flickered in Ray's oxygen-starved brain like a fading flair that illuminated nothing. Life and death and everything in between was all summed up here: in this sick desperate coupling.

Ray was far-off by then, displaced, watching the two bodies fucking on the floor like they were gas clouds in outer-space. And then his mind suddenly cleared for one terrifying instant. The cliché is that your whole life flashes before you right before extinction. But Ray had only one final panicked thought before his brain exploded to black and it was so helpless, hopeless, and impossibly sad that it alone would have been hell entire had it lasted any longer than a dying moment: he wanted to call Charlotte one last time before he died. He wanted to tell her that, in spite of everything, he loved her.

Five days passed—five days of his life that Ray would never get back, not that he'd want them back, days of being fed by tubes, breathed by tubes, drained by tubes, a slab of bruised meat. You could almost say that Ray was dead those days, although, technically, he wasn't even in a coma, or anything approaching one. He was only heavily medicated to the point of oblivion. He remembered nothing of those days: the whole time would always remain a total blank, a caesura in his chronology. He was at Beth Israel Hospital when he woke up, or maybe it was St. Luke. He kept telling himself to ask, but never did, and, really, what difference did it make? He'd been moved from one or the other after being raced by ambulance to some other place altogether for emergency care.

He was found by an old Chinese man who'd gone up to the room to smoke dope or do tai chi exercises or, most likely, to scavenge for whatever the two queer tuna-eyes who'd rented the room may have left behind. That's how the story went, anyway. Ray was lying on the floor covered in blood and filth, looking quite dead. The extended Chinese family who owned the building debated among themselves for the better part of two days whether to get involved or leave Ray on a park bench somewhere; in the meantime, they applied herbal poultices, spooned tea into him, and poked at him with acupuncture needles. When Ray didn't die, they cleaned him up, and called the police. Their efforts had either saved his life, or increased his risk of brain damage, only time would tell.

These were the details that Ray didn't remember, the blanks that had to be filled in, or not, and they didn't seem as important to him as they did to everyone else. He didn't panic when he regained consciousness like they thought he would. One of the things Ray did remember was telling himself that if he woke up at all, he'd wake up more or less the way he did: in dramatically bad shape. He was expecting the immobilizing restraints, the monitors, the over-bright lights, the tubes and needles, and the dull, ever-present pain everywhere. He was expecting all the uncomprehending faces like a visiting congress from another planet.

He'd been severely beaten, obviously, and it would require far too long a list to enumerate all of his various injuries and breakages, but among those of most immediate concern were the shattered jaw, the pulverized hip, the crushed eye sockets, the smashed ribs and splintered vertebrae. There was the severe bruising of his liver, kidneys, and pancreas, the rupture of his spleen, the puncturing of his right lung and the pericardial sac around his heart. There were the multiple concussions and the ominously spreading bruise that shadowed his brain. There was the missing kneecap.

He was lucky, if Ray heard that ludicrous assessment once, he'd heard it a million times already, to even be alive. He was told, almost the moment he woke, that he'd been given a blood test for AIDS and a whole army of other venereal diseases. So far, he was in the clear. They told him this with great gravity, as if the news were supposed to relieve him, or were of any great concern to him at all. He learned that it literally hurt to blink, to breathe, to live.

The police came and went, came and went, like clouds in the sky.

Ray found it convenient that his jaw was wired shut. In his condition, he couldn't reasonably be expected to answer their tiresome questions. They tried to work out a rudimentary signal system by which he'd communicate by tapping a finger, one tap for "yes," two for "no," or vice versa, Ray could never remember, but it hardly mattered, he generally feigned sleepiness or confusion or whatever.

There was a wet crunching sound in his left ear as if he were always eating cornflakes. It tended to render any sounds coming from the outside world unintelligible. But when were they anything but? Ray kept his own counsel and decided almost immediately to tell the detectives that he remembered absolutely nothing about the attack, and that was mostly true, although he thought he could tell them what they wanted to know most of all, if he really cared to. They wanted to catch who'd done this to him, but to Ray's way of thinking, they were really missing the point.

Beth visited, of course. Every goddamn day. She sat by Ray's bed and looked up at the television which always seemed to be playing, sometimes with the volume up, sometimes mute, but always showing something, twenty-four-hours-a-day. Beth often put her hand over his uncrushed one and talked about stuff that happened at work, the weather, the news, whatever inane show happened to be on TV and Ray couldn't move. He often pretended to be asleep just to get her to shut the fuck up, but it seldom worked.

At lunch-time, she usually brought Ray a Snapple and, at his request, read him the bottle cap. He didn't mind hearing her say things like, "about 18% of animal owners share their beds with their pets" or "the first ballpoint pen was sold in 1945 for twelve dollars."

That's pretty much how it went for days and days and days as he slowly healed. He started taking physical therapy. He sipped apple juice from a box in the day room. He looked at magazines. He watched reruns and talk shows and E! Hollywood stories of celebrities and so many of them looked like Charlotte, laughed like Charlotte, talked like Charlotte that Ray began to wonder if she were just a figment of his imagination.

Sometimes it seemed to Ray as if the whole affair had been a movie he'd seen or a book he'd read or that one of the shows that were always on TV had somehow seeped into his unconscious as he slept and taken on a reality of its own. The doctors had warned him of something like this. They told him that after a severe head trauma such as the one he'd suffered there might be some lapses, some gaps, some ghosts in the machine. His thoughts ran in a closed loop, the same thing over and over. It may not have really happened, but, in his mind anyway, his affair with Charlotte was more real than life itself.

One afternoon, Beth leaned over to whisper into his ear that he had a visitor. She'd been watching a Jason Bourne marathon on TV: six straight hours of Matt Damon. Ray could have sworn she was watching it out of spite, but maybe the head trauma had just made him paranoid. Ray didn't get many visitors. He hadn't wanted any. He didn't want any now. Without opening his eyes, he mumbled through the wires still holding the bottom of his face together.

"Who is it?"

Beth whispered conspiratorially. "I think it's the cops again."

Ray sighed. He figured he'd pretend to be dozing, or doped, or deaf, the usual. Ray was used to the cops by now. They weren't very patient and they weren't too smart but this one turned out to be different. Before Ray could even answer her, Beth was already on her way out of the room to show the man in and Ray simply closed his eyes and waited for the inevitable. He had laid there and waited and waited and waited and kept his eyes closed. Ray could sense the cop just sitting there, watching him—watching and watching and watching, like he could sit there for centuries. At first, Ray figured his visitor would give up after a while, conclude Ray was unconscious, and just go away like all the others. But the cop didn't go anywhere and didn't try to ask any questions. In the end, it was Ray who gave up and opened his eyes and wasn't too surprised to see Sam-I-Am.

"So Mr. Pierce," he said, "they tell me you'll live."

Ray forced the words through his bruised face. "I can only hope they're lying to make me feel better."

The black suit, shades, and ear-piece were gone: the whole Secret Service schtick had been stashed. Sam was wearing a dark sweatshirt, jeans, and the brown leather jacket that looked like it had been through a thousand adventures. His hair, usually pulled back in a grizzled ponytail, was hanging free, draped around his broad shoulders. His slouch hat was sitting on the nightstand.

He cocked an eyebrow. "You don't seem that glad to see me."

"I don't think I like green eggs and ham, Sam-I-Am."

Sam reached into his jacket and pulled out a cigarillo. He fired it up. There was, apparently, no place in the city they could forbid him to smoke. "Very good Mr. Pierce," he said from behind a veil of bluish smog. "They can break your bones, your dignity, your spirit…even your hope. But a sense of humor cannot be broken."

Ray looked pointedly at the smoke. "Can I have one?"

Sam examined the burning cigarillo between his thumb and finger-stump. "Sorry. It's against the law. Besides, these things will kill you. Don't you read those warnings we put on all the packages?"

Ray did something that was supposed to be a laugh, except it hurt. When he stopped doing it, he asked: "What the hell happened? Why did that freak think I killed Rossi?"

"Rossi told him that you did."

Ray closed his eyes and let the nausea pass. He opened them again. It hadn't passed.

"They tell me I've got some kind of unspecified brain damage. Is that why I'm not following?"

"Rossi told you he'd send an email if something happened to him, right? Well, something did happen. He was killed and the email went to you. And that email told you to contact Sindy. You see, Rossi was convinced you were the one sent to kill him and, of course, you were fucking his wife. So he figured to kill two birds with stone. He'd get his revenge against you from beyond the grave."

Ray discovered that if he squinted out of one eye his head hurt a little less. "You knew, didn't you?"

"It's my job to know these things, Mr. Pierce. And to find out the things I don't. What I didn't know was the identity of John Rossi's source inside the senator's inner circle. I had to smoke that person out. So Rossi was liquidated, ironically enough, to find the man who was protecting him. The email was sent and you met the mystery woman, so to speak. *Voila.* We met 'her,' too. One of the senator's own bodyguards." Sam shook his head. "Love makes a man do strange things."

"You were at the bar?"

"One of my people. Jeremy."

Ray stared blankly.

"The man who tried to pick you up," Sam said.

A dim memory of the good-looking Brit floated back about halfway to Ray, just close enough.

"Yes, I remember. So he didn't really find me captivating after all? Jeez, to add insult to injury. And now, just look at me."

Sam reached down and tapped the ash from his cigarillo into the bedpan at his feet. "Yeah, sorry about the beating and the rape. We didn't really mean for that to happen. Well, not to that extent anyway. We had to wait long enough to make sure Sindy was of no further intelligence value. I assure you we moved in as soon as feasible."

"You killed her?"

"We chatted first…and then, well, let's say we made a contribution to the fertility of our heartland's depleted soil. We mustn't suffer traitors, Mr. Pierce."

"And what if there is still someone out there who knows the truth?"

"Then we always have you to pin everything on."

"Is that why you've let me live…" Ray tried to wiggle up in the bed; it was a painful mistake, not to mention pointless. "Hey, what the hell are you doing. What is that?"

Sam had reached into his jacket and pulled out a black leather case which he unzipped to reveal a shooter's works: syringe, rubber tube, and a bottle with a greasy amber residue.

"Just something to help you relax Mr. Pierce."

Ray stared at Sam-I-Am with utter disbelief. "Are you going to kill me *now*? After all this?"

Ray thought of reaching for the button by his working hand. The button that would alert the nurse, but something held him back, some sense of the essential uselessness of such a gesture.

Sam nodded, acknowledging Ray's good sense. "If I were going to kill you, I'd have dismissed the nurses or simply disconnected the alarm. I really don't need the drama right now. Calm down, Mr. Pierce."

The syringe prepped, he lay it on the table and tightly tied off Ray's unresisting arm around the right bicep with the rubber tube. He thumped at a promising vein. The injection went in nice and slow, like a waltz at Christmas or something. Sam sat back down and Ray didn't feel any different than he did before. He kept waiting for something to happen but when nothing did he finally said, "So?"

Sam scraped his chair closer to the bed, smoked a while in silence, and then said this: "Remember I told you that when the time was right, I'd tell you what love is really all about?"

Ray nodded, as far as his neck brace and steel halo allowed. It was less a nod, really, than a tripling of his chin. That hurt, too.

"Well, Mr. Pierce. That time is now." Sam-I-Am finished the cigarillo, crushing it out in a malignantly ugly flower arrangement sent by his old colleagues at *AdBiz*. Beth had recognized the flowers: "Bird-of-Paradise," she'd told him. "It's probably not a true story," Sam shrugged, "but it sums things up better than any true story. Lies are always better at telling the truth. Fiction tells us what the truth *felt* like—which often doesn't follow from what happened—but ends up closer to reality all the same. That's why we tell stories in the end."

Sam looked up at the TV where Matt Damon was running away from another explosion. He picked up the remote Beth had left out of Ray's reach on the night stand. He waved it in the direction of the TV.

"Do you mind?"

"Please."

Sam extinguished the TV. "Don't know what it is. But something about that guy really gives me the jeepers-creepers." He put the remote down. "Did your parents ever tell you stories when they put you to bed at night, Mr. Pierce? Probably, right? Well, the story I'm going to tell you now is like a fairy tale. That's how I'd like you to consider it. It's the fairy tale they should have told you instead of filling your head with all the useless bullshit they filled it with. Now close your eyes and try to relax, while I tell you the true story of love."

Ray found his eyes already slowly closing, almost in spite of himself, the injected sedative, probably, he told himself. He heard Sam scratch another match, light another cigarillo.

"When Josef Stalin was on his death-bed," Sam began, improbably enough, pausing to shake the flame off the match, "he summoned the two men in line to succeed him for one final test. To each he handed a bird and asked them to imagine it were the Russian people. 'Show me,' he said, 'how you'd earn their love and devotion.' The first man, afraid the bird would fly away, clutched it so tightly that he instantly crushed it to a pulp."

Sam paused for a while, smoking. In the peaceful quiet, Ray heard the humming and beeping of the machines monitoring his life. After a time, Sam resumed, his voice soothing, almost hypnotic.

"The second man, seeing his rival's mistake and determined not to repeat it, loosened his hand too much and the bird escaped his grasp and flew out a nearby window. Disgusted, Stalin spat out one of those uniquely Russian curses and called to his bodyguard for one last bird. This one Stalin held himself and slowly, methodically, plucked out all its feathers, one by one. 'There,' he said when he was done. He showed the two men the naked bird cowering in his open hand. 'And he is even grateful for the human warmth coming from my palm.' You see, Mr. Pierce," Sam said, letting a few moments pass for the story to sink in. "Love isn't for sissies. Love isn't for the faint of heart. What they told you is all wrong. Love is for the wolf, not the lamb. You've got to be ruthless. You've got to be merciless. To love someone, you've got to be cruel, you've got to be *hardcore*."

Ray slowly opened his eyes. Sam was standing over him now, looking down, and the look on the older man's face was almost...*wistful*.

"Will I ever see her again?" Ray mumbled, slipping towards the twilight of oblivion.

It was the only question left to ask. The only question ever.

Sam leant over the pillow and kissed Ray flush on his broken mouth. When he straightened up again, Ray wondered whose lipstick he was tasting.

"That Mr. Pierce," he said, "depends entirely on you. Sweet dreams."

--compiled from the last entries of the online blog Cruelty, attributed to Raymond Henry Pierce, currently #3 on the FBI's Most Wanted list for questioning in connection with the suspected murder and/or kidnapping of seventeen missing women

It's Beth who pushes my wheelchair out the front door of the hospital when it's time for me to go home almost fourteen months later. It's one of those really sunny, but still chilly days, a Monday, I think. We're going to her place: that's where I'll be staying for the foreseeable future, since I'm compelled to have one. I'm wearing black drawstring pants cut up the side to accommodate the thick soft cast on my fractured left leg, which is still supposedly mending, or maybe it's the ruptured Achilles heel that's mending, so much is mending, I haven't bothered to ask.

Beth, by the way, seems very happy, very excited, almost in a sexual sense, to be pushing my wheelchair. She's rented a suburban minivan, just like a real-life soccer mom, to drive me to her new uptown apartment. When we get there, I see she's made all kinds of various adjustments to the place during the last few months to accommodate my current state of decrepitude. She claims she told me all this back at the hospital as I lay recuperating, but if she did, I was probably either unconscious or I wasn't paying attention.

She wheels me around the place, pointing out the ramps between the rooms, the special light switches, and hands-free phones, stuff like that. There's a couple of handles bolted to the walls by the bathtub so I don't drown, and two more on either side of the toilet, so I can get up all by myself without breaking my neck after I take a shit. Just the thought of my new life as it's laid out in this handicap playground is enough to make me need the toilet. I tell Beth I want to take a leak and she looks crushed when I turn down her offer for help.

Weeks pass. I take lots and lots of painkillers, pretending to be in pain so that I can feel nothing at all. I watch lots of TV: Britney still loves Justin, J.Lo doesn't love Mark, Bruce wants Demi back. Brad and Angelina are together, no they're not, yes they are, no they aren't. No one seems to know anything for sure. The best part of the day is when Beth is at work and I have the place to myself. She's set up a work-station in the corner of the living room but I don't do anything there except cruise the internet for porn, sports scores, porn, and Google hits for Charlotte.

They want me back at AdBiz when I feel up to it. My old boss contacted me in the hospital—a rethink in the publisher's office has dictated a new editorial direction, they always liked my work, etc etc. Interpretation: someone's ass is on the line and they want a possible fall-guy. I don't think I'll be feeling up to it any time soon. I still have the office get-well card they sent along with that cancerous flower arrangement. I think I remember signing one exactly like it last year for some nitwit in accounts payable who managed to contract lymphoma. The card has a drawing of a sniffling apple with a thermometer sticking out of its mouth. What does Human Resources do? Buy them in bulk for croaking employees? Of all the questions I've been asked, the one I've grown most tired of hearing is, "Boy I'll bet you're glad to be alive."

Usually, in the afternoons, when she hasn't got a lunch-meeting, Beth comes home and we have lunch together. I prefer it when she brings back sandwiches from Cosi's. On the weekends, we take strolls through Central Park. Beth pushes me in my wheelchair among the budding trees. She parks me in front of a lake or meadow. She lays a blanket on my lap. It's really quite idyllic. She seems almost proud of me, like I'm her child, or some kind of trophy. Did I mention that she's having an affair?

..............*for weeks now, the doctor's been insisting that there's no physical reason for me not to be walking on my own. His nagging has gotten to be so relentlessly aggressive and insulting—and now there's some threats regarding the insurance coverage—that I've finally relented and consented to use the pair of special aluminum crutches the physical therapist has supplied and when I get tired, a walker. Beth seems as disappointed as I am. She insists we keep the wheelchair "just in case" (and she says this with a curious shine in her eyes) I have a "setback."*

On the whole, Beth is patient to a fault. She cleans up after me and endures my frequent fits of brooding and ill-temper without complaint. On our walks, for instance, she'll spend two hours or so accompanying me on my halting perambulations of the park trails, interrupted by my need to rest and catch my breath on a park bench every fifty yards or so. Afterwards, she brings me home and gets me settled in front of the TV with my cheezits and anti-inflammation pills. Then she changes into her form-fitting lycra jogging suit and runs her daily five miles around the reservoir. I don't remember her ever looking so fit and sexy. Say what you will about our situation: she's thriving.

Did I mention that she's having an affair? Oh yes, Zack is a hotshot young attorney that works at Dorfmann Holloway, a real up-and-comer, pun intended. She's not trying to hide it either, I'll hand her that. In my condition, after all, it's important for me to be able to get ahold of her at all times. She leaves me her number at this or that restaurant, party, or theater event just in case I can't reach her by cell. She's even given me her number at Zack's, where I've had to call her once or twice while she's lying beside him in bed, I'm sure of it.

As far as I know, the relationship with Eric ended shortly after I walked out on her that first time. It's not a topic we talk about. I've never even mentioned it to Eric. Never got the chance. He dropped out of circulation last July. There are rumors he's living somewhere in the French countryside—or Arizona. Beth talks to me about all kinds of other things, though, things that I'm not interested in at all: it's horrible or lulling, depending on whether or not I'm paying attention. If I really can't bear it and I want her to shut up, I'll grimace, grab my hip or knee, and beg her for another painkiller. One day, however, I remember perking right up when she told me that she was talking to her friend Danielle and it seems that no one has seen or heard from Lara for close to a month now.

What happened the night I was assaulted is another topic that we don't talk about. Beth doesn't ask how I came to be found beaten close to death in a

Chinatown flophouse, half-strangled, dressed in women's underwear, traces of another man's semen in my shattered mouth and ruptured anus. Without having to discuss the matter, we both understand that sexual relations between us are out of the question. Instead, she gently strokes my back when I wake up moaning with bad dreams in the middle of the night. When, at last, I'm certain that she's finally fallen back to sleep, I roll over to face the wall and masturbate into the sheets. Guess who I'm thinking of?

. . . . . .Lately, I've taken to going to the park by myself on sunny afternoons. I stash the crutches in some out-of-the-way niche and walk briskly along the trails. Sometimes I'll buy a pretzel or a hot dog from a vendor. I'll sit on a park bench dedicated to the loving memory of some dead person and watch the squirrels and pigeons fight each other for garbage. Sometimes, if I'm quick enough, I'll even catch sight of a sleek grey rat hopping into the damp shadows near an archway or disappearing into a storm drain.

I'll watch the office girls on their lunch hours and kids in the playgrounds and illicit lovers meeting for afternoon trysts. I look for people who have no futures, people who could one day just vanish without a trace: they are all over the place. Right here, for instance, is an ad from "a cute teacher who'll go over your knee or bend over the desk for spanking good times" and here's one offering a "rim job for a real man," promising to "do what the wife or girlfriend won't." Here's a thirty-eight-year-old guy who's looking for a married man. He says, "let me smell your wife's dirty panties and I'll suck you off. No reciprocation necessary," he assures me. Wow, what a giver. I'll read the paper or not and lots of time I'll just sit there and think, but mostly I'm not thinking of anything at all. I smile out at everything and nothing in particular, like a billboard selling something no one needs.

If I am thinking at all, though, what I'm thinking is what I thought that first morning being pushed out of the hospital by Beth into all that sun light. It was like the horror of being born all over again. For months, I'd been hearing how unlikely it was that I had survived what had happened. "Lucky," is the word everyone kept repeating. It was unanimous: I was lucky to be alive. "You must have survived for a reason," they all insisted. "There must be something you were meant to do with your life." But no one had any idea what that might be. And me—I hadn't a clue.

Going out the doors of the hospital, I felt dazzled to be in the sun. After all those days healing in artificial light, I'd forgotten, it seemed, just how unforgiving and uncompromisingly fierce the naked sun could be. I shrank from it like a vampire. Squinting and blinking, I fumbled the dark glasses onto my nose. I don't think I've taken them off since. The temperature of the sun, I once read under the bottle cap of a Snapple Mango Madness, can reach fifteen million degrees.

It was a Monday, probably, or maybe a Wednesday, but definitely one of those sunny but cold days that you get between seasons, and I felt a kind of dazed wonder, but not of gratitude or happiness or relief or anything like that.

What I felt, as close as I can describe it, is what I feel now: a kind of resigned surprise, and then, a spiteful contempt, but for who or what, I still can't say. Perhaps it was for the sun itself…insinuating, interrogatory, singling me out. Or, maybe, it was directed at the utter absence of whoever or whatever I'm addressing when I walk up the sunlit paths of the park, muttering over and over, I'm alive, goddammit, I'm still alive.

Because they were right, you know, all of them. I did survive for a reason.

Tonight I can't sleep. On the nightstand the digital clock reads 4.12am. But Beth always keeps it set half-an-hour earlier than the real time, as if she can't wait to see a new day, to find out what comes next, and wants to hurry the story along. The clock says 4.12am but it's set a half-hour ahead and I don't feel like doing the math. What comes next? More of the same that's come before, but not anymore. Lying beside me, curled like a fetus, she's been asleep for hours.

I'm already at the edge of my side of the bed, just as I always am, and I quietly sit up. I let my legs down carefully off the bed, waiting several minutes for the left one to limber up sufficiently. I reach for my cane and climb to my feet. Out of habit, I find myself cringing every time the floors creak until I've safely cleared the room. I hobble slowly down the hall to the living room.

In the little alcove by the door to the hallway, I stop to catch my breath and let my heart slow down. Something inside me is trying to get out, and it feels like it's using my heart as a battering-ram to do it. It was a dream that woke me, the same dream I've been having since Sam-I-Am came to visit me in the hospital. I don't believe in dreams anymore, but this one just won't give up.

*It starts with me driving on an empty highway, at night, in a violent rain.
There's something at the side of my car, moving fast, at least seventy-five-miles-per-
hour because that's how fast I'm driving, something long-legged, loping along the
breakdown lane. But I can't make out what it is. Whatever it is, it suddenly
turns on the speed and bolts across the road right in front of the car. Two stick-
like legs and nothing above it but a diffuse changeable shape, like blowing rain—*

*I hit the brakes, grab the steering wheel, and skid the car into a ditch. I
must have hit my head and passed out because when I wake up I'm out of the car
and walking in the rain towards a shack.*

*Beth is inside. She's sitting on a black cushion against one of the weathered
walls. Her legs are folded under her like a Buddha's. In the dream she's an old
woman, with a wizened, hook-nosed face. She nods and smiles like she's been
expecting me and gesticulates with her hand to the empty cushion in front of her. I
sit there, like she's the teacher and I'm the pupil.*

*The shack is a mess: beads, dried fish, old magazines, assorted handmade
gew-gaws, roots, dried flowers, newspapers—all of this chaos lit by kerosene
lanterns. In the midst of everything, on what looks like a hand-made wooden
table, is a computer, scanner, and fax machine.*

*Beth is packing a water pipe with dried leaves and buds and now she's
holding it out to me, carefully, in both hands.*

"What is it," I ask. "Marijuana?"

*Beth shrugs a shoulder, smiles, looks off, and bats her eyes, as if to coyly
say, "Oh, who knows? Who knows? Maybe this, maybe that."*

*I notice there is a gap between her yellowed, front teeth. She points to her
head, and then indicates the pipe. She says something I don't understand—it's a
language I can't identify that she's speaking, maybe Transylvanian?*

*I take the water pipe and inhale deeply when she lights it. To my surprise
I feel spacey immediately. When I touch my skin with my fingertips, I feel like
I'm touching someone else. I hold up my hands or intend to hold them up, but they
remain in my lap, disconnected, like a mannequins hands.*

*"She's infected me," I try to explain to her. "She's spread her
incoherence into my system, her chaos, her cancer—it's in me now."*

*I'm talking about Charlotte, naturally. But Beth doesn't seem to
understand what I'm trying to tell her, even though she's nodding
"understandingly." I'm holding my stomach, which suddenly feels like it's splitting*

open. The pain is excruciating, and I place my hands over it, feeling something like a giant tumor or the knob of a small head in my lower abdomen.

"I want to tell you the truth," I gasp, "the truth about myself." I try to say more, but I find that I'm having trouble breathing. I panic. I manage to gasp, "Am I dying?"

Beth, still an old woman, smiles, and shrugs.

I suddenly feel like I'm going to vomit. I try to get up, head for a bathroom, but I'm too dizzy and weak. All I can manage is to crawl on my hands and knees like an animal. My face is covered with sweat and tears and drool and I'm heaving and gasping. It's not enough until I taste the bile—and then—

Blood slaps the tiled floor—something wet with limbs. I stare at it in horror. Whatever it is flops around blindly, tubers and open mouths like blue suction cups, like dozens and dozens of parasitic assholes. I grab at my throat, strangling, still retching. The worst part of it all is that the goddamn thing is still attached to me, it's rooted to something inside me by a thick main tube, like a length of slimy, muscular intestine, spewing filth, around which my lips beg wordlessly for help.

Another wave of panic grips me—I'm choking to death, choking to death on this living, gasping, breathing wet thing that looks like part of my own viscera, as if I've been turned inside-out, something that looks like a semi-transparent octopus, joined at the head with a smaller version of itself. Ripping away at my shirt, clawing for breath, what I see is horrifying. The flesh of my torso has indeed split open from chin to crotch as if I've been laid apart for autopsy. Even to a layman's eyes, what I see is clearly inoperable: it's the other end of the thing half-vomited on the floor. I see what I can only describe as an intricate system of roots, rootlets, filaments, and fibrous nettings that is indistinguishable from the internal organs to which it has insinuated itself like a vital connective tissue.

With each attempt to vomit, I can feel the fixed tug of the thing deep inside me, sutured, it seems, into and around my pelvis and throughout my inner organs. With every attempt to expel it, all the tiny black knots that hold it, tighten.

Looking up in desperation, I see Beth smiling, nodding, her faded eyes laughing in her withered, wrinkled face. With her long dry hair and gap teeth and wizened face she looks like some kind of gypsy. She makes a mock sympathetic expression, again bats her eyes flirtatiously, and sucks on what looks like a dried papaya.

She won't help, or can't help. She just sucks on her dried papaya and watches impassively, like I was on TV.

I'll choke to death for sure if I can't get this thing up, that much I understand, but to do so I'd have to accomplish an impossibility: I'd have to finish turning myself inside out.

There's only one thing to do and even the thought of it is enough to kill me. What I have to do, I realize, is overcome my instinctive reflex to gag. I have to overcome my disgust. What I have to do is swallow this thing all over again. I have to do the exact opposite of what I've been trying to do all along, what it seems I've been trying to do all my life. I have to do the opposite of my natural reaction which was to try and get well. Whatever else this thing slopping around on the floor might be, I realize now that it's synonymous with my life. I've been going about it all wrong. No shit, Sherlock, right? But who could have guessed the truth?

If I want to survive, if I want to live, I have to get sicker.

That's when I always wake up.

Now I'm standing in front of the closet door, which, after another thirty seconds or so, I open. Propping my cane against the jamb, I get down on my knees before the boxes stacked inside. Yesterday afternoon Beth brought some of my summer clothes out of storage. It's late August already, I think. Along with the clothes, she's brought some of the personal things I requested, a list of them, in fact, that was much longer than necessary and meant to disguise the importance of the only object I'm really interested in seeing from my former life.

I thought she'd object to my request for my old laptop, too much of a link to my old life is what I figured she'd think, and I readied myself with excuses to counter her objections, about how I needed it for work, that it had a lot of important personal and business information, investments, tax returns, client numbers, that kind of thing. But, to my surprise, Beth didn't object at all to bringing me the laptop, and now I realize why: she'd already been through it and erased anything that she thought might pose a threat. She knew the laptop was now basically a clean slate. Editor that she is, what she did was edit my past and she's cut Charlotte out of it.

Reaching into the appropriately marked box, I lift the black rectangle from out of a pile of folded rayon shirts. It reminds me of those black boxes they always *try to retrieve after an airplane crash to explain what might have happened. That's what the computer is now—the black box that survived the disaster of my former life. I set the laptop on the floor and lift the cover. I touch the power switch, hold my breath, and pray the battery still carries a charge because I don't know where the adaptor is. There's a tense moment—and then the screen flickers weakly to life.*

As I wait for the computer to boot, I contemplate what I might find, if the answers I've been searching for are hidden there, enigmatic and ominous, as spells in a high-tech black magic grimoire. Looking behind me, I half-expect to hear Beth coming down the hallway. Or to find her already standing in the doorway behind me, arms folded under her breasts, a smug, knowingness stuck to her face like silver duct tape. But the doorway is empty; everything is quiet.

There are several different theories to explain the common phenomenon of déjà vu. From a relatively harmless variety of stroke to a natural lapse in the processing time of the brain between an event and it's recording—I wonder which, if any of them, can explain the sensation that I've already experienced the "memory" of what I'm writing now before it's even happened. How do you explain, for instance, that from the first moment I laid eyes on her I felt as if I'd known Charlotte forever? The doctors have already warned me about these kinds of mental anomalies. If they hadn't, I'd almost believe what I was experiencing were indeed magic or destiny, or, at the very least, a kind of ESP.

What I'm reading is a series of emails to Charlotte that haven't been written yet, or rather, written with reference to things I haven't yet done, but already remember. I would remember, I'm certain, if I'd killed her, wouldn't I? That isn't something I could possibly have forgotten—in spite of everything. I'm sure of it. Aren't I? On the other hand, why does what I'm reading bring back such vivid memories?

The text is embedded in a long and tedious technical download about using Microsoft Powerpoint. You scroll through the first fifty pages and the last fifty pages and you don't realize you're looking at the same ten pages of text cut-and-pasted over and over again. More importantly, you don't bother to read the middle. It's there, all of it, the pages of this journal, and tonight I'm putting it online before erasing it from my computer. I'm putting it online—my whole story—so that the world will never forget, just like the Holocaust survivors who never want the history of their catastrophe to fade away. To tell what it was like.

Once upon a time. What is it Stalin said? One death is a tragedy, a million deaths is merely a statistic.

You see, I finally understand my mistake, the mistake that Sam had tried to help me correct. I wonder now how I could ever have worshipped her as I did: meat-bag of organs, bones, nasal hair, glands, pus, gastric juices, urine and bacteria that she is—how did that all become translated into an object of poetry? Love is a miracle, no? No. But it wasn't love I felt at all.

It's embarrassing, really, that it took me so long to learn.

They need more, Sam explained, more victims, more sacrifices to the cause. The party needs someone who can provide them. Haskins will announce his candidacy for president early next year. These good people need new blood to save the world. They need energy. They need lives. They need someone who loves enough, someone devoted enough to make the necessary sacrifices. They need a new priest for a new kind of religion, which is really the oldest religion of all. Charlotte would be interested in meeting that kind of man. Was I interested?

Yes, I see my mistake.

I see now the softness of what I'd felt in the past, of all I'd done wrong in my affair with Charlotte, the pleading, the pleasing, and the longing and I know now that love is none of those things. I thought it was, but it's not. Love is hard. Love is cruel. Love is merciless. Love is selfish. Love goes to the strong, the vicious, the ruthless, and the victorious. It goes to the unashamed. It goes to the bold and the unforgiving. Love doesn't apologize, doesn't compromise, it doesn't play by the rules. Love is hardcore. That's what I am now—a hardcore romeo.

I sit here on the floor for a long time. I might be crying, but I'm not. By now, I've already powered down and closed the laptop, but I don't move. I might be laughing, but I'm not. In the windows behind me, the sky is brightening, the wall in front of me, too. The sun, as always, is coming up. Beth should be stirring soon, judging by the light, no matter what time it is. Her clock radio has already gone off and I recognize Smashmouth's remake of the old Monkees tune, "I'm a Believer."

I smile as the new day, cold and bright and empty, is reborn all around me. One day, just like all the others, identical, from now on, from this moment until forever, like clones, so many of them, so perfectly ordinary, so absolutely identical, so dead and swarming and overwhelming they can't be stopped, like an army of zombies, they never end, and I'm condemned to live each and every last goddamned one of them and I look upon it all and I smile and I say, "It is good." I take a deep breath. There are some words scrawled on the wall behind me. I recognize for the first time the shade of lipstick that Charlotte slashed across our wrists the very first time we met. That's the shade these words are written in. I know that color all-so-well: dried blood.

Let me be honest: Beth isn't getting up this morning. I need a Diet Snapple. I wonder if there are any left in the refrigerator. Antarctica is the driest, coldest, windiest, and highest continent on earth. *I hear the sirens growing louder. I wonder if they are coming for me this time. I hope they are. I hope they can stop me. No, I don't, that's a lie. Let's all, at last, stop telling lies, shall we? If I've sinned, it's only because I've loved too much. It's not like they show it in books and movies.*

THIS IS HOW MONSTERS ARE MADE

Don't miss these other exciting titles
charting the no-man's land beyond
contemporary literature

THE AFTERHUMAN PRESS
...what's next in books

Aftherhuman
by Michael Cross

The Maniac Manifesto
by Nick Caligari

Fake Girls
by Matthew Sloan